RICH IN PARADISE

Julia Fitzgerald

C

CENTURY

LONDON SYDNEY AUCKLAND JOHANNESBURG

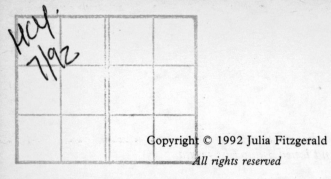

The right of Julia Fitzgerald to be identified as the author of this
work has been asserted by her in accordance with the Copyright,
Designs and Patents Act 1988.

First published in Great Britain in 1992 by
Random Century Group
20 Vauxhall Bridge Road, London SW1V 2SA

Century Hutchinson South Africa (Pty) Ltd
PO Box 337, Bergvlei 2012, South Africa

Random Century Australia Pty Ltd
20 Alfred Street, Milsons Point, Sydney, NSW 2061
Australia

Random Century New Zealand Ltd
PO Box 40-086, Glenfield, Auckland 10
New Zealand

British Library Cataloguing in Publication Data

Phototypeset by Pure Tech Corporation, Pondicherry, India
Printed in Great Britain

The BEST THING in the WORLD

What's the best thing in the world?
June-rose, by May-dew impearled;
Sweet south-wind, that means no rain;
Truth, not cruel to a friend;
Pleasure, not in haste to end;
Beauty, not self-decked and curled
Till its pride is over-plain;
Light, that never makes you wink;
Memory, that gives no pain;
Love, when, *so*, you're loved again.
What's the best thing in the world?
– Something out of it, I think.

ELIZABETH BARRETT BROWNING

OTHER BOOKS BY JULIA FITZGERALD:

Beauty of the Devil
Castle of the Enchantress
Daughter of the Gods
Desert Queen
Earth Queen, Sky King
Firebird
Flame of the East
Jewelled Serpent
Kiss From Aphrodite
Pasodoble
Princess and the Pagan
Royal Slave
Salamander
Scarlet Woman
Slave Lady
Taboo
Venus Rising

Chapter 1

The seasons might as well not have existed in the Downley Home for Distressed Minors, for few of the girls had the opportunity or inclination to enjoy or study them. It was from her observation of the leaves of the beech tree that Bellinda measured the time of year. Now the sparkling, snuff-gold tints were fading to pale bark brown and then to the colour of old cream silk. From shining gold coins, the leaves became fragments of tattered rag.

The frosty ground bit into the thinly shod feet of the orphans as they trailed to church on Sunday morning, Bellinda at their head with the Governess, footsteps halting, beside her. Fingers rigid and chalk blue with cold, their toes tingling from the ice clinging to their boots, the children had to sit for an hour through the Vicar's monotonous and uninspired sermon on grievous sin and the hellfire that would surely be its punishment.

Beside Bellinda the Governess was trembling, her hands letting slip her hymn book repeatedly. It was not the cold but an excess of geneva gin that was making her shake. Her swollen eyes were pouched in puffy flesh, her cheeks a vein-streaked mauve. She was leaning heavily against Bellinda, and shortly her head dropped and she began to snore. Gently Bellinda nudged her, but to no avail. The snoring increased, and heads began to turn. Even the Vicar noticed, casting a shrivelling glance in their direction.

'Ma'am,' Bellinda hissed, 'Ma'am, please wake up!'

'Look at that woman, Mama!' a little voice piped up from behind them. 'She thinks that it is bedtime!'

'Ma'am!' Bellinda tried again; it was time to stand up and sing, but if she moved, the Governess would tip over into Bellinda's seat. Taking a deep breath, she heaved at the sleeping woman's arm, while Sara on the opposite side pulled at the other flaccid arm. Slowly, they helped the Governess to her feet where she tottered, opened bleary eyes and looked unseeingly about her. The hymn went on interminably and Bellinda's back ached with the effort, but she stood firm. If people realized how bad matters were, the Governess would be dismissed and some unmanageable stranger would take her place. Bellinda shuddered at the thought. Things at the moment were difficult and exhausting, but not impossible. The Governess was a kindly woman at heart, and when she was sober she did care for them in her own peculiar way. Besides, Bellinda was fond of her. The Governess was, like herself, a woman without family or loved ones, and for those in that situation Bellinda would always find affection.

Mercifully the service finished swiftly and the congregration shuffled out, noses pink-tipped with cold, for the church had no heating. Bellinda caught a brief glance of the Vicar's shrunken wife, who was, as ever, twisting and untwisting her hands together, and then of the Vicar himself, a man who had never cared to meet her eye at any of the services. It was shyness, maybe, or fear of women, for a man who had chosen such a petrified wife must surely be terrified of the whole female sex.

The Governess seemed slightly recovered in the snow-scented air, despite her unladylike belching. Heads high, Bellinda, Sara and the crocodile of orphans retraced their steps to the chilly, tomb-like building they called home. Cook had prepared a warming midday meal for them, a soup made skilfully from one small joint of bacon, three large bags of the cheapest flour and a sack of old, withered potatoes. With it was yesterday's rock-hard bread, 'wood shavings' as the girls called it, for even at its best it had that same rough texture. 'You'll get splinters from eating that,' Sara would jest, but it was not amusing when the coarse, flavourless bread was their main fare at most meals. Sometimes it came with lard scrapings, sometimes with runny jam made from bruised fruit and water, sometimes with what they called Cook's 'slap on', for this was not untasty, made of leftovers pounded to a pulp and flavoured with whatever spice was available.

The Governess sat at the head of the long table and picked at her food, her eyes dull. Her mug of tea was liberally sugared, but the orphans were allowed no such favours. Sipping noisily, she looked at them, one after the other, at their cropped, neatly combed hair, their pale, drawn faces. Her eyes came to rest on Bellinda's hair, so dark, almost ebony but not quite, and grown longer than the regulation cuts of the younger girls.

Cook called Bellinda's hair colour 'burnt cork brown' but it was quite pretty and with curling tongs and satin ribbons it would look very becoming, not that the girl would ever know such luxuries, the Governess mused. It was Bellinda she worried about most of all. She was no ordinary child; her attractiveness was increasing all the time, despite the wretched diet that was all the budget would allow, and those penetrating green eyes were unnerving. Had the Governess known such a word as eldritch then she would have applied it to Bellinda's eyes. If one stared into their depths, there was a hint of otherworldly things, of hidden places and ancient secrets, of mysteries and marvels. It was uncomfortable to do so, however, so the Governess had not repeated it beyond the first time or two, the second time to see if what she had at first suspected could possibly be true. What was in that green deepness? At first glance, the pupils were still and steady as a woodland pool, and then the water would begin to ripple . . .

'Ma'am.' It was Bellinda's voice and she had not even seen her approaching. 'Cook wants to know if muffins will suit for tea. She has got some misshapes from James Herbert's in Dashwood Avenue.'

3

'Muffins?' The Governess's face brightened. Even though they would be rough little beasts with stalky protrusions that poked into her painful gums, they would be warm and drenched in fat. She would eat six at the very least, for the thick, stodgy soup did not agree with her digestion at all. 'Yes, muffins will suit very amiably indeed for tea. Ask Cook to fill my mug, will you, and bring it to my withdrawing room.'

Although sounding very grand, the Governess's drawing room was a shabby little cubby hole with a battered armchair and couch and a side table on which lay a grubby lace cloth stained with tea. There was a small, pitiful fire struggling for life in the grate, and the Governess propped herself before it, her palms round the hot mug for comfort.

'Sit there, Bellinda.' She pointed to the armchair.

'Yes, Ma'am.' Now there would be a lecture, for there always was when the Governess sobered up, however briefly. In these moods, she believed herself quite capable of executing her duties efficiently and would be struck by guilt at the thought of Bellinda having to carry the burden that should have been hers alone.

'Bellinda, you cannot remain here for very much longer. You are seventeen now and that is two years beyond the age allowed by the Board's regulations. I will find you work in one of the dairies –'

'I am content here, Ma'am, thank you.' How many times had she told the Governess so, thankful to remain where she was with Sara? And indeed what was the alternative? The majority of the girls were put into service or apprenticed as dairy workers if there was a vacancy.

'But not happy, eh? No, you are not happy. You will wish to take a husband one day, if that thought has not already come to you. Life on a farm would be hard but, generally speaking, farmers are faithful husbands. There would always be enough to eat – butter, cream, fresh milk every day, bacon . . .'

4

'I have no wish whatsoever for marriage, Ma'am.' Bellinda leaned forward to snatch up a burning twig that had been spat from the flames, endangering the old rag rug. Flinging it back into the grate hastily, she said, 'I have no wish to tie myself to any man, farmer or no. I want a life of my own, not to be any man's slave.'

'You are young now but one day you will have to take that step or bear the brunt of spinsterdom, as I have done. Bellinda, there is no sadder creature than an unmarried woman, however virtuous she be. Let her pray on her knees all night and day and piety drop from her pores, yet she will still be sneered at. A woman who cannot catch herself a man is the sorriest of all females.' Tears suddenly flooded the Governess's eyes.

'I think I can live with that, Ma'am.'

'Oh my dear child, you have no idea what it is like, the contempt that will be levelled at you!'

'I shall withstand it.' Bellinda's expression was determined.

The Governess felt her short flush of energy draining. The child truly had no idea, for the orphanage had cushioned her against the world in many ways. The girls were not allowed to mix with other children, for fear of tainting them, for the large majority of the orphans were illegitimate, the fruit of sin. Bastards were not loved in a society built upon the respectability of wedlock and the family.

Once, a girl had peered over the wall of the Home and spoken to the orphans and they had rushed to talk to her. She had even been offered a mug of milk, when they rarely saw such a treat themselves, but the girl's mother had hastened up, her face the picture of horror.

'Come away at once, Mary Louise,' she had ordered, 'those are the children of sinners!'

Bellinda, her face furious, had called after the retreating pair, 'Suffer the little children to come unto me!' but the woman had hurried all the faster.

5

Now the Governess reminded Bellinda of that incident. 'There will be insults flung at you, and you will be avoided as if you were diseased. Marriage would bring you respectability, as nothing else can for an illegitimate child. I have in mind for you a widowed farmer whose wife died last year. He is elderly, but that should not affect your fortunes. Indeed it could brighten them. I have had a word with him and he would not hold your illegitimacy against you. Care for him well and all that he has shall be yours –'

'Ma'am, I will take my chances in the world.' The thought of an elderly husband chilled her, but not as much as the prospect of marrying in the hope of his early death.

'A romantic notion, my dear, but people will ask for proof. The fact that you have lived here has marked your reputation with a scarlet ribbon. Some good, kind man is your only hope. Even then, it will not be easy. People always probe into your past.' The Governess leaned forward, lowering her voice. 'My dear, that is why I am here. I could have married, but I am a hopeless liar.' The Governess's hands became agitated, the tea slopping in her mug. 'The man I loved wanted to meet my family but I had none to show to him, and his mother was even more pressing. When they found out that I did not know who my father was, they shunned me.' Tears rolled down the veined cheeks. 'I could have made something of myself if only I had not been illegitimate!'

Bellinda took one of the square, rough hands. 'Ma'am, look how well you have done for all of us. You have been a mother to so many girls over the years in place of the few you might have given birth to.'

The Governess snatched back her fingers. 'You cannot dupe me. I am a drunkard and a weakling. Had it been yourself in my place, how much better this Home would have been run! Bellinda –' the voice was now a croak – 'I want to see you settled before I die. What

6

other hope can there be for an illegitimate girl but to marry?'

The Governess then yawned heartily, her lids drooping. These days her energy was soon spent. Gently Bellinda took the mug from her hand and placed it on the table. Even before she reached the door the snores had begun. Some people could sleep so heavily. She wished she had that ability.

'What did she want?' Sara was waiting in the corridor, her hands tucked into her armpits for warmth, her freckles standing out like ginger dots against her pallid complexion.

Bellinda looked at the fourteen-year-old whom she loved like a sister. 'She thinks I should marry a good, kind farmer and settle happily into marriage on a generous diet of cream, butter, fresh milk and bacon.'

'Oh Bell, she did not tell you to leave, did she?' Sara's chin trembled. She knew that her friend was still at the orphanage only because of the Governess's drinking. But for Bell, the woman would have been exposed years ago.

'I am afraid she did. My only hope is to be a devoted wife and scrub the dairy every day and milk the cows and collect the eggs – taking time off now and again to produce a son, of course. Farmers need sons to help them in the fields.'

'So you are going to do it?' Sara bit on her lips. Her only friend was Bellinda. What would she do without her?

'Can you see me milking cows?' Bellinda's eyes twinkled. 'No, I am not going to do it. I shall stay here to look after you all.'

'Will they let you do that?'

'They will have to.' Bellinda's jaw set in an uncompromising line.

Vanity Groves-Hawkes was a young woman of decided opinion. She always planned some great act of largesse at Christmas time and this year would be no different.

In London with her papa she had seen a heart-wrench-ing play where a young orphan girl was taken in by a wealthy and aristocratic family, the girl vowing undying loyalty and commitment to the eldest daughter. In a touching scene that brought the play to an end, the grateful orphan, now eighteen and sensibly dressed in a high-necked gown of cocoa-brown cotton, knelt be-fore the beautiful daughter of the house, whose name was Eleanora, and swore that she would serve her until the last breath left her body.

Tears had misted Vanity's eyes at those words. How wonderful, how touching! She wanted to do something as inspiring as that; she wanted to be like the beautiful Eleanora and earn such tender devotion.

It was not that they did not have plenty of servants at Carlyon House, for they did, but these were men and women who would work elsewhere if they did not work for her papa. What she wanted was a gratefully devoted servant, a girl who would never forget that she had been lifted from the gutter by Vanity Groves-Haw-kes.

'Mama, I wish to adopt an orphan for the Christmas season,' she announced to Marguerite Groves-Hawkes next morning, taking her mother entirely by storm.

Blanching, for she knew only too well her daughter's predilection for undertaking charitable deeds at this time of year, Marguerite gave a brave little laugh.

'Sweetheart, where would we find an orphan at this late date?'

'In an orphanage of course, Mama. There are three within twenty miles of Carlyon House, so Papa told me.'

'Papa told you that, did he?' Marguerite made a mental note to speak to her husband that night. The last thing Vanity needed was to be encouraged in her wild notions.

'Yes, Mama. He knows of them for he always gives them money at this time of year. Do you not recall how the children from the Fairley Orphanage serenaded us with carols in church last December?'

'No, I do not recall, sweetheart.' Marguerite put down her brush, letting her thick flaxen curls cascade about her shoulders. Her hair was one of her most attractive features and she employed it to the utmost.

'They sang very sweetly. Then the girls from the Downley Home for Distressed Minors sent you a beautiful sampler in gratitude for Papa's gift. Surely you remember that?'

'I think so, yes, so I do.' It had been a crumpled light brown square of cloth horribly stitched in reds and pinks and harsh greens, the stitches so tight that the cloth resembled a piece of quilting. Still, they had not been given the superb education allotted her own daughter, so one could not expect them to produce exquisite embroidery.

'We shall visit the Downley Home first, Mama, for they have shown gratitude whereas the other children have not.'

Picking up her silver-backed brush, Marguerite began to brush her hair again, craving the soothing motion. All she had ever asked for was a happy, contented family life and to that end she had expended virtually all her energies. Whatever her husband or her children desired, she always did her best to encourage and support them, seeing that as her duty, but when Vanity made one of her pronouncements, she dreaded the outcome. How did one 'adopt an orphan' for Christmas?

'Sweetheart, are you quite positive that you wish to go through with this? What will transpire after Christmas?'

'Maybe we could adopt the orphan permanently, Mama.' Then as she saw Marguerite flinching, Vanity quickly added: 'She would be so useful about the house. Matilde could teach her how to be a lady's maid.' Matilde was Marguerite's French maid, an elderly, sallow-faced woman with a permanent nasal inflammation that made her sniff constantly. She had retired early that day with a savage cold.

9

Marguerite allowed herself to breathe again. 'Then you had better make sure that the orphan is of an age for such tasks, sweetheart. Lady's maids must have delicate fingers, a light touch, a sympathetic nature. They must be presentable in their dress and adaptable, too, and show an ability for languages, but most importantly, they must be plain of face. If you can find all of these in one orphan, then by all means bring one to the house for Christmas, my love.' Lowering her golden head, Marguerite brushed vigorously.

In their winter finery Vanity and her mama descended on the Downley Home one bleak December afternoon. Marguerite was elegantly robed in a plum velvet cape lined with miniver, beneath it a plum velvet skirt and jacket recently made for her at Taliere's, one of the top Paris couture houses. On her dainty feet were gleaming black leather boots buttoned up the sides, and on her head a black velvet toque decorated with bobbing black egret feathers. Vanity wore sapphire-blue velvet, of an almost exactly matching design, but with a girlish bonnet trimmed with blue satin ribbons. On her hands were blue gloves of fine and delicate leather to match the silver-clasped purse in which she carried a fragile lace handkerchief, a golden guinea (what she called her good luck charm), a phial of sal volatile should her mama feel faint, and a packet of her favourite peppermint lozenges.

'What a grim place!' Marguerite shuddered as they looked at the gaunt building that had stood so solidly since the Middle Ages when wayfarers and itinerants had come to its doors for succour. In those days, monks had lived there, working the land and baking the unleavened bread which they had then distributed. Vanity proceeded to tell her mama of this, for she had looked up the Downley Home in one of Papa's local history books.

'The monks were dispossessed by Henry VIII, Mama, and thrown out into the streets. There was a terrible scandal for they found a woman in —'

'No, do not tell me, I do not wish to hear anything unpleasant!'

'Oh Mama, it was not unpleasant. They found out that the Abbot had a mistress and five children and –'

'Vanity!' Her voice was a controlled shriek.

Marguerite was rescued by the sound of the door being unlocked, the key grating harshly as it turned, and then the massive oaken edifice swung wide and there stood the Governess, her mauve cheeks split into the most congenial smile that she could muster. The letter had arrived from Carlyon House only the day before, by foot messenger, detailing what Mrs Groves-Hawkes required of them. Panic had erupted as soon as Bellinda had finished reading out the message to the Governess, whose command of English was poor. The orphanage had been swept and dusted and polished, the Governess had donned her Sunday best, as had the girls, and now the moment was here. One of the wealthiest families in Buckinghamshire wished to take in one of the girls. It was a miracle.

'Madam, we are deeply honoured by your visit!' The Governess dipped into a swaying curtsey, her Sunday best boots creaking loudly. When she rose, her face was flushed with purple, the colour accentuated by the spotless white cap that covered her wispy hair. 'I am Mildred Elizabeth Waring, Madam, Governess of the Downley Home, and this is my young assistant, Bellinda, who is an orphan herself.'

Bellinda knew that the Governess was babbling on, but she could hardly stop her in front of these two splendidly dressed women. From the pallor of their winter-blown faces, they looked greatly in need of mulled wine and hot cakes, both of which awaited them in the Governess's little room – the stained lace cloth had been soaked in cold tea overnight and dried by the fire, so that now it was the colour of fresh biscuits, the stains completely concealed. They were unable to do anything for the shabby, battered furniture save polish what could be polished, but they had worked hard.

At last the visitors were led to the little room where the fire blazed – Sara had been out since dawn collecting sticks and twigs in the woods – and the tray of warming refreshments awaited them.

Bellinda saw the looks of horror in their visitors' eyes as they surveyed the ancient furniture on which they were required to sit.

'I thought my husband gave you a generous donation each Christmas, to enable you to care for the children,' Marguerite said, looking about her in dismay.

'Indeed he does, and for that we are unendingly grateful, Madam, but as you say, the money is for the children and this is my own humble little sitting room. I spend nothing on myself.' The Governess managed another smile while Bellinda thought of all the empty geneva bottles she had cleared out from beneath the couch and behind the cushion, from inside the coal scuttle and the little wall cupboard. However, if one discounted the alcohol, the Governess spoke true. Taking sugar in her tea was the only luxury she had that the children did not.

'Those who are in charge of the young should set an example,' Marguerite sniffed.

'Madam, these young girls are going into service when they leave here. It is unlikely that any of them will ever see furniture of a better quality than this, except to clean it.'

'Of course.' Cautiously Marguerite sipped the spiced wine. It had a sour aftertaste and she cupped it in her hands for warmth but did not take another mouthful.

'Mama.' Vanity's voice was pressuring.

'Oh yes, the children, we wish to see them.'

'But of course. They are awaiting your visit. How excited they have been knowing that you were coming, Madam. One would have thought that Her Majesty was to visit us!' Emitting a gay little laugh, the Governess led Vanity and her mama out of the room and into the main hall.

12

As they made their way, Vanity eyed Bellinda. About her own age, the orphaned girl had a surprisingly pleasant voice, not one of those coarse, rasping croaks the lower classes so often possessed. What was more, she held herself well and looked extremely capable. Her complexion was good, and her eyes an unusual colour that reminded Vanity of the bright, uncompromising greens one saw in Scottish tartans. It was a shame about her hair, of course, that dark, almost black colour that was actually an odd shade of liquorice. Vanity adored golden hair, and the girl that she chose would have flaxen ringlets and wide blue eyes, despite what Mama had said about ensuring that one's female servants were plain. She had visualized her orphan down to the last, tiny detail.

The hall was icy cold but the girls stood stiffly in rows like concubines awaiting their sultan's attentions. Backs rigid, faces scrubbed, hearts pounding, they watched as the little group approached. Sara, who had been out collecting firewood since seven of the clock, was shaking with weariness and there was a tightness in her lungs, as if a hand were squeezing them ruthlessly. Next to her, Maureen was almost panting with excitement. Did these grand ladies guess what their visit meant to these girls? Maureen had been almost in tears from the thrill, convinced that she would be chosen, for she had prayed so hard that she knew her prayers must surely be answered. Nora and Lily, the two youngest, barely knew what the visit was for, but they stood hand in hand, their faces bright. Any change from their dull routine was exhilarating. Some had been sick after their morning meal, their stomachs churning at the thought that they might be picked out.

Here came the sultan now, or was it Prince Charming with the mislaid glass slipper? Sara watched in abject trepidation. At Carlyon House there would be men, and that sex she feared more than anything on earth. At the orphanage there were no males, apart from a rare visit from the Board, who took little interest in the girls – and if they did decide on an inspection, then she had her adored Bell to protect her like a mother. Bell was the only person she had left now. Scowling fiercely, determined not to be chosen, Sara tried to make herself look as ugly as possible.

Chapter 2

Almost an hour had passed and Vanity could not make up her mind. Not one of the girls possessed the golden curls and wide blue eyes that she had dreamed of, nor did any of them come anywhere near to her ideal of prettiness. Conscious of the bold green stare of the girl called Bellinda, Vanity retraced her steps along the lines of orphans.

'Can they all embroider?' she asked Bellinda.

'Not to the standard that you would require, Ma'am.'

'Can any of them sing or play the pianoforte?'

'I do not believe that any of them have ever seen a pianoforte, Miss Groves-Hawkes, and their singing is confined to what is required of them in church.'

Vanity cast Bellinda a glance. Was she being insolent? But Bellinda's face was serene, and there seemed to be nothing there to suggest impertinence.

'Can you embroider?'

'A little. I have no particular skill.'

'Can you sing?'

'No, I am afraid that I cannot.'

'You are a poor lot, are you not . . . ' Vanity sucked in her lips.

'Had we been born into a home such as Carlyon House, then I am sure that we would all have acquired exemplary skills, Ma'am, but the Lord God decreed otherwise.' Bellinda's green eyes met Vanity's hazel ones squarely. Being ill accustomed to the lower classes answering her back, Vanity was at a loss as to how she should respond. She wished that her mama were beside her but Marguerite was sitting on a bench, one finger coiled in a flaxen ringlet as inattentively as a sleepy child. It was a sign that her mother's patience was running out.

Vanity came to a halt in front of Sara who had screwed up her freckled face for the fifth time, jutting out her jaw.

'This girl needs spectacles,' was Vanity's pronouncement, but Bellinda was so busy trying to keep a straight face that she did not come back with a sharp reply this time. 'What is your name?'

'Sara, Miss,' Sara hissed through her contorted mouth.

'I had a dog with freckles once, but not so many as yours. Does she get called Freckles by the other orphans?' Vanity turned to Bellinda, who was speechless for a few moments at such insensitivity.

'No one calls me Freckles!' Sara hissed angrily. Three years before, the vilest of men had nicknamed her that and she still felt sick every time she remembered it.

'There is no one who would be so callous, Ma'am.' Bellinda raised her voice to cover up Sara's angry words. Its tone was icy. 'Everyone here calls Sara by her Christian name.'

'I see that you have spirit.' Vanity glanced again at her mother, who was now twirling her fingers through two curls, her eyes dreamy and far away. Vanity usually welcomed that look on her mother's face for it meant that she might take command of the situation, but in this place she felt far from capable. Shaken, almost. These girls were unsettling with their cropped hair, their pasty faces and drab clothes and so many with that beaten look in their eyes . . . In her own unique way, she was experiencing her first genuine feelings of compassion for the poor but as she had so little familiarity with it, beyond her annual Christmas alms-giving, she was finding it deeply unsettling. Yet at the same time she was having second thoughts about taking an orphan for a servant. Better, perhaps, to invite a girl simply as a guest over Christmas, and decide later if she wanted to keep her on as lady's maid.

'I will see that this girl gets spectacles,' Vanity said crisply, turning to Bellinda, 'and she will spend Christmas with us at Carlyon House. It is shocking that no

16

one has seen to her disability. Poor girl, how she must have suffered!' And how grateful she will be to me after I have helped her, Vanity added silently.

'No!' Sara cried out, the tears bursting from her eyes as Vanity went to join her mother. Bellinda put a hand on her arm, cautioning her. 'It will only be for a few weeks, Sara, and you will have a marvellous time.'

Vanity's ears were sharp. Turning, seeing the tears rolling down Sara's face, she looked perplexed. Tears and denials were not what she had anticipated, not from the orphan who was going to adore her.

Sara took advantage of the moment. 'I shall not go without Bellinda!' she cried.

Vanity went pink. Shows of emotion disturbed her as much as they did her papa.

'Listen to Bellinda, Sara. She is correct in saying that you will have a marvellous time, and everything that you desire. So shall you, Bellinda, for I have no wish to separate you if it causes distress.'

Sara's sight would be transformed and she would worship Vanity devotedly in return, while Bellinda would be shown how to comport herself with courtesy and good manners. When Bellinda was returned to the orphanage, she would be able to teach these poor unfortunates how to respect their superiors. No one got anywhere in the world by answering back.

'Mama, I have made my choice. I wish to take that girl there – the one with all the freckles – and Bellinda, who is her friend.'

'Two?' Marguerite woke in dismay from her reverie. 'But sweetheart, we decided upon one only –'

'Did we truly, Mama? I do not think that we actually clarified how many –'

'You said one orphan, Vanity!'

'Did I, Mama?' Vanity said airily, knowing that she always got her way. 'I truly think that it must be two, for Sara wept on being told that she would be parted from her friend over Christmas and we came here to spread joy, not misery, did we not, Mama?'

Marguerite stared across the room at the freckled girl who looked exceedingly repugnant to her with all those gingery blotches. She had advised her daughter to select a plain girl, not a freak.

'That is the one?'

'Yes, Mama. The poor child needs spectacles, and there may be something amiss with her jaw, but Papa's physician will see to it, will he not? She will be so grateful when she can see properly, Mama!'

Marguerite was desperate to be back at her fireside in her elegant boudoir, a steaming cup of chocolate in her hands, her chilled feet being rubbed by Matilde. She was so cold and unconscionably bored that she would have agreed to almost anything at that moment.

Seeing her resistance crumbling – as it always did where her daughter's wishes were concerned – Vanity barely waited for Marguerite's verbal permission.

Beaming happily, Vanity retraced her steps to where the Governess stood, teetering on her aching legs and struggling for self-control as the craving for geneva built up inside her.

'We shall take the two girls, Sara and Bellinda, for they do not wish to be parted.'

The Governess opened her mouth to shout out her denial, to cry that No, they could not take Bellinda for the Home would collapse into a shambles without her, that Bellinda was her right hand, her mainstay, her guardian angel, but no words would come. Instead there was a strange lightness in the region of her liver, as if she would float away, high above the heads of all those in the hall. Then came the pain of anguish, but it was emotional, not physical, for which when she had recovered a little she would be inordinately grateful.

Had she seen pictures of it in a thousand books and paintings of it in a hundred galleries, Bellinda could never have truly envisaged the full meaning of life as it was lived at Carlyon House. Sara too was speechless. They felt as if they had been gently lifted from a bundle

18

of rags and placed on swansdown and velvet. As guests of the Groves-Hawkes family, they were to have servants to wait on them, men and women who were eager to do whatever they wished, to bring them rich buttery cake and plum pudding if they should desire it in the middle of the night, to wash and iron their clothes, brush their hair and polish their boots.

Carlyon House had the very latest in bathrooms, a massive, echoing chamber with a blue and white tiled floor, a voluminous, pit-deep bath, a vast, porcelain basin and, most astonishing of all, a lavatory that not only flushed but was decorated lavishly inside with blue flowers and green leaves. Although the sound of the water gurgling and threshing through the pipes was terrifying, as if a great torrent were coming at them, they wanted to hear it over and over. Sara's hand was constantly at the gleaming mahogany pull, tugging at the chain and waiting in wonderment for the noise to begin. Then she would cling to Bell, her legs quivering.

They had been left alone in the bathroom to bathe, although Mrs Jermyn, the housekeeper, had tut-tutted a great deal over that. Clean, neat and presentable as they were, that did not change the fact that they were working-class orphans with an unspeakable past. The thought of bastards – and how that word made her tingle – so much as touching her master and mistress's possessions made Mrs Jermyn feel sick and a little dizzy. Bastards touching, holding, feeling, seeing, and no doubt planning to steal . . . How could Miss Vanity have brought them here and how could the mistress have sanctioned it? She had always thought Miss Vanity such a sensible girl, taking after her father.

'Sara, this water is so hot, and look at that soap, and *smell* it – it's like roses!'

'There are seven choices of bath oil.' Sara could count and read a little, but with difficulty. The letters became muddled in her head, and when it came to writing them down, she could only manage words such as a child of five or six might concoct. Bellinda had tried to coach her, but with little effect, for Sara would hold her head as if in pain.

'There is knotted string in my head, Bellinda, when I think of words. I can never write them as you do,' she had said, tears in her eyes.

'They all have lovely names.' Bellinda looked closely at the labels. 'White Lily, Vin de Rose – but let us use the cologne.' They had been told to try whatever they wished, though Mrs Jermyn had swiftly removed the mistress's most precious and favourite oils and powders.

'Bastards, bastards,' Mrs Jermyn kept muttering as she paced up and down outside, 'bastards in the master's new bathroom, bastards!'

Inside, steam was misting the glossy new porcelain and flushing the girls' faces. French cologne went into the water and after it some of the White Lily, chosen by Sara, causing it to cloud like milk.

'Oh, look at that!' Sara cried, hastily unbuttoning her shabby boots and tearing off her sensible brown dress and much-darned shift. She wore no cosy flannel drawers, for the budget did not run to what could not be seen. Stripped, her body was revealed for what it was, waxily pale, scrawny and hollow chested. Two of her ribs projected above the others, making a hard ball of bone almost the size of a child's fist.

'Get in, but let me test first that it is not too hot.' Bellinda dangled her fingers in the milky water. 'Just right,' she said. Grinning, Sara climbed into the enormous bath, its sides jutting high above her shoulders. Giggling, she clasped at a slippery ball of rose-scented soap and looked at Bellinda, who grinned down at her, loofah at the ready.

The water soon became grey, and yet like herself Sara had an all-over wash every three days, using a rough lye soap that scorched off more dirt than it dissolved. There was a rose-scented shampoo for Sara's hair, and she squealed when the soapy water cascaded down her flushed cheeks and into her eyes.

20

Outside the door, hearing what she considered to be inhuman noises of debauched revelry, Mrs Jermyn went on muttering to herself, 'Bastards, bastards in the master's new bathroom!' her face dotted with the sweat of revulsion and disgust.

'Oh Bell, this water feels so soft!' Sara lathered the soap on to her arms and legs, rubbing and squeezing.

'There are oils in the White Lily that soften the water. Now use this little brush on your nails.'

The brush was carved from ivory in the shape of a swan, the swan's feathers being yellow bristles. There was an entire set of ivory swan brushes ranged on the bath's edge, and flowered porcelain dishes for holding the soaps and the little lumps of what looked like grey cinders that they would later find out were volcanic pumice, used by ladies to keep their feet smooth.

'Bell, pull the chain again!' Sara urged, her eyes sparkling.

'I do not think that we should keep doing it, my love. We shall annoy the family.'

'Oh please, Bell!'

'Very well.' Eyes glinting, Bellinda did as she was urged. Tugging at the mahogany pull, she waited for the thunderous threshing to start, while Sara clutched the soap to her chest and screwed up her eyes in dread and excitement.

'It sounds just like a flood coming at us and yet it stops and cannot reach us,' Sara said. 'There was a flood like that in London once, after a storm, and the water swilled round our ankles . . . Mama was with me . . . ' Her face twisted and pain replaced the look of glee.

'Tell me about your mama, my love.' Bellinda knelt down at the bath's side.

'I-I cannot remember what happened next, but you know what I have told you, Bell. One day she will come for me. She has it all planned.'

'Yes, my love, I know she has.' Reaching for the enormous bath flannel in which to wrap Sara, she hid her expression. Sara was kept happy by her belief that her mother would come for her one day, and who was Bellinda to say that she was wrong? There was no doubt at all that Sara had once belonged to wealthy parents.

Rubbing the thin body in the soft, absorbent towel, Bellinda thought of her own mother, a mystery figure who had never taken shape or form in her mind for she had never known her. But then she shook sad thoughts from her head – it was her turn for the unbelievable luxury of a bath.

'What happens now, Bell?' Sara asked as Bellinda finally rose from the tub.

'Harding the maid is to take us into Miss Vanity's room where we shall be given clothes.'

'Clothes?' Sara's eyes lit up. Once, when she was small, she had been dressed in lace-edged gowns trimmed with satin ribbon, with flowered bonnets and soft kid slippers. Once, so long ago . . .

'They have some dresses for us to try on, and boots too I believe.'

'Not Miss Vanity's?'

'Oh no, new ones brought here for us to try. "On approval" Harding called it.'

A tapping came at the door, and Bellinda opened it to see Harding standing there in her spruce black and white uniform, her white cap tipped slightly forward on her thin brown hair. She had a small flattish nose and very full lips which would always rob her of any prettiness, but her blue eyes danced with mischief. Sara liked her very much already.

'Leddies, come this way,' Harding said in imperious tones, a giggle swiftly following. Laughing, the three girls made their way to the room where the fairytale princess slept – or that was how Sara would always think of it. Miss Vanity's bedroom was swathed in rose pink satin, creamy lace frills and pink silk rosebuds. The floor was covered in a thick Persian carpet in colours of strawberries and cream, and the massive mahogany wardrobe was flung open to show a rack of dresses waiting for them.

'Just as if we were princesses ourselves,' Sara would say later when they were alone. She knew all about princesses, for Bellinda had read her the tale of the fur slipper and Prince Charming, and the one about Sleeping Beauty.

Running to the wardrobe, her mouth wide, Sara searched amongst the boots, scattering in confusion the pairs that she found.

'What are ye doin', Miss Sara?' Harding wanted to know.

'Looking for a fur slipper, of course,' Sara replied, sitting back on her heels. She had almost thought that there might be one there, for while part of her said, 'How foolish!' another part passionately wanted to find such a slipper.

'Whoo-hoo, yur'll get a fur slipper, Sara me girl, and on yur backside not yur foot,' said Harding in her rolling Buckinghamshire accent. She was a warm friendly creature but she rarely spoke without some warning on her lips. 'There's slippers for ye, but they be made of felt, and felt will jest have to be good enough fur ye.'

Bellinda was barely listening. She could not take her eyes from the racks of dresses that had been brought here specially for them, on approval. Such colours! Blues like the sky and pinks as bright as rosy cheeks, greens like the shiny apples at Wycombe market and yellows sharp as the lemon they had been given for what Miss Vanity called luncheon, but which they had always known as dinner.

In their excitement, it never occurred to the two girls that they were on approval as much as the clothes, for their fairytale was being lived. Real and alive at this moment, how could it ever die?

The scented shampoo had made their hair shine. Sara's had a red tinge to its tawny depths, Bellinda now saw, and an apple-green dress would contrast well.

23

There was one of soft, smooth wool that would suit her to perfection. It was so light that it seemed like a thick cotton and yet the warmth was far superior. Beneath it would go a multiplicity of fresh white petticoats, a chemise trimmed with broderie anglaise, and a pair of red flannel drawers that Harding called 'under-neaths' for propriety's sake, although she was not averse to coming out with words like backside when she chose.

There were also the corsets. In the Downley Home, what could not be seen was not included in the budget, and all but the oldest girls were left unlaced. It would have been quite shocking to Marguerite had she known, for the voluptuous female figure was con-sidered quite indecent unless safely imprisoned in a good strong pair of stays. Bellinda had worn corsets for two years now, a pair that she had soon outgrown and which dug into her ribs most painfully if she did not sit up very straight. Marguerite would have applauded that, however. Immoral thoughts bred swiftly in slack bodies. Tight lacing kept out corruption.

Bellinda's outgrown corsets had been made to suit the crinoline of the 1860s, which was a very different shape from the now fashionable sheath-slim skirts at the rear of which there was ruched gathering and per-haps a generous bow if one could afford it. Poor girls had never been able to afford crinolines, of course, but Bellinda's corset had come in a chest of clothes sent to the home by a lady whose daughter had died. Five crinoline dresses, without the vast hooped cages that would have kept them aloft, had been cut down to make clothes for the girls, and Bellinda had been told to keep the corset.

Now before her on the bed she saw a display of fashionable corsets in the new hourglass shape called the cuirass, and in materials that made her shiver with delight. There was gleaming satin, hand-made lace, figured silk and one corset that was reinforced with strips of creamy leather so soft that they felt like velvet. Satin bows and lace encrusted the tops.

'Take yur pick,' said Harding, and the two girls delved amongst the corsets, stroking and smoothing and touching. Sara chose a figured silk in primrose yellow and snowdrop white, and Bellinda one in dark-blue satin, the top heavily embroidered in terracotta and tangerine daisies, the shaped stitching, to give an elegant line, in terracotta and peach silks.

Laced into the satin creation, Bellinda felt instantly adult. Outgrown clothes kept one a child, but this magnificent construction made her a woman.

Sara was whirling round the room, hands at her waist, enjoying the feel of its tiny handspan. By bedtime, she would be thinking otherwise, Bellinda knew, for as the day wore on, corsets seemed to shrink in size and cut into all the most vulnerable places.

'Here, Miss Sara, get yur dress on afore anyone comes in, then I'll comb your hair for it's all in a cagmag,' Harding scolded, holding out the apple-green gown, which Sara grabbed from her most rudely and flung over her head.

Encased in the brand-new finery, Sara looked her age at last instead of a scrawny child squeezed into a brown dress. Harding combed her tangled hair and tied it back with a green velvet ribbon.

'There, ye see, ye mumpet, yur do look like a princess, even wi'out fur slippers.'

Sara was speechless as she surveyed herself in the cheval glass. There stood someone on the verge of maturity, not a bad-looking girl after all if only she had not been spattered with those horrendous ginger freckles. Her eyes were a shiny brown with wonderment.

'Now Miss Bellinda, what'll yur choose?'

Stepping forward, Bellinda took out a brown dress. Not the dull, uninspired donkey brown of the orphanage dresses but a fine pale golden brown, like the shells of hazelnuts, it was trimmed with bands of rich gold velvet. Harding passed her a gold velvet ribbon that

25

made her oak-brown tresses look even closer to black. Against it, Bellinda's complexion gleamed as pale as fresh milk, with a luminous quality that drew attention to her startling green eyes.

'The mistress 'as a brooch the exact same shade as yur eyes, Miss Bellinda,' Harding told her. 'An emerald et is. Have ye ivver seen an emerald?'

'No.'

'The mistress will wear et at Christmas to please the maister, although her's not overly fond of green. Her thinks it's an unlucky colour.'

'That doesn't mean I should change, does it?' Sara wanted to know, eyes half teasing. When you had suffered as much misfortune as she had, it could not really make things worse if you wore green dress, petticoats, drawers and boots, in bed and out of it.

'You look lovely, Sara, like a real young lady of the house.' Bellinda smoothed back Sara's tawny hair. There were always a few wisps at the forehead that were determined to spring out of place.

'I was the young lady of the house once . . . ' Sara's brown eyes misted and she caught her lips between her teeth.

'Come along, we ain't got all night.' Harding's voice was unnaturally crisp. She could not abide displays of emotion. 'The maister is to meet yur for dinner and if yur not all spruced up ready it'll be me as gets the blame,' she told the girls.

Bellinda and Sara had not seen Vanity's mother since that morning, for luncheon had been served in the nursery, where Vanity's young brother Robert had looked at them with curious eyes but said very little over the meal.

The sound of a gong thundered through the house, and Sara turned white beneath her freckles, all the delight in her new clothes disappearing. Now they would meet the master, Thomas Groves-Hawkes, who, descended from a long line of wealthy country gentlemen, collected antiques from all corners of the

26

world, so Miss Vanity had told them, but that did not
trouble Sara. What terrified her was that Thomas
Groves-Hawkes was an adult male, a breed of creature
that she had learned to hate and fear in her three years
on the London streets before the Society of Our Lord
the Saviour had rescued her and brought her to the
Downley Home.

Chapter 3

Sara saw nothing and heard nothing as she walked slowly down the beautiful staircase to the main hall, Bellinda's hand tightly grasping hers. Her heart banging, she seemed to have lost the ability to breathe and she knew that there were red spots of colour on her cheeks, though doubtless the freckles would help to hide them. Hearing a male voice, she drew back, but Bellinda tugged at her hand.

'We must be brave,' she whispered. 'They want to be kind to us.'

'Oh if only that was the truth,' Sara whispered back.

She heard the male voice again, laughing out loud, a gentleman's voice, confident, resonant. Oh, she knew about those voices. She knew about men who spoke like that and who did terrible, abominable things to her body . . .

Sweat broke out all over her skin and she knew that it would stain the beautiful broderie anglaise underwear. If only there was no master here, if only –

'Sara!' Bellinda was hissing at her. 'Remember your manners when we are introduced. You must bob a curtsey and not speak unless you are spoken to first. And do not forget to say Please and Thank you.'

Say Please and Thank you for tearing at my body, for biting me so I bleed, for digging your nails into my skin and pushing your tongue in my mouth, thought Sara, wanting to cry out, to scream: No, I can't meet them, I can't! Three years of her life had been spent at the mercy of so-called gentlemen. At the age of eleven she had been forced to behave like a woman, an old, old woman, while deep inside she had been a screaming, petrified child. There would always be that terrified little girl demanding attention, demanding succour yet believing that it would never come.

The dining room was a connoisseur's dream with its Louis Quatorze furniture, its ceiling painted with pink-cheeked cherubs frolicking amidst nymphs draped in what appeared to be bed sheets, their plump rosy bodies spilling out from the white folds. Beneath their feet lay a priceless Aubusson carpet that had once belonged to Madame de Pompadour, and on the rosewood table blazed candelabra that had stood in Marie Antoinette's writing room at Versailles. All of these facts they would learn in time, but for now their impression was one of light and beauty, before their eyes fell on the family who were gathered to greet them.

The mistress's face was cold. She had not wanted to treat this pair of orphans as family guests, but her husband had overruled her, saying that this marvellous charitable gesture of Vanity's would be the making of their daughter.

'Do you not realize what a pampered, sequestered life she leads here? Girls go from the schoolroom to the marriage bed and their eyes remain closed to the realities of life. How can they raise children when they know so little?'

Marguerite had turned pale. She had gone from the schoolroom to the marriage bed, as her husband put it, and she took the criticism directly against herself, even though her husband had not intended that she should.

'Girls are tender creatures. Would you have their pretty minds destroyed by the sights they see in the outside world? Beggars without hands and diseased women plying their verminous trade in the streets? What possible good would that do to Vanity? Is it your intention that she should teach our grandchildren about – about venereal diseases?' Marguerite flushed hotly as she said the last two words. She knew of these abominable things but one did not speak of them. Decency must prevail at all times. However, she must show that one could learn a great deal in the safety of one's home. One did not have to reside with the filthy ragged paupers.

Her visit to the Downley Home had disturbed her. Had she been a compassionate woman, she would have welcomed the opportunity to widen her education, to acknowledge that something else – a not always pleasant something else – lay beyond her front door. But such an acknowledgement would open channels that she had endeavoured to keep closed all her life. Spending extortionate amounts on extravagant clothes and bonnets, and decking herself in the pearls, rubies and amethysts that her husband bought her, was her major line of defence. While she did these things she was an important woman, very important, and as such she had no need to trouble herself about anything she considered beneath her. Marguerite not only judged others by their outer appearance; she also judged herself in this manner.

If she once admitted that there were people in need then she would have to expend her precious energies in charitable deeds. Marguerite abhorred the thought. She nurtured her energy, holding it close to her breast like an infant lest it should desert her. She would not even mount a horse to ride in Rotten Row when they were staying in London, although it was the apogee of fashion. Having watched her mother dying of the consumption, she had a terror of becoming weak and pale and helpless.

To Bellinda and Sara, Marguerite appeared as a vision of radiant and highborn womanhood. It did not matter that she was not beautiful save for her wonderful flaxen hair, for she was handsome and her fashion sense was superb. Elegance can conceal a multitude of physical failings. Yet neither of them could guess at the fear and the racing thoughts that now ranged themselves behind that gloriously decked facade, the way that Marguerite's heart would pound and miss a beat so that she thought she would not be able to breathe or speak.

On her part, she saw two pauper girls of unknown parentage, dressed in gowns that they would never otherwise have been able to wear, their expressions wary, their manners hesitant. The leader of the two had classical features that might well develop into what passed for beauty amongst the lower classes, but thankfully the younger girl would be forever denied such an advantage because of the abomination of ginger freckles that coated her face.

Let your female Servants be Sallow of Skin with Hair the colour of House Mice. Keep Them dressed in Gowns that drape them from their Chins to their Heels and see that at all Times they wear high boots tightly laced to cover entirely their Ankles and Calves. Ideally, they should be incapable of Reading or Writing unless this is Deemed Essential for their Household Tasks. The Inculcation of Education into the Lower Classes incites Calumny and Rebellion. A peaceful Household is one that is Ruled by Well Trained, strictly disciplined Servants, ones who know Their Place and do not have their Heads filled with Fantastical Nonsense about bettering Themselves.

That cautionary warning of her grandmother's came into Marguerite's mind. The Lady Fleur Leveson had composed a household book which she had filled with hints, recipes, cautions and warnings for the new wife. Marguerite's mother, Elizabeth, had been raised on Fleur's Diary, as the family called it, and when Marguerite was seventeen, she had been given the book in her turn, to prepare her for wedlock.

'I disagreed only once with your grandmother,' Elizabeth had told her daughter. 'I hired a girl who was pretty. It ended in horrendous disaster.'

Marguerite had been five and thirty before she found out what that disaster had been and why her brother was sent to Europe a year earlier than planned. She learned that she had a niece in Scotland, who was

31

supported by her brother but whom he was never to see, by order of their father. The thought of her own dear son Robert falling foul of some seductive maidservant and having to be sent away made her shiver with horror. He was only ten now, but one day . . .

When Marguerite's eyes met Bellinda's, she had to stop herself from looking away. Forthright, bold and analytical, they were not the eyes of a foundling girl. She knows my secrets, thought Marguerite and she clenched her teeth together so tightly that her jaw ached. I wish she had never come here. Vanity should never have invited her. The moment that the festivities are over, she must go . . . Even working-class beauty was to be feared.

That man! Please God do not let me have to touch him! Sara was praying as the master of the house came ever nearer.

Knowing her dear friend intimately, Bellinda was aware of the intake of breath, the trembling of the freckled hands. Sara had told her smatterings about her life in the city, but not in any great detail. That it had been a time of terrible hardship and painful experience Bellinda had no doubt, for what else could it be for a waif without family and home who must wander the London streets begging a living? Sara's eyes filled with tears and her body shook when she talked of those three years that had fallen between the time she had lost her mother and the time that the Society of Our Lord the Saviour had rescued her and brought her to the Downley Home.

Thomas Groves-Hawkes was of middle height but his excellent deportment made him appear taller. Certainly to the stricken Sara he was giant sized and utterly forbidding. Born of parents who had never given a thought for the poor, and coming late to the realization of their privations, he could not do enough in recompense. Annually, he gave gifts of money to such institutions as the Downley Home and there was even a generous sum for the Matilda Lumley Home for Distressed Gentlewomen, a general term that concealed the fact that it took in middle-class females who had through their own stupidity, ignorance and pulchritude found themselves in an 'interesting condition' outside the sanctity of marriage. Thomas did not inquire too deeply if at all into the running of the institutions that he supported. His secretary, Edward, would do the inquiring and if the institution appeared reputable, then the funding would begin. If some of the money went into the pockets of the uncommitted then Thomas would never know. That it went out of his pockets was all that he asked.

Basically, he was an honest man, shrewd in the ways of business but lacking in judgement where men and women were concerned. He sought happiness, overlooking much in his desire to gain that state, blocking out many facts that it would have been in his better interest to know.

Bellinda saw behind the dapper appearance immediately, to the winsome child he had been, a fact which he would have been entirely shocked and dismayed to know. She liked him on sight, feeling a deep compassion for him. From what she had seen of the elegant Marguerite Groves-Hawkes, he had chosen a wife who appeared to put him first, but in fact put herself first. He had not yet discovered that and might never do so. She doubted that he would wish to learn it, for it would certainly not increase his happiness.

Bobbing her curtsey, she in her turn never guessed that Thomas thought her charming and graceful, secretly wishing that his own daughter could move with such fluid grace. Vanity bobbed and twitched and flicked her head from side to side like a bird while Bellinda undulated as if she had endured years of deportment lessons. Thomas and Bellinda took to one another on sight, but only Marguerite realized it. The self-centred possess a sharp intuition where their own security is concerned, and Marguerite's complacency had deserted her now that she saw the way in which

her husband was looking at the girl. It was not her
sensuality nor her erotic appeal, she was sure. Bellinda's intelligent expression, that questioning, questing
face was a challenge to him. While he might have
compassion for the younger orphan, for the older one
he would have greater plans. She could almost see him
thinking: I will have her educated; she will share the
children's tutor. I will make a young lady of her.

Marguerite felt her heart lurch into a panic-stricken
beating, as if it would leap out of her breast. As Bellinda gave her serene, intelligent smile, her clear green
eyes meeting Thomas's grey ones, Marguerite vowed
to stun her husband with a new night robe as fast as
she could be fitted for one. Something in a delicate,
transparent lawn that would reveal tantalizing glimpses
of her nakedness beneath it . . . Unlike many women of
her age and class, she was not afraid of what took place
in the bedroom.

Possibly transparent lawn would be too obvious?
Satin was a very sensual material. Or she would choose
the finest Parisian lace, a deep peachy pink trimmed
with bars of glossy satin. Hawkes would forget any face
but hers once he was in her bed. Her confidence
renewed at the thought, she relaxed a little, her heart-
beat slowing, her body cooling. It was foolish to doubt
that she would maintain her superior position in her
husband's affections. What was an orphanage brat
compared to herself? She had been idiotic to think that
the girl could endanger her marriage.

Unaware of Marguerite's tormented thoughts, Thomas and Bellinda smiled at one another, liking what
they saw, and, feeling a little happier for their meeting,
sat down to dinner.

Vanity, who had watched the greetings tautly, for she
wished nothing to go amiss, found herself smiling
broadly with relief. All was well. Her father found Bellinda and Sara amiable and the latter had been transformed by her new clothes, that dreadful grimace
having vanished. She would have the child's eyes tested

34

all the same, for lady's maids were required to sew a delicate stitch. Bowing her head, she listened to her papa saying grace, and believed that she would have her way after all.

Sara and Robert were decorating the tree with Vanity and Bellinda's help. Ceiling high, the lush-branched fir would have dwarfed a smaller room. Swathes of gleaming silver ribbon criss-crossed the dark green foliage in readiness to shimmer like moonlight when the candles were lit. To hang on the branches there were miniature figurines in porcelain, their faces painted with charming expressions. There were ladies in parasol-wide crinolines, gentlemen in frock coats and tall hats, boys and girls in gay tartans and checks, with hoops and sticks or dolls in their hands. Even the tiny dolls had perfect faces, their cheeks rosy red, their real hair eyelashes framing wide blue eyes, their mouths open to show minute pearly teeth.

Robert did not like Sara. He thought her very ugly indeed. However he knew that his papa was fully supportive of her presence in their home, and if he did not show kindness to the orphan girl then he would incite Papa's anger. Vanity too would display her irritation, and his sister's ill temper was to be avoided at all costs. Stumbling over the words, he forced himself to converse with Sara, passing the decorations to her so that she could attach them to the tree herself, and helping her when she found the silver tying tapes too slippery to make into bows.

'See, you can make them into knots instead. Mama will not mind. Who can see whether they are bows or knots with all this thick foliage to conceal the ribbons?'

Robert flushed as he spoke, his small, square body held stiffly. He did not want to touch the girl with freckles. Maybe it was a disease? Maybe he would catch those dreadful blotches himself?

'Thank you, Master Robert, I shall do as you say,' Sara said in her politest voice, the one that her own

35

mama had coached her to use on social occasions, and Robert looked at her strangely, thinking that she was making fun of him, but there was no sign of malice in her eyes.

Vanity beamed. Sara was already showing all the signs of being a sensible, well-behaved and grateful girl. How quick she was to learn, her phrases so decorous, her please and thank you never forgotten. She could be everything that Vanity hoped, giving her life in devoted service to her mistress.

Vanity had noticed Papa looking at Bellinda when he thought that he was unobserved, but she could not perceive anything unseemly in his gaze. It was as if he were weighing Bellinda in the balance, his mind saying first Yes, then No, then Possibly – and then returning to Yes. As these thoughts were also obsessing Vanity, she saw nothing untoward in others thinking them, too.

This afternoon Penelope Fritzby and her brothers were taking tea with them. It would be a further test for their two foundling guests. Penelope's brothers were everything one could desire in young men – dashing, eligible, heart-stoppingly handsome. If one of them so much as spoke to Sara beyond a formal greeting, then Sara would not become a lady's maid at Carlyon House.

'The tree looks beautiful, doesn't it, Bell? I remember when . . . ' Sara's voice tailed off. 'Yes, I do remember that we had a tree like that and I helped Mama to decorate it just as we have done today. Papa came in and lifted me high above his head and said that I was to be the Fairy Queen on top of the tree, and Mama laughed and said she would make me a silver gown and wings and I would be the prettiest Fairy Queen ever seen . . . '

When Bellinda turned from washing in the flowered china bowl, she saw tears rolling down Sara's face.

'Oh, my dear, you must not cry like that when we are having such a wonderful time.' She scooped Sara into her arms.

'What if Mama comes to collect me and I am not there and she goes away again and I never see her?' Sara's brown eyes were wide and staring.

'If your mama comes for you then the Governess will tell her that you are at Carlyon House, of course, and she will come here for you.'

'They – the family will not stop her taking me, will they?' Sara was trembling like a small child.

'How could they? Your mama is your mama and no one can stop her from doing whatever she wishes with you.'

'You are sure of that? They are a very powerful family, they have so much money and everyone talks of them as if they are royalty. Harding said that they have friends at the Queen's palace . . . '

'In their own way they are, but they would never do anything improper, I am sure. They would never come between a mother and her beloved daughter.'

Sara's eyes were dreamy now. 'My mama loved me very dearly, you know, Bell. She used to dress me in pink satin, the softest smoothest satin you ever touched, and there were tiny pink rosebuds on the skirt and pink bows at the neck, and my hair would be trained into ringlets with hot tongs like Vanity uses . . . And Mama would call me her most beautiful baby girl, although I was a lot older than a baby. I remember everything she said to me, but I don't – don't remember why she went away.'

The little voice trailed off, the shivers of dread receding as Bellinda held her. The Governess had often told her that Sara had originally come from a good family before being rescued from 'a wretched depravedness in the London gutters'. She had been found in filthy rags, her arms locked at the shoulders from holding out her hands to beg for hours on end. Bellinda had rubbed those bony little shoulders at every opportunity to bring back normal use to them, trying to coax Sara to talk of her past life in the hope that spilling out her troubles would spare her the wretched nightmares that

37

she suffered, but Sara rarely spoke of her three lost years beyond saying that she had been eleven when her mother and father left her and fourteen when she was brought to the Downley Home. There had been an attempt to trace the parents, but to no avail.

'There will be a better chance of your mama finding you here, you know, for she will hear about you being at Carlyon House. You know how people gossip. They will say, "There is a new girl, an orphan girl called Sara at Carlyon House, and she has so many freckles you would not believe it," and your mama will say, "How wonderful! That is my Sara. I will go and fetch her now." '

More tears were rolling down Sara's cheeks but they were tears of happiness now, as they always were when Bellinda spoke to her in this comforting way.

'Yes, she will say that and then she will come to the door and it will open and she will take me into her arms and we shall never be parted again!'

'That is how it will be, my little love. Now, had we not better prepare for these visitors who are coming to tea? Remember that we are guests here and we must not speak unless we are spoken to, nor must we draw attention to ourselves in any way. Keep your eyes lowered, Sara, and I shall do likewise.'

'M-men, they are men!' Sara wailed.

'No, my love, they are boys. The eldest is only a few months older than your Bell, and still studying. They will not harm you.'

Whatever had happened in Sara's past, she knew that it must have been shocking, but what mattered to her now was that Sara was safe and well and in her care.

The Fritzby boys were all incredibly good-looking, and they knew it. Lounging at the fireside, their long, muscular legs outflung, their lean-boned faces rosy from the flames, they were sipping Indian tea from dainty cups that looked doll size in their huge hands. The eldest, Leon, had thick blond hair growing in a peak on his forehead, its brightness making his eyes all the more blue. The second eldest, Garth, had eyes of a light honey brown, his hair being an even deeper gold. The youngest was Carl. Sixteen, with the dark-brown eyes and lustrous golden hair of his brothers, and still having the self-consciousness of youth, he tended to take grateful shelter behind the dictates of etiquette and a plate piled high with plum cake.

When the introductions were complete, Sara and Bellinda sat down on the small chaise longue that Vanity directed them towards. There was no room for anyone to take a seat with them, which was how it was intended to be. Mindful of their lower estate, they sat with eyes downcast, sipping at the deliciously scented tea and eating plum cake slowly and cautiously so that they would not drip crumbs, choke, or show a bulging cheek.

The conversation went on around them as if they were not there. Penelope Fritzby did not need to take a breath between her words, or so it seemed to her listeners on the chaise longue. Animatedly, she babbled on about her activities, all of them sounding of the most ordinary variety yet which she plainly found personally thrilling. It was gossip for the withdrawing room, banal, harmless and the dullest of fare, but Vanity too seemed enlivened by it, or so Bellinda thought from her flushed face – or was that caused by the presence of the Fritzby brothers?

One thing that one learned from being penniless, friendless and without family, was that one's opinions mattered naught, one's conversation was unwanted and one's presence was on sufferance. These lessons now blossomed for the two girls. They sat quietly, backs straight, sipping their tea silently, and behaving as if they were of no consequence whatsoever. Tolerance extended only so far; if they interrupted, or proffered a viewpoint, Vanity would put them back in their place instantly, they knew.

At one point Penelope, being a kindly girl, did attempt to converse with them, asking them if they were enjoying their stay, but Leon's loud guffaw at something his brother said completely muffled Bellinda's reply. Sara went pink, for it was all too easy to believe that the laughter was directed at them, that they were being jeered at. In her time, Sara had suffered more than her share of ridicule because of her freckles. Why should it be different here?

The worst moment came when Carl took a small clockwork figure out of his pocket, wound it, and put it on the rosewood table to show how it worked. The arms jerked up and down, beating little wooden sticks on to a red and blue tin drum, the figure in its soldier's garb marching furiously with rigid legs then tipping over the edge of the table to fall at Sara's feet.

Not thinking, she reached down to pick it up and as she did so, Carl's fingers brushed hers. She shrank back as if he had struck her, all the colour draining from her face. They were just boys, she reminded herself, just young boys, not men, not those vile, cruel men, but all the same she felt sick, the plum cake settling like a stone in her stomach.

'It is not broken?' Vanity inquired, apparently not having noticed Sara's dismay.

'No, thankfully it is not. It is for Cousin Louis. He is eight in January.' Carl's voice was strong and mellifluous. It melted from his throat like beaten gold. Sara's heart pounded and continued to pound until the boys and their chatterbox sister had gone.

That night she dreamed of a golden-haired boy who, dressed like an angel, descended from massed white clouds to take her by the hand. 'You will be safe with me, Sara,' said the angel, who had Carl's beaten-gold voice, and for the first time for three years, Sara did not flinch away from someone of the opposite sex but let him lead her upwards into the massed white clouds to safety and happiness.

Chapter 4

Robert had a cough and was being dosed by Nanny with blackcurrant syrup.

'Do you think that the contagion might have arrived on a letter?' Vanity said, her imagination rife.

Nanny looked at her with narrowed eyes. 'Miss Vanity, I have never believed in these newfangled insects they call grims. For one thing I have nivver seen one myself, so doubt they exist. Mark my words, some men have made themselves a grand fortune having us believe in so'thing what cannot be seen and then brewing remedies to kill it. Remember Robert's favourite tale, "The King's New Clothes". Not one wishing to be called fools, all but a boy said they could see the King's new clothes when he was in his birthday suit and not in his new clothes at all. I have it in mind to invent something invisible meself and then make a fortune from marketing a remedy against it.' Nanny folded her thick, capable arms across her billowing bosom.

In his bed, Robert giggled. 'Nanny, when I have my own company, you will be first to be asked to sit on the board.' Then he began to cough again and more blackcurrant syrup was administered.

'Keep those orphans out of here,' Nanny instructed. 'That Sara looks thin as a pickle spoon. We don't want her picking up some of these invisible grims, nor giving Master Robert any.'

'They are called germs, Nanny, not grims,' Robert corrected, licking the sticky home-made concoction from his lips. 'And why should I want girls in my bedroom, especially pauper girls?'

So Sara and Bellinda did not see Robert for two days but were given reports on his progress by Harding.

'U'll be well very soon and back playing with his soldiers,' she told them. 'It ain't nothing but a meek little cough.'

Robert, his early courtesy abandoned, had been most unfriendly to Sara, so she could not feel empathy for his confinement to bed. In fact it was a relief not to have his cold eyes upon her all the time. Instead, she thought of golden-haired Carl and yearned to know when he would be visiting again. There was of course no way that she could ask Vanity.

'I want a tin soldier that beats a drum, like the one Carl showed us!' Robert announced, and a servant was sent over to the Fritzby household, returning with empty hands for the gift had already been dispatched to the Fritzbys' cousin. Robert went scarlet with rage and sulked for the rest of the day. Not until his papa came home with a clockwork dog that barked when its tail was levered up and down did he smile. The dog barked incessantly for the next three days until Robert grew bored with it and it joined the great pile of discarded toys in the nursery.

One morning Sara picked up the dog. It reminded her of a toy that she once owned, a kitten that miaowed when its stomach was pressed. Her papa had brought it for her from a foreign country that he had visited on business. She had called the kitten Alice, after the Queen's daughter, and Alice had gone everywhere with her from that moment on. Until the terrible day when –

'That is my dog!' Coming into the nursery and seeing the pauper girl touching the toy, Robert snatched it from her hands.

'I know it is,' she replied, her heart thudding.

'Then why are you touching it without my permission?'

'I am sorry.' Sara looked away from the hard black eyes, the flushed cheeks. Robert was to be indulged until he was fully recovered, or so his mama had ordered.

42

'You are a bitch!' Robert hissed, using a word that would have shocked his parents deeply, but which was nothing new to Sara, who gazed at him in silence. Who knows what would have happened next if Sara, for once, had not been saved. Screwing up his face, Robert put a hand to his cheek, for a surfeit of blackcurrant syrup had given him the toothache. He went away, calling for Nanny and forgetting his persecution of the hated interloper.

Looking out over the gardens from the nursery window, the toy dog pressed tightly in her hands, Sara tried to recall something more of that time with her parents, but the memory had receded. All she could recall was the name of her toy cat. What had happened to Alice? If only she knew that. And if only she knew what had happened to her beloved mother.

When Bellinda and Vanity returned from a trip to the milliner's, their cloaks wet with sleet, their faces glowing, Sara said nothing about Robert's behaviour. That plus the hostile glares from Mrs Jermyn were the only things that marred Carlyon House, yet why should she expect anything to be otherwise? Even if Robert scolded her on the hour, every hour, this life she was now enjoying would be heaven.

'Sara, you look very pale.' Bellinda took her hand. 'And you feel hot. Are you all right?'

'Oh yes.' But she did not feel all right, and that night she began an attack of the coughing that she had not suffered for some months, not since Bellinda had fed her up on extra treats inveigled from the Governess – fresh butter and milk and even a little wild honey bought at the market in Wycombe. A dark-skinned Romany boy had sold her the honey, saying that it would bring back a corpse from the dead. It had certainly worked wonders on Sara's chestiness but now the cough was back, and Sara was confined to bed with a large bottle of blackcurrant syrup all to herself. Now and again, Nanny would peek in at her and mutter about 'confounded grims' and how everyone had been 'maudlin' ill' since they were discovered, which was not strictly true. And there was one terrible moment when the door opened and Sara saw Mrs Jermyn glaring at her, the look of a fiend in her eyes. The word she heard the housekeeper mutter was far more insulting than what Robert had called her, but thankfully the woman soon went away.

Bellinda sat beside her bed for hours at a time, feeding her warm milk sweetened with dark brown sugar and a little coddled egg when she could take it. The cough syrup stuck to her teeth, very thick and very sweet, but it did ease her chest.

'I shall be well soon, Mama.' Sara looked up at Bellinda with glazed eyes. 'Where is Alice? I cannot find her in the bed.'

'I do not know where she is.' Bellinda smoothed back the dark, sweat-dampened hair. Was Alice Sara's sister then?

'I want Alice!' Tears filled Sara's eyes and then she fell into a sudden sleep, and for the remainder of the night was quiet. Bellinda did not leave her bedside, but sat there nodding in her chair, her hand in Sara's.

She woke to the sound of a board creaking. In her sleepy state it sounded like the crack of a whip. Startled, she looked up. The master of the house was staring down at her.

'Sir!' She leapt to her feet.

'Sit down, Bellinda. How is the invalid progressing?'

'She is recovering well, sir, thanks to your kindness and the good food that she is receiving here.'

'You would not have had eggs and cream and black-currant syrup at the orphanage?'

'Never, Sir, for the budget would not have run to it.'

'What would you have had there?'

'Porridge oats, bread, jam made without sugar, pickled onions and sour cheese bought at a reduced price at market. Not because the Governess wishes us to have such plain fare, sir, oh no, it is not because of that,' she hastened to add. 'It is the budget, sir. We are totally dependent on the budget.'

'I see.' A chasm yawned before Thomas Groves-Hawkes. He did not doubt that Bellinda was telling the truth and yet he had never suspected that children in orphanages were fed such paltry fare. It was correct of course not to overfeed children with rich foods such as red meats and fruit cakes, for their immature digestions could not tolerate such excesses, but sugarless jam, and sour cheese? Would his children have welcomed these? Yes, if they had no option and knew no better, said his conscience, a conscience that had woken late in him and was all the more troublesome for that.

'When do you have mutton, or beef?'

'Never, sir.'

'Cocoa or eggnog? No, of course you would not have eggnog if you did not have eggs.' He smiled apologetically, his patrician features softening.

Bellinda was clenching her hands tightly. She knew that she must look terrible sitting there with her hair coming loose from its ribbon, her skirt crushed, her boots half unbuttoned to ease her tired feet. Nanny had given her an apron to wear while she was tending Sara and there were two dark syrup stains on it already. If only she could be invisible now, like Nanny's grims!

'It seems that I have a great deal to learn about life.' Thomas gave a sigh that was almost heartrending, as if there were a mountain of misery bottled deep inside him.

Bellinda did not know what to say. It would be rude of her to either agree or disagree. She waited, sleepiness creeping back up on her and conscious of how cold the room was now. She must add fuel to the fire when the master had gone.

But he did not go. To her astonishment, almost alarm, he sat down in the nearest chair and looked about the room, at the mirrors edged with pretty porcelain flowers in pinks and blues, the curtains of finest cream lawn, the scatter rugs of Turkey weave in dark blues and rouge reds. Such luxury for his children, yet in the Downley Home they dined on bread, sugarless jam, and sour cheese.

'I shall send more money to the Downley Home,' he said finally. 'Tell your Governess that she must let me know if there is anything in particular that she has need of. No, I shall tell her myself. You will not be seeing her until after Christmas, will you?'

'No, Sir.' Bellinda felt a heaviness enfold her. After Christmas all this would end and it would be back to the porridge and the freezing bed, breaking the ice on the washing bowls in the morning and shivering in church during the service because the budget did not run to warm underneaths. Once, her life had been uncomfortable but bearable. Now, after this, it would be intolerable.

For a time Thomas said very little, and strangely it did not seem to matter. Even in silence, they were in accord. They understood one another, he, the man who had never wanted for anything and she, the young woman who had nothing. If want was all there was to it, then they were worlds apart, but if each could offer something to the other, then it was a different matter entirely.

'Bellinda, Vanity tells me that you love beautiful things.'

'Yes, sir.'

'That is not an easy characteristic to possess when you do not have the money to furnish your desires.'

'I can enjoy looking at other people's beautiful possessions, Sir, like the wonderful ceiling in the dining room, and the French screen in the withdrawing room, with the painting of Madame de Pompadour.' Her tongue stumbling over the foreign pronunciation, she felt her face flame.

'You have an unusual name, Bellinda. Tell me how did you get that?'

She blushed even more as she told him. 'When I was a few days old, I was found on the steps of a hospice

46

just as the bells were ringing, so they called me Bell. The monks could not take me in, of course, so I was taken to the orphanage, and there the warden added a few more letters to my name to make it easier to say. Most people who know me shorten it to Bell, anyway.'

'Do you know what Bellinda means?'

'No Sir, only that I was named for the bells.'

'Bellinda is Italian. It means "beautiful serpent".'

'A snake is not a good thing, Sir –'

'A snake can be a very good thing, Bellinda, it all depends on one's beliefs. Very many hundreds of years ago, the serpent was sacred to the Great Mother Goddess who was worshipped and revered by virtually the entire world.'

'I do not understand how something as dangerous as a serpent could be sacred to anyone, Sir.' She knew what sacred meant, but only in relation to the church service and the hymns that she sang there.

'You have to understand what life was like many hundreds, thousands of years ago, when men were terrified of such natural events as eclipses of the moon and sun, when the world suddenly growing dark was an evil omen, a portent of violence, death and disaster, maybe the ending of all that they held most dear. The serpent lives beneath the earth, and the Great Goddess was Mother Earth. The serpent sloughs its skin, appearing as if by some miracle to renew its life and be reborn afresh. It coils in a serpentine shape and that shape can be seen painted and carved on so many vessels from the time of the Great Goddess. There were ancient rites, very sacred and mysterious ones, involving the snake. The serpent was as important to the people of the ancient world as the Cross of Jesus is to us.'

'I see, Sir.' Bellinda was trying to digest this extraordinary information. Country people respected the snake, but only, so she had thought, because it could bite and cause death.

'Women governed religion in those days, Bellinda, while men had very much of a back seat.' Something about that idea seemed to amuse him, for his eyes crinkled. 'Religious rites involved behaviour that we would consider highly indecent today. We spoke of Madame de Pompadour just now. The manner in which she elevated herself in the world was shocking, yet had she been born into the ancient world, she would have been a high priestess, and she, not the King, would have held the reins of power. What do you know of the Pompadour, Bellinda?'

Thomas's grey eyes were inscrutable. Bellinda wished that she dare turn up the lamp so that she could see more of his expression.

'Only what Vanity told me, Sir. That she was the – the favourite of the King of France and spent a very great deal on clothes and jewels and wigs.'

Vanity had in fact said that the Pompadour had spent nearly as much on gowns, jewels and accessories as Marguerite, but Bellinda could never have repeated that.

'Would you like to be in her position, Bellinda?'

'Sir, it is a pointless question for I shall never be wealthy enough to buy such finery.'

Thomas had not meant that and now he did not know if the girl were simply very innocent or had neatly deflected the true purpose of his question. Whichever, he suddenly felt ashamed of himself. Whatever other men might say of their wives, Marguerite never refused him her favours in bed, actually seeming to enjoy the rites of marriage. He had no need of a mistress, or even a dalliance, and if he attempted to seduce this girl into one, he would destroy more than one life. He would be extremely foolish to behave in such a way under his wife's roof, yet the girl was intriguing, and he had found his thoughts increasingly centred upon her. In his experience, poor women kept their eyes lowered and mumbled, 'Yes Sir' and 'No Sir'. They did not hold up their heads proudly and stare one straight in the face, nor did they reply to one's questions with such directness.

48

In behaving as she did, Bellinda had brought a great truth home to him. Torn the scales from his eyes, as it were. Despite his belief that he was now enlightened, he had been living behind a veil, seeing only what he wished to see, hearing only what he wished to hear. The poor and destitute, the homeless, the dispossessed, those born on the wrong side of the blanket, what were they to him, what could they be to him? At his birth he had been wrapped in lace shawls once worn by a French princess who had sold them to his father when she was fleeing from the Terror. He had been the much-desired son, born after four sons had died in infancy. Never had there been a more pampered and protected child. He must see nothing distressing, hear nothing upsetting; he must be kept from the world's most awful truths, or so his mother had commanded.

Servants had not been allowed to tend him unless they were in sparkling health. If they displayed so much as a sniffle, they were banned from his presence until they were well again. When he ventured out in his little carriage with the bright coat of arms of the Hawkes family, he was not taken where he might see poverty or baseness. When he was fifteen years old, his mother had spoken of his favoured childhood, telling him that it had been her idea, that he had her to thank for all the beautiful memories of his early years. Her eyes had glowed as she had talked of his 'idyll'. When he had done the Grand Tour at the age of nineteen, a year later than his father wished because his mother shrank at the thought of what he would see in Europe, he had looked on his first ragged and barefoot urchins, his first tattered beggars and wailing infants falling from their drunken mothers' arms. In his ignorance, he had put it all down to being in a foreign place, being quite sure that nothing like that could be seen in England.

'The French are depraved,' he had told his tutor, who was travelling with him, 'and that beggar without arms . . . Ugh! Thank God we shall be home shortly.'

His tutor had looked at him pityingly, knowing full well what his mother had decreed. 'Do not disillusion my son!' she had commanded before they left for Europe. How he would have liked to describe some of the appalling sights he had seen in the Rookeries of London, yet he was forbidden to do so on pain of dismissal.

A favoured childhood! Thomas's mouth twisted wryly, for it seemed to him that the ignorant bliss his mother had planned for him was in reality the clanging emptiness of a fool. With every day that passed, coming to realize how little he knew, he had despaired of ever catching up. He would gasp out loud at things he heard, at the tales of hardship and tragedy and untimely death that were the reality of the world so long concealed from him, and however much he learned, he thought that he would never know enough.

This girl sitting before him in her crumpled gown with her hair undressed and her boots unbuttoned knew more about the real world than he ever could. Compared to him she was weighted down with knowledge and experience, all that he had been denied. Within her was all that he longed to know, to feel, to hear and see. He had to struggle with himself not to reach out and touch her. It was as if all the richness kept from him in his childhood were embodied within her. His palms tingling, his half-lifted arms were reaching out, when the child in the bed gave a moaning sigh and rocked her head from side to side. It was enough to bring him to his senses, and how distant they had been from him. What might he not have done but for that interruption? For in that sudden and frightening moment Thomas Groves-Hawkes realized that his feeling for Bellinda was more than an ambivalence of pity and emotion. Her serene beauty had captivated him. Other thoughts invaded now – thoughts that should not be there.

Rising hastily to his feet, he stumbled out, narrowly missing tripping over a footstool. Bellinda heard his retreat down the corridor and as the sound faded into the distance, she sat there, her mouth puckered, wondering. If she was a beautiful serpent, what was he?

'Oh dear God!'

Turning up the lamp by the bedside as Sara woke with a fit of coughing, Bellinda saw scarlet stains on the pillow. Blood! Sara was coughing blood. Looking around her for something that would mop it up without being spoiled, she saw only the cloth that lay on the medicine tray. Hastily pulling it from beneath the bottle of blackcurrant syrup, she wiped Sara's mouth.

'It is red.' Sara looked at the stained cloth and then at the blotches on the pillow. 'Why is it red, Bell?'

'Your cough has made your throat raw, that is all. It will heal, my love.' She spoke reassuringly, but feeling a coldness bathing her heart so that it lodged in her breast like a snow-covered stone. Sara had consumption, the flux that ate out the lungs until they could no longer take in breath. Other girls had died of it at the Home. It was a fact of life, and no one was free of it, not even the rich. What was more, it was highly contagious.

Bellinda was not thinking of herself but of the reaction of the master and mistress of the house if they found out. There would be no Christmas at Carlyon House for Sara if they knew . . . She would be sent away, back to the cold, meagre life of the Home to shiver beneath a threadbare blanket and dine on sour cheese. Bellinda had not had time to become fond of the people in Carlyon House but she loved Sara to distraction. All they had was one another and they would never be separated. If necessary, she would lie to keep Sara at Carlyon House. She would lie, dissemble and conceal and do whatever was necessary to save her Sara's life.

The wardrobes were awash with underlinen. No one would miss a petticoat or two. In secret, Bellinda cut one into handkerchief-sized pieces to hold at Sara's mouth, then placed a larger piece over the pillow so that any blood that was spattered would be caught in it. She washed the bloodstained linen in the little alcove outside the sick room where there was a small sink, and put it to dry on the fireguard, keeping some whole petticoats handy to drape over it should she hear anyone coming.

The coughing did seem to improve, however, much to her relief. She sat patiently spooning nourishing broth and milky possets into Sara's mouth, urging her to eat. Reminding her of their miserable fare at the Home.

'They will be eating sawdust sausages at the Home now, Sara, and cinder bread,' she said, making Sara giggle with her descriptions of the food. 'Eat, for you must build up your strength. There is honey toast to follow if you finish all this.'

Vanity swept in unexpectedly, her hazel eyes sharp. 'What, not better yet, Sara? Are you planning to spend Christmas in bed being waited upon?'

'Oh no, Miss Vanity, she will be well by then,' Bellinda replied swiftly, and in fact Sara was improving.

'I have told Robert off for giving you his cough. I bring people here as companions and then they are ill, thanks to him!' Vanity pouted, her eyes winging round the room. Bellinda held herself tautly, dreading that Vanity would notice the white cloths drying on the fire guard, but she did not. 'The tree looks wonderful – oh, but of course you helped us decorate it, did you not?' She looked at Sara piercingly, as if guessing what was wrong with her.

'Are the master and the mistress well?' Bellinda inquired politely.

'They are indeed. Thank you for asking, Bellinda. Are you not becoming bored with your sick-room duties?'

'I always care for Sara, she is like a sister to me,' Bellinda answered gravely.

'If I told you to come downstairs and read to me then you would be required to obey,' was Vanity's somewhat haughty response.

'Indeed I would and I am ever mindful of your great kindness in having us here and of how much we owe you, Miss Vanity,' Bellinda said, her voice as warm as she could make it.

It was exactly the right note to assume. Vanity smiled, and stood up. 'But of course I would not dream of taking you from your sister, as you call her. One must be faithful to one's dear ones. Tell Harding if there is anything you need for the invalid.'

'Chicken broth'll bring the colour back to ur cheeks,' Harding said when she brought in their lunch. Harding was kind and did not turn up her nose at them like some of the other servants who thought themselves almost as grand as their employers.

'Not chicken broth again!' Sara complained, and Bellinda spoke almost crossly to her.

'Sara, you had never tasted chicken until we came here.'

'Oh yes I had! Mama always gave it to me when I was ill,' Sara cried.

Harding raised her brows at Bellinda. 'Her likes to think her wus raised a lady, don't her?'

Bellinda lowered her voice. 'Sara did come from a good family, Harding, one that was quite rich from what I can gather. Somehow she lost them – but she will not talk of it, so I cannot tell you anything else. Maybe they abandoned her. Maybe she was abducted by thieves. Who knows?'

'Ooh!' Harding's eyes opened wide. 'There wus an infant took by gypsies 'bout two years gone. 'Bout March it was. Stole hur from hur bassinet they did and her wus nivver seen again. There was a terrible commotion and 'undreds of men set out in search of hur, but naught wus found. Hur mother did die of a broken heart.' Harding looked at Sara, her eyes narrowed as if by doing this she might be able to guess her true identity. 'Poor little mumpet.' Harding gave a deep sigh, then mindful of her duties, smoothed down her apron and sped away to her next task.

53

Sara was already halfway through the broth, crumbling the fresh white yeasty bread into the dish and spooning it up greedily. 'You were right, Bell,' she said. 'It was all that coughing that made my throat bleed. But now it has healed, hasn't it? And I shan't miss Christmas?'

'My love, you are not going to miss it. I shall see to that.'

Bellinda meant what she said. If there could have been some way of extracting her own sturdy health, her strong blood, and giving it to Sara then she would have done it at once and with all the love in the world.

Chapter 5

The most joyful moment each morning leading up to Christmas Day involved the Advent calendar that Thomas had given his children, Vanity and Robert taking it in turns to peel back the little flaps that would reveal all manner of wonderful holy scenes.

Bellinda enjoyed this moment enormously, for putting aside some of her dignity, Vanity would behave with a gleeful abandon. Surprisingly, Robert did not, despite his being only ten years old – or maybe it was the presence of the two pauper upstarts, as Bellinda had heard him call them.

Today the scene was of the Virgin Mary riding the donkey to Bethlehem, Joseph trudging along beside her.

'Mary and Joseph going to the Holy City!' Vanity cried, her face shining. 'Do you not think that Mary is very beautiful, Papa?

'The artist who executed the painting is from Paris. The French have a particular eye for beauty,' Thomas replied.

A voice broke through their conversation. It was Sara, her face white and strained. 'That is not Mary and Joseph, that is my mama and papa coming to Wycombe to fetch me home! They will be here very soon. I have been waiting such a long time for them.'

There was an embarrassed silence and then Robert said, 'If their arrival means that you are to leave us, Sara, then no one will be more pleased than I.'

'Robert, go to my study!' Thomas commanded, his voice thunderous.

'But Papa – '

'At once, I say!'

Scowling, Robert obeyed, brushing roughly against Sara as he went.

'I must apologize for my son. He has the Hawkes temper but that is no excuse for being so rude. He has been spoiled and he cannot adjust to others receiving the attention that he thinks is his entirely.'

'Oh Papa, that is not fair!' Vanity cried. 'He is not jealous of me!'

'Vanity, I did not ask for your opinion, thank you. Sara, I can only say that I am sorry for what Robert said. It was unforgivable of him when you are guests in our house. He will apologize to you himself when he has recovered himself.'

Sara was silent, not knowing what to say, but Bellinda's hand was on her shoulder so she felt safe despite the scene. It was as if a rough wind had whirled itself about her head, but there was tranquillity now.

'Sara would not wish to be the cause of any upset while we are here,' Bellinda said quietly. 'Perhaps it would be better if we did not stay. Christmas is a time for families to be together, not to be divided.'

'Christmas is a time for charity, for helping those in need, Bellinda. Vanity invited you both here for the festivities and here you will stay.'

Later that day, Robert did come to apologize to Sara and he did it with good grace although his jaw was tight with anger. Sara's response surprised both him and Bellinda.

'Master Robert, I want you to be very happy this Christmas, and the last thing I wish is for you to be sad. I hope that you will forgive me for being the cause of the scene that upset you.'

Robert, who had been crumpling his face to stop a scowl forming, looked at Sara in astonishment. She had spoken like a young lady of good breeding, Vanity herself could not have made a sweeter apology. He would have been a savage not to accept it and put his resentment aside.

'I hope that we shall be friends from now on, Sara,' he heard himself saying, much to his own amazement.

56

'And you can play with my clockwork dog as much as you like,' he added.

'Oh thank you, Master Robert!' Sara beamed, her pale face brightening.

After tea, Robert put the toy into Sara's hands himself, almost managing a smile. For the rest of that day she sat in her chair in the nursery, the dog in her lap, and now and again she would pat its head and whisper, 'There, there, Alice, you are safe now.'

In the wash house Mary Alewin, the head laundrywoman, was battling with the mistress's latest purchase, the Thomas Bradford rotary washing machine. It had been invented to replace the old box mangle that needed a great deal of elbow grease to turn its wheel. The new mangle turned so swiftly by comparison that one needed to be constantly alert or fingers could be trapped and the arm swept up into the rollers and crushed.

When Mary had finished the mangling, and piled the folded sheets into the big zinc bath, she heaved it out into the gardens. Two of those sheets had come from Sara's sick bed for it was Mary Alewin who had washed the blood off them. The sheets were too large for Bellinda to manage in secret, and she had taken Mary into her confidence.

'How's that Sara?' Mary asked Cook, knowing that the elderly woman shared her fondness for children.

'She's up and about today but looking peaky, Harding says.'

'Do yur think Miss Vanity will keep her on?'

''Tis said she might, for there's none more grateful than those rescued from adversity. And from what I've heard 'bout the Downley Home 'tis sparse fare up there. Now if the maister instructed me, I'd be making them pies an' puddings by the dozen and Arthur could take 'em up every week.'

'On top of everything else ye have to do, Cook? What aboyt the mistress's dinner parties – there were thirty invited last time, so yur said.'

'If I had another hand in the kitchen I could do it.'

Mary changed the subject sharply. 'Cook, your niece had the consumption, didn't she?'

'And what if her did?' Cook bristled. 'I was never in contact with her, so there was no risk of – '

'Oh I didn't mean that, Cook. I just wanted to ask how it affects people. I mean, can yur get well again?'

'Her didn't but then her lived in the city in one of those dark slums and her would never cook herself a proper meal. Her lived off bread and dripping, nor would her drink milk. If yur wealthy then ye can pay to go to a drier clime, but even then it's usually fatal.'

'Fatal?' Mary's heart gave a jolt.

'And it's easily caught, so it gets passed from one to another in the family and they all dies afore ye knows it. Once the blood starts coming up, well, what can ye expect?'

Mary leaned back, her cup of tea slopping on to her skirt. She was thinking of all that blood on the sheets and how she had rubbed it with her hands to loosen it. The water had been quite scarlet. Would the consumption be carried in the blood, would it have those invisible things in it that Nanny talked of? Mary did not want to ask herself the next question. Banging down her cup, she hurried off with a muttered comment about work to finish.

Cook watched her going, her mouth twitching crossly, for she had been looking forward to a good gossip. Mary Alewin had not been the same since that Jake fellow had come into her life. Cook thought of her own George, dead these twelve years from an accident shortly before they were to be married. There had never been another man in her life. Why was it that those who loved children the most were denied them?

Vanity was showing Bellinda her papa's collection of Chinese porcelain, fragile and gleaming as if touched by moonlight.

58

'Papa inherited these from Grandpapa Hawkes. He was a great traveller and he went to the East as frequently as possible. Grandmama Hawkes was not a good traveller and so she stayed at home and completed two hundred embroidered tablecloths and twelve altar cloths. Personally, I would have gone with Grandpapa rather than sit at home and sew, but she suffered from the *mal de mer* – that's sea sickness, Bellinda – and she would not risk the long voyages. Would you have gone with him had you been she, Bellinda?'

'Maybe. It sounds very exciting.' Bellinda's palms were tingling with the longing to touch the beautiful poreclain.

Vanity rattled on. 'Do not tell anyone but he had a Chinese favourite, you know, like Madame de Pompadour was King Louis's favourite. She was what is called a *horizontale*, that is French for one who lies down with men, you know. They say that we have yellow-skinned relatives somewhere in the East. They say that about Mary Alewin, too. Have you seen her yellow skin?'

Bellinda shook her head, wondering if she was going to be confronted with the matter of the stained sheets.

'What can one expect with men being men and doing all this travelling away from their homes? If wives would only take the trouble to make their husbands happy in bed, then husbands would be faithful. A happy man would not dally with a mistress and curse his descendants with yellow skin!'

'Do you have plans to marry, Miss Vanity?' Bellinda swept the conversation away from Mary Alewin.

'Indeed I do, but not until the right man comes along! I would have liked to marry Carl but he is too young for me. It might be Garth or Leon, or it might not. Papa says that I shall be free to choose and he will not force me into anything.' Vanity tossed her curls.

'You are very fortunate.' Bellinda's eyes were on the huge gleaming vase that stood on a plinth in the corner of the Chinese Room. There were golden dragons coiling round it and blood-red flowers of a kind she had never seen before. Her fingers itched to trace the delicate porcelain, for when she touched beauty she absorbed it deep into her soul, and how lacking in beauty her life had been.

'Do you like that? It is very, very old and quite priceless, Papa says. It once belonged to an Emperor in China of the Ming, or was it the Sung dynasty? I always get confused with dynasties. Ask Papa. He will tell you.'

'May I touch it?' Bellinda could not hold back any longer.

'I do not think Papa would care to risk that, Bellinda, you're not used to such fragile things. Just looking will have to satisfy.' Vanity did not realize how condescending she sounded.

'Of course.' Bellinda's calm voice betrayed nothing of how Vanity's words had stung her.

Sara was listening, her eyes on the two young women. So Vanity would have married Carl had he been older . . . Sara felt sick when she heard those words. Carl was the golden–voiced angel who came to her in her dreams and spoke to her as if she were his beloved. He belonged to her, not to Vanity. Vanity had so much, a whole wide world too much, while she, Sara, had nothing.

'Sara, are you taking notice of what I say about Papa's collection?' In preparation for training the younger girl as her maid, Vanity's voice always became more imperious when she spoke to her. 'It is exceedingly famous and people come from all over Europe to see it. No one is allowed in this room without a senior member of the family to accompany them.' Vanity had not yet informed Sara of her plans, and the child looked so drained of life since her illness that one did wonder what should be done with her.

'The collection is most breathtaking, Miss Vanity,' Sara replied. 'My papa was interested in Oriental porcelain, too.'

Vanity and Bellinda looked at Sara as if she had grown two heads. She had the ability to produce these extraordinary remarks, spoken in that high, carefully modulated voice that suggested a middle-class upbringing.

Over her head, Vanity mouthed 'Did he?' but all that Bellinda could do was shrug. She was beginning to doubt Sara's utterances, for the girl could produce little information about her past when they were alone, yet could come out with these amazing statements in company. It could be that Sara enjoyed being the centre of attention and must concoct fibs to maintain that place.

Attention now was on the little group of figurines on the ormolu table. An immensely fat man carved from topaz jade caught Bellinda's eye. Grinning from ear to ear, he wore a brief Oriental robe, and on his broad forehead was a smoky yellow jewel.

'Do not look into the jewel, girls. It is said that if you do so, you will lose your senses. I myself have never dared to take the risk for in this world one needs all the senses one can assemble.'

Sara was tempted. They could see her eyes wavering on the jewel, her head jutting forward, but she thought better of it.

'Very wise, young woman,' Vanity said.

Bellinda's eyes were now on a graceful statuette of a beautiful woman sitting in the middle of an open flower. In her arms was a child. It was the woman's expression that enraptured her with its serenity and sweetness. As she gazed on that radiant face, she felt herself being swept towards some unfamiliar, strange and disturbing destiny and she wanted to submit to it at once with a meekness that was not in her nature.

'Who is the lady and why is she sitting on a flower?'

'Oh, that is Kuan Yin. She is the Chinese Goddess of Mercy, the Mother Goddess of the East, rather like the Catholic Virgin Mary. That is a lotus bloom she is sitting on but why she does so I cannot tell you. You will have to ask Papa. He knows everything there is to know.' Vanity's eyes came to rest on Sara and there was a coldness in them.

'Are you going to tell us that it is not Kuan Yin but your mother holding you in her lap when you were small?' she asked the younger girl who looked away, her lower lip trembling.

'No, it is not my mother,' Sara said, her voice low.

'What a relief! Had it been she then we would have had to alter the whole of Oriental history for you, Sara.'

For someone gently raised, Vanity had a very insensitive nature and Bellinda could not keep the hostility from her expression.

'This is my favourite cabinet.' Vanity moved across the room. 'Look at these – do you know what they were for?'

The two girls looked at the long, curving golden spikes lying on a pillow of cream silk edged with gilded tassels.

'Are they Chinese daggers?' Sara asked.

'No, they are not Chinese daggers.'

'Chinese knives?'

'No, they are not Chinese knives. Let me give you a clue.' Vanity held up her hands, fingers splayed.

'Are they Chinese fingers?'

'Of course not!' Lifting out four of the golden crescents, Vanity pushed them on to her fingertips. 'See, they are false nails.'

'But with those on you could not comb your hair or fasten your buttons!'

'The Chinese Emperors did not do anything so mundane as that. They wore these false nails to show that they did not need to dirty their hands with common everday tasks. For that, they had thousands of willing servants. They were worshipped as gods, you see.'

Vanity reached out, lightly scraping the nails down Sara's arm, but the younger girl leapt back as if stung, her face ashen.

'Did that upset you? I am sorry.' Vanity did not sound sorry at all. She was thinking that lady's maids had to be calm and unflappable and that perhaps Sara was not the right material after all. Silly child, did she not know that this was her greatest chance in life, her only chance, and that she should be showing abject gratitude?

Vanity now moved across to the cabinet that contained the rare collection of jade, but Bellinda's thoughts were on the Goddess of Mercy. She was feeling again that inexorable pull and trying with all her might to rationalize it. The statuette was foreign, and foreign things could be odd and disturbing, even frightening. She was dazzled by the beauty of the room's contents and that was why she imagined that Kuan Yin was speaking to her. If only she could hear the words clearly . . . Irresistibly drawn, she looked back at the statuette.

Kuan Yin was gazing straight into her eyes, and her arms were extended, offering the child to Bellinda. Bellinda's mouth fell open, a little gasp escaping it. She was so shaken that she dared not look back again. For the remainder of their time in the Chinese Room she kept her back to the Goddess of Mercy, but was so preoccupied that she did not notice how distressed Sara was after Vanity had pressed the golden nails into her arm.

'Get away, get away!'

Sara's cries woke Bellinda, and she was beside her on the bed before the girl's eyes were properly open. Taking Sara in her arms, she said, 'You are only dreaming, Sara, only dreaming. Bell is here to take care of you.'

For a few moments of frenzy, Sara pushed at her wildly and then her head sank against Bellinda's breast as she wakened fully. 'He was going to scratch me, Bell, the beast was going to scratch me! That's what he liked to do . . . He had long nails all sharp and he would scratch me until he fetched blood.'

'It was only a dream, my love. You are thinking of the Chinese emperors and their false nails.'

'No! He was a real man, a terrible man. He used to – he used to – Bell, you know what men and women do to have children? He used to do that to me, all the time. He enticed me, that's what the Society people said, he enticed me and because I was so young I did not know what he intended. He shut me in the dark and then he did that to me, for days and days.' Sara was shaking violently. 'Then he said I was too old for him and he had me thrown out. I was freed, but all I had to wear was an old rag of a dress that was too small for me, and no shoes. I did not know where I was, or what my name was. All I could remember was Sara, but that was not my name. It was my mother's name! Bell, I have remembered my mother's name!' Tears swept down Sara's pinched white face.

'Can you remember her last name?'

'Sara, Sara . . . No, I cannot, but I shall try. It might have begun with B, or V. Oh, I don't know.' Fresh tears came. 'When will she come for me, oh when?'

There was silence for a time as Bellinda cradled her close, wondering if Sara's horrific tale came from memory or nightmare. Then from the depths of her arms, Sara whispered. 'I think there was sickness. Mama and Papa were sick, very sick of the cholera and they died, and someone, a servant, I think, was paid to take me to Papa's friends but she went off with the money and left me in the street. Soho it was, yes, it was in Soho that she left me.' Sara was holding out her hand towards the lamplight. 'Look at the scratches, Bell. He did that to me.'

Bellinda took the small hand in hers. It was totally unblemished, and she kissed it and held it to her cheek. How desperately tragic this child's life had been, so bitter was the memory of her parents' deaths that until now she had erased it, pretending that they were still alive.

'Kissing heals scratches quicker than anything else in the world,' she said, 'and when you look at your hand in a few moments, all the scratches will be gone.' Slowly she counted, one, two, three, four, five, and then she showed Sara her hand again and the younger girl gave a tremulous smile at the sight of its unmarked flesh.

If only the inner scars could be healed as swiftly.

Chapter 6

'Darling, are you quite sure you want to go through with it?' Marguerite was reclining on a blue velvet chaise longue that had once graced Malmaison before the Empress Josephine had sold some of her furniture to recoup a debt. She was wearing a new morning gown of greengage velvet trimmed with tiered frills of hand-made lace. Her fichu was of matching lace. The new cuirass corset gave her the neatest of waists and a far more striking bust line. One would not have guessed that she had borne children. 'She looks such a surly child to me. I have not yet seen her smile.'

'She has been ill, Mama, and that was Robert's fault, you know.'

'Blame cannot be apportioned for illness, darling –'

'I know that, Mama.' Secretly Vanity herself doubted that Sara was suitable material for lady's maid training, but she refused to agree too easily with her mother. Certainly Sara could speak well enough, which was greatly in her favour, but she did not seem quite right in the head. Those utterances of hers were quite beyond understanding; out would come all manner of unexpected pronouncements almost as if she were vying to outdo her patrons in some way. What one dearly wanted from the creature was heartfelt gratitude, a goodly portion of meekness and sharp, shiny manners at all times, as Papa called them.

The other orphan, Bellinda, was a far stronger character, Vanity thought, than the pathetic Sara. Had Bellinda been given the benefit of a proper, decent upbringing then she would have made a remarkably excellent lady, but of course she came from God knows where, having been born of some unspeakable union. There was no hope for foundling females. They either succumbed to the gutter, or lived shadowy existences on the verge of immorality. Madame de Pompadour had come from a very poor family. Fish had been her family name and she had certainly swum upwards against the tide. Emma, Lady Hamilton had begun life as a serving wench and had ended it in a pauper's attic in Paris because of her debauchery. And if one wanted to add to the list, there was an entire string of *horizon-tales* who had assumed that position with the present heir to the throne, Edward, Prince of Wales. His brother Clarence was no better: the rumours about him were quite shocking. It was unbelievable what men did when they thought themselves unobserved, but word got round all the same and Vanity was a skilled eaves-dropper; it helped to lighten life's tedium considerably.

Vanity was intrigued by scandal. What made men commit adultery when they had beautiful wives and glorious children? What made women commit the un-speakable act outside the sanctity of wedlock? Did they not understand that they were ruining their lives for ever? All reputation gone, what did they have left to offer a decent man?

'Vanity, I am talking to you. Where are your wits?'

'I am sorry, Mama, I was thinking of what you said before.'

'And what was that?'

'About Sara not smiling. She should be smiling, for we have done so much for her. She is an odd creature. When I showed her the golden fingernails in the Chinese Room she leapt back as if I had stung her.' Vanity did not reveal that she had actually scratched the nails deep into Sara's arm to test her self-control.

'Servants must be implacable at all times, sweetheart. Skittish girls have no place in a well-run orderly house-hold. I remember your Grandmama Hawkes once gave a luncheon for an extremely important gentleman who had brought some priceless jade for your grandpapa's collection. In the middle of the luncheon, a mouse appeared in the kitchen and one of the girls from below stairs came screaming into the luncheon room and landed in the man's lap.'

'How dreadful! What happened?'

'Something even more unfortunate. The man, obviously not in his right mind, married the chit. Disgraceful. Of course he could never be received at decent tables again. One cannot allow anything to happen in one's household that is out of one's control. Do you comprehend, Vanity? When you marry, you must have servants who are both diplomatic and discreet. Imagine what that Sara girl might say out loud if one of her odd moments was upon her! I have been thinking about getting you a French maid, one ready trained. I know you wished to do a good deed and rescue a waif, but one cannot allow the waif to upset the entire household, can one, darling?'

Vanity sighed. A French-trained maid would be all very well, but such a servant would be quite capable of obtaining work in any wealthy household and so would not display the gratitude and loyalty that Vanity desired. 'I had thought about that, Mama, and I shall think on it some more, I promise you. There may yet be hope.'

Marguerite continued as if her daughter had not spoken. 'We cannot uproot the creature now, of course. Let us get Christmas over and then she can go back to the Home. Give her some of your cast-offs, and a basket of food and some trinkets and she will be quite content, I am sure. The Governess at the Home can find work in one of the dairies for her, a little hard toil will take out that high and mighty streak better than anything.'

'You could be right, Mama.' Lips pressed tightly together, Vanity took out her embroidery. She was decorating a mulberry velvet waistcoat for her father as his Christmas gift and had only one small patch of dark green leaves to complete. For her mother there was a set of one dozen fragile lawn handkerchiefs, each embroidered with a spray of roses. For Robert, there were

embroidered slippers. Vanity had a delicate and in-
spired touch with her needlework, inherited from
Grandmama Hawkes who had preferred sewing to the
sea, but she had no intention of being confined to
the house with her sewing after her marriage. Wherever her husband went, she would go too. Let anyone
try to stop her!

'Quickly, I hear your father's footsteps!' Marguerite
hissed, and Vanity was closing the lid of her sewing box
as Thomas stepped into the solar.

'Ah, here are my beautiful girls. How are you, Marguerite my heart?'

'Very well, my dear.' Marguerite pressed her fingers
into Thomas's neck as he bent down to kiss her, to
remind him of the passionate night that they had spent.
Reclining in her greengage velvet morning gown, her
superb waist nipped in by the fashionable corset so that
her creamy breasts looked even fuller. Marguerite had
never appeared more attractive. It did not matter that
she lacked beauty, for she was fresh skinned and her
tumbling flaxen curls retained the glossy luxuriance of
a girl's. No wrinkles marred her complexion, but the
tiny mole at her mouth's corner caused her hours of
irritation. In all their years of marriage she had never
dared ask Thomas if he liked that mole, or hated it, for
if the answer were in the negative she would die of
embarrassment and humiliation.

Sometimes she dreamt that the mole had grown big-
ger and was now a hideous growth on her face, and
then she would wake with a little cry.

'Did you hear about the foundling – the freckled one,
that is? Vanity showed her the Chinese nails and they
positively terrified her!' Marguerite laughed up at her
husband. 'I must say I find this orphan a rather tiresome and unsettling creature. 'She comes out with these
utterances, as if to tell us she is grander than we are.
It will not do, Hawkes!'

Swinging her tiny feet to the ground, Marguerite sat
up. 'Where is Harding with the tea?' Swishing across

the room, her silk petticoats rustling, Marguerite tugged angrily at the bell. She could simply have rung the small hand bell nearby, but she knew what a magnificent figure she presented to titillate her husband's passions. There was nothing feeble or retiring about Marguerite, unlike so many of the wives they knew who retreated to their beds with various incapacitating symptoms, imagined or otherwise. She was strong and sturdy; she had produced two children without any of the usual problems, and she was not afraid of conceiving more.

Harding appeared, her cheeks rosy, her cap askew. 'Pardon, Ma'am, but Mary Alewin is to marry and we been drinkin' to hur 'ealth.'

'Mary Alewin is to marry! Did you know about this, Hawkes?'

'Why yes, my love. Mary's young man asked my permission some days ago. I meant to tell you.'

'They should have asked me first! Mary should have come to me!' Marguerite glared at her husband. 'They are my servants and I must be informed first.'

'Of course, my love,' Thomas soothed, comparing Bellinda's serene dignity, her ability to cope with the unexpected, with Marguerite's obsession with the running of the household, who did what and when and why. She would have been so very much more at home at Versailles where the strictest etiquette governed all.

Harding could not wait to get out of the room. In her haste, she let a madeleine fall to the floor from her pocket where she had hastily pushed it. Marguerite let out a shriek of horror.

'Sorry, Ma'am.' Harding scuttled to retrieve the cake and then could not think what to do with it. Three glasses of Cook's elderberry wine had numbed her senses. Finally, she pushed it back into the pocket of her apron, bobbed a curtsey and flew.

'They should have celebrated with us!' Marguerite accused. 'Now we cannot offer them alcohol or they will be running amok.'

'My dear, they are not wild beasts to be chained in their lair. They have a right to celebrate when and where they wish.'

'They do? Then they must dine with us tonight, Hawkes. Lady Gooding and Sir Edward will not mind one jot if they find a washerwoman and her intended sitting beside them. Indeed, I would think that Teresa needs nothing more than a long diatribe on the merits of washday!'

Picking up the train of her gown, Marguerite stormed from the room.

'Oops, I think that I have offended your mama.' Thomas's pale eyes twinkled.

'She will survive.' Vanity had no time for her mother's tantrums. Tantrums meant that one had lost control. One day she would tell her mother that. 'Papa, I might keep Sara on as my maid. What do you think? Should I do that?'

'Have you discussed this with your mother?'

'Yes, Papa. She is against it. She does not like Sara.'

'If your mother does not like the child then it would be ruinous to go against her. She would make the child's life a misery, you know.'

'Yes, I know, Papa, but I did so want to have her as my maid. In so many ways she would be suitable.'

'Your mother has trained you well, my dear.' There was an ironic note in Thomas's voice which was completely lost on his daughter.

'Yes, she has, Papa.' Vanity waited for her father to continue but he was silent for some time.

A servant brought in a large engraved silver tray laden with silver comfit dishes piled with sweetmeats, and plates crammed high with gingerbread, rich fruit cake, Madeira and Genoa cake. The Georgian teapot was shaped like a cupola. It had once belonged to the Prince Regent, having been styled to blend with his folly at Brighton. At one point, starved by debts, he had sold a chestful of silver to Thomas's great-grandfather, a staunch Royalist who had given him an excellent price for it. Behind the larger tray came a smaller one borne by Harding and on which lay another eight dishes of madeleines, plum cake, Victoria sponge slices, and scones with little individual pots of jam, butter and cream.

Vanity would dearly have liked to launch herself at the food, but her papa was obviously intending to say more and she could not ignore him. She might not love him too greatly but she did respect him. When the servants had withdrawn she said, 'Papa, are you not proud of me?'

This did bring his attention back to her and he ceased his pacing up and down.

'Of course I am proud of you, my dear. You are my very own daughter so how could I not be?'

'It is just that, oh, sometimes I think that you prefer Robert.'

Thomas was not going to be drawn into discussing favourites, or admitting that Robert was indeed his favourite.

'Wise parents do not have favourites, my dear. I love both my children equally.'

'Mama does not, you know, Papa. She loves only herself –'

'Vanity! That is not true!'

'But it is, Papa. If you were poor tomorrow, she would leave you.'

'That is ridiculous. Where do you get these fanciful ideas?'

Thomas looked closely at his daughter, at the rather hard planes of her face, the unblemished complexion and the small, clear eyes. Her mouth was too small for beauty, her nose too large. Had she been born to poorer parents she might well have ended up as a governess in some indifferent household. However, as the daughter of Thomas Groves-Hawkes she would have no difficulty in finding herself an important husband. Thomas had worked closely with Prince Albert on his plans for the Great Exhibition, drawing together

72

all those who could assist in providing magnificent displays of antiquities. There had been talk of a knighthood, and then the Prince had tragically died of typhoid.

However, Thomas's work was not forgotten, and he still visited the Queen at Windsor when they would talk over those happy days before the Prince's death. Her Majesty could not hear enough of Thomas's anecdotes about her late husband, wishing to listen to them over and over again. For Vanity there would be suitors of worth and substance, men closer to the hub of society, someone near to the Queen perhaps. There was after all no speedier mode of advancement. Thomas had always sensed a restlessness in Vanity, a desire for excitement and gossip. She would become increasingly bored in the countryside but life at court, or attached to one who must spend time at court, would change her way of thinking, broadening her mind. Preferably the man must have a title, or be in line to inherit one. It was his great desire to have a title for his daughter. The Groves-Hawkes had money, reputation and standing. A title was the next ambition.

'I see what I see, Papa.' Vanity's crisp voice brought him back from his dreams.

'And so do I, my dear. Hunger has made you ill tempered, I vow. We shall not wait for your mama to return.' Thomas sat on the Malmaison sofa and with his own hands lifted the Prince Regent's teapot and poured the pale golden liquid into the delicate Sèvres teacups that had once belonged to Madame de Pompadour.

Bellinda was haunted by the little statuette of Kuan Yin. Somehow she must hold that delicate figure in her hands and look into the porcelain eyes again. Was Kuan Yin trying to tell her something or was she imagining it? It was a wild notion and she was not one to value such things; all the same, she could not free her mind of it. She knew that no one was allowed in the Chinese Room without a member of the family, and

73

she had considered asking Vanity to take her in there again, but thought better of it. She did not like asking favours of the girl for she sensed that favours would be required in return and they might not always be pleasant ones. Besides, Vanity's tongue was as sharp as the Emperor's false fingernails when she was in one of her acerbic moods, and these seemed to have predominated of late.

That night she stared out at the stars from her room, knowing that she was the only one still awake in the entire house. It was a strange feeling, almost one of power. She might have been the only human being awake in the entire world. When the moon-faced clock in the hall chimed twelve, she made her way down to the Chinese Room.

The hall was silvery with moonlight, and avoiding all the creaking floorboards she made her way to the door. Her heart was thumping as she gently turned the handle and stepped inside. In the darkness there was a strong odour of things foreign – spicy, disturbing and unearthly. Lighting the lamp by the door, she stood for a time adjusting to the muddy yellow light, seeing the strange unfamiliar shapes trembling into the shadows as if they were preparing to leap out at her and grab. Biting on her lip, she walked towards the figurine of Kuan Yin.

The Goddess was leaning out towards her exactly as she remembered, her slanting eyes beseeching, as if to say Have mercy! The child she was offering was smiling – yes, smiling up at Bellinda. Taken aback, she let out a gusty breath. How stupid of her! The Goddess was fashioned in that pose, her eyes had been shaped to look entreating. There was no mystery in it and she had been a fool to believe that there was.

'The things of the Orient are strange and unsettling,' she had read in Thomas's library. 'Men have travelled in the Orient and they have come home vastly different, changed in many subtle ways. The East and West should not mingle, for the East is deep in mysteries that we can never understand.'

74

What point in thinking of that now? Touching a statue could not change her in any way at all, and the face of Kuan Yin was as gentle as that of the Virgin herself. How could she be harmed? The statue was porcelain, cold, soulless. Even if she held it, even if she held it close to her breast, it could not hurt her.

Heart pounding, she took the Goddess and the child into her hands.

'What have you to say to me, Kuan Yin?'

Bellinda looked into the slanting eyes only to have them stare back into hers with the same frigid gaze that any statuette would offer. Disappointed, almost aggrieved, she went to put the figurine back on its stand, and it was then that she felt the slight movement, the thud thud thud as if a heart were beating deep inside the china. The shock of it made her arms jerk wildly and to her horror the figurine slipped out of her grasp to shatter into fragments at her feet.

Chapter 7

'Bellinda!'

She heard the voice of Thomas Groves-Hawkes as if he spoke to her in a dream. Turning slowly, she looked into his eyes while the shock of what she had done turned her inch by inch from warm to cold.

'What do you think you are doing?'

The figurine was now in Thomas's hands. It was not broken as she had thought.

'But I saw the pieces shatter – '

'In your fear you saw it shatter, but as you can see, it is not damaged.' There was a light in Thomas's eyes that she did not perceive. 'Here, if you want to hold it, take it now. You cannot appreciate true beauty if you do not touch it.'

Holding out the figurine, he waited for her to take it from him.

'I – I could not. How can you trust me after this?' She backed away, her hands bunched at her thighs.

'Bellinda, you should have asked me if you wanted to see more of the treasures. From what Vanity said, I gathered that you did not enjoy your visit to the Chinese Room.'

'I enjoyed it very much, Sir!'

'So you returned . . . ?'

'Yes, I returned.' She looked down at the floor, shamefaced.

'Take the lady from me.' Again he held out the figurine and this time Bellinda took it, but her hands were trembling. 'She is the Goddess of Mercy in her homeland, the protectress of women and children and those in dire need. If you were a Chinese girl then you would pray to her and make offerings, rather as we do to the Virgin Mary in the West.'

This time Bellinda knew that the sensation of a heart beating deep within the statue was her own heart pounding, the throbbing of it pulsing against the china. Was it because she held this most precious object or because the master of the house was so close to her, so close that she could smell the brandy on his breath? He was old enough to be her father yet she could sense something more than paternal interest in her.

'Miss Vanity told me a little about her, Sir, but I would like to know more.'

'Kuan Yin also helps those who are sick. She is ever conscious of the suffering in the world.'

Thomas stopped speaking, watching Bellinda's fingers caress the figurine. She had a gentle touch, like one who is accustomed to the fragilities of precious relics. By rights she should have had square hands, solid and rough, but her fingers were supple as eels and infinitely tender. How he would love them caressing him! That thought brought a rage of colour to his cheeks and a twisted feeling in his belly. If he were to believe the popular ethos of the day, women were Satan's temptation and if one lay with them, one would fall along with them, as Satan had fallen. But this girl was so innocent, so unworldly. He was sure that she was a virgin and that if he despoiled her, it would be the cruellest thing he had ever done. Even so his arms began to rise in readiness to pull her close. He wanted that soft fresh youthful skin against his own, he wanted to kiss those frank green eyes and –

'Hawkes!'

It was Marguerite resplendent in midnight-blue velvet, the Groves diamonds glittering at her breasts, ears and wrists. With her flaxen ringlets trembling, her ivory skin flushed and the icy fire of the diamonds blazing on her body, she looked like an avenging Valkyrie.

'Yes, my love.' How smooth his voice was and how calm. No one could have guessed what had been in his mind, the thoughts of naked white flesh and curving

77

hips, the dark, moist haven where he longed to bury himself. 'Bellinda is admiring the statue of Kuan Yin.'

'At this hour?' Marguerite looked outraged. She and Thomas had been out for dinner with Lord and Lady Templeton, arriving home to see a light in the Chinese Room. That this girl should be in here unattended, touching these priceless treasures!

'She was so involved in her appreciation she forgot the hour, my love.'

'No one is allowed in here alone. Why did you not ask Miss Vanity to show you round, Bellinda?'

'She was helping to make the masks for Christmas Day, Ma'am, and a headache came on so she went to bed early. I did not want to disturb her.'

'And so you took your chance? Yes, I see.' Marguerite's face was stretched into vitriolic lines. 'Hawkes, send her to bed and then come into the library.' The mistress of the house swept out.

Harding always left a tray in the library for them when they had been out, brandy for Thomas and something rich and fortifying for Marguerite. Tonight it was dark, fruity plum cake with a glass of milk standing beneath a lace cover but she paid the food no notice. Shutting the door behind them, she turned on her husband.

'It is just as well that I changed my mind about going straight to bed, is it not? Hawkes, you are so foolish you would have given the girl that figurine! The look on her face! I thought she was going to weep from joy – and well she might be if allowed to hold such a priceless object. Next you will be inviting all the servants into the Chinese Room and telling them to choose what they wish for Christmas!'

She stamped her foot, exactly as a small child might, and had he not been so shaken himself he might have laughed at her tantrum and turned his back on her, but tonight he could not. Marguerite, ever materially oriented, had thankfully not sensed what was truly in his mind. She had seen only value and its possible loss, and for that he must be grateful.

78

'My love, the child has a gift for beauty. She appreciates it and I thought I might teach her something about the collection.'

'Like what? That foundlings are fit to be curators? Really, Hawkes, you are the silliest man at times. If you want to give the child some gift, then find her some fairing. What difference would she know?'

'I had no intention of giving the child the statuette! I was merely telling her about it.'

Marguerite walked towards the fire, conscious of the elegant beauty she was displaying. Tonight she had achieved what some would say was impossible: the male guests who had sat at Lord and Lady Templeton's table had looked at her breasts and not at the Groves diamonds, famous though they were. She was beyond the age when women were said to be finished, and yet she glowed with life and health. If only her husband would appreciate it! Turning, she looked at Thomas with a sad light in her eyes that he had never seen there before. She had spent hours before the mirror rehearsing it.

'Hawkes, I feel that there is an increasing void between us. It began when those girls came here. They have turned the household upside down. It was the most witless idea to have them here and I would blame Vanity entirely if she were old enough to blame. But she was merely trying to follow your teachings about charity – and look where it has got us all! It has left me feeling . . . feeling estranged from you!'

Thomas's mouth fell open. This was the last thing he had expected from his sometimes wilful but usually devoted wife. The shock of her words was so great that he sank down on an armchair beside the fire, staring silently into the scarlet coals. He wished he knew what to say, but he was lost for words.

It was Marguerite's trump card and she had played it superbly. Even she had not been expecting such a magnificent reaction from her husband. He looked like a man who was finished. Triumph blazed in her breast;

79

she could not keep the gloating look from her eyes and it was there when he looked up.

'Marguerite, I married you because I thought you the most glorious creature I had ever set eyes on. I still do. I shall always think that, but if you wish us to live separate lives – though, I hope, remaining together in this house for the sake of our children – I shall not stand in your way.' He got to his feet, not believing that he had said what he had, a clenched sensation in his chest, his legs fluttering like paper in the breeze.

'Hawkes!' she called after him, the colour stripped from her face, but he did not turn back and when she reached their bedroom, she found that he had locked himself in his dressing room. Only once before had he slept on the couch in there and that was their first row, the week after they had returned from honeymoon. She could not even recall what it had been about but the making up had been joyously sweet. Her maid would be asleep; there was no one now to unlace her. She had been looking forward to her husband helping her to undress, for she had been aching to seduce him. The role of temptress suited her admirably. To have a man worshipping at her feet was intoxicating. Now there was no one to kiss her and marvel over her white breasts and say how smooth was her skin and how pale and soft her hair. Her ploy to reignite his waning passion for herself had gone disastrously wrong.

Taking up her ostrich fan, she tore it into tiny fragments, until her dark velvet gown was covered in drifts of snowy feathers and the air misty with them.

'What have you been up to, Bellinda? Mama is in the most furious mood.'

'I went into the Chinese Room without permission. I am most awfully sorry, Miss Vanity. I shall apologize again to your mama if it will help.'

'It would not help, I am afraid. She is beyond all reach at the moment.' Vanity thought of her mother's boudoir as she had seen it this morning, with the curtains of the wonderful bed cut into tatters and the light film of ostrich feathers lying like snow everywhere. Worse, the painting of her father's mother that hung in the room had been drenched with an assortment of Parisian *parfums* that had seriously damaged the brushwork. Marguerite had always complained about having to look at her mother-in-law while she was lying in bed, and now she never would again. The painting was ruined.

'I did not mean any harm, Miss Vanity – '

'Oh, they all say that. Bellinda, you know right from wrong, do you not? So why did you venture in there? Mama says that you were planning to take some treasures and run off with them, but I do not believe that.'

Bellinda went bright red. 'I would never have done that! I only wanted to look at the little statuette again.'

'You should have waited until I was better. Now the household is in turmoil and Mama and Papa are not speaking. But I shall speak in your favour to Mama. You will be allowed to remain until after Christmas, as will Sara, of course.'

Vanity, stubborn as she could be in pursuit of her own wishes, had finally discarded her fantasy of Sara as her devoted lady's maid. Marguerite had so taken against the child that it was quite impossible. Vanity sighed. After Christmas, she would speak to Mama about finding a trained French maid.

Thomas was translating a strange book written in Latin by a man who signed himself Witch Finder, and who had been given the task of searching out witches during the time of Thomas Cromwell. The book had arrived with a batch of old histories that he had bought. So far he had translated only half a chapter, but he was already finding himself thinking quite fondly of an age where any woman who rebelled against her husband and behaved oddly was considered quite likely to be in league with the Devil and thus liable for a stringent punishment. The scold's bridle . . . How he would love to see Marguerite locked into that!

Sara and Bellinda were banished to the nursery for the evening when friends of the Groves-Hawkes were to be entertained. From that room they could hear nothing of the jollity, but Alice the clockwork dog was on Sara's knee. Harding had brought them a tray piled high with some of the same dishes that were being served in the grand dining room and they were more than happy to have a quiet and cosy evening alone.

Bellinda was reading aloud from an article on deportment in one of Vanity's magazines.

'The female who works on the land will have a ruddy complexion and brown arms. She will wipe her nose on her sleeve and slap her lips when she eats. She will speak in coarse, uncultured tones and laugh raucously. A lady must at all times keep in mind such low behaviour and ensure that she does not emulate it. A lady keeps her voice low and controlled. She eats silently and does not slap her lips together. She uses a handkerchief at all times. She does not laugh out loud but low and gently. She wears a sun bonnet at all times to protect her complexion . . . '

'So ladies are white and farm girls are brown? But Mary Alewin is brown and she is a lady.'

'The differences are not always clear, my love, and it depends who is doing the judging. To this author, Mary Alewin would not be a lady whether she was white, brown or green.'

The door of the room creaked suddenly, warning them of someone's approach. It was Miss Vanity. Both getting up, they bobbed a curtsey but she waved at them to sit down. She was tightly encased in a rose-pink satin gown with a fichu of delicate Honiton lace. Round her throat was a single string of pink pearls and in her hand a pink ostrich-feather fan.

'I was becoming very bored downstairs, girls. Mama has invited some Earl's son and she has in mind that I shall fall madly in love with him and be married by the spring, but I do not like him. He is a very greedy fellow and he stuffs his mouth when he eats. But he is important and so I have to be polite to him. A cousin of the Dashwoods is dining with us too and he is much more fun, but alas he is married.'

'We were not doing anything that would amuse you, Miss Vanity,' Bellinda said, putting down the magazine. 'It is very quiet here.'

'I can see that it is.' Heedless of her satin gown, Vanity plonked herself on the padded top of one of the toy trunks, stretching out her toes to the fire. 'Do you know what Papa is planning for you, Bellinda? No, I can see that you are innocent of his intentions. I told him that you could read and write as well as I can and so he is going to employ you.'

Bellinda stared in surprise. 'I do not understand. What could I do in the master's employ?'

'He is to teach you everything that there is to know about antiquities, Bellinda. He tried with me once, you know, but I am not that interested. Like Mama, I find all these old pots and dishes unutterably dull, but you obviously think they're marvellous, which is how Papa feels, too.'

Bellinda felt herself flushing. 'I do not think that I could do anything like that. I know nothing about them.'

'Exactly. So Papa is going to teach you. Then you can make an inventory of all his treasures, with a brief description of each one, so that he knows exactly what he has, what it looks like, where it came from and how. You see, we know about the lords and ladies who fled here during the French Terror, and what they sold to our ancestors, but what if these facts are forgotten? What if future generations of our family do not realize that such and such a thing belonged to the Prince Regent, or to the Empress Josephine, for example? Papa feels very strongly about such matters. He wants it all recorded.'

'What about the master's secretary? I would have thought – '

'His time is already fully taken up with Papa's other business. So you see, Bellinda, you are to be honoured.'

It had been a beautiful evening until that moment. Had she known that the mistress liked her, then Bellinda would have been overjoyed, but Marguerite bristled at the sight of her. She had no desire to stay where she was not wanted. And what of Sara?

She must have spoken the words aloud, for Vanity said, 'Sara will go back to the Downley Home in January, and when she is fifteen, I shall see that she is found a suitable position in a very good household. Because of her frailty, she will not be expected to scrub floors and blacklead grates. I will make sure that she gets a kindly mistress. Does that satisfy you, Bellinda?'

'Yes, Miss Vanity.' That Vanity should be taking such an interest in them was unusual to say the least. They must be grateful, even if it meant that they would be separated in the New Year.

When Vanity had gone, Sara looked at her friend, her brown eyes glowing. 'It will not matter, Bell. Mama is coming for me at Christmas, remember? You will be happy here at Carlyon House and I shall be happy with my mama. She will be taking me home.'

Bellinda hugged Sara close, saying nothing, but there was stark pain in her eyes. Sara was fortunate that a good post would be found for her, for she would not have lasted long as a skivvy in an unkind household. They must be grateful and give thanks that Vanity was interested in them, but how it rankled that they should be so dependent upon the whims of the rich, who could use them like Master Robert's chess pieces, as if they had no feelings or emotions of their own. She had watched Master Robert and Miss Vanity playing chess, and she supposed that this move could well be called a checkmate.

Chapter 8

Sometimes Sara thought that she was on the Christmas tree, in the shimmering silver dress that her mama had made for her, and those were her happiest times. All around her Carlyon House was throbbing with activity, the air rich with the scent of spices, herbs and sherry-soaked fruits. Not even Harding had time for a word, and now that Bell was shut away with the master every morning, Sara felt very lonely.

Seeing Sara wandering around below stairs with a forlorn expression, Cook called her into the kitchens.

'Come in, my little mumpet, ye look pale as a suet dumpling. Here, sit ye down and drink some o' this.'

Cook plonked a mug of creamy milk before Sara, followed by a dish of almonds and raisins, then, her arms floury, she set to work on the pastry she was making.

'Ye can allus come in here when the others is occupied, Sara. I allus have time for a little chat. Just pop in and we can have a chinwag.'

'Thank you, Cook.' Sara sipped at the milk, a rim of white froth gathering on her upper lip. It was warm in the kitchen and there were lovely smells that reminded her of a kitchen long ago, where she had sat just like this and been made much of by her mama's servants.

'Families are allus run off their feet at Christmas, dear, and ye mustn't think they've forgot ye. They've got their secret wrapping to do. All those presents, y'know. Miss Vanity has hand made every gift she's giving. She 'as been busy on them since August. I think there's a little smidgin of a something for you too, Sara.'

'For me? But I have nothing to give in return.'

'We can soon sort that out, my dear.' Cook was thinking of the hope chest that she had never used.

85

'I'll not have that creature listening to the kitchen gossip, Mags, it's not proper!' Jane Jermyn stood with hands on hips, her face raw red with fury.

'Jane, ye must remember her is but a little 'un and Christmas do mean a lot to they.'

'Mags, you are the most sentimental woman on God's good earth, but you must put sentiment aside this time. What if she overhears our private talk and carries it back upstairs?'

'I shall make sure that her do not hear it.' Cook crashed down the pastry she was making, covered it liberally with flour and banged at it with her wooden rolling pin.

'You cannot be on guard all the time. Servants do gossip. 'Tis their way.'

'Not afore the child they do not. I make sure on that!' Cook banged the pastry so hard that the flour sprinkler jumped two inches into the air.

'Mags, we should not even be holding this conversation. You must not encourage the child. She might be a spy – '

'A spy? Jane Jermyn, you 'ave lost yur wits!' Cook shook out more flour, not noticing or not caring that some of it drifted on to the housekeeper's immaculate black dress.

'Mags, you clob head, look what you dun!' Mrs Jermyn lapsed into the colloquial that she strove so hard to conceal in her efforts to elevate herself, for while it was forbidden for others to rise above their station, she considered it all right for her. 'You 'ave made a right cagmag of my dress. Now ull 'ave to change! You besom, this be my second-best dress!'

'Jane Jermyn, I ain't no besom and dun ye go a-callin' me that or ull clob head you with this rollin' pin!' Cook wielded the wooden weapon threateningly and Jane retreated, her teeth clenched tightly together.

After she had cooled down, Cook thought of her plan. She was ever one for making peace where others strove to make war. If Sara made some small gift for Jane at Christmastide, then would it not win the housekeeper over, or at least placate her a little? Jane was a prickly creature, ever mindful of her own importance and quite ruthless in her quest for security. Cook knew the truth about her, of course. How she had been the twelfth child of a family of fifteen, her father a chairmaker with poor health who had preferred drink to work. Her mother had taken in washing to keep the family going, and hard labour had finished her at the age of thirty-nine, when she had fallen dead in her little wash house. The father had not seemed at all upset, so Jane had told her, and after hanging round the cottage complaining bitterly about his lot for some weeks, he had vanished, leaving Jane and her three elder sisters to care for the rest of the family.

It was a common enough story. Families were too large and too poor, and if the mother or father failed, there was no respite for the children. The workhouses were always waiting for those who fell on hard times. Jane and her sisters had brought up the family, going out to work to bring in money. Jane had risen above her less ambitious sisters, who were only parlour maids. A hard streak there was in Jane Jermyn: perhaps it was the same hard streak that had made her father walk out on his family or maybe it was a cover for all the hurt she had known? Cook hoped that it was the latter.

As she cut up the fruit for the tarts, she thought of her hope chest and the linen that she had been saving for a marriage that had never happened. There were one or two bits of lace in there. Sara could make a lace collar for Jane, perhaps, or edge a handkerchief for her. A good little deed like that might bring a smile to the housekeeper's face.

Sara had been walking along the passage to the kitchen when she heard the two voices raised. Stopping, she clung to the stone wall with her fingers. Cook and

Mrs Jermyn were arguing about something, and instinctively she knew what that something was. Unable to move because her legs were trembling so much, she heard every word. Mrs Jermyn had called her a spy, but she was nothing of the sort. Wherever she went, people accused her of doing wrong. Robert thought she was trying to steal his toys. Mrs Jermyn thought she was snooping on her. And the mistress . . . The mistress looked at her with the coldest contempt she had ever known.

If this was real, true life then she did not want to live it. She had thought that happiness was bound to come if only she was protected from the men who had abused her body, but it had not; and now that she knew it would not, she closed in upon herself.

As the housekeeper swept out of the kitchen, muttering abuse between clenched teeth, Sara hid behind the door of the buttery, then went back upstairs, her step slow. If it caused trouble when she went into the kitchens then she would not go again. Thank heavens her mama would be here soon, for she could not go on like this much longer.

It was traditional in Carlyon House that the servants exchanged their gifts on the morning of Christmas Eve. From that morning when the candles were lit on the tree and the gifts taken out from under the fragrant green arms, Bellinda was happy. Cook had given her and Sara some squares of linen and from these they had worked laboriously to make small handkerchiefs for everyone in the family and for each of the senior servants. The men had a plain square, the women a smaller square edged with old lace.

Mrs Jermyn looked down at her lace-edged handkerchief with astonishment. The gift had put her in a very embarrassing situation. She knew what she should say but she did not wish to say it.

'Come on, Jane,' Cook hissed, 'do they right thing by the child. Say thank ye.'

'Thank you, Sara,' Jane said, her voice squeezed from her throat.

'We have a little something for you, too, Sara,' Cook now said, handing a parcel to her.

Sara looked at the package, her eyes shining.

'Open it then, we are ull waiting to see what be in it.'

Tearing at the wrapping paper, Sara uncovered a soft brown scarf, its ends fringed and bobbled with white. She could not believe that it was hers and tears came into her eyes as she tried to thank everyone.

'Chose it to match your eyes we did,' said Cook, her face flushed with delight.

'You are all so very kind.'

'Now open yours, Bell.' Cook handed Bellinda her gift.

Inside the paper was a soft leather purse, and inside the purse were ten shillings, 'from all the servants of Carlyon House'.

Bellinda said her thank yous, her eyes bright, but she was conscious of the tight-mouthed expression on the housekeeper's face. It was almost a sneer today.

Thomas was still shut in his dressing room, sleeping on the couch. He would never have thought it but he was finding his new monastic existence remarkably refreshing, and almost welcomed the estrangement from his wife, despite frequent quarrels.

Marguerite was very demanding in bed. He knew that he should be grateful for her generosity, but at the moment all he felt was a deep ennui. Other men had grumbled to him of their frigid, uncooperative wives, but how could he tell them that his wife was if anything oversexed? What would they say? It was not an acceptable topic, for ladies were not meant to enjoy sexual conjunction; they endured it. Was he then to say that his wife was not a lady? No, the matter was too complex for that. Unfortunately he did not feel that he was capable of analysing her. She was spirited and handsome; she had always been faithful. She did not flirt or encourage other men. She seemed totally satisfied with him, yet was he satisfied with her? There was something oddly missing from their relationship, something that he had never guessed at until Bellinda had come to Carlyon House.

Bellinda, beautiful serpent. Lying on the couch, hands behind his head, he imagined her in the Garden of Eden, her oak-dark hair spread wide around her moon-pale body, her breasts rising and full, the nipples pinkish brown. Her legs were shapely, he knew even without seeing them. Full white thighs, tender dimpled knees and tiny ankles. She was sitting against a tree, one leg raised so that he could see the dark bush between her thighs. Her arms were linked round her knee and she was smiling gently, looking at someone with those almost shocking green eyes. Who was she looking at, his beautiful serpent, his temptress?

'Let it be me,' he whispered beneath his breath, 'let it be me!'

Then in his imagination, he was in her arms, pushing back the heavy dark waves of hair with trembling hands and resting his head on her breasts. When her arms curved round him, to hold, to cage, the breath choked in his throat as if a hand were clamping him there. Gasping, he rolled over on to his belly and thrust his hips against the padding of the couch, throttling his groans with his palms across his mouth.

Even in the plain light brown dress that Vanity had deemed suitable for her, Bell looked beautiful. Only with difficulty could Thomas keep his eyes from her during the church service, throwing all his energies into singing the Christmas hymns. Beside him, Marguerite was glorious in velvet the colour of holly berries, a little green hat tipped to the front of her head and decorated with asprey feathers and one bright red rose. She was by far the most handsome woman in the church, and she knew it. He should have had eyes only for her; he

90

should have been enraptured by her, but he was not. Whatever had been between them had evaporated. He had heard other men talk of the joy vanishing from their marriages and he had pitied them, never thinking that it could happen to him. Now he realized that only a fool expected to continue loving his wife indefinitely. The gloss eventually got knocked off the gingerbread, and then there was nothing left but crumbs to snatch at.

If she had only shown an interest in his collections, but she viewed his antiques and curios as valuable possessions, nothing more, things to add to the Groves-Hawkes glory, while he looked upon them as heritage and inheritance, living history in his hands, to be cherished as he treasured his ancestry. A wry smile twisted his mouth as he thought of the ruined portrait of Adela, his mother. That destruction had been symbolic, he now saw. Adela had raised him to see only beauty, and now he was left with nothing but that while all else eluded him . . .

Bellinda was singing heartily, as was Sara. After the special breakfast that was being prepared for them, the family gifts were to be opened, and Sara had talked of nothing else except that moment when her mama would come for her.

'She will be here today!' she had cried on waking. 'She knows that I am waiting for her!'

'What will you do if she does not come, my love?'

'Oh but she will, she will!' Sara's eyes were shining, their sight set on far horizons that Bellinda could not see, places where Bellinda could not go. She found that quite disturbing.

The service over, the family trooped out, Vanity in pale coral velvet edged with miniver, Robert in his tweed suit with a cape over his shoulders. Behind them came the servants in their best clothes, hands together, heads lowered. The Vicar beamed at everyone, his wife's hands twirling round and round one another even faster than usual, as if in chase. She wore a dress of dull purple that made her skin look blotchy and sallow. Marguerite stood beside her for some time, forcing empty chatter from her lips so that everyone could see how glorious she looked beside the frumpish Vicar's wife. The latter was so overwhelmed at being picked out for this honour that she blushed a bright vermilion and looked about to faint.

'Get the sal volatile ready!' Bell hissed to Sara. 'Will you catch her or shall I?'

'Not me!' Sara hissed back.

The house was gleaming when they returned, scented with beeswax and pine needles. Brabam was waiting at the door with punch glasses filled with a deliciously warming negus, and then they made their way into the white drawing room to open their presents.

'Yull's lucky girls,' Harding had said, 'getting two lots of presents.'

There was indeed a gift for each of them from every member of the family, a light brown merino wool cape for Sara, with brown leather gloves, and for Bellinda a merino cape in a sensible dark brown. Marguerite had chosen it to make her look dowdy, but instead the dark colour made her eyes even brighter, her skin more translucent. Robert gave them a quill pen each, and writing paper tied in blue ribbons, and Vanity gave them eau de cologne and scented soap in pink satin-covered boxes.

Then Sara handed out the handkerchiefs they had made, the plain ones for the gentlemen and the lace-edged ones for the ladies. Vanity looked pleased with hers, but Marguerite held hers at her fingertips as if it were soiled. Sara lowered her head, for she wanted to say something sharp to the mistress of the house, something sharp and rude and offensive, but she knew that she must not for Bell's sake. But when Mama had ridden up in her handsome carriage, all dressed in velvet and furs, her tinkling voice calling out for her beloved daughter, then the mistress of this house would have to change her tune!

'Mama, that woman has been most unpleasant,' Sara would say, and Mama would stride up to Marguerite and slap her face hard, first one cheek then the other.

'No one is unpleasant to my beloved daughter!' she would cry and Marguerite would fall to her knees and beg forgiveness. Sara found herself beaming broadly at the thought.

When the gifts had been exchanged, refreshments were brought in by Harding, and Robert and Vanity then recited verses by Tennyson and Wordsworth. Their parents watched them with delight and admiration, but when Marguerite tried to exchange a glance with Thomas, his eyes were cold. She felt a chilly sensation of shrinking inside. She had badly miscalculated. She had thought that he would come running, begging and pleading with her, but he was keeping his distance and looking far from unhappy about it. Something must be done, and quickly.

Bellinda gave a reading from the Bible, verses chosen by Vanity, and then Sara recited a verse from memory, a verse that she had been carefully learning for some weeks with Bell's help. The verse had been selected as an appeasement.

God made the lady of the house so fair of face
And the servant who waits on her and always knows his place.
God knowing what is best for all, oversees the human race
Master and mistress at the head, their servants at a slower pace.

Even Marguerite applauded Sara, but her face remained sour.

When Brabam brought in the huge goose, Robert shouted out loud with glee, and Sara laughed too. Soon everyone was smiling, and the happiness lasted right through to the iced Christmas pudding. Then

93

Sara did the strangest thing. Listening with her head on one side, she said, 'There she is now,' and getting to her feet without permission and walking out of the room to the front door, she struggled with the heavy handle, breathing heavily as she pulled open the door and stepped out on to the wind-blasted porch.

'Mama!' she cried, and ran down the steps on to the drive, her arms raised, but those who hurried after her could see no one there to greet her. They stood watching the unsettling scene, not sure what to say or do while Bellinda ran after Sara, calling her back into the house, but not knowing whether she would obey.

Chapter 9

'She will not stay in this house one day longer!' Marguerite cried. 'She is an actress, she will do anything to get our attention! She has upset this family from the day she arrived here and now she has ruined our happy Christmas Day!'

'I think you are right, my dear.' Thomas sat by the window of his dressing room, looking out at the bleak, frost-hardened garden.

'Think? I do not think, I know! She is the most cunning child ever born but she will be cunning elsewhere after this and not at Carlyon House. Hawkes, are you listening to me?'

'Of course, my dear.' Thomas turned to face his outraged wife. She was never more beautiful than in her peach silk nightrobe, the lace inserts arranged to display her prominent nipples, her flaxen curls loose about her shoulders. He imagined that Isolde would have looked something like this, but he was no Tristan and he could not rouse even the slightest passion for her. What he yearned for were green eyes alight with intelligence and earth-dark hair tumbling down a slender back: his beautiful serpent.

'Hawkes.' Marguerite sat down beside her husband, coiling her hands through his, the nightrobe taut against her magnificent body. 'What has happened to us? I am sorry for what I said earlier, and you can't really believe that I don't want you in my bed. Do you not love me any more?'

'Of course I love you, my darling.' His voice was flat. 'How could I not when you are the most wonderful wife in the world?'

She leaned against him, relief making her limp. She was so sure that she was losing him yet he was an honest man. Surely he would not lie to her.

'Darling, shall we spend the night together?' she went on. 'Shall we try to put things right?'

He wanted to shout: All you ever need to put things right is sex, but what about me, what about me? You spend hours having dress fittings and arranging your hair when you could be showing an interest in my collections, but you never do, do you? You only have enthusiasm for your own concerns. Could you blame me if I made love to Bellinda?

He had gone pale, for the rush of words in his mind had been so savage that he had almost spoken aloud. Marguerite, watching him pale, could not understand why he should react like this. Why did he keep away from her now? Could it be . . .

'Hawkes, you have not . . . you have not contracted an ailment, have you?' she said, her voice a whisper.

He looked at her in horror. 'You think that I would take such risks? Never!'

'Then why keep me at arm's length, my darling?' She leaned against him sinuously, her French perfume filling his nostrils.

There was only one way that he could stop this. 'I do not wish the child Sara to be flung out as if she were a leper. I wish her to stay here. Her health is variable, you only have to look at the dark rings beneath her eyes. A few months of Cook's best offerings and she will be transformed. My love, if she were your child would you not wish people to be kind to her?'

'She is a bastard, so how could she be mine?' Marguerite said in disgust. 'I would never stoop to such filthy behaviour, and how could you accuse me of it?' Pulling away from him, she stormed to the doorway of her bedroom. 'Hawkes, you disappoint me. I do not see that we have any common ground between us now. Whenever we speak, you choose to insult me. You side with imbeciles against me and when I need your help

96

and your love, you reject me!' Tears welled up in her eyes. She believed every word she was saying, which was why she was such a superb actress.

Thomas looked at her with bleak eyes. He knew what she wanted; she wanted him to rush to her and beg her forgiveness. She never did want anything less than his total capitulation. This time, however, she was not going to get it. Rising to his feet, he flung on his clothes and strode out of the room as if she were not there. Let her stew. Let her stew.

Marguerite sat at her dressing table, brush in hand. What was wrong with her? She tended her looks with such diligence; she wanted to keep her beauty for her husband's delight, yet he was alienated from her now, behaving as if she were repugnant to him. Suspecting that there must be another woman involved, she went through all the females of their acquaintance.

Amelia, Lady Brough had always made a play for Hawkes. She was a very attractive young woman with flame-red hair and sultry hazel eyes which she used to excellent effect. Had she seduced Hawkes?

Then there was Maisie Willoughby Brighton, the American heiress they had met at the Dashwoods' in November. Maisie was outrageous, bred of the wild, uninhibited society of New York. She had kissed Hawkes in front of everyone, claiming that he reminded her of her dear brother. Marguerite had laughed with everyone else, but her nails had dug deep pits into the palms of her hands. When they got home, Hawkes had made love to her violently and she had guessed that he was thinking of the full-breasted Maisie.

Clutching her hands together, she lowered her head. She knew that she was sexually attractive, for that showed in the eyes of every man she had ever met. When she thought of the lovers she could have had! Yet she had always remained faithful to Hawkes, nursing the sentimental notion that fidelity was of paramount importance. She had considered herself fortunate until now because her husband was faithful in return – or so she had thought.

What should she do? She looked into the mirror again, the mirror that had always been her friend, her consolation and confidante. There were the familiar features she had known all her life, the luxuriant flaxen hair, the wide apart light-blue eyes, the sensual mouth and strong, even teeth. It was a face that called for jewels and ornamentation. Without diamonds, rubies or sapphires, it was nothing. That was why she had married Hawkes, because of his family's famous jewel collection. One emerald necklace was reputed to have come from Cleopatra's palace in Alexandria. And there were the diamonds that had once graced the neck of Catherine de' Medici. Now *that* was the sort of heritage that appealed to Marguerite. Who cared whether some famous derriére had sat upon a certain chaise longue or a famous mouth had drunk from a certain tea set? Chaise longues and tea sets could not be worn. They were no adornment to the person, but jewels were . . . they were the heart and soul of history itself.

When she put on Catherine de' Medici's diamonds, she became that great and indomitable Queen of France. When she wore Cleopatra's emeralds, she imagined herself as Isis reborn.

Hawkes never suspected, of course. How could she tell him such things? He would never understand, nor would she ever understand how his eyes could light up over lumps of yellow jade or cold, skimpily decorated vases from the Orient.

Opening her jewel box, she took out the Medici diamonds, touching them as if they were delicate as silk. Gently she lifted them to her throat, letting them lie against her skin for a moment or two before she fastened the clasp. Now she was illuminated, the diamonds flashing and sparkling in the mirror. Now her eyes glowed, her face shone and the power that had been Queen Catherine's rose up inside her like an uncoiling serpent.

Catherine had been hated and despised when she first came to France as wife of the future Henry II. He had ignored her, the plain Italian girl, expending all his passions upon his ageless mistress, Diane de Poitiers. For ten years Catherine had been barren and only her good relationship with her father-in-law had prevented her public disgrace and an acrimonious divorce. Francis I could never resist a woman's wiles. Then Catherine had borne her first child, and more had come after, child upon child, yet she had known all along that she was only in her husband's bed because his mistress had advised it. France had needed heirs. Then Henri II had died of an agonizing wound at the joust and Catherine had come into her own as Regent of France.

Never give up hope. Never submit. Never retreat. Those were the messages that Catherine's diamonds rendered to Marguerite, and she did not resist them.

'Ye were unkind to that poor little mite.' Cook stood with her legs planted apart, her big red hands on her hips. 'Her be sobbing brokenhearted in ur room and 'tis no wonder.'

'I have told you before, Mags, that child is no good, in fact she is evil. She has had this whole household revolving round her since she came here and look where it's got us!' Jane Jermyn glowered. She agreed totally with her mistress where Sara was concerned.

'But her's being sent on ur way now, isn't she, and so ye'll not 'ave to force a smile at her again.'

'That cannot be too soon!' Mrs Jermyn stood up, her jaw clenched. Why did she keep coming to talk to this odious woman? She would never come again!

'Can ye not recall when ye were a young 'un and unsteady on yur feet, Jane? Would ye not 'ave given anything to 'ave had some friendly support?'

'Yes, but I was not an imbecile, was I? That girl makes my flesh creep. She is not right in the head. The mistress was told that she is possessed by the Devil and they have kept it quiet so as not to shock us.'

'Possessed by the Devil!' Cook's hands curled. She was imagining what it would be like to pick up her massive rolling pin and bring it down smartly on Jane Jermyn's head. Crack she would go and crack and crack again until the stupid old besom came to her senses. 'She be no more possessed o' the Devil than the Vicar who gave us our sermon!'

'Well that is where you are wrong, Mags, for it was he who told the mistress about it. He said the child had all the signs and she must be got out of the house before the poison spread.'

That made Cook's mouth drop open. What reply could she bring to that? The Vicar was a dour man but he was godly. If he thought there was devilishness in poor little Sara then maybe there was. She swallowed noisily while Mrs Jermyn's eyes glowed with victory.

That poor child. What would become of her now?

Bellinda felt numb as she packed Sara's few belongings. Sara was at last asleep after sobbing all evening. Bellinda had done her best to comfort her although she knew that only Sara's real mother could have done so now.

'She did not come! She did not come!' Sara had wailed, heartbroken. 'I heard her carriage outside, I heard her voice, but she was not there!'

'Oh my love, if she could be here then she would, you know that. Wherever she is she must think of you constantly.'

'I think of her constantly too, Bell. She was so very beautiful. She had a shining smile and big blue eyes and lovely curls. I do not think that I shall ever see her again now . . . '

Turning her face into Bellinda's shoulder she had wept uncontrollably.

By order of the mistress, Sara was to take two of her new gowns, her underneaths, her new merino cape and the warm petticoats. She was also to be allowed to take a basket of meat pies, plum cake and egg custards for the orphans and there was a cherry cake and two jars of strawberry preserve for the Governess herself, but what consolation would these be to Sara after all the riches she had seen at Carlyon House? She was being banished, and there was nothing that Bellinda could do about it. She herself had been ordered to remain, for she was to continue making the inventory of the master's treasures. Doing that had thrilled her, but now it lay bitter in her mouth like the aftertaste of a foul medicine. She did not want to be parted from Sara. No one understood Sara or cared for her as she did.

'Will you come and see me, Bell?' Sara had whispered as she relaxed into sleep.

'Of course, every week. I have one and a half days off and I will come then. I will bring you nice things to eat.' She had the ten shillings that the servants had given her. That would last some time if spent on such things as pies, dried fruit, nuts and milk.

'If you do not come to see me I shall die,' Sara sighed. 'You are my dear sister.'

'Yes, I am your sister and you are mine, dear Sara, and we shall always be together, whatever happens.'

There was a faint smile on Sara's pinched and tear-puffed face as she went to sleep, but Bellinda's face was grim. In God's name, what was wrong with the mistress who had commanded, 'Get that imbecile out of Carlyon House by morning!' And what of Mrs Jermyn, who had muttered beneath her breath, 'Bastards always bring trouble with them. Never have a bastard in the house! They should throw that Bellinda out too.'

Bellinda wanted to hide away when the carriage took Sara, but Sara had begged her to wave goodbye so she did, standing in the frost-silvered garden as the huge carriage wheeled away, Sara's ashen little face peering from its side window. She had the terrible feeling that she would never see her friend again, that Marguerite Groves-Hawkes had cut the thread of their linked destinies as surely as Clotho, that one of the three Fates who decided when life should end. She had read about Clotho in one of the master's books, and in her mind's eye the Fate had Marguerite's face, the cold ice-blue eyes, the merciless heart.

The carriage out of sight, she turned back into the house where she had expected to find such happiness, retreating to the Chinese Room where she was listing the pieces in the jade cabinet. She had made a start, struggling to keep her writing as neat as possible, mindful of the rulings the Governess had made: keep the arm relaxed and do not tense the fingers beyond the strength needed to hold the pen. Keep the paper square in front of you as you write. Do not stick out your tongue. She had never done that, but Sara did as she tried to spell. She saw Sara so vividly doing that, when she first came to the Downley Home. Poor little Sara. If you were poor, you might as well be dead, for no one cared if you lived or died.

'How are you managing, Bellinda?'

She looked up startled for she had not heard the master come in.

'Very well, Sir, thank you.'

'Which is your favourite jade, Bellinda? Which colour do you prefer?'

'I like the creamy yellow best, Sir.'

'Jade comes in many colours but most people believe that it only comes in green. Look at these pieces here . . . ' He gestured to the box that contained the smallest items. 'What colours can you see there?'

'Greyish-green, dark green with black streaks through it – '

'Those are called veins, Bellinda. What else?'

'Greenish-yellow, dark brown, greyish-white, white with green veins and white with brownish specks, red, blue, and grey with black veins.'

'As you can see, jade comes in many colours. Some of these pieces are very very old. Have you heard of Marco Polo?' She shook her head. 'In the fourteenth century he explored the Orient and at the court of the

Great Chan – that is, the Chinese Emperor – he saw jade for the first time, but he did not recognize it as we do now, of course, for he had never seen its like before. He called it a very hard stone. The Spanish returned from conquering the Aztecs and brought with them Europe's first sight of jade, which they believed would cure them of kidney diseases. So jade became called nephrite, which refers to the kidneys, the French translated this as *l'ejade* and due to a transcribing error, this became *le jade* from which we get the well-known word.

'There has been a great deal of confusion where jade is concerned. Other stones have been called jade when they are nothing of the sort – for example, jasper. A very clever French chemist decided to sort out the differences just a few years ago and now we know what they are. The stones brought into Europe by the Spaniards were jadeite, for even jade itself can be divided into two, jade and jadeite. Later, I will tell you how you might try to discern between the two, but for now I wish you to describe as best you can every piece you find.'

'Yes, Sir.' Bellinda could not hide the bleakness in her eyes. How she would have loved all this had Sara been cosily chatting in the kitchens with Cook or playing in the nursery with Robert's toys.

The morning passed slowly, for she was determined to make her writing both neat and legible. Her wrist ached after a time and she rubbed it energetically. Her eyes came to rest on the delicate figurine of Kuan Yin.

Could one pray to an Oriental goddess? Would she hear in the same way as the Mother of God? The Vicar had recently given a sermon on false idols and in that he had included the devils and demons worshipped by that Church which was an offence in God's face. She had not known to which he referred until Miss Vanity talked of the sermon later. It had been the Catholic Church. She had wanted to ask how God's Church could be an offence in His eyes, but had not dared. Miss Vanity and her parents were Protestants and they had seemed to be in accord with what the Vicar said.

She was trying to keep her thoughts away from Sara, yet seeing the tiny child on Kuan Yin's lap she could not help but think of her dear friend. Why did any god, Christian or otherwise, allow children to suffer so hideously?

'Bellinda, you were in a daydream then.' It was Vanity, beautifully dressed in midnight-blue velvet ruffled with Brussels lace, a multi-layered crimson silk bow giving the fashionable bustle line.

Bellinda looked up, her eyes clearing slowly. A piece of ancient jade in her palm, she had been in China with Marco Polo, seeing the Great Chan for the first time. In her imagination he was a fearsome sight, huge and broad shouldered, robed in heavy bright yellow silk embroidered with coiling flowers and leaves, and he was wearing those long, curving false nails that had so scared Sara.

'Can I help you, Miss Vanity?'

'I just came in to see how you were faring. Papa has left you alone, I see. Obviously he must trust you greatly.'

'The master has a business meeting,' Bellinda said, then wished she had not spoken, for Vanity's eyes hardened. 'I did know that, thank you, Bellinda,' she said coldly.

'Of course, Miss Vanity, I am sorry.'

'What do you think of this stuff?' Vanity said, gesturing towards the jade. 'Truly think, I mean. Do you like it or is it just boring old lumps of stone to you, like it is to Mama?'

Bellinda did not have to lie. 'I am thrilled to be allowed to touch such fabled pieces of jade. They are alive with history.'

Vanity looked at her oddly. 'That pronouncement would have done justice to Sara at her most bizarre,' she said. 'Do not tell me that you have visions of the past when you touch these ugly old stones?' There was scorn in her voice.

Bellinda could not stop herself from blushing, for that was exactly what did happen when she held these beautiful pieces, or in fact any of the artefacts in this room. She had only to hold one in her palm and scenes from history would rush into her mind, some so vivid that they seemed to be happening before her eyes. She had been enjoying that tremendously until this moment. Vanity had a great ability to throw iced water over everything.

'You do not mean to say that I am correct?' There was a breathy, excited quality in Vanity's voice. Unknown to her mama, she and two of her friends had been trying to raise the spirits with a Ouija board. Seances had become enormously popular the last few years, and there had been rumours that even the Queen had tried to contact Prince Albert, although this was shrouded in secrecy for fear it might offend some of the Queen's more conservative subjects.

'I am sure that everyone imagines historic scenes when they touch things like these – '

'But that is just it, Bellinda, they do not. I certainly do not and the idea of Mama doing so is quite ludicrous! Even Papa has never said anything like that. He enjoys holding the jade and looking at it, but that is all. Bellinda – ' Vanity pushed a small yellow carving into Bellinda's hand – 'tell me what you see now?'

Silence hung in the room as Bellinda tried to assemble her thoughts. Was she going to be ridiculed if she obeyed? Miss Vanity could be very sharp, very ruthless when she chose. Was this some trick to discredit her?

The carving felt like soft, warm satin in her palm. She relaxed, her eyes half closed, and instantly she was in the Great Chan's court again, the Emperor with his strange, fierce face glaring at Marco Polo, who was on his knees before him making a very deep bow, his face almost touching the ground. The Great Chan had a yellow face and his eyes were narrow and slanting almost evilly, his nose flat and broad-nostrilled. His mouth was a slit and hanging down on either side of it was a thin black moustache. He was lifting his arm and pointing one of those claw-nailed fingers at Marco

105

Polo, his slit of a mouth opening and his eyes flashing angrily. What was he going to say?

She was about to learn when Vanity snatched the jade from her rudely. She had heard footsteps outside the door. If that was Mama then there must be no chance of her finding Bellinda in what looked like a trance, her eyes glazed.

'That will be all for today,' she said crisply. 'I shall come and see how you are getting on tomorrow.'

Bellinda barely heard Vanity leaving, nor did she hear the voices outside the door as Marguerite questioned her daughter as to her papa's whereabouts. Vanity and Bellinda had known where Thomas was, but his wife had not.

The Downley Home was shudderingly cold. Cook had left, for Maureen – who was now in charge because the Governess was ill – had been rude to the elderly woman who had done her best for the orphans and foundlings for the past ten years. Maureen had called her a fat old fool and a thief and she had gone, tears streaming down her wrinkled cheeks. The other girls greeted Sara warmly, full of questions about Carlyon House and the family who lived there, but she felt so drained of energy that she wished only to sleep. Nora and Lily, the two youngest, stood by her bed staring down at her with intense curiosity. They should have been in bed hours ago but there was no one to oversee them now, for Maureen spent a great deal of time away from the Home with her men friends.

One night Nora and Lily had heard laughter coming from the Governess's parlour and they had peeped in through the half-open door to see Maureen without any clothes on. She was sitting astride a strange man with bushy side whiskers. He was not wearing any clothes either and he was thrusting his body upwards against Maureen's, harder and harder, his face getting redder and redder, then he cried out a very rude word and collapsed.

Nora and Lilly had clutched at each other, their cheeks hot. They had never seen anything so horrible. Even though they did not understand what was happening, it was upsetting. It was wrong and wicked to take off your clothes in front of a man, very wrong. You should be married first and then you could take them off in front of your husband, but only then. That much they knew.

Shaking, they ran back to their beds still holding hands, but it was a long time before they could get to sleep.

'What was she doing, Nora? Why was he so red in the face? He looked as if he 'ad been running.'

'Maybe he had, but he wouldn't go running in his bare skin, would he?'

'Maybe he 'ad been running round the room?'

''Tis too small for that, silly.'

'Maureen should not 'ave taken her clothes off in front of him. It is wrong.'

'Nora, you do not think that 'e'll come up here and do that to us, do you?'

Lily shivered, huddling down under the thin cover. 'I would scream if he came near me, Nora. Scream and scream!'

'But who would come to save us now the Governess is sick?'

They lay in silence, hearts thudding, contemplating this terrifying fact. Since Bellinda had gone no one had cared for them. The Governess had been drinking heavily and not eating and had soon been unable to rise from her bed. Then Maureen had taken the money that was to buy food and pay Cook. The Board had come well before Christmas to see that they had stocks of wood for the range and sacks of flour and potatoes, but they would not be back until the warmer weather, as was their custom. Consciences could be salved with a few sticks of wood and sacks of potatoes.

Finally the two girls slept, but in their dreams there was a naked man chasing them, his face bright red from

107

running. Just when they thought that he was going to catch them, Bellinda appeared, her face white with fury.

'Leave them alone!' she cried. 'Leave them alone!' The man shrank back, his arms across his face.

'Do not 'it me, do not 'it me!' he sobbed.

'I will spare you if you leave my girls alone,' Bellinda told him, and the man sobbed that he would not harm them, that he would go at once. Smiling, Bellinda placed a hand on each girl's shoulder. 'You are safe now, my loves,' she said in that lovely warm voice that they remembered so well and longed for. 'He will not dare to come back again while I am here.'

And in their sleep, their now peaceful sleep, they knew that she spoke true. They would be safe while Bellinda was there.

Chapter 10

'Bellinda, Mama has asked me to speak to you. You were seen going to the kitchens and now that you are officially employed by Papa, it is not seemly that you consort with the servants. You may speak to Mama's personal maid if you desire company, but you may not go below stairs.'

'I have spoken to Cook a number of times and no one has told me this.'

'There is no argument about it, Bellinda. You may not consort with the servants below stairs and that is that.'

Vanity was relishing her moment of power to the full.

'You may speak to Mrs Jermyn if you wish, but no one else below stairs.'

'I see.' Bellinda thought of the frosty atmosphere in the upper quarters of the house, and the warm, amiable atmosphere below stairs, and wished with all her heart that she had been hired to work in the kitchens beneath Cook's kindly gaze.

'I hope you do see, Bellinda, for Mama is extremely sensitive to disobedience since Sara's behaviour so upset us all. Carlyon House has always been a place of peace and happiness and that is how we wish it to continue.'

'Yes, Miss Vanity.'

'That is all, Bellinda. You may go now.'

'Thank you, Miss Vanity.' Bellinda stepped out of the withdrawing room where Vanity had been sitting in queenly state to administer her instructions. Two weeks without Sara and she was already feeling restless and isolated.

On her first day off, she had put on her cape and bonnet and made for the front door, but Mrs Jermyn had appeared out of nowhere.

'Where do you think you are going?'

'I am going to visit a friend, Mrs Jermyn.'

'And what friend would you have?' the woman sneered.

'I do have friends, Mrs Jermyn.' Bellinda kept her shoulders squared, her head high.

'The mistress wishes to speak with you. Wait here.' Mrs Jermyn vanished up the wide, graceful stairway and Bellinda stood in the hallway for an interminable time awaiting her return. Finally the housekeeper came down the stairs, moving as slowly as was humanly possible without coming to a halt.

'The mistress will see you now,' she said, her small dark eyes glinting maliciously.

'Thank you, Mrs Jermyn.'

Bellinda made her way up the stairs, conscious of those ruthless eyes boring into her back as she moved. What had Sara called Mrs Jermyn? A pot of lye, yes, that seemed a very apt description.

The mistress was sitting regally upon a chaise longue, beside her a pile of the latest French fashion magazines.

'Bellinda, I believe that you were planning to go out.' The mistress's eyes were the palest ice blue, like her heart, thought Bellinda. 'Where were you going?'

'To visit a friend, Ma'am.'

'What friend, Bellinda?'

'A girl at the Downley Home, Ma'am.'

'Would I know this girl?'

'Yes, Ma'am.'

'It would not be that imbecile, would it?' The ice-blue eyes were like pieces of the coldest, snowiest waste land as they stared at her.

'I do not know any imbeciles, Ma'am,' Bellinda said bravely.

'I think you do, Bellinda.' Marguerite changed tack. 'I have never heard anyone called by your name. I do not like it.' From today you will be called by your last name, whatever that is.'

'I do not have a last name, Ma'am.'

'Oh for Heaven's sake, you are the most difficult girl! How could you not have a last name? Do I have to *invent* one for you?'

'If you wish, Ma'am,' Bellinda said, knowing full well that whatever Marguerite decided, she would do without hindrance from anyone.

'Then you shall be called – ' she snapped her fingers in the air once or twice – 'George. Yes, Bellinda George. That suits you well.'

Bellinda stood there in silence, seeing right through this intensely self-involved, cold-hearted woman who manipulated her family so ruthlessly and so skilfully that they did not even realize it.

'Well, girl, have you lost your voice? Did you not hear me? You will be called George from now on.'

'Yes, Ma'am.' Bellinda felt the crazy urge to laugh out loud. She was familiar with the custom of servants being called by their last names, but to suddenly have a man's name . . .

'And I do not want you visiting that Sara, do you hear me? She has brought disrepute upon our family and there must be no more contact with her. She is a bad influence upon Robert and I cannot have him harmed. You will tell Mrs Jermyn where you wish to spend your days off and she will tell you whether that can be allowed. Besides, I have some work I wish you to do for me. I need someone to read to me each day.' Marguerite did not want to admit it but her eyesight was failing and she would die rather than admit to that. Jane Jermyn's accent was atrocious and she could not abide being read to in that ugly voice. Bellinda had a smooth, strong voice. She would be ideal for the task.

'Ma'am, I am worried that Sara might be ill – '

'You are not to visit her, do you hear?' Marguerite glared. 'Mary Alewin is to look in upon the orphans on the master's behalf. She will let us know how Sara is, but there must be no personal contact, do you understand?'

'Yes, I understand.' Bellinda's voice was bitter. She understood only too well. She was to be a prisoner at

Carlyon House, the place that was to have been her Heaven.

'You can go now.' Marguerite picked up a magazine, staring intently at a magnificent ballgown designed by Worth but seeing only a blur where once she would have seen the graceful lines.

Her lips tightly shut, Bellinda withdrew from the scent-drenched, suffocatingly hot room, reaching the cool landing with relief. There she clutched at the banisters, bending over them, her eyes tightly shut.

She was not to visit Sara. She was not to go below stairs to speak to Cook. She was to be called George from now on.

What had the Governess always said? 'There's one law for the rich and one for the poor.' How right she was!

Mary Alewin was wrapped up well against the violent winds that swept across Plomer Hill. She had walked up the hill in the track of the coal cart, feeling sympathy for the horse as it struggled to find its footing in the muddy ruts that the night's rain and a slight easing in the weather had brought. It was an old horse and should have been put out to grass long ago. She would never treat her own animals so harshly when she and Jake had their farm. God made the animals as well as the people, so how could you be cruel to one and kind to the other?

She was carrying a basket filled with Cook's pies, bread, butter, preserves and biscuits for 'they orphans', a secret gift Mary had smuggled out of the house. She was to look in on the orphans, on the master's instructions, and see how they were faring. She was a little wary of coming into contact with the children of sinners, for how often had the Vicar said that sin rubbed off, that you must stay away from everything to do with it.

She was saying a prayer as she came in sight of the gaunt orphanage. It was bleak in this spot, but in the distance there were trees standing like black spidery fingers against the skyline, and there was one beech near the Home itself, its branches as bare as January could make them. Hundreds of years before, this had been an almshouse, so someone had told her, but the old King, Harry, had broken up all the monks' and nuns' houses and stopped them praying to their false idols. That had been a very good thing, of course. She had a mental image of God weeping in Heaven because people were praying to plaster images instead of to Him. Idolatry was the world's greatest evil, so the Vicar said.

The wind had decided to snap her skirt against her legs as she walked up the pathway to the Home, and she fought to pull the material into a more respectable position before she reached up to pull the rusty old bell. When no sound came from it, she knocked hard to make herself heard above the wind. She stood there for some time before trying the handle. Finding the door unlocked, she stepped into the musty-smelling hall. The walls were dark brown and thoroughly depressing. There was the smell of trapped, rotting water, a nasty damp patch somewhere perhaps. She shivered, feeling the coldness press in upon her. This was the only building where she had ever felt the cold more keenly than she did outside.

'Hello,' she called, and again, 'hello, be anyone there?'

Hearing no response, she walked down the hall and looked into one of the rooms. Maybe this was what sin smelt of, this musty, rotting smell? The shabby, untidy room was empty and that too smelt of decay. There had not been a window opened nor a fire in the grate since the Governess had fallen ill. The big hall was echoingly empty save for the benches and chairs and the panes in one of the high thin windows were shattered. Leaves and twiggy debris had blown in through it and lay scattered in little piles on the table and floor.

Back into the hall Mary Alewin went. Was the place deserted? Maybe they had moved the orphans somewhere else?

Then she heard a board creak and a scared voice called down, 'Who be they?'

'Hello, this is Mary Alewin from Carlyon House. Be your Governess there?'

'Her be sick abed.' Nora's little face appeared round the banister. 'Have you brought a message from Bellinda?'

'Her sends you all 'ur love. What's yur name?'

'Nora. Is Bellinda coming back?'

'No, her be employed by the master of Carlyon House now. He has sent me to find out how things are with you.'

'The Governess is in her bed very ill. Do you want to see her?'

'I better had, I suppose.' Mary followed Nora up the first set of stairs, along the landing and up a smaller flight. This was where recalcitrant monks had been locked until they repented, but she did not know that, nor did her sturdy mind sense any of the sufferings that had taken place here all those centuries before.

'Who are you?' the Governess screeched, trying to sit up in bed. Her face was puffy, her eyes almost hidden in the water-filled flesh.

'I've brung you some food from Carlyon House, Ma'am, and inquiries from the master who wishes to know how you all be faring.'

'Did you say food?'

'I did.' Having helped the sick woman to sit up, Mary fed her a pie and some bread and cheese.

'Do you have any wine?' The puffy eyes were beady.

'No, I do not.' Mary sounded outraged. A teetotaller herself, she had never liked the notion of a woman drinking. It was the downward path for the lower classes if they started on that. 'I have milk here. Do you have a cup?'

The Governess pointed to a dust-laden table in the far corner where there was a jumble of cups and dishes, greasy and caked with old food.

'How is Bellinda? Is she well? It is bad news about poor little Sara. Why has Bellinda not come to see her?'

'Bad news?' Mary's face collapsed. 'Bell would have come but the mistress forbade it.'

'Forbade it? How could she do such a heartless thing? Sara lives for her Bellinda and she will not be much longer for this earth.' She wanted to ask if the Board could come and see to things, but she dreaded what would happen if they did, so she stayed silent. She would be sacked in disgrace, instead of being able to hand over the reins of the Home in a last burst of glory as she planned, for she was due to retire on a pension in the spring. She still had nowhere to go and the thought of being cast out in mid-winter was terrifying. She would die if she had to leave her bed. 'It would make all the difference to Sara if Bellinda could see her.'

'The mistress has forbade it, I told you, and when she forbades something, it stays forbade.'

'The wicked besom!' The Governess flushed crimson. 'I have had naught but trouble since Bellinda went. One of the girls took over the budget and she spent the money on furbelows and her man friends. She came in and laughed at me now and then, for I could not rise from my bed and slap her around the head as I longed to do. And now she has run away, and all the winter money is gone . . . How are we to manage? But you must not tell the Board, do you hear? If you did, they would fling me out and I have nowhere on earth to go.' A tear rolled down her puffy cheek. 'By spring it will be different. I shall be well then and when the new Governor comes, I can hand it all over to him happily.'

'Will you have somewhere to go then?'

'I am hoping. Listen, you must get Bellinda here to the child. How could I live with myself if she died without seeing her friend again? Little enough do these girls have, little enough. A kiss and a loving word from Bell and she would die happy.'

'I never thought Sara to be a bad one, but the mistress did, and her wishes overrule.'

'So you told me! If you could get some food to us we should be mightily thankful, but it must be done in secret or the Board will hear and that will mean catastrophe. Can you do it, do you think?'

'I will try.' Mary Alewin leaned back, the enormity of such a task settling on her shoulders like stone. Where would she get food for all these girls, and how would she get it up that hill and all in secret?

There comes a time when common sense must rule, and now was that time. Bellinda was ready to set out for the Downley Home, not sure what she would find. Mary Alewin had told her what she had heard and seen there.

'I shall find the food for them,' Bellinda said with determination. 'Do not inform the master about the stolen budget. I shall deal with it. Tell him by all means that the girls could do with more comforts, but nothing else. Tell him that the Governess needs delicacies to restore her health, for she has had little enough of those. And please, please, do not tell the truth to the mistress!'

'As if I would!' Mary looked hurt. ''Atween you and me, I think her be a shocker, but that is only 'atween you and me, Bell.'

Cook refilled the basket with pies, buns, butter and cakes, freshly baked loaves and ginger biscuits, and Bellinda prepared herself for the moment when she would leave Carlyon House.

Heaven had reached out its shining finger and touched her lightly on the shoulder, but only lightly. Now the golden finger had withdrawn and the darkness of base earth was all she saw. Heaven and earth, one golden, tempting and bright with marvels, and one dour and dark and athwart with troubles.

Before she left there was one special goodbye she must say. In the Chinese Room, its dark corners gently gilded by lamps, there stood the statuette of Kuan Yin, she who would not ascend to Heaven until all on Earth were safe. Bellinda would have the morning alone with her as she completed the final entries on the master's collection of jade.

Kuan Yin had never looked more radiant, her face sweetly smiling, her eyes tenderly pleading. Unable to stop herself, Bellinda lifted the figurine from its ebony base, and immediately she saw the children. Were these the ones whom the goddess loved so much that she would not desert them? Young and slender, their faces pale and drawn, they stood hand in hand as if waiting for some command. She was so surprised at seeing them all that she did not take heed of their clothes for some while. They were not in the robes of Oriental children, their hair pulled up into tight knots. They wore Western clothes, plain, unkempt dresses of cheap material, their hair uncombed and loose round their ears, their feet more often than not bare.

'These are the ones you love, Kuan Yin,' she whispered, anticipating an immediate reply and disappointed when none came. She must have offended the goddess in some way. She was about to replace the figurine when the words washed over her.

'You too are Kuan Yin.'

'I am Kuan Yin?' she asked, puzzled.

There was no response. The waiting children had vanished and she was alone again. It was almost noon and she must go.

It was the tweeny's half day, so she would have some assistance in carrying the food up the hill. The tweeny would leave by the servants' exit and she by the front door, as she was forbidden to go below stairs.

Her bonnet tied tightly beneath her chin and her cape buttoned at her neck, her few worldly possessions tucked into the pockets of her petticoats, she walked through the hall of Carlyon House and opened the front door, not looking round as she closed it behind her.

Beyond the main drive she met up with the tweeny, Lizzie Herbert, and together they set off across the fields towards the woods that would lead them to Plomer Hill.

Lizzie was quite small and she puffed and panted a great deal as they went up the steep hill, having no breath left for conversation. Bellinda was glad of that. She had nothing to say to anyone at this moment. She had put Carlyon House behind her as finally as if it had never existed. It had become a prison and now she was free.

'I turns off 'ere,' Lizzie panted. 'My ma lives down that lane.'

'Thank you for your help, Lizzie.'

'You won't tell none that I 'elped you, will ee?'

'Of course not. Goodbye, Lizzie.'

'G'bye, Miss Bellinda.'

The skies lowered over her, drenched in a wetness that would soon descend. Hurrying now, she made for the Downley Home as the first drops blew into her face.

Chapter 11

She was too late. Sara's bed was empty. The girls lay tucked beneath their darned blankets, but Sara's bed was flat, the covers taken from it to reveal the ugly striped mattress.

She stood in the doorway feeling as if someone had punched her heart. If Sara had gone, there was no reason for her to be here.

Then she heard the little voice. 'Is that you, Bell? Sara's in Nora's bed to keep warm.'

She made a gasping sound and there was a strange whistling in her ears. Then over it, she heard Sara's voice calling, and within seconds she was at her friends bedside.

There was not even a half-burned candle to illuminate the pale little faces that stared up at her. The girls went to bed extra early in winter to try to keep warm.

'Sara 'as the fever, Bell,' said Nora, 'and she be shakin' and shiverin'. I done my best to keep 'ur warm.'

'I am sure you have, Nora. That is very good of you.'

Sara was looking up at her with over-bright eyes, the hot, acrid scent of fever rising from her body.

'I have come back, Sara, and I shall not be leaving again,' Bellinda whispered. 'Sleep now and I shall see you again in the morning.'

'I was not a bad girl,' Sara said, her teeth chattering. 'I was not a bad girl.'

'No, you were a good girl. Sleep now, my dear, and you will feel stronger in the morning.'

Taking off her cape, Bellinda placed it across the bed for extra warmth. Then she went up to the Governess's bedroom. From it came the stench of unwashed body and an overflowing chamber pot. In the darkness, she stumbled over a rent in the threadbare carpet.

'Bloody hell, who is that?' came an outraged voice from the bed.

'It is Bellinda, Ma'am. I am sorry if I woke you.'

'Bellinda! Am I dreaming? Get a candle from the dressing table and there is a tinderbox in the drawer. Let me see your face.'

The candle lit, they looked at one another.

'So it is you. I thought I'd never see you again. Did that Mary tell you what happened? Last week bloody Maureen stole the budget and went off with a fancy man.'

Bellinda had never heard the Governess swear before and it was strange to hear it now, but she had no doubt that the woman had been driven to it.

'Maureen was the thief, was she?' Bell sat down on the bed.

'That little sneak! She told me a tale of all she would do with the money, and then when I told her where it was hid, off she went with it, and the girls have had to live on oats and old potatoes.'

'I have brought more food with me, Ma'am. Are you hungry now?'

'Ravenous!' The Governess clutched her hands across her bosom in anticipation of the feast to come, and as she did so there came the gentle clink of glass against glass.

Sighing, Bellinda threw back the covers to reveal a collection of geneva bottles, all empty.

'Oh, Ma'am, you've been ruining your health!'

'I never was any good without you to care for me, Bell. It's been a hard act to keep up, me the strong, competent one, all-wise, all-knowing, when I have this feeling of frailty inside me all the time. Put it down to being an unwanted child. I have to staunch the pain somehow.' The Governess's eyes were pleading.

'You might have been unwanted all those years ago but you are not now, are you? We have all wanted you, and needed you, for many years. You have been the mainstay of this Home, Ma'am. The girls need you. I need you. Where would we be without you? You are the only mother we have ever known.'

'The only mother . . . ' The Governess's puffy cheeks trembled and a tear gleamed on her cheek. 'Is that how you think of me?'

'Yes, we think of you as our mother and we need you. We cannot survive without you, Ma'am, so you must get well and strong again soon. Do you promise me that you will?'

The voice was a croak but it spoke the right words. 'I promise, my dear, I promise.'

'With all your heart?'

'With all my heart.'

Bending over, Bellinda kissed the damp, rose-stained cheek and it was as if the Governess began to breathe differently, to take in the air and benefit from it. As if she had taken on a new lease of life. She had always condemned herself harshly for her self-imagined frailty, healing her pain with alcohol, but every word that Bellinda had said was true. The girls could not survive without her. She had a good heart and a stronger spirit than she suspected, and Bellinda would see that she recovered her full health and strength. She would nurse her and feed her nourishing fresh food, and within a very few weeks the Governess would be on her feet again and ruling the roost as of old. Bellinda vowed it as she held the sick woman's cold hands in hers and squeezed them tightly with all the love that she bore for her.

On her way out, Bellinda lifted up the chamber pot and took it to the old privy on the second landing where she emptied it and rinsed it with water from the jug, a number of drowned insects appearing as she poured.

Later, as the Governess ate heartily, and Bellinda made up a fire in the tiny grate, she heard the entire tale.

'I would have got the authorities on to that Maureen but then I would have had to tell the Board and they

121

would have thrown me out and I have nowhere to go. If I can just stay here until spring, I shall be all right. I will get my pension then. I would have to lose it if they sacked me.'

'No one is going to tell them. I have a little money, and that will tide us along.' The ten shillings she had been given at Christmas would be the saving of them. 'There will be stew in the pot for dinner tomorrow.'

The Governess caught her hand. 'I was torn in two when you went, Bell. I wanted a better life for you, for I am not a heartless woman. I hoped that Carlyon House would lead to a great future for you, but look what it did to Sara. Did they throw you out?'

'I left of my own accord.'

'You left? Will they not come after you?'

'No. Why should they do that? Poor young women are ten a penny these days. They will get some parson's daughter to take my place and that will be that. But she will have to be plain as a pikestaff to satisfy the mistress.'

'The mistress must have her servants plain, eh? So why did she tolerate you?'

Bellinda had never looked more beautiful to the Governess, with her dark hair swathed in a coil and her skin gleaming white in the candlelight, the intelligent green eyes bright with emotion as she talked of her ordeal.

'She called me a stolid country girl, Ma'am. She said I would do well on a farm.'

The Governess giggled hoarsely. 'I once said that, if I recall.'

'You meant it kindly and she meant it cruelly, Ma'am.' Bellinda began to clear away the remains of the meal. The fire was busily crackling now and the room had lost its unpleasant clamminess. 'Shall you want anything else before you go to sleep?'

'Just the chamber pot, my dear.'

After lighting a fire in the parlour grate, Bellinda curled up on the old sofa fully dressed. Thankfully there was

122

still a good pile of firewood outside the kitchen door so she could keep the fires going. In the morning she would carry Sara down to the parlour and turn it into a sick room. No one who was ill should be left in that chilly dormitory. It was some time before she slept, and if she dreamt she remembered nothing of it.

It was still dark when she woke to hear a wailing, a thin, eerie sound. At first she thought it was one of the girls and then realized it was a cat. Turning over she tried to sleep again, but without success. Getting up, she jabbed the fire into life and put more twigs on it. When they were burning well, she added some logs, dusted the parlour and swept the carpet, opening the small window to clear the air. In the dormitory the girls still slept and her heart went out to them as she closed the door gently.

In the vast kitchens with their scrubbed stone floors she struggled to get the massive, unwieldy range alight. It seemed to devour the kindling, flare for a few moments and then die. Cook had dealt with all this, and Bellinda had never thought to find out for herself. Maybe kindling was too insubstantial for such a big range? Going outside, she found some larger firewood and pushed it into the black hole. Finally, the flames gathered strength, clutching at the wood for life, and she breathed a sigh of relief, rubbing a sooty hand across her forehead.

The big iron pot was almost too heavy to lift. Heaving it into position, she filled it with water and salt then waited for it to boil before adding porridge oats. At least the girls would have a hot breakfast today. How had they cooked their porridge without the help of the range? She had a horrible vision of oats mixed with cold water.

The kitchen was warming now. Searching the shelves she found flour, sugar and spices. She had brought butter with her from Carlyon House, so she had the ingredients for biscuits. She had watched Cook making them once, so she knew how to go about it.

Mixing and rolling, she cut the biscuits into circles with the rim of a mug and placed them on the baking sheets. If only she could conquer the complexities of the range. Each shelf had a different heat, or did you put in some foods for longer than others? She wished she could remember. Pushing the trays into the oven, she closed the door. The girls would not be fussy if their biscuits were not crisp enough.

The porridge was thick and bubbling by now and the old clock showed that it was after eight. Someone had been winding it regularly. She went into the refectory, but as she opened the door the wind burst into the room in a great gust and she saw leaves and broken window glass on the floor. So much for that. They would eat in the kitchen from now on.

By nine of the clock the girls were eating their porridge and spiced biscuits as if they had never seen food before. Bell had sat them round the range so that they could warm themselves, and their cheeks were rosy already. Leaving Polly in charge, she went up to the dormitory to see to Sara.

Sara slept as if she could not wake, her body burning to the touch. Now and again her mouth twisted as if she were having an unpleasant dream, then her lids would flutter and she would make a little sound before settling quietly again. Gently Bellinda wrapped her in the coverlet and carried her down to the parlour sofa. She did not stir even when tucked up there, a pillow beneath her tawny head. Piling more wood on the fire, and leaving the door ajar in case Sara called out, Bellinda went back to the kitchens.

The girls were behaving themselves. Polly had heated some water and they were washing the battered wooden porridge bowls. Keeping warm in a smaller pot was Sara's breakfast, and Bellinda took this through to her.

Somehow Sara had managed to sit herself up. In the half light her face now looked even paler and her hair even more straggly. There was a look of sheer terror in her eyes.

'Bell, Bell! I am going to die. I know it.' Her voice was shaky and trembling.

Bellinda rushed to take Sara in her arms and hold her tightly.

'Oh, Sara. You must not even think such things,' Bellinda said while gently caressing Sara's sweating forehead.

'But I am, Bell. Nobody gets over the flux. Nobody!'

'What nonsense! Of course they do. All you have to do is build up your strength.'

'That's not what Maureen told me,' Sara said weakly. 'She reckoned people always die of it.'

How could anyone be so cruel? If only Sara had told her earlier instead of brooding over Maureen's dreadful words. The spirit of the patient had to be kept high at all costs. Terrible damage had been done, but Bellinda was determined to undo it.

'You must sit up some more and eat this porridge,' she said, stuffing the pillow behind Sara's back to make her more comfortable.

'Bell, I am just not hungry. I could not eat a thing,' Sara wheezed.

'You can and you shall,' Bellinda insisted. 'Now come along, you must eat while the food is still hot.'

As Bellinda picked up the bowl of porridge, Sara opened her mouth, ready for the first spoonful. Although Bellinda could tell that Sara was making a real effort, the porridge just rolled around inside her mouth before dribbling out over her chin.

'Oh, Sara, please try. Please try harder.'

Sara attempted a second spoonful, but again the grey mush trickled out from her lips.

Wiping away the food from Sara's chin, Bellinda realized that Maureen's cruel prophecy would soon be coming true. Poor Sara was declining fast. No matter what was done, it could not be long before her beloved friend would be gone for ever.

Chapter 12

There was to be no respite. Every precious moment threatened to be Sara's last. Bellinda felt torn. Part of her wanted Sara to be finally relieved of her suffering, part of her wanted the beloved child to hold on to life – just a little longer, for there could be no hope now. The consumption had taken its full hold.

'Bell, Bell, I really did have a rich mama, you know,' Sara gasped. 'She would have come back for me soon. I know she would.'

'Of course she would have done,' Bellinda soothed as she fought back her tears. 'Did you think I ever doubted it, my little love? Did you ever think that?'

Sara gave a beaming smile. It was as if the illness had suddenly vanished. Her face no longer seemed shrunken. It was round and bright and her freckles glowed like ripe oranges and those mischievous, impish eyes were gazing adoringly up at Bellinda.

'Mama is coming for me,' Sara said excitedly but there was a hoarseness in her voice now. 'I can hear her footsteps. You can always tell Mama's footsteps. Always! Can't you hear them too, Bell? Can't you hear them?'

'Yes, yes I can!' Bellinda pretended.

'She'll be coming through that door any moment.' Sara pointed weakly.

'Of course she will, Sara. Are you not thrilled? At last you are going to see your mama. At last!'

Sara's brown eyes were shining with joy. 'Yes, yes I am, Bell. Yes I am!'

'She will be coming through that door at any moment. Look! Is this not her?'

'Mama! Oh Mama, at last you are here. At last!' Although there was no one there, Mama seemed as real to Bellinda as to Sara. How splendid the child's mother appeared. Bellinda saw her dressed in soft violet, a well-cut jacket with a crisp white linen collar and a wide skirt. She was carrying a parasol and wearing a bonnet decorated by two red silk roses and fastened by a wide blue bow. Gentle, indigo eyes shone deeply from a face of clear-skinned perfection as she gave a warm and loving smile. To Sara she was Mama. To Bellinda she was Kuan Yin.

'Sara has told me so much about you, Ma'am,' Bellinda said, almost choking on her tears. 'I am overjoyed to meet you.'

'Bell has been such a friend to me, Mama. She must come with us. Can she, Mama? Can she?'

There was a pause while Mama answered.

'She can, Mama? That is wonderful! Did you hear that, Bell? You can come with us. You can!'

'Oh Sara, that is indeed wonderful,' Bellinda sobbed. 'What kindness your mama is showing. What kindness!'

'Mama has always been so kind, Bell. You must not cry. Please do not cry.'

Bellinda gulped upon the choking tears. She would have to be brave. Nothing must spoil the illusion. 'I am just overcome a little, that is all. Nothing more.'

'Then you will come with us?'

Bellinda squeezed Sara's hand. 'Neither Mama nor I shall ever leave your side, my little love. We will always be together, we three. Always!'

'Yes always, Bell. Alwa . . . '

As Sara's voice faded, her mouth curled into a sweet, loving smile. Her eyes were now frozen in adoration, staring sightlessly at where Mama had stood.

The whole of Bellinda's body convulsed as grief swept through her like a dark tidal wave. For a moment she could not breathe, then the tears flooded from her eyes and she could hear her own wretched wailing. Her only friend was gone.

She raged at the Grim Reaper for taking such innocence, cheating Sara of a life full of happiness. For in that tragic moment she believed, just as Sara had done, that soon her mama would have come to take her away from the squalid orphanage. Sara had always believed that. Despite everything Sara had always been so full of hope. Now at last she was with the mother and father she so dearly loved.

For any orphan there could only ever be one end – a pauper's grave. For Sara to be ignominiously cast amongst other bodies, a mere foot or so from the surface in a shallow hole dug by local drunkards, was unthinkable. Bellinda was determined that this should not be so. The Governess readily agreed with her that it would be far more fitting to bury Sara deep beneath the beech tree. The digging was to be done by Bellinda, the Governess and the orphans. There had been protests that such a task was for men but Bellinda was soon able to convince everyone that not only would it save money that the orphanage could ill afford, but also the performing of such an act would be the showing of a deep and proper respect.

To Bellinda's relief the Vicar grudgingly agreed not only to the burial place but also to giving a full and proper service before Sara was laid to rest. In contrast to the Vicar's attitude, the verger seemed more than willing not only to act as a pallbearer but to arrange for three other locals to assist him. Bellinda and the Governess then ensured that each of the undernourished orphans was only allowed to do a little digging at a time. It was a long and arduous process but after three days the task was complete. Between two exposed roots was now a deep hole, completed just one day before the funeral.

Throughout the readings and the singing of hymns, Bellinda forced herself to remain calm and composed. While many of the children sobbed, she fought back her tears, preparing herself for what would soon have to be done. When the time came she took in a deep breath, straightened, and then with her head held high she walked to the front of the church. Trembling, she began her speech.

'Sara will never be forgotten. Like the beech tree that she will be lying beneath, her memory will stand like a beacon. How blessed we all were to have shared in her dreams. Somewhere in another life her mama and papa will be waiting for her. Truly I hope so, for the life that she led in these times could not have been more wretched. Rest in peace, my little love. Rest in peace.'

Her voice had echoed around the walls of the church and she knew those words would be etched into her memory for ever. Truly, she dearly hoped that Sara would indeed find happiness in her new life, for she believed what Thomas Groves-Hawkes had told her about the ancient beliefs of reincarnation.

The burial was a tearful ordeal. Many of the orphans wept, as did the Governess when the roughly fashioned wooden coffin was lowered into the hole. Still, Bellinda fought back the temptation to cry; as in any other crisis, it was she who was expected to take charge, to be in full command of herself and others. Only when the burial was finally over did she allow herself the luxury of going to the room where Sara had died, there to weep copiously until there were no more tears and her body was totally exhausted by grieving.

Then she lay upon the deathbed, tormented by the cruel memory of Sara's final days. Bitterly she recalled how Sara had been treated at Carlyon House. Although the Governess had paid a visit to Carlyon and told them of Sara's death, none of the family had contacted the orphanage. Bellinda had regarded Thomas Groves-Hawkes as a kind man, but she now realized that he was too dominated by a selfish wife and a spoilt daughter to ever become a true philanthropist.

'Bellinda, Bellinda.'

She turned her head away from the pillow, recognizing the voice of the Governess. The woman came to her side and gently put a hand upon the orphan's trembling shoulder. Bellinda raised herself up and then flung her arms around the Governess.

'What reason can there be for such a tragedy?' she sobbed. 'What reason can there be?'

'Hush now, Bellinda,' the Governess soothed. 'God has a reason for everything. Death is but a lesson for the living. Sara's illness has cured me of my drinking habits. I have not touched a drop these past days, nor never shall again.'

'You have not?' Bellinda was stunned, the revelation providing a momentary release from her sorrow.

'Not one drop,' the Governess answered proudly. 'And what is more, you will find the Home a far better-run place than it used to be. I depended too much upon you, Bellinda, far too much.'

'I will always be here to help you.'

'No, child, that would not be right. You are not like the other girls, you have a destiny. You belong in the outside world now.'

'I never belonged at Carlyon House,' Bellinda said bitterly.

The Governess shook her head before her face crumpled into a smile. 'Be that as it may, Bellinda, I have a feeling that one day many other people will be depending on you. Life has a lot in store for you, my girl. A lot in store!'

'But where can I live but here?'

'I have a little money saved, enough to take you to London.'

'But, Ma'am, you will be needing all your savings for your retirement,' Bellinda protested. 'Besides, I cannot leave the children so soon after Sara's death.'

The Governess took hold of Bellinda's shoulders. 'You can and you shall. I know as well as anyone else what a terrible place the city is, but there are good positions to be had for girls as bright as you.'

'I want no position but to be here with the children.'

'Bellinda, I have managed to change my slubbornly ways so that you will not feel so obligated to stay.' The

130

Governess's eyes burned with an unaccustomed zeal. 'London awaits you, my child, but first you must try to sleep.'

After crying some more, Bellinda did finally manage to drift off to sleep. Despite her grief, sheer exhaustion ensured that she slept solidly without dreaming. As soon as she awoke, she thought about what the Governess had said. Were her words not true? Now that Sara was gone and the Governess was coping better, was she really needed so much?

A walk around the orphanage confirmed what the Governess had told her. There was nothing to keep her here and some inner voice, that of Kuan Yin perhaps, was telling her that her destiny now lay in the great and awesome city that had always fascinated her. Sara had been a living testament as to what a cruel and merciless place it was, but was it not also somewhere where ambitions might actually be fulfilled?

Finally she went to see the Governess, who offered her tea as soon as she entered. Bellinda sipped at the brew, thinking carefully about what to say.

'Please do not be offended, Ma'am,' she began carefully, 'but I cannot accept your offer of money for my stay in London. You will be needing every penny yourself.'

'But child, you cannot go to London without some kind of provision,' the Governess protested, her cheeks now flushed to a bright crimson. 'What utter madness. You must take *some* money, I insist!'

'No, Ma'am,' Bellinda said firmly. 'I shall not take one penny from you. I must put my trust in Kuan Yin.'

'Who? What are you talking about, girl?'

Bellinda knew that even if she tried to explain, the Governess would be unlikely to understand. How could she? The effect that the ancient goddess was having was still a mystery to Bellinda, let alone anyone else.

'Oh, it is a saying that Thomas Groves-Hawkes once used,' she said casually. 'I think it just means putting your trust in God.'

131

'Well, rich people have a pretentious way of talking at times, and no sense for that matter. I'd like to see one of them go anywhere without a well-filled purse, especially London.'

'That may well be so but I refuse to take any of your own money, Ma'am,' Bellinda insisted. 'It would not be right.'

The Governess shook her head in despair. 'Oh Bellinda, be assured it would indeed be right and proper for you to take it.' After giving a resigned sigh she then said, 'However, I know there is indeed a stubborn streak in you. Already I am beginning to wish that I had not suggested you go to London.'

Bellinda got up from her seat and gave the old woman a hug. 'Ma'am, you cannot know how much I shall miss you and your kindness.'

The old woman's face was etched in sadness. 'I fear that I shall miss you even more. It was not just because I depended upon you so much that you were always my favourite. There is something very special about you, Bellinda.'

'I have never thought of myself as anyone special. I believe in leaving such illusions to someone like Miss Vanity.'

'There is nothing special about that little madam, a common scullery maid has better qualities than she.'

Bellinda laughed. 'An unkind thing to say, Ma'am, but how true. How very true.'

The Governess shared in her laughter before pouring more tea. Then together they watched the fire, its dancing flames crackling loudly before eventually ebbing, the logs becoming nothing more than soft, glowing embers. Throughout its burning they had talked without interruption, reflecting upon what had happened at Carlyon House, how the Governess's health had improved so much, now that she had stopped drinking, and reminiscing with deep affection upon the antics of Sara.

Bellinda then rested some more. Tomorrow at first light, she would begin her journey. It was going to be the most testing time of her life, there could be no doubt of that. However, curiously, she was not afraid. She *did* belong to the world outside the orhanage, the world beyond Wycombe. She thought of Kuan Yin's smiling face, the only really good memory she had of Carlyon, and immediately it brought her peace of mind. Once again she was able to sleep well.

The following morning she explained to the orphans the reasons for her decision. It was hard to make some of the younger ones understand, and heart-wrenching to see them cry. The poor little mites had been through enough, now she was deserting them. If only she did not have to do it so soon, but all her instincts told her that the time to act was now. Her work was done at the Downley Home, an inner voice was telling her that she was needed elsewhere.

Her farewells to the orphans were not to be hurried. Each one of them merited her full attention. Many cried a little and it was difficult for her to hold back her own tears. Not until now had she fully understood just how fond they all were of her. With all her heart she promised that very soon she would be seeing them again. Once she had managed to secure a good position, then part of her earnings would be sent to the Downley Home. It was to help people such as themselves that she was going to London.

Lily and Nora wanted to watch her walk down the hill but she told them to stay inside for fear of catching a chill. After she had kissed each of them upon her tearstained cheek and wiped away the tears from her own eyes, she picked up the small bag that the Governess had given her and went outside. Thick grey clouds were draping heavily over the Chilterns, casting the countryside in a deep and forbidding gloom. It was no day for travelling, especially for someone like herself who did not even have her fare money. Shivering, more through uncertainty than the cold, she waited for the Governess to join her.

133

'Is your mind still set upon this venture?' the Governess asked as she came and stood beside her.

Momentarily Bellinda wavered. The temptation was strong. Was this not madness? Was not even somewhere as barren as this orphanage a safer place than an unknown city?

'I cannot reverse my decision now,' she answered solemnly. 'I must go and seek whatever destiny awaits me.'

'Stubborn as ever, Bellinda, stubborn as ever.'

Bellinda looked into the sad old woman's face with its deep lines and rose-stained cheeks. 'Yes, stubborn as ever, Ma'am,' she told her. 'Stubborn as ever.'

'Well, you stay that way, child.' As ever the Governess's voice was a hoarse croak. 'Be obedient to whatever mistress or master employs you but never lose that independent streak. God is counting on you not to do that.'

'I shall write to you, Ma'am, as soon as I can.'

The old woman clasped the girl's hand. 'I shall be living for that day, Bellinda. Now best you hurry to town. With luck there might be someone taking some furniture up to London. And here – ' she pressed some coins into Bellinda's palm – 'take these, at least there'll be enough to get you some of Mr Herbert's muffins to eat on the way.'

Without protest Bellinda took the money. 'Thank you so much, Ma'am. How can I ever forget your kindness?'

Although the old woman was smiling, her eyes were glistening with tears. 'It is your kindness that will never be forgotten, not mine.'

Bellinda kissed the Governess on the forehead, took one final look at the beech tree where Sara was buried, allowed her gaze to roam over the dark walls of the Downley Home for Distressed Minors, and then turned towards Plomer Hill.

She hurried down the hill until she was in High Wycombe itself, and after purchasing some muffins from James Herbert's in Dashwood Avenue, went to the John Williams chair factory in Desborough Park Road.

'So you'm a wanting a lift to London, eh?' The man who spoke to her had thick muttonchop sideburns and lecherous eyes. 'Well I reckons a young girl like you couldn't be finer company, eh?'

Before he could grab her arm, Bellinda backed away. Already she had become very afraid of this man. If this was what wagon drivers were like, she would walk all the way.

'Never mind him, Missy,' a voice from behind told her. 'Silas'll never be trusted to drive a wagon to London.'

Bellinda turned and saw the face of a man whose nature seemed much more kindly. Although he too sported bushy sideburns, he could not have been more unlike his workmate.

'Mind you, I won't be trusted either if the foreman catches me taking on passengers. Best you go and wait outside. I'll be out there shortly.'

Standing outside the factory was a wagon heaving with chairs, stacked so skilfully that there could have been as many as thirty, perhaps more. Already, Bellinda was feeling sorry for the poor horses which would haul this heavy load. Then remembering about the foreman, she kept a discreet distance away while remaining vigilant for the driver's emergence from the factory.

When he did eventually come out he introduced himself as Harry and told her to go round the corner and he would pick her up from there. To her relief he kept to his word and she soon found herself perched up high on a hard wooden bench seat beside him, fighting to keep her balance as the cart pitched, rolled and juddered; the iron-shod wheels clattered loudly over the deeply rutted London Road.

As Bellinda had expected, Harry was soon wanting to know the reason for her journey. She had no wish

135

to admit that she had little money and was putting all her trust in Kuan Yin. She had always hated to appear foolish to anyone.

'Well, I's glad to hear you got yourself some arrangements for when you get there, Missy, for I'd hates to think of you all alone in that big wicked place,' Harry told her as the cart continued to creak under the massive weight of the chairs and to lurch violently as the wheels encountered yet another rut. 'Thieves and all sorts live there, you'll see. You'll stay in your master and mistress's house and not put a foot outside if you got any sense. I's never happier than when I knows I'm on my way back to Wycombe.'

After that they did not talk for a while. There was no real point in tormenting herself with thoughts of her uncertain future. Thomas Groves-Hawkes had once told her that in the East there were people who had such absolute control over their minds and bodies that they could perform all sorts of incredible feats, including lying upon a bed of nails without coming to any harm. Bellinda felt she could never aspire to such incredible achievements, but if she tried hard enough she might just be able to banish thoughts about the future for the time being.

Several carts and a mail coach passed them in the opposite direction, but Bellinda paid them only scant attention. She was far too preoccupied with the beauties of the surrounding countryside. The woodlands were just coming in to leaf. Even on such a gloomy day everywhere seemed bright and verdant. It was a time of rebirth, of renewal. Could it be symbolic of Sara's reincarnation? She saw a magpie swoop past before cresting the tops of the trees. How magnificent, how free it seemed to be. Sara was free now, of that she had become truly convinced.

Beaconsfield provided them with a short but welcome rest. While the two horses were being watered, Harry bought Bellinda a meat pie. She fought the temptation to take a large bite. Even though she was hungry it was still no excuse to behave greedily, and she would display the same manners as she had at Carlyon House. Harry watched her eat before showing her a fatherly smile.

'Proper little lady, that's what you is,' he chuckled.

They journeyed onwards, past vast fields of stubble, tiny cottages with windows from which people would often wave to them, and wagons and coaches heading in the opposite direction. When darkness began to fall Harry explained that he usually spent the night beneath a pile of old topcoats, stretching out across the full span of the seat. He invited Bellinda to sleep there while he would lay himself down beneath the cart. Bellinda protested that it should be she who slept on the ground. Harry was not to be dissuaded, insisting that his tough old bones could withstand the dampness better than her young delicate ones.

Shivering, Bellinda awoke to the sound of birds singing. Never before had their songs clarioned with such joy. Like church bells on a Sunday morning, their trilling filled her with optimism as she gazed up at a morning sky that was hosting soft white swansdown clouds. She remained in that state of mind as they journeyed onwards and Harry entertained her with amusing and affectionate stories about his two young sons and two older daughters.

It was only when they reached the outskirts of London that her spirits suddenly became low. Compared to High Wycombe and Beaconsfield it was shabby and dismal. The terraced houses were rundown and uncared for, and poverty was no stranger to the inhabitants. If only she really did have somewhere to go. Like a dark filthy maw, London was already engulfing her. She wanted to take pity on a poor waif who stretched an arm up towards her as they passed. The girl's pale grey eyes were full of desperation. She tossed down one of the Governess's coins, while reflecting that very soon her own life might well be the same as the waif's.

Harry reined the horses to a halt outside a massive soot-encrusted warehouse. The journey was over.

'I don't likes to think of you all alone in this city,' he said gravely. 'If I had more time I'd be making sure you got to where you's going, but truth is I got to get these chairs unloaded and then it's back to Wycombe as fast as these old nags'll take me, otherwise I'll be out of a job.'

'No harm shall come to me,' Bellinda assured him with a false air of confidence. 'Orphans are very good at looking after themselves, you know.'

As she climbed down from the wagon, Harry dipped into the pocket of his battered coat and pulled out some coins.

'Here,' he said urgently, pressing them into her hand, 'I knows you wouldn't be daft enough to come here without any money at all. But believe me, Missy, you'll be needing every penny you got to survive in this place.'

Pride did not get the better of her, gladly she took the money. London was beginning to terrify her. It had been madness to come here without financial security. Reluctantly she made her farewells, thanking the fatherly man for his kindness.

She forced herself to walk in a strong and positive stride along the gloomy and forbidding street. Nervously she hurried past a man, cap pulled low over his eyes, who was lurking menacingly in a doorway. She gagged upon the stench of raw sewage rising from the ground. Conditions here seemed worse than in the orphanage. Harry had told her that at the end of this street was a main road where she could catch an omnibus, a vehicle he described as like a horse and carriage but much larger and capable of carrying a lot more people, to take her into the city centre.

Bellinda looked up at a darkening sky and saw a pale, ghostly moon peer down at her from between clouds as black and grimy as the streets. Never in her life had she been in greater dread of the night.

Chapter 13

Bellinda shivered against the cold – or was she shivering against something else? Her own fears perhaps? The street she had now reached was as busy as High Wycombe on market day. Everywhere were people, all in a hurry, all with somewhere to go, no doubt. Even those in tattered and dirty clothing were probably able to jingle more silver in their pockets than the tiny sum she had in her purse. An orphan who now belonged nowhere at all, what hope of finding work and accommodation did she have?

The street echoed with the sound of hooves clattering upon the road as carriage after carriage rolled by at dangerously high speeds. What if a small child should suddenly run out into the path of these charging horses? People would probably shrug and say it was 'just one of those things'. Yes, the carefree way in which the drivers handled their horses was surely symbolic of how cheaply life was regarded here. How could she have come to such an assumption so early? Was Kuan Yin guiding her thoughts? Perhaps, but in truth Bellinda had already seen enough misery and degradation on her journey through the outskirts to realize that death could only be regarded as a welcome release for some.

Harry had mentioned something called an omnibus. So far she had not seen any carriages carrying lots of passengers; only vehicles containing the privileged had passed by. Surely there had to be something to convey the poor to their destinations. She would ask someone.

'Omnibuses is it, ducks?' said a sallow-faced woman holding the hand of a shabbily dressed child. 'Well now, they says one runs along this road at times, but don't ask me when. Never had much call to find out, see. Don't know 'ow much they charge but I know riding on one ain't cheap.'

'It's not!'

The woman studied Bellinda with her sad and tired eyes. 'Seems a shame to disappoint yer, but truth is only well-off people usually takes 'em.' Then she brightened. 'Still yer look a smartly dressed young gel. Maybe it won't seem so much to yer.'

'Probably not,' Bellinda bluffed before thanking the woman for her help. With her paltry resources, a ride on an omnibus would be a luxury indeed. The Governess's bag was beginning to weigh heavy, but she could only trudge along in search of her destiny. Whatever that was.

Perhaps there were hostels of some kind, cheap accommodation for travellers. Nothing could be worse than the orphanage, and the city would surely be at its most perilous as the night crept on. Finding somewhere to stay had to be her main priority. Again, she would have to ask.

A burly man was drunkenly lurching towards her. Bellinda would certainly not be asking him! There was something very threatening about him, a lascivious expression that frightened her.

'Well now, a young gel all on 'er own – ' spittle dribbled from his plump lips as he spoke – 'can only mean one fing 'round 'ere.'

Bellinda tried to sidestep him but the drunkard staggered over to block her path. 'No need to be like that, little miss, I know I'm an ugly cove but gels can't afford to be choosy in yer game.'

'Get out of my way!' Bellinda demanded as forcefully as she could. '*Get* out of my way!'

The drunkard grabbed her arm, his thick fingers digging into her. 'What's a matter, yer little cow?' he growled. 'Scared I'll be too big fer yer?'

Bellinda did not understand what the man, whose breath reeked of alcohol, meant by being too big for her as she desperately tried to free herself from his

140

grasp. It was impossible, until she swung her heavy bag up into his groin. The impact was hard enough to surprise him. Gasping, he let go.

She hurried away as he shouted, 'Come back 'ere. I'm a good payer. Come back!'

Again Bellinda did not understand what the drunken brute was talking about, but his words terrified her. Encumbered by the bag, she ran as fast as she could, threading her way through the crowded night until she was exhausted. Dreading what she might see, she looked back. There was a crook-backed man selling hot roasted chestnuts and a young girl trying to sell a bunch of faded flowers to the passers-by who, thankfully, did not include the drunkard.

Running had made Bellinda hungry. She would buy some roast chestnuts, for there seemed little prospect of finding anything cheaper. She parted with one of her precious farthings and took the bag of hot chestnuts from the crook-back. She felt so sorry for this poor wretch cursed by such an affliction that had she not been destitute herself she would have given him an extra farthing for nuts roasted to such delicious perfection. After finishing them, she felt thirsty. However, thirst was something she could endure.

Now that her hunger was sated, Bellinda asked the chestnut man if he knew where cheap accommodation could be found.

'Nowhere te go fer the night.' The chestnut seller stroked a stubbled chin. 'Now that takes some finking about, don't it.'

'I would be most grateful for any advice,' Bellinda said eagerly.

'Well my advice te yer is te go te . . . ' as he pondered over the problem, with bare fingers he flicked over some chestnuts roasting on the grill ' . . . go an' see Missus 'Ardmore.'

'Mrs Hardmore?'

'That's the lady, she's a friend a mine, see. She'll look after yer.'

'Oh thank you for your kindness, Sir,' Bellinda enthused.

The chestnut man grinned. 'Well now, Sir is it? There ain't many folks what shows me that kind of respect.'

'I was so fearful of having to spend the night on the street,' she told him. 'I cannot tell you how relieved I am to find somewhere to sleep.'

'Well if yer gots some money, then Missus 'Ardmore'll see te yer. Now, what yer wants te do is go round the corner te the Green Man. She'll be in there at this time of night, will Missus 'Ardmore. Doesn't like te be disturbed when she's at the geneva, but tell 'er Mad Matthew sent yer and she'll understand.'

Bellinda thanked him and hurried to the next turn. As soon as she entered the side street she could hear raucous laughter and noisy conversation. She had never been inside a public house and had no real wish to do so now. Had not the drunkard who had tried to molest her probably been imbibing in such a place? If only Mrs Hardmore were not here.

Once inside Bellinda found herself wanting to cough. The air was dense with smoke. The place could not have been more crowded. Finding the woman amongst so many people would not be easy.

'I am looking for a Mrs Hardmore?' she asked of a girl not much older than herself.

'What d'yer want with that old bag?' asked the girl, whose face was thickly layered in a garish rouge makeup. 'She's no good fer us gels. Drunk 'alf the time, that's what she is. They might knock yer about a bit, but give me a good fella te do the looking after, any day.'

Bewildered, Bellinda did her best to explain above the din that she was seeking accommodation.

In one gulp the girl downed half a glassful of geneva. 'So old 'Ardmore's a respectable landlady now,' she scoffed. 'Well she ain't been no good at any other job so she might as well try 'er 'and at that, I suppose.'

'Where will I find her?'

'Propping up the bar, o' course. Can't miss 'er, big woman with a patch over one eye.'

Bellinda thanked the girl and made her way to the bar. Mrs Hardmore was easy to spot. Leaning against the bar was a grossly fat woman, her left eye covered by a patch. In one hand she was holding a glass, and in the other a clay pipe. Bellinda took in a deep breath and hesitantly approached this formidable-looking woman.

'Well what do yer want with me?' the woman demanded, glaring with her one eye. 'I ain't in the business of taking on gels any more. Menfolk don't like it, see. Threatened to slit me throat they did, if I got involved in their business.'

Bellinda gasped. 'How dreadful, Ma'am, but it is not work that I seek from you, only a night's accommodation. Mad Matthew recommended that I speak with you.'

Mrs Hardmore looked bewildered. 'No wonder they call that old hunchback mad. 'Ardly got anywhere to sleep meself . . . O' course, come up from the country have yer, dearie?' Bellinda nodded and the woman's expression became more kindly. 'Well that's different, ain't it? How much yer got?'

'I have only a little.'

'Yes but 'ow much is a little?' Mrs Hardmore insisted.

Bellinda took out her purse, intending to count its contents, but Mrs Hardmore snatched it from her grasp. 'Come on, gel, I ain't got all night. Let's see what's in 'ere.' She tipped the contents into an open palm. 'Well this ain't gonna get yer far.'

'But, Ma'am, it is all I have,' Bellinda said dejectedly.

Mrs Hardmore inspected the money again before looking up at Bellinda and smiling. 'Well then, dearie, it'll 'ave te do, won't it? Course what with Mad Matthew wanting 'is cut fer sending yer te me, it's gonna cost yer all o' this.'

'It is? But, Ma'am, I have no other money at all.'

Mrs Hardmore tipped the money back into the purse and angrily stuffed it into Bellinda's hand. 'There, yer ungrateful little bitch, take it back. Yer ain't gonna find anywhere for that price. I was only trying te 'elp yer and that's all the thanks I get.'

'Ma'am, I did not mean to offend you.'

Mrs Hardmore's face crumpled into a smile. 'Well you give me what's in there and there'll be a room for yer at er . . . at er . . . number twenty-five of the Mile End Road. Just tell 'em I sent yer.'

'Oh Ma'am, I cannot be grateful enough. And to-morrow, shall I find work easily?'

Mrs Hardmore turned to the ruddy-faced barman who had been listening to their conversation. 'I reckon a pretty young gel like 'er'll 'ave no trouble in finding work, don't you?'

'She'll do fine. Might even give her some business meself when next I get paid.'

Mrs Hardmore threw back her head and guffawed. 'See, dearie, you'll 'ave no trouble getting customers. No trouble at all!'

Bellinda felt encouraged that there seemed a real chance of finding work, but at the moment her only thoughts were to find somewhere to sleep. She was totally exhausted. Profusely she thanked Mrs Hard-more for her kindness and hurried off to find the house in the Mile End Road, the road she now knew to be the one she had first travelled along. She had hoped to thank Mad Matthew once again for his kindness, but he was no longer selling his chestnuts. In a way she was glad, for there was now an even sharper chill in the air than before. Like herself, he too should now be tucked up in a warm bed somewhere.

It was almost too dark to see the house numbers but luckily number twenty-five was illuminated by a nearby gaslamp. She banged the knocker and stood shivering, waiting for an answer.

After what seemed like an eternity it was opened by a thin-faced woman wearing a nightcap and holding a flickering candle. 'What d'yer want?' she demanded.

'I have been sent to you by Mrs Hardmore, she tells me that you have a room for the night.'

'Room fer the night? Missus 'Ardmore? What yer talking about, girl?'

Confused, Bellinda explained.

'You've bin 'ad,' the woman said unsympathetically. 'I've never 'eard of Missus 'Ardmore and there ain't no rooms 'ere. Ten little 'uns are in this 'ouse, them and me 'usband o' course. Now best I gets back to 'im afore 'e loses 'is temper about being disturbed at this time o' night.'

The door was then slammed shut. Bellinda felt powerless to do anything but stand there in the cold, tears of hopelessness swelling in her eyes. Surely the chestnut seller would not have tricked her so callously? And Mrs Hardmore had seemed genuinely willing to help. What foolery! She had been duped. Why had she been so absurdly trusting? Now she was utterly penniless, alone and destitute in one of the cruellest places in the world. Well, cruel it might be but that was still no excuse for injustice! She would return to the Green Man and confront Mrs Hardmore, who would not be allowed to keep that money without a fight!

'Dunno where she's gone,' the barman said uninterestedly. 'Missus 'Ardmore comes and goes as she pleases, always 'as done.'

No doubt he was in league with the villainous woman, but Bellinda was determined not to give in. 'You must know where she lives, she has my money and I have nowhere to sleep. Can you condone such actions?'

The barman banged the pewter mug he had been about to fill on to the bar. 'Listen 'ere yer silly little cow, what people does 'ere is none o' my business. You was stupid enough to get taken in. Well trusting people in this city's the number one sin.'

'I can see that now,' Bellinda said bitterly, fighting hard against the temptation to cry again. 'I should never have been so trusting.'

'Tell yer what – the barman's expression was now more mellow – 'might be some room upstairs fer yer.

Don't like te see a young lass like yerself spending the night on the streets.'

'Oh Sir, I cannot thank you enough.'

He stretched out a fleshy hand and tried to fondle her chin. 'Come on now, nothing's fer free in this world. I'm gonna do yer good and proper, me gel, and it ain't gonna cost me a farthing.'

'I don't understand. What do you mean, do me?' Bellinda asked suspiciously.

The bald-headed man who had been listening to their conversation grabbed hold of her arm. ''E's meaning te lift up yer skirt, stick it right up between them pretty legs o' yours and, like e' says, do yer good and proper.' As she struggled to free herself he gave a toothless leer. 'Tell yer what, after 'e's finished with yer, I'll do yer meself. Give yer a shilling, I will.'

Bellinda now realized what they were suggesting, as well as the drunkard in the street. No, she had not sunk so low as to offer her body for obscene pleasures. 'Let go of me,' she demanded. 'No one is going to do me, least of all either of you!'

'Let 'er sleep on the street till she comes te 'er senses, Tom,' the bald man snarled after letting her go.

The barman shook his head at her. 'Lost yerself the chance of a warm bed yer 'ave,' he said contemptuously. 'Now seeing yer ain't got any money fer spending, you can get out o' this place right now!'

'I have no wish to stay,' Bellinda said with all the calmness she could muster. 'One day I shall make sure that you and your kind will never be able to violate young girls again.'

The bald man guffawed. 'Now there's a task. Must be thousands of little gels only too willing to lift their skirts up fer us blokes.'

Bellinda thought that this was probably true. What foul beasts so many men were. She glared at them in disgust before venturing out into the cold night air again.

*

146

Now more than ever, Bellinda was regretting leaving the orphanage. Perhaps, tonight, she would die of exposure. Did she really care any more? What was there to live for? Sara was gone, leaving her to face alone a world of cruel disillusionment. Only the instinct for survival was ensuring that she play out this pitiless charade to its bitter conclusion.

That driving instinct told her that she should keep walking, for exercise kept you warm. But whether it could keep one alive during such a bitterly cold night was another matter. However, total exhaustion could not be far away. Then she would have no choice but to seek some kind of shelter and wait for the morning.

The high street had quietened now. Few carriages passed, and there were less people on the pavement. Bellinda was thankful, her chances of being molested could only be that much reduced.

She came to a vast building, and in the gaslight could just read the large letters spread across its facade: Shoreditch Railway Station. Why not shelter there? At least she would be under cover.

Not even Carlyon House was as vast as this place. Bellinda imagined that a cathedral could hardly be more impressive. Yet in its way this too was a cathedral, built in homage to man's ingenuity in producing steam-propelled machines running upon rail tracks that, according to Thomas Groves-Hawkes, stretched for hundreds of miles. How proud he had sounded when describing this wondrous novelty for the rich, for surely it would be they who would most benefit. Still, no matter, the station would provide some of kind of refuge.

Standing beside a platform was one of the legendary engines. Perhaps, had circumstances been different, Bellinda would have wanted to satisfy her curiosity by inspecting this dormant metal dragon, still breathing wisps of faint smoke from a chimney stack that rose high from its squat, ugly body. However, the task of finding shelter and warmth now obsessed her.

At least the station was not quite as cold as the streets, though there was a cruel chill in the air for there were no means of warming this grimy edifice. There were several long bench seats but every one seemed occupied by a wretched soul like herself either sleeping or staring glumly at the platforms.

'Ere ducks, over 'ere. Come on, don't be shy. There's room fer yer 'ere if we shift up a bit.'

The words had been spoken by a toothless old woman whose unkempt grey hair straggled from beneath an ornate bonnet. The decorative flowers were now faded and battered and its pale-blue satin was streaked in grime. What a bitter parody of wealth this homeless woman created by the wearing of a rich woman's hat.

After her experiences she was wary of any offer of hospitality, but some instinct told Bellinda that this woman was no thief. And what if her instincts were wrong? Did it matter? After all, what was there left to steal, except the two petticoats, corsets, and toiletries in a bag that seemed to grow heavier and heavier. Cautiously Bellinda seated herself in the vacant spot, thanking the woman for her kindness.

'Fink nuffing of it, ducks, won't be 'ere fer much longer anyway.'

'You won't?'

'Nah, Peelers'll be round 'ere soon, then we'll all 'ave te shift.'

'Who are the Peelers?'

'Never 'eard o' the Peelers?' The old woman's grey eyes flared in amazement. 'Where yer bin all yer life? That's what the law's called round these parts, after old Bob Peel what started 'em.'

'Oh, you mean the policemen. But surely they would not be so unkind?'

'They'll be unkind enough, ducks. Make no mistake about that!'

Bellinda shivered at the thought of being evicted into the streets again; the heat from the woman's body

148

pressed against her own had provided her with some warmth. 'How long will it be before they come?' she asked despondently.

'Any minute now I don't doubt, but don't yer worry. There's a graveyard near 'ere. Might not be respectful but a lot us goes there and lights a fire.' Her eyes twinkled mischievously. 'So far the dead ain't complained. Probably likes a bit o' company.'

Bellinda smiled. 'When someone as warm-hearted as you sleeps on their grave, then I'm sure no corpse would dream of complaining.'

'Now that's a nice fing fer yer te say.' Affectionately she patted Bellinda on the knee with a hand in a threadbare mitten. 'Funny 'ow yer can tell but I fought to meself as soon as I clapped eyes on yer that you was a nice girl who shouldn't be 'ere.

'What's your name?'

'Betsy, they calls me Betsy.' Then she gave a laugh that echoed against the station walls. Someone on one of the other seats hissed at her to be quiet. 'Never known why cos Florey's me real name,' she continued, unconcerned by the protest.

'Betsy suits you best,' Bellinda told her. 'As for me, I am an orphan who never had a proper name so they called me Bellinda, for bells could be heard when I was born.'

'Nuffing wrong with Bellinda, ducks, that's a beautiful name. A real beauty.'

'Yes,' Bellinda agreed proudly. 'I like it too.'

'Well, now we know who each other is, we can goes te sleep. You look all in, Bellinda.'

Bellinda smiled at Betsy before closing her eyes. The seat was hard, the station cold, but at that moment it did not matter. Bellinda was no longer on her feet, and more important she was beside someone who seemed kind and trustworthy. Better to be in the company of pungent Betsy than a perfumed member of the Groves-Hawkes family with their shallow and selfish ways. For one moment the terrible memory of Sara's death

149

haunted her yet again. Then there was peace, a warm slumbrous peace that turned to a kind and protective darkness.

'Oi, you, wake up!'

Somewhere beyond, a cruel voice was beckoning. Bellinda would ignore it. Kuan Yin would keep intruders away from the beautiful garden where blue hyacinths gently blended with a sumptuous carpet of freesias, roses and buttercups. The voice shouted again and the flowers began to rise high from the ground, protecting her.

'Wake up!' The voice was an explosion, scattering the flowers up into an angry red sky.

Now awake, Bellinda found herself gazing up at a bewhiskered face that even in the dim gaslight seemed to glow with animosity.

'That's better,' he said triumphantly. 'Now that you're with us I can tell you what I've told the others. This station's no resting place for scum like you. Why, proper ladies and gentlemen sit on those seats waiting for the trains!'

'That may be, but I and my friends are not scum!' Bellinda told him angrily.

'Well scum or not, I want you lot out of here. Otherwise I'm blowing my whistle.'

Betsy tapped Bellinda on the knee. 'Come on, ducks. We wouldn't be wanting the constable 'ere te blow 'is whistle now, would we?'

The short sleep seemed only to have made her more exhausted, and Betsy had to help her to stand up.

'Yer kind ain't nuffing but bastards!' the woman growled at the policeman. 'Ow would you like it if yer had nowhere te sleep fer the night?'

The policeman looked chastened. 'I wouldn't,' he said quietly. 'But truth is, I got a job to do just like anyone else.'

Betsy turned to Bellinda. ''Ear that? This gentleman 'ere says 'e's got a job. Wish I could say the same, don't you, ducks?'

150

Bellinda nodded, and she and all the other homeless trudged wearily out of the station into the cold night air.

Bellinda's teeth began to chatter and her whole body shivered violently. She was almost regretting having entered the station, for being cast out again was a cruel torture.

'Now don't yer 'ave that worried expression on yer face,' Betsy scolded mildly. 'Like I said, there's a graveyard nearby. We all goes there and lights a fire.'

Although the wrought-iron gate of the graveyard was locked, one of the homeless, a youngish man wearing a brimless top hat, managed to open the padlock without the aid of a key. Betsy told Bellinda that he had been a thief until seeing one of his friends hanged at the gallows. He had lost his nerve and now preferred the life of a beggar.

The graveyard was even more eerie than she had expected. What if some angry spirit rose from the grave? Who could blame it when so many people were desecrating this sacred resting place of the departed?

She was led to the centre amidst a cluster of gravestones. From battered bags and from inside worn coats, kindling wood was suddenly produced.

'Told yer we was organized,' Betsy said proudly. 'Won't be much of a fire, but enough te keep us warm fer a little while.'

The fire was soon crackling and spitting. Although there was little heat generated from such a small fire, the glow did provide some comfort. Orphans whose bodies could no longer withstand the cold of the night had been known to die in their sleep. Was this to be her own fate, she wondered, as she followed the others' example and laid herself down upon the ground as close to the fire as possible. Her bag would serve as a pillow and her coat as a blanket. Perhaps in her dreams she would return to that garden again. Or perhaps not . . .

Once again someone was telling her to wake up, but this time the voice was more kindly, more reassuring.

'Sorry te wake yer, ducks,' Betsy was saying as, wearily, Bellinda sat herself up and rested her back against a gravestone. So she had not died during the night, though she felt barely alive. The ground had been bone hard and covered by frost. Not only was her body aching from the hardness but the frost had soaked into her clothing. 'Trouble is the verger'll be 'ere soon. Don't want 'im te find out we comes 'ere, do we?'

Bellinda could find no energy to speak. She just shook her head from side to side in agreement before weakly getting to her feet. In the grey dawn the homeless made their way back into the streets.

'Well, what yer gonna do teday?' Betsy asked as they leaned against the railings outside the churchyard.

'Try and find work,' Bellinda replied dejectedly.

'Well yer young and that's in yer favour. What yer got in mind?'

'My one aim in life is to gain a position that enables me to help others.'

'People like us,' Betsy said after a bout of heavy coughing.

Bellinda put a hand on the old woman's shoulder. 'Yes, Betsy, people like you.'

'Well I could do with a bit o' 'elp,' Betsy managed to say before another bout of heavy coughing. 'Meantime I'll just 'ave te keep on begging though, won't I?'

Sara feared that like Sara, Betsy had the flux; the body could only endure so much hardship. 'One day I shall ensure that no one has to beg on the streets of London.'

'Then I wishes yer all the luck in the world, ducks. But first yer got te find yerself a job.'

'Where is the best place to try?'

'Not round 'ere, that's fer sure. Well leastways not for such a nice little girl as you.' She coughed again before continuing. 'Up West is where yer want te be. That's where the rich live.'

'Then that is where I shall go.'

'I'll takes yer there, feel like a bit o' a walk, I does.'

'How far is it, are you sure you want to come with me?'

'It's a few miles, but course I'm sure'. She gave Bellinda a toothless smile. ''Avin' yer fer company these past 'ours 'as bin the best thing te 'appen te me fer a long time.'

'Oh, Betsy, if only I could find a job for you too.'

Betsy gave a bitter laugh. 'Ducks, yer gonna 'ave an 'ard enough time finding work fer yerself.'

Bellinda feared Betsy's words to be true. Were work easy to find then there would not be so many poor. What did Fate have in store for her? Death, starvation perhaps? If that were so then she must accept her death with good grace, for it would be the wish of Kuan Yin that she leave the miseries of this life and go on to the next.

Before starting their journey, they had breakfast. This consisted of two pieces of stale bread that Betsy produced from her coat pocket. At first Bellinda refused, determined that her companion eat both pieces, but the old woman insisted, so she took a piece, doing her best to brush away the dirt. Its taste was foul, but no matter, it did help to stave off the hunger.

The journey seemed endless. It had never taken long to walk through High Wycombe before reaching the country again. In London it was nothing but busy streets thronging with people.

At a place that Betsy told her was Covent Garden, Bellinda noticed a small girl standing at the roadside. She seemed to be waiting for someone. Further along were several others no more than ten years of age, all with brightly rouged faces and again seemingly waiting.

'Betsy, why are there so many young girls here at this time of the morning?' she asked. 'I know enough of London to realize what a dangerous place it is.'

'Well there's some gentlemen what likes te do a bit o' business 'afore they goes te work.'

'Business? What kind of business?'

Betsy gave another one of her bitter laughs. 'What kind o' business does yer think?'

'You can't mean – ' Bellinda was too horrified to go on.

''Fraid I do, ducks. I've seen little gels of maybe no more than seven years old up against a wall with some man ramming into the poor little mite.'

'Betsy, this cannot be true. What vile beast would . . .'

'World's never bin short o' vile beasts.'

'But surely such a thing is against the law?'

Betsy shrugged. 'Don't think so, Peelers is more concerned with kicking the likes of us outta stations.'

'Oh, what utter wickedness,' Bellinda gasped, tears now streaming down her cheeks. 'What kind of people are the rich to allow this to go on?'

'Bellinda, who does yer fink's the best customers? I know it ain't right, but a littl'un can earn 'erself an 'ansome sum, more than an older girl quite often.'

'You seem to approve,' Bellinda said angrily.

'Nah, course I don't. But there's nuffing the likes o' us can do about it.'

'Oh yes there is!'

'Ducks, yer can't change the way o' the world.'

'Betsy, have I not told you that one day I intend to gain a position of influence? Have I not told you that!'

Betsy smiled. 'Yes, ducks, you did, and d'yer know, funny fing is I believes yer.' She looked at Bellinda pensively. 'Can't put me finger on it but there's something different about yer, me gel.'

'You are not the first to say that, Betsy.'

'Won't be the last neither. Now come along, ducks. Mayfair's still a long way off, so best yer puts a step in it.'

Mayfair could not have been a greater contrast to the teeming slums. Tall, pristine houses rose proudly from smooth pavements. A man in an immaculate grey frock coat and absurdly tall hat eyed them with contempt as he passed. Bellinda wondered whether he had an assignation with one of the child prostitutes – or was she being too harsh? Not every man was like that. She could never have imagined Thomas Groves-Hawkes ever behaving so despicably despite his selfish ways. No, it would be wrong to judge all men so harshly. But she vowed that one day the vile exceptions would be brought to justice.

'Well, ducks, this where we says goodbye.'

'But why, Betsy?'

''Cos if folk sees me with yer it won't look good. I got beggar written all over me, I 'ave.'

'Oh Betsy, you must have more pride in yourself, you have a heart worth a hundred times more than the fine ladies and gentlemen here.'

'Nice of yer te say so, ducks, but truth is yer gonna find it 'ard enough te get yerself a job as it is, without my 'indrance.'

Bellinda wrapped her arms around the old woman's bony shoulders and hugged her tightly. 'Thank you for your kindness, dear Betsy,' she said softly. 'Thank you so much.'

'Now you look after yerself, ducks. Promise? And remember, if yer gets no luck then come back ter the graveyard tonight. I'll 'ave a little something fer yer supper.'

Bellinda hugged her again and promised that even if she did manage to find employment she would still visit the graveyard in the near future.

Betsy had advised her not to knock on the front doors of the houses for she was bound to be turned away; better to go down the iron stairs that led to the basements where the servants dwelled. Bellinda decided to be systematic. She would try the first house on the left and work her way along to the end of the street, then down the right-hand side until every house had been tried.

'What do you want?' a thickset man demanded as she knocked at the basement door of the first house.

'I am trying to find work,' she began. 'I have come from – '

'Well there ain't none 'ere,' he interrupted.

'Then I am sorry to have troubled you,' Bellinda said, disappointed.

'Well even if there was yer ain't going about it right. Masters and mistresses want letters of reference before they takes on staff.'

'Oh but I have one, from the Governess of the Downley orphanage in High Wycombe.'

'Well that might be in yer favour, but no one's going te take on a girl that can't even keep herself clean.'

'I can explain that, you see I did have money for a night's board and lodging but – '

'I ain't got time te listen te all that. Like I said, there ain't no jobs 'ere,' the man growled before slamming the door in Bellinda's face.

Refusing to be disheartened, she immediately tried the house next door. This time a starch-aproned woman answered. She wasted no time in telling Bellinda that there were no jobs for 'street sluts'.

Still refusing to be disheartened Bellinda tried the third house, the fourth, the fifth, until every house on the left-hand side had been tried. Although tired and exhausted she forced herself over the road, almost being run down by a passing carriage, before continuing on the right-hand side. Again the reply was always the same, and often with the added reminder that there were plenty of people looking for work in service. Bellinda refused to give up. Kuan Yin would be her strength, her spirit. Although she could barely stand now, she was convinced that determination would triumph over adversity. She would find work, and waiting for her would be a warm bed. Sleep, how she longed for sleep!

Three more houses to go. Mind over matter. One of them would welcome her.

'Yes, what does thee want?' a ruddy-faced woman demanded.

'I was inquiring about vacancies.'

'Well our tweeny's just died. Mistress don't want to be bothered with finding a new one.'

Bellinda had wanted something less menial than being a skivvy, but now realized she had little option

156

but to accept any job on offer. 'Oh Ma'am, I would be most grateful for any work. Most grateful.'

'But thee looks so dirty, girl. Even tweenies have to keep themselves in proper order in this house.'

'Ma'am, I was forced to spend the night on the streets, for my money was stolen.'

The woman stroked her double chin. 'Well that's not surprising in this city. You can wear the dead girl's uniform. But it'll come out of your wages, mind.'

'Of course,' Bellinda agreed readily. 'I do have a letter of reference from the Downley Home in High Wycombe.'

'Orphan are thee? Well that should make you want to work harder. Not everyone takes on orphans.'

'I am used to hard work, Ma'am.'

'Should hope so indeed, because work is what you'll be doing here, my girl, and it's all got to be satisfactory.' The cook then opened the door wider. 'Well, no point standing outside, is there? Best you come in.'

Inside, the cook studied Bellinda with her hard, beady eyes. 'You don't look like you're going to be much use to me today, you look all in. I'll let you have a good sleep for the rest of the day. But make no mistake, my girl – ' she wagged a finger at Bellinda – 'at five o'clock tomorrow morning I'll be wanting you up and ready for more work than you've ever done in your life.'

Bellinda thanked her once again, before being led up the back stairs. She barely had the energy to keep climbing, passing floor after floor until finally they could go no further.

'Here,' the cook said, opening a creaking door, 'this is your room. You're to keep it as clean as the rest of the house. I'll have no slubbornness anywhere. Does thee understand?'

'Yes, Ma'am.'

'From now on it's "Yes, Mrs Ramsbottom". Now you get yourself into that bed, there's cold water in a jug and soap beside it.'

The room was cold and the water in the jug even colder. The bed looked as sparse and as hard as the ones at the orphanage. Why had she left? What purpose was there in travelling to London to become nothing more than a tweeny, the lowest of the low in the servants' world? It was a cruel irony.

The bed would be far more comfortable than the graveyard, and Bellinda was longing to climb into it, but she undressed and then endured the torture of washing in the icy water. In her threadbare nightdress she slid beneath the sheets and found the bed no warmer than the room. Her teeth chattered and her body quivered as she remembered the pan-heated beds at Carlyon House. How warm and cosy they had been. Always, there was one law for the rich.

What of her dreams of doing great works of charity? Dreams indeed! Since when were tweenies allowed dreams? She could wish for nothing more than a good sleep, before starting a job she knew she would hate.

Chapter 14

As there was neither candle nor clock in her room, Bellinda had no means of knowing what time it was when she woke. She remained in the bed, now warmed by her body, lying on her back and thinking in the darkness. Her mind wandered from the orphanage to Carlyon House and then back to the orphanage. Always, her thoughts were dominated by Sara. It still seemed impossible that she was gone. What purpose had her death served?

She recalled how at ease Sara had been in the ways of etiquette at Carlyon House for, unlike herself, Sara had experienced that life style before. Bellinda recalled how, when first confronted by a confusing array of cutlery at the Groves-Hawkes table, she had been uncertain as to which to use first. Vanity was about to show her the correct one to take when Sara, much to Vanity's annoyance, advised her to start by using the ones furthest away from the plate. Bellinda smiled at the recollection.

Then a darker memory came: Sara, her own dear Sara, had once been one of those brutalized waifs she had seen in Covent Garden. Sara had told her of the cruel use some depraved man had made of her and Bellinda, horrified and sickened though she was, had not truly believed her. Until now – now that she had seen the child prostitutes for herself.

Lying in pitch darkness, Bellinda felt the full and terrible import of cold realization strike home. She gasped as she imagined the dreadful obscenities that must have been performed upon Sara's tiny, innocent body. Yet it was not her body that men's lust had destroyed, but her mind. What purpose was there to this cruel world? Her own body trembled and tears flooded as she wept and wept over the tragedy of Sara's life.

'Thee're no use to me lying in that bed.'

Bellinda turned her tearstained face away from the pillow and looked up. Illuminated by a candleflame were the harsh features of Mrs Ramsbottom.

'Come on, get up, girl. The dead girl's uniform's been washed, so no reason why thee can't start wearing it.'

'Thank you, Mrs Ramsbottom,' Bellinda said, wiping away the tears. 'Please tell me, what did the last tweeny die of?'

'Couldn't tell thee,' the cook said casually. 'All I knows is, one minute she was scrubbing stairs and the next she was dead. Never seemed able to stand hard work, did that girl. I hopes thee turns out to be something a bit better or out the door thee goes!'

Bellinda refused to give this tyrant the satisfaction of hearing her obediently say 'Yes, Mrs Ramsbottom'. She just got out of bed and took the uniform. As soon as she had done so Mrs Ramsbottom was gone, leaving her to dress in darkness.

The uniform was far too big for her. It would surely prove uncomfortable to wear. Gloomily she descended the stairs to the kitchen.

'Thee can start on the hob,' Mrs Ramsbottom told her. 'Hasn't been blacked proper since that useless girl died.'

Bellinda had rarely blacked the hob at the orphanage, there always seemed more important tasks to perform. This particular range hardly needed full attention but, as at Carlyon, everything had to be absolutely immaculate, lest the idle eyes of their masters and mistresses be displeased by even the slightest speck of dirt. Knowing Mrs Ramsbottom's expectations, she worked quickly.

'Too slow by half to be satisfactory,' the woman complained as soon as Bellinda told her the task had been completed. 'Should have finished half an hour

160

ago.' She gave an exaggerated sigh. 'Most unsatisfactory. Still, thee better get on with the stairs now. See if thee can't make up the time.'

'Very well, Mrs Ramsbottom,' Bellinda said calmly, refraining from pointing out that she had worked as quickly as she could.

'By the way, you better give me tha name.'

'Bellinda, I am called Bellinda.'

'No, I did not mean tha first name. It's surnames in this household, I don't hold with familiarity.'

'I have no surname.'

'No surname! That's orphanages for thee. Well the last tweeny's name was Brown, so you might as well be Brown too.'

Marguerite Groves-Hawkes had tried to rename her. Now Mrs Ramsbottom was doing the same. 'I would rather be called Bellinda, Mrs Ramsbottom,' she said.

'From now on tha name is *Brown*, young lady, whether thee likes it or not!' Mrs Ramsbottom's pig-like eyes flared. 'Now you get on with those stairs.'

Bellinda was then handed a lighted candle mounted on a small tray, and warned not to knock it over while she worked for fear of starting a fire. She was also told to keep out of the way of the master and mistress.

As Bellinda cleaned the first step she wondered what catastrophe had made Mrs Ramsbottom such an objectionable person. Perhaps the poor woman had been widowed, or perhaps she had lost a son or daughter? Whenever you felt animosity towards someone, was it not a good idea to try guessing what had made them so unhappy that they wanted to make other people's lives a misery?

The over-sized uniform was now beginning to feel very uncomfortable, constantly crumpling in the wrong places and forming ridges that dug into her. Would she be forced to wear this garment, polish these stairs and say 'Yes Mrs Ramsbottom, No Mrs Ramsbottom,' for the rest of her life? It would seem so.

After she had completed her task the cook again informed her that the standard of her work was still unsatisfactory. She was then told that some bread and dripping awaited her in the kitchen, where she could join the kitchen maid for a twenty-minute break.

'I'm Hardwick,' a young girl almost as freckled as Sara told her.

'Well, unlike Mrs Ramsbottom I believe in calling people by their christian names,' Bellinda said with a smile.

'Then it's Liza.'

'I'm Bellinda, and despite what Cook might want to think, I have no other name.'

'Now then – ' Liza's eyes twinkled mischievously – 'I bet she calls yer Brown after the last tweeny what died.'

Bellinda laughed heartily. Mrs Ramsbottom burst in from the next room. 'We shall have no such vulgar mirth in this household. Mr Briar and me wants some peace during our break. Remember that, Brown!'

After Cook had slammed the door shut, Liza giggled impishly. 'Silly old fool, finks she's God almighty she does.'

'What's Mr Briar like?'

Liza snorted loudly. 'Im? 'E's worse than Mrs Ramsbottom.'

'Goodness, can that be possible?'

They both laughed quietly before saying in unison, 'It's possible!'

Bellinda liked Liza and was glad that she had found someone whose company she could enjoy.

Her next chore was to clean and dust the master's bedroom. It was a large imposing room, with heavy burgundy curtains draped in such a way as to virtually exclude the sunlight. Thanks to the teachings of Thomas Groves-Hawkes, Bellinda found it easy to identify much of the furniture that she dusted.

She knew the ornate clock on the mantelpiece to be ormolu, and the chairs? Were they Adam or Sheraton? She was not sure. There were also several examples of what her mentor had said was the most fashionable pottery of all, Staffordshire. What would happen were she to break one of these ornaments? The consequences would be all too obvious. Like anyone else of her kind, she was to live day by day upon the very edge of destitution, for just one slip and she would be out on the streets again.

Knowing that Mrs Ramsbottom would be expecting everything to be 'satisfactory', Bellinda did her work as quickly and as thoroughly as she could before reporting back to the kitchen. Liza was squatting upon a short stool, the carcase of a part-plucked chicken dangling between her legs, while Mrs Ramsbottom was rolling out pastry.

'Ah, here at last are thee? Can't say before time. Well tha can help in the kitchen until this afternoon,' Mrs Ramsbottom said, her thick arms flexing as she rolled the heavy pin backwards and forwards, pulverizing the dough. 'Then for the rest of the day you can do the whole house from top to bottom – and I mean every room. Course under normal circumstances, tweenies are supposed to keep themselves unseen by the mistress and master, but seeing Mrs Gage is poorly and in bed, you'll just have to do tha work discreetly. Besides, I dare say she'll be wanting to take a look at thee, seeing tha just joined.'

The first course of the day was to be cold salmon in aspic, followed by roast chicken with a sumptuous selection of vegetables, and finally an apple pie flavoured with what Cook described as her 'special spices'.

After the pie had been placed upon the dumb waiter and heaved up so that Mr Briar could serve it to the Gage family, they busied themselves tidying up the kitchen before the crow-like Mr Briar returned to inform them that the used plates and cutlery were to be brought down. After the washing-up had been completed the staff had their own lunch. This consisted of what had been left over from the main course. Little remained of the chicken, and that went on to the plates

163

of Mrs Ramsbottom and Mr Briar. Only potatoes, carrots, cabbage, parsnips and gravy were served to Bellinda, Liza, and the coachman, who was referred to by Mrs Ramsbottom as Cooper.

Once again the butler and Mrs Ramsbottom went into the small room next door while the other three ate at the kitchen table.

'Let me introduce meself,' the coachman said breezily. 'The name's Tom, Tom Cooper.'

Bellinda introduced herself, explaining that her surname was not Brown and that Bellinda was her only name. She liked the stockily built young coachman, who seemed as friendly and cheerful as Liza. She could also tell that he was a little in awe of her. Was this to be her first romance? No, Tom might well make a good companion but she was not destined for him.

The rest of their conversation was concerned with her description of Downley and High Wycombe, for both these townfolk seemed fascinated by the country world beyond London. Then it was time to get back to work and for Bellinda that would mean every nook and cranny in the vast house. It was bound to be a tiresome and soul-destroying task but at least she would get the opportunity to meet Mrs Gage.

'Who is it?' a dainty voice asked after Bellinda knocked on the door.

'It is the new between maid, Ma'am. Is it convenient to come and see to your room?'

'Convenient? How could such a disturbance ever be convenient?' Through the door, Mrs Gage's faint voice was barely audible. 'Still, you'd better come inside, I suppose.'

Mrs Gage was sitting upright in a magnificent half-tester bed. Almost dwarfed by a red heavily draped canopy, the mistress of the house gave Bellinda the impression of being a frail and sickly woman.

With humourless grey eyes Mrs Gage studied Bellinda. 'So you are our new between maid,' she said wanly.

164

'Yes, Ma'am.'

'And what is your name?'

No doubt Cook would have demanded that she say Brown, but why should she? 'My name is Bellinda,' she answered proudly.

'Bellinda, now that is quite a charming name. How did a between maid come to have such a delightful name?'

'Bells were ringing when I was born, Ma'am.'

Mrs Gage clasped her long and bony hands together. 'Oh what romance! How poetic!'

'Thank you, Ma'am.'

Mrs Gage's weak smile vanished, her expression hardened. 'Yes, girl, well you'd better get about your business and be quiet about it.' She sighed, a long exasperated sigh. 'Of course, what I truly require is someone to read this book to me.'

'I can read, Ma'am.'

'Oh heavens above, girl! I am not referring to the ability to read in an elementary fashion,' Mrs Gage said irritably. 'I refer to proper diction, and an actual understanding of the words being read.' She gave a faint but cynical laugh. 'Tell me, what would an ill-educated girl like you know of Thackeray?'

'I have only read *Vanity Fair*, Ma'am.'

Mrs Gage's narrow jaw dropped. 'And what, pray, did you think of Becky Sharp?'

'A cunning schemer who deserved more retribution than Mr Thackeray saw fit to mete out to her at the end.'

'Well I have yet to finish the book, but no punishment could be too great for that wanton woman, and as for that Rawdon Crawley with his foul, drunken ways, well . . .'

Bellinda remembered Rawdon Crawley to have been a somewhat sympathetic character but decided it would not be correct to argue with one's mistress. 'It is a memorable book, Ma'am,' she said cautiously.

'Yes, I must confess that I am intrigued by it, despite the explicit descriptions of such wanton debauchery.'

Debauchery! Had this woman not seen the debauchery that occurred but a short walk from her own doorstep?

Mrs Gage then eyed Bellinda quizzically. 'Are you capable of reading to me, I wonder? Here, girl, sit at the side of the bed and begin.' She handed over a beautiful leather-bound copy of *Vanity Fair*.

Bellinda had read only two passages when Mrs Gage stopped her. 'Oh my dear, what intonation, pronunciation, diction, and sympathy with the text. Never have I been read to with such expertise. Never!'

'Thank you, Ma'am.'

'It is I who must thank you,' she enthused. 'Continue, pray continue.'

Bellinda continued to read until she was hoarse. Hurriedly Mrs Gage poured her a glass of water and bade her to drink before resuming.

'Oh, I think that is enough for today,' she said wearily after another chapter had been finished. 'Being read to can be very tiring, but you must come back tomorrow.'

'Very well, Ma'am,' Bellinda said hoarsely, her throat dry.

Gladly she took some more water before leaving Mrs Gage to sniff delicately at her sal volatile. She then continued with her chores, until she came to the library. Bellinda had been looking forward to dusting all the books but her heart sank when she discovered that Mrs Ramsbottom was in there.

'Thee can go upstairs right now and pack tha things,' the cook said angrily. 'Thee shall not be allowed to stay in this house one minute longer.'

'I can explain, Mrs Ramsbottom,' Bellinda said calmly.

'Explain! How can thee explain tha disappearance for more than two hours?'

'I have been reading to Mrs Gage.'

For a moment Mrs Ramsbottom was speechless. 'You've been what?'

'Mrs Gage asked me to read to her.'

'But that's no job for a tweeny. Mr Briar has a very nice reading voice. He could have done that.'

'Mrs Gage seems to like the way I read to her, she wants me to read to her tomorrow afternoon as well.'

'Whatever next!' Mrs Ramsbottom shook her head in disgust. 'Just what is the world coming to when a mere tweeny is allowed to do other people's work?' she said before storming out of the room.

Although having to read for such long stretches was tiring to the throat, Bellinda much preferred this task to being Mrs Ramsbottom's skivvy. For the next three afternoons she read out the adventures of Becky Sharp to Mrs Gage, who seemed to be appreciating her ability more and more.

It was on the fourth day that Bellinda's mistress turned to her and asked, 'How are you with children, my dear?'

For a moment Bellinda was too startled to answer. 'I am at ease with them, Ma'am,' she replied, wondering why she had been asked. 'Most at the orphanage were younger than myself so I . . . ' She stopped herself from saying that in truth, it was she who had mostly looked after them. For it would not have looked well for the Governess.

'Did you assist the Governess in the children's welfare?'

'Yes I did assist, Ma'am.'

'Oh, Bellinda,' Mrs Gage sighed. 'I am still far too tired to attend to such tiresome matters as finding a nanny for our dear son. What a pity that you are an orphan. I know my husband would insist upon employing someone with a reference from people of a higher status than an orphanage.'

A nanny? Was this not the kind of work she was truly seeking? If only she were able to produce something other than a reference from the Governess. But of course! 'I stayed at Carlyon House for a little while,' she said hastily.

Mrs Gage's pale eyes brightened. 'My dear Bellinda. You have stayed with the Groves-Hawkes?'

'Yes, Ma'am, throughout the Christmas period. I assisted Mr Groves-Hawkes in the listing of his antiques. It was most interesting work.'

'I'm sure it was. I think you should know that I and my dear husband hold the Groves-Hawkes in the highest esteem.'

'They are people of great standing,' Bellinda said, refraining from saying what she truly thought of that selfish and heartless family.

'They are indeed, and so charming. Oh that Vanity, what a delightful child.'

Bellinda made no comment.

'Well, have no fear, I shall write to them. I shall write to them now!'

'Oh, thank you, Ma'am.'

'Of course, it will now mean having to find another between maid,' Mrs Gage said as Bellinda brought writing materials over to the bed. 'Oh, that Mrs Ramsbottom! She can be so incompetent at times! Knowing your qualifications she should have brought you straight to me. She knew we were looking for a nanny.'

'I do not think she was aware of my stay at Carlyon House, Ma'am.'

'Well she should have been. Now best you get on with your cleaning work while I deal with this letter.'

It was only after she had left Mrs Gage that Bellinda was able to give more thought to the matter. By now Briar would be sending the letter on its way. How would the Groves-Hawkes act upon receiving it? She had hardly left Carlyon under the best of circumstances. If it was to be dealt with by Marguerite Grove-Hawkes then Mrs Gage might well receive a reference that was by no means complimentary. What then? Not only would she fail to gain the post of nurse but might even lose her job as a tweeny. What had she done? Foolishness!

168

Chapter 15

'What can be in that letter, dearest, for you to find it so engrossing?'

'Oh, mere business matters, my love,' Thomas Groves-Hawkes lied to his wife.

'Then must you be so tiresomely self-involved at the breakfast table?' Marguerite asked irritably.

'I'm afraid so,' Thomas answered sharply, now reading the letter from Mrs Harriet Gage for the third time.

So Bellinda was in London, at the home of the Gages. Upon the first reading he had only just managed to stifle a gasp. How that girl was haunting him, his green-eyed beauty. His? Could she ever be that? Oh, what inestimable bliss mere contemplation brought to his troubled mind. Would he ever be granted the chance to caress that milk-white body blessed with the velvet smoothness of youth? Bellinda, had she not become his *raison d'être*? Did not his very soul belong to her? For what else could be said of a man who ached night and day just to be near this heavenly child?

Had Marguerite seen this letter she would undoubtedly wish to send a most derogatory reference to Mrs Gage. It was therefore imperative that the whole matter remain a secret. Bellinda must be granted every opportunity to become a nanny.

Secrets! Once he had no secrets at all from his beloved wife. How infatuation destroyed without mercy, driving its victim to commit one godless act after another. One day he would have to atone for these sins not only of thought, but soon of deed too. Not now! Nothing else was important, save the urgent dispatch of a most laudable reference to Mrs Harriet Gage.

Bellinda was now convinced more than ever that very
soon she would be out on to the chilly London streets
again. Had she not left Carlyon House without permission? In a constant state of anguish and depression,
Bellinda continued with her work as a tweeny and
reader to Mrs Gage. Even after a whole week, she had
still not seen either the master of the house nor the
young son. She gathered that Mr Gage was out at
business for most of the day while little Jamie had a
nanny borrowed from a nearby family while her own
charges were being attended to by a French counter-
part during a stay in Paris. The woman kept herself
aloof from all the other servants, including Mrs Ramsbottom and Mr Briar.

One morning Mrs Ramsbottom told Bellinda to go
and see Mr Gage in his study. Trembling, she knocked
on the study door.

'Ah, come in, Bellinda.'

She entered and was confronted by a round, imperious man with heavy jowls and bushy muttonchop whiskers. Like her own, his eyes were green, and there did
seem to be a friendly twinkle in them.

'Well now, what have we here?' His tone seemed
friendly too. 'I never expected you to be so young and
pretty. Our dear Jamie will be thinking of you more as
an elder sister than a nanny.' He tugged at his double
chin and smiled. 'Still, that's not a bad situation. He
should have been blessed with brothers and sisters. You
will be most suitable.'

'I shall!'

'Yes indeed, my dear. I can assure you that my good
friend Thomas Groves-Hawkes could not have been
more praising of your abilities.' He waved the letter at
her. 'It would appear that you made quite an impression upon him, young lady. 'What a godsend your arrival at this house has proved. First you help my wife
recover from her vapours by reading to her, and now
you are to become a constant companion to our

beloved son. I say welcome to this household, Bellinda. I say welcome!'

That night Bellinda climbed beneath the chilled sheets of her bed more happily than for some time. The Governess had been right after all. She had found herself a position of merit. What was little Jamie like? The thought tantalized her. That night she slept soundly and contentedly.

To her disappointment she discovered from Mrs Gage that the Frobishers were not due back from France until the end of the week. She apologized to Bellinda for not allowing her the opportunity to meet Jamie, explaining that as the temporary nanny was still in attendance, it would be unsettling for the 'precious child' to meet her replacement.

Bellinda was at a loss to understand the reasoning behind this but accepted that a parent would know best how to deal with her own child. Besides, was it not just a few more days before her tweenying was over?

Now fully aware of Bellinda's impending promotion, Mrs Ramsbottom did not miss the slightest chance to criticize. She would get down on her knees to stare at a place where Bellinda had just worked, and invariably say, 'Thee has missed that bit there. Tha work is unsatisfactory. Most unsatisfactory!' And, 'How long does an orphan with sloppy ways think she's going to last as a nanny?'

Bellinda remained silent. How she pitied this woman who used her position to make herself as unpleasant as she could. How lonely she had to be. Perhaps she too had lost someone very close. Would it not have been better to turn to others for friendship and comfort? If only the world were populated by people like Sara and Betsy, and of course the Governess who, despite her slubbornly ways, had always possessed an honest heart.

As the days passed Mrs Ramsbottom became more and more vindictive. Bellinda did not care. One of her duties was to clean Jamie's room while the nanny took him out for his afternoon walk. Never could any child have owned so many toys. There was a clockwork soldier which she could not wait to see marching, a metal steam engine that was a miniature of the machine she had seen at the station, and an imposing medieval fortress that occupied almost a quarter of the room. However, despite such masculine toys, the room itself seemed more suitable for a girl. The window was draped by a pale blue lace-edged curtain. The wallpaper was resplendent with a bright floral design and upon his bed were soft downy blue pillows, very similar to those that Vanity had rested her head upon. His clothes were also of a girlish style – small knickerbocker suits in satin or soft velvet with frilled white collars. She recalled that Robert Groves-Hawkes' clothes were much more masculine, as was his room. However these observations did not detract from her feeling of excitement and anticipation whenever she entered the room.

The animosity towards her came not only from Mrs Ramsbottom. Emily the parlour maid had now returned from leave after nursing her dying sister. Perhaps it was the death of her relative, but the thin, sour-faced girl seemed to regard servants of lower rank than herself with sneering contempt. As for the temporary nanny? All her meals were taken to her own room or Jamie's, much to the chagrin of Mrs Ramsbottom who regarded such a demand as trying to make herself like the master and the mistress of the house.

One more day, then Bellinda would meet her charge. Upon the small table at Mrs Gage's bedside was his portrait. It was a finely painted miniature of a boy with sky-blue eyes and soft golden locks in a velvet suit.

She was now reading to her mistress in the drawing room for Mrs Gage had fully recovered. The book was John Bunyan's *Pilgrim's Progress*. Enthusiastically, Harriet Gage was journeying with Bunyan for the third time. However, Bellinda thought the whole tome very dull and today was finding it difficult to concentrate; her mind was too occupied by the prospect of meeting Jamie.

'You seem a little nervous, my dear,' Mrs Gage said gently after Bellinda had finished a chapter.

'I am sorry, Mrs Gage, perhaps I am a little unnerved by the prospect of meeting your son for the first time,' she confessed.

'Oh child!' Mrs Gage's stone-grey eyes were sparkling. 'Such nonsense. I can assure you that he is the most adorable child. One simply has to give him whatever he wants. A more lovable and obedient son one could never wish for.' She sighed wistfully. 'My dear husband did so want more children but I think that God has blessed us well. Is he not worth a hundred other children? Upon meeting him I am sure you will agree.'

Bellinda smiled at her mistress. 'I'm sure I will, Ma'am.'

She then began to read the next chapter. Somehow *Pilgrim's Progress* did not seem so dull after all.

'I hear that you are to be young Jamie's nanny when I'm gone.'

Bellinda put down her scrubbing brush and looked up. Standing above her was the temporary nanny. She had the windblown complexion of a country woman and there was certainly a lilt to her voice that no Londoner possessed. 'Yes, that is right,' she said cautiously.

'Well I cannot be more grateful to the master and mistress of this house for providing me with such gainful employment while the family I work for were in France but . . . ' she shook her head ' . . . it is not my place to say . . . ' again she shook her head ' . . . well, the child is so ungovernable.'

Bellinda had always believed that there was never born a completely ungovernable child. It had been proved many times at the orphanage that with the right amount of firmness and kindness, even the naughtiest child could soon be persuaded that good behaviour was of benefit not only to herself, but all the others. However, she did not express this view, but politely said, 'I must thank you for warning me.'

'Well, me dear, thought it best to say something.' She shrugged her plump shoulders. 'He's so unruly and you're so young. I just hope you can cope.'

'I can but do my best,' Bellinda told her. 'And I must thank you for your warning and wish you well for the future.'

The nanny smiled. 'That's kind of you, me dear. What a pity we never had more of a chance to talk. But the truth is, you're best not to leave him for a minute. You never know what the little brat will get up to.'

Continuing with her chores, Bellinda wondered if Jamie could really be as bad as suggested. Mrs Gage had referred to her son as adorable. So who was she to believe? She remembered how disobedient Maisie had been at the orphanage and how it had become necessary to give her a gentle smack. From that day onwards the child had shown nothing but love and respect for Bellinda. The Governess had always praised her for her way of instilling self-discipline into the smaller children without having to resort to harshness. Could Jamie be any greater challenge than Maisie? Impossible!

She slept well that night, her days of tweenying finally over.

Jamie was indeed as adorable as his portrait and Mrs Gage had suggested. His eyes were amethyst, gleaming with a boyish exuberance. His hair was the colour of corn on a bright summer's day and his smile was innocent, sweet and uncalculating. Why had that other nurse been so disparaging? It was too early to tell, but there really did seem nothing to suggest that this child was a brat.

'Hello, I am so glad to meet you,' he said, giving her a beguiling smile.

'And I am pleased to meet you, Jamie.'

Jamie said no more but turned to his mother and smiled approvingly.

'Well, now that the introductions have been dealt with I shall leave you with my son, Bellinda.' Mrs Gage knelt down and kissed Jamie on the cheek. He looked up at her adoringly and Bellinda wished that just once she had known what it was like to be kissed by a doting mother.

'You seem to have many interesting toys, Jamie,' she said as soon as they were alone.

'I could do with some more, Bellinda,' he said nonchalantly. 'Papa just doesn't know how boring it is having to play with the same things every day.'

The children at the orphanage had virtually no toys at all, and even young Robert Groves-Hawkes did not have such a vast array. How could he want more? Was it her place to ask such a question? 'Is there nothing amongst such a splendid selection to amuse you?' she said, unable to control her curiosity.

His expression changed to petulant arrogance, reminding her of Vanity. 'But you are here to amuse me, Bellinda,' he said pompously. 'That is why Mama has given you to me. I hope you're better than that other woman and the one before her. They were all so boring.' Then he was smiling again. 'Still, they were old, very old. You're not like that. You're more like a sister.' He nodded. 'Yes, that's what you are, the big sister I should always have had!'

Bellinda laughed. 'Oh Jamie, I could not be more delighted. I have never had a little brother.'

His expression hardened. 'No, that cannot be,' he said pensively. 'Mama told me that you are an orphan so you must never pretend that I am your brother.'

Bellinda flinched. What kind of a world was it where even small children were so conscious of background and position? 'Tell me, Jamie, do you not do any learning?' she asked, now eager to change the subject.

'You mean doing sums and trying to write words?'

'Yes, do your father and mother instruct you, or is there a governess who visits?'

'Mama tried to make me do those things once and so did Papa, but it was all so boring.' He picked up a

175

soldier and studied it. 'I get bored playing with these, but as for lessons? They are just unbearable.'

'But Jamie, what will happen when you grow up?'

Angrily, he stamped the floor. 'I'm not going to grow up. Never!'

'But Jamie, everyone grows up in the end whether they like it or not.'

'I'm not going to. Grown-ups are dull. That's why I think I'm going to like you, Bellinda.'

Although worried about the child's lack of interest in education, she still found him very likeable, and persuaded herself that the occasional flashes of arrogance were merely the mimicking of his elders. Truly, she hoped that she could guide him into accepting that growing up was inevitable.

However, that would have to wait. This was a time for play. Bellinda encouraged him to demonstrate all of his toys. She was particularly impressed by the model theatre with its cut-out players, and even more impressed by Jamie's imagination. Using the cut-outs, he performed a play of his own creation: a story of children captured by evil foreigners who were trying to force them to grow up. His ability to change his voice to suit the characters could not have been more impressive.

'Perhaps you are going to be a great actor some day,' she said after the finale when all the evil foreigners had been banished.

'No, Bellinda, having to learn lines would be too boring.'

'I see,' she said disappointedly while tucking him into his bed for his midday nap.

He had just fallen asleep when the nursery door was opened by her mistress. 'Bellinda, we have a visitor and he wishes to speak with you.'

'But what visitor would wish to speak with me, Ma'am?'

Mrs Gage smiled. 'My dear child, it is none other than the one who recommended you for this post, Mr Thomas Groves-Hawkes.'

Chapter 16

Trembling, Bellinda entered the library. Thomas Groves-Hawkes was standing by the window. They were to be alone together. He turned towards her and smiled awkwardly.

'Good morning, Sir.' Bellinda knew that her voice sounded edgy but she had no control over it. Why had he come here?

'My dear child, there is no need to be so formal.' He was smiling – but awkwardly, as if he were concealing a guilty secret.

'Forgive me, I am just a little overcome, Sir.'

'Well then I am to blame for that. I should have given you proper warning of my visit.' He tried another smile. 'But my dear Bellinda, I am not the only one to spring surprises. What about you?'

'Me Sir?'

'Yes, my dear, sweet innocent child. Can you not imagine the amazement I felt upon opening Mrs Gage's letter, thus discovering that you had left the orphanage and travelled to London?'

'I must thank you for your letter of reference, Sir.'

He shook his head and his grey eyes were filled with frustration. 'Oh Bellinda, must we be so formal? Can you not call me Thomas?'

Bellinda was too stunned to answer. How could she ever address the master of Carlyon House as anything other than Sir?

'Bellinda, I beg you not to think of me as a superior.'

A wild uncontrollable rage suddenly surged through her. Bitter memories of how Sara had been treated flooded into her mind. Common sense, rationality and restraint were engulfed by those dark waters. 'Sir, I promise you that I do not think of either yourself or your family as my superior!'

Anger flashed in his eyes, it was obvious that he was not used to being spoken to in such a way. Soon she would be on the streets again, probably for ever. She did not care.

There was another flash of anger but then no more. Instead she saw an almost timid expression. Despite the imposing austerity of his demeanour there would always be a tragic, vulnerable quality about Thomas Groves-Hawkes, a quality she suspected that even his own family was unaware of.

'I fear you refer to the way that you and Sara were treated at Carlyon House?' he asked gravely.

'I suppose I do, Sir,' she said cautiously.

'It was my dear wife, Marguerite, who disliked Sara,' he said apologetically. 'She found the child's behaviour rather . . . er, distressing.' He now looked at her with the eyes of a chastised little boy. 'I implore you to show compassion now, Bellinda. Have I not atoned just a little by securing this position for you?'

'You have, Sir.'

'Then can you not find it in that generous heart of yours to grant me just a little forgiveness?'

Standing before her was a fully grown man, attired in an immaculately tailored frock coat, his hair centre-parted to fastidious perfection. Yes, he had all the trappings of wealth and authority. Yet all she could now see was a sadness and vulnerability.

'Sir, I can never forget your generosity towards me,' she told him.

He smiled, this time a warm gratified smile. 'It would appear that the rest of my selfish family have yet to earn any appeasement in your heart?'

She did not answer.

'It is but what they deserve,' he said pensively. 'But please understand that it is not easy to accept into the house one who is so pure as yourself.'

178

Bellinda blushed. 'Sir, you flatter me beyond my worth.'

'How can anyone flatter you beyond your worth, Bellinda?' he said admiringly.

Again, Bellinda blushed.

'I must apologize, it is not right for me to embarrass you so. I did not come here to do that.' He dug a hand deep inside his frock coat and retrieved a leather purse. 'Here, Bellinda, take this money as a token of my esteem. That uniform of yours looks most uncomfortable.'

'It is, Sir,' she agreed.

'Then buy yourself a new one, my child,' he said, handing her the purse.

Bellinda thanked him before he departed. Now alone in the library, she wondered why she was not feeling relieved that her burst of rage had not lost her a position in the Gage household. Curiously, she now saw the incident in a different light. Thomas Groves-Hawkes might even have tolerated more frankness, for all she knew. At times he seemed to be showing the adoration that he should have reserved for his wife. She gazed out of the window, up at an icy sky. She had always assumed that his had been a world of warm summery skies, protected from the cold realities of life amongst the poor. She had been wrong. Sadness lingered deep and heavy within the soul of that man. Desperately he was seeking solace. Escape, perhaps? With herself? She could not tell. Troubled, Bellinda left the library and went in search of Mrs Gage.

'Ah Bellinda, you are just in time to begin a little reading while dear Jamie is still at rest.'

'Should I not be ensuring that he is still comfortable, Ma'am?'

'Heavens no, my dear, he will be fast asleep, of that I can assure you. Is he not the most compliant of children?'

'Yes, Ma'am,' Bellinda agreed, although really wanting to mention the boy's unhealthy preoccupation with remaining a child for ever.

179

'I knew you would agree.' She gave a satisfied smile. 'Now, let us resume *Pilgrim's Progress*. I cannot wait to hear your mellifluous reading voice. No wonder Mr Groves-Hawkes was so impressed by you, no wonder.'

Bellinda read to Mrs Gage for over an hour before returning to Jamie's room. He was now awake, looking up from his pillow with those adorable blue eyes.

'Oh Bellinda,' he said dreamily, 'I did enjoy my sleep today.'

She smiled down at him and said in an unashamedly motherly tone, 'What a little cherub you are, Master Jamie.'

'Cherub? What's a cherub?'

'You don't know what a cherub is? Well there's a thing. A cherub is a child with tiny wings who can fly up, up into the clouds. He is a little angel who never grows up.'

Jamie giggled with delight. 'Oh Bellinda, how wonderful. How wonderful! You must help me make some wings so that I can fly.'

Bellinda laughed. 'My dear child, man cannot fly. Oh what a sweet dream! If only we could.'

Jamie looked sad. 'It just isn't right, is it, Bellinda? Birds aren't very clever yet they can fly.'

'That is God's will, Jamie. He made all things for a purpose.'

'I hate God!'

'Jamie, you must not say such a thing.' Ever since she had discovered Kuan Yin, Bellinda had found her traditional Christian beliefs being challenged, but duty compelled her to correct him. 'There is an order to the world, Jamie. We all have our place. We cannot avoid the fact that we will never fly or that we must become adults.'

'If God would let me fly then I wouldn't mind growing up,' he said pensively.

'A hard bargain for our Lord to agree to. But tell me, if you were able to fly, where would you go?'

Jamie sat upright and grinned impishly. 'Well to begin with, I would fly far away from here.'

'Oh I guessed that, but where exactly?'

'To the Empire, of course. Yes I would fly to the Empire.'

'And where is the Empire?'

'Oh I don't know where it is but grown-ups are always talking about it, aren't they?'

'Jamie, the Empire is a lot of places. Didn't you know that?'

'Of course not,' he answered indignantly. 'Learning about places is boring unless you can go there.'

'Well I couldn't tell you all the places in the Empire but I know there is India, parts of South Africa, and – '

Jamie clasped his hands to his ears. 'I don't want to hear about all that. Learning is dull. I just want to fly there, that's all.'

Bellinda felt utterly defeated. The child was living in a world of his own, just as Sara had done at times. If the Gages were not careful they would find themselves with a son incapable of taking his proper place in society.

She said no more about flying but prepared him for his afternoon walk in Hyde Park, wrapping him in a thick red pelisse with matching muffs and woollen hat. Taking his hand she led him outside. Even the more refined streets of Mayfair were still dangerous places. Horse-drawn carriages and hansom cabs hurtled to and fro, without heed for any pedestrian.

Bellinda was apprehensive about crossing but it was Jamie who finally urged her to go, even though a coach seemed to be bearing down upon them. Gripping his tiny hand, she hastened to the other side and to her surprise, discovered that the coach still had not reached the spot where they had crossed.

'You see, Bellinda, you can get over the road if you hurry,' he told her.

'Please remember, dear, that I am a country lass, and Wycombe was never as busy as London.'

181

'Then you must learn to fly, Bellinda. We must both learn to fly!'

How irresistible this child was, gazing up at her with his mischievous eyes. How tempting it was to immerse herself in his trouble-free make-believe world.

She had never seen Hyde Park before. It was almost as if a piece of the countryside had been planted in the heart of the capital. Just as in the fields by High Wycombe, trees abounded, stark and bare, against a winter sky striated by iron grey clouds. It would have been a sombre, lonely place were it not for the people. There were plenty of afternoon strollers, mostly gentlemen in tall hats, sometimes escorting ladies dressed in the finest of clothes. It was soothing sight, such a contrast to the London she had first encountered. Here was open air and tranquillity. A place where one could feel safe.

'I like going to the park, don't you, Bellinda?'

'Yes, very much, Jamie. I never realized that Hyde Park was as vast as this.'

There was a mischievous glint in his eyes as he looked up at her. 'There's a lot you haven't realized,' he said impishly. 'Now, will you let go of my hand?'

'Why?'

'Because I want to walk on my own. I have always been allowed to do so in the past.'

'Well I must have your word that you won't run away.'

'Why should I want to run away from you, Bellinda?' he asked sweetly.

'I cannot imagine, my little cherub,' she said suspiciously before letting go of his hand.

Joyfully he ran across the green sward. Bellinda chased after him and clutched the giggling child. 'You're not going to get away from me that easily, young Master Jamie!'

Jamie wrapped his tiny arms around her legs. 'Oh Bell, I never want to get away from you. You're my real mother. No one else.'

Bellinda knelt down and kissed him upon the cheek. 'Oh, Jamie, I can never replace your mother,' she said softly.

Tears swelled and began to trail down his cheeks. Gently she kissed them dry. 'Jamie, that does not mean that I don't love you. Trust in me and I can guide you a little.'

They walked in silence for a while, sensing a symbiosis growing between them. Was this right, Bellinda asked of herself. Jamie now seemingly wanted to replace his own mother with her. What was to become of such a situation?

There was a chilling silence at the breakfast table of the Groves-Hawkes family. Vanity and her brother endured the situation until her patience could stand the hostile atmosphere no more.

'Papa, I think it best that Robert and I leave. You and Mama obviously have matters to discuss.'

Marguerite's cold blue eyes flared at her daughter. 'How dare you be so insolent!'

'Mama, I am not being insolent, merely practical,' Vanity said haughtily, pushing her chair aside. 'Come, Robert, our presence is not needed here.'

'Sit down at once!'

'Let them go, Marguerite,' her father said irritably.

'Oh, so not only do you seem to lack control over yourself, but your son and daughter as well!'

'That is absurd, my dear,' he riposted.

'May Robert and I go before the battle begins?' Vanity asked sarcastically.

'Yes, go. For Heaven's sake go!' Thomas Groves-Hawkes snapped.

Closing the dining room door behind her, Vanity turned to Robert with a triumphamt smile.

'I can't see what there is to smile about,' he complained.

'Oh you little fool,' she said in the same haughty tone she had used to her parents. 'Can you not see?'

'See what?'

'Buffoon! If parents are not in control of themselves then they can hardly be in control of us, can they?'

'I suppose not,' Robert answered gleefully. 'I suppose not!'

The hostile silence between Thomas and Marguerite was interrupted by the entry of a serving maid.

'Do you not have the courtesy to knock before coming in?' Marguerite demanded. 'Go away. You may clear the table later.'

'Yes, Ma'am.'

Alone again, they breakfasted in silence until the volcano within Marguerite finally erupted. 'You had no right to go to London like that. No right at all!' she raged.

'I have every right to do as I please.'

'And what, pray, could be so urgent that you felt compelled to rush away without giving notice of your intention or making a proper farewell?'

Angrily Thomas clattered his knife and fork down on to his unfinished food. 'Sometimes impromptu visits are essential. Were you acquainted with the world beyond the choosing of clothes and social gatherings, you would have realized this a long time ago.'

Marguerite sniffed at her vial of sal volatile. 'Why must I be so insulted?' she wailed. 'What has become of us? What ever induced you to take a . . . to take a . . . '

'To take a what?' Thomas demanded.

'You know what I mean. You unfaithful swine!'

Thomas flinched. Had Marguerite found out about his obsession with Bellinda? No, it was impossible. Only he had seen that letter from Mrs Gage. She could not know. 'What a fertile imagination you have, my dear,' he said calmly. 'As this is one of the rare occasions when you have actually taken an interest in my affairs, then I should explain that it was an urgent matter of business that took me to London.'

'Liar! Since when has business other than your precious antiques ever been a matter of urgency to you?'

'Marguerite, truly you are a fool at times. Granted I have indeed accrued a good fortune, but money can soon be lost if it is not put to good use.'

'How dare you call me a fool! How dare you patronize me!'

'I am not patronizing you,' Thomas growled through gritted teeth. 'I am simply telling you the truth.'

'Who did you go to see?'

'I saw various people in the city, Marguerite. One does not simply go to see one person.'

'How convenient, so many people to provide a good alibi.'

'Alibi?' Thomas was reaching boiling point. 'Am I to be quizzed in my own home? Even had I committed some misdemeanour then I can assure you that it would be the place of the police to investigate me and not you!'

Marguerite sniffed at her sal volatile again before tears began to stream down her cheeks. 'Oh Hawkes, what has become of us? Am I still not the most beautiful of women?'

'In my eyes you are the most beautiful woman in the world,' he lied.

'I am? Oh Hawkes, if only I could believe you. If only I could.'

'What else can I say to convince you?'

'Must I go into details? We have not . . . have not . . . '

'Had sex for some time?'

Marguerite gasped.

'The word offends you? I am surprised, for it has always been one of your prime pursuits. Do you think life revolves around such activities?'

'How dare you suggest that I am nothing more than . . . a woman of ill repute!'

'Marguerite, your reputation could not be more impeccable, it's just that there are things beyond what one does in bed.'

Marguerite sniffed, more tears streaming down her cheeks. 'You no longer love me, I know it. You have been unfaithful. Perhaps you went to one of those places.' She looked at him with eyes that were pitiful in their intensity. 'Oh yes, Hawkes, I am not as naive as you might suppose. Does not London abound with girls willing to give themselves to any man with a few shillings in his pocket?'

Thomas banged a fist on the table, causing the cutlery to jump into the air. 'You go too far!' he roared. 'How dare you accuse me of such debauchery!'

His wife lowered her eyes and then looked up again, her anger seemingly abated. 'Dearest Hawkes, please in God's name tell me that you have not been unfaithful to me, that your impromptu visit to London was indeed a matter of business.'

Lies, deceit, there was no other escape. 'My darling Marguerite, I went to London upon an urgent matter of business.'

'And nothing else?' she asked coquettishly.

'Nothing else, I swear it.' His heart was pounding, he could feel sweat oozing into his clothes. 'Believe me, my most blessed Marguerite, I have eyes for none but you.'

'Oh Hawkes, you cannot imagine how I have longed to hear such words.' Her blue eyes were no longer icy but the gentler hue of pebbles caressed by the flowing waters of a stream. There had been a time when that look had so beguiled him, but no more. 'Come, let us retire to the boudoir.'

'My dear, it is nine o'clock in the morning!' he protested.

'And did that ever concern you when we were newly married?'

'Of course not, but – '

'But nothing, dear husband, I insist that our love be rekindled.'

'But – '

'Hawkes, I insist!'

What escape was there? His insincere declaration of love for her had already damned him. To deceive with

186

words was easy enough, but how could he expect his body to lie?

Marguerite stood up, gazing at him coquettishly while toying with her flaxen ringlets. She was behaving like a small girl. Once such behaviour would have excited him, but not now. There was something almost pathetic about a middle-aged woman trying to resurrect her girlhood. Youth and innocence were but a fleeting gift to women, a gift that had been reclaimed in Marguerite's case and bestowed in abundance on the beautiful Bellinda.

Even at this moment when his wife longed for his attention, Bellinda was haunting him. Marguerite told him that he was to wait a 'discreet' time before going to the bedroom. As she spoke, he noticed her full breasts heaving beneath her morning gown. There had been a time when such indications of what was to follow would have driven him to a frenzy. Alas, no longer.

What was he to do? The fires of passion had surged through his body many times in the past days, but it had not been Marguerite who ignited them. Were she an old and haggard farmer's wife, she would have no less appeal to his desires than now. All he wanted was Bellinda.

From the window he vacantly stared out at the Buckinghamshire countryside. The fields were rimed with hoar frost, despite the presence of a winter sun glowing serenely beyond bare trees. Bellinda was that sun, only she now had the power to melt the frost that chilled his heart. He watched the sun slowly rise above the stark outlines of the trees before reluctantly going to join Marguerite in the bedroom.

She had changed into the china-blue gown she had worn upon their wedding night. To his knowledge it was the only item of clothing she had ever retained for longer than a year. How handsome her figure was. Surely there were very few women who could still fit into a garment first worn before their children were born. There could be no doubt that Marguerite was the envy of wives and husbands who had unavoidably fattened with age. Yet despite the fact that she was palming her hands over voluptuous breasts swelling beneath the soft fabric, Thomas was unmoved. Clumsily, he undressed . . .

'Hawkes, what is wrong with you?' Marguerite demanded after the third hopeless attempt.

He did not answer. What could he say? Instead he rolled away from her and stared blankly at the ceiling.

'Is something the matter? I was right. Your passions belong to someone else.'

'Beloved, I swear that's not true. I swear it!'

With an angry swish of the bedclothes Marguerite sat up and stared down at him. 'Liar!' she screamed. 'Get out of my bed. Get out!'

Sheepishly, Thomas obeyed. He knew he had insulted her by his lack of action. Riddled by guilt, he endured her tirade as she lashed insult after insult upon him. He had once learned that medieval monks often beat themselves as a penance. Marguerite's scorn was his own penance. As she continued to deride he found that he was almost enjoying the degradation.

Thomas hurriedly dressed and left the bedroom, his mind in a turmoil of guilt, regret and – yes, even now – longing for Bellinda. He returned to the dining room and ordered the maid to bring some tea. As he waited, he fought for control of his mind. Unknowingly, that beautiful and innocent girl had destroyed him.

When fresh tea was brought to him Thomas ignored it. He had no wish to linger in the dining room. He had no wish to linger at Carlyon. Once again, London and Bellinda beckoned.

Chapter 17

'We're going to play a game today, Jamie.'

The boy looked up at Bellinda and smiled adoringly. 'I like playing games with you. It's always a lot of fun.'

'Well, I do my best, young master,' she told him affectionately. 'I do my best.'

'So what is this game?'

'It's called beat the nanny!'

'That means beating you at something, Bellinda,' he said mischievously. 'I like that idea very much. Very much indeed!'

'Then let's see what you can do better than me, shall we? Let's play Figures. I was never good at that. It will give you a bit of a chance.'

'How do you play Figures?'

'Never played Figures? My! My!' Bellinda scolded jokingly. 'The rules are simple. We both add up some numbers and whoever gets them right is the winner.'

'That sounds fun, but how are we going to know who is right and who is wrong?'

'Now that is a very good question,' Bellinda said, while she struggled to think of an answer. 'A very good question indeed.'

'Well how are we going to know?' Jamie demanded after tiring of Bellinda's silence. 'You've got to tell me.'

Suddenly, inspiration came to her. 'The General can be the judge. He's bound to be good at such things because he's always having to count his men.'

'So he is!' Jamie enthused.

'Tell you what, we'll start by counting some of his soldiers. You first and then me.'

Jamie had already told her how many tin soldiers were in the General's army. It would give him the opportunity to win the first game. She smiled as Jamie pretended to count. Then it was her turn. 'Well I make it sixty-four.'

'Sixty-four!' he scoffed. 'You'd better ask the General, Bellinda.'

She knelt down and lowered her head before the figure who sat astride a static white charger. 'Sir, Jamie and I would be most grateful if you could tell us how many soldiers you command.' She paused. 'Eighty-nine! Surely, Sir, that cannot be true?'

'It is. It is!' Jamie told her. 'I'm right and you are wrong, Bellinda.'

'Now there's a thing,' she said, shaking her head in mock disgust. 'I told you I wasn't very good at this game.'

'Let's play some more.'

'Very well, supposing the General had to fight another army of one hundred? How many soldiers would be on the battlefield?'

Jamie frowned. 'How is anyone supposed to know that?'

'By adding the totals of the two armies together, I suppose.'

'I haven't got enough fingers to count that many,' Jamie protested.

'But you don't need fingers, all you have to do is think how many is eighty-nine and one hundred all together.'

'Well that's easy, you only have to say it the other way round – one hundred and eighty-nine!' Jamie cried triumphantly.

Frowning doubtfully, Bellinda consulted the General again. 'Why, you're right,' she exclaimed after receiving the toy's answer. 'What a clever boy you are!'

'Of course I am,' beamed Jamie complacently.

He was actually a very intelligent boy and eager to learn, provided that he thought he was playing a game. Soon she would try to teach him how to read and write. Bellinda would not rest until her tiny friend was the cleverest seven-year-old in the land!

190

★

It was madness to go back to London again. Madness! As his personal carriage pitched and rolled towards the capital, Thomas Groves-Hawkes wondered how far his obsession with Bellinda would finally take him.

His usual room at the Savoy was unavailable, and the one offered did not have a view of the river. Marguerite would have been most displeased. It mattered little to Thomas. All that mattered was being near Bellinda. How that thought excited him. Yet he would have to be disciplined. Yes, his love for her must remain secret. Secret at all costs!

'Why, Mr Groves-Hawkes! We have the honour of another visit,' Mrs Gage said when he joined her at afternoon tea. 'Have you come to see Bellinda? I can tell you that we are extremely pleased with her. Not only is she a competent nanny but is teaching Jamie like a proper governess.' Mrs Gage's pale eyes suddenly brightened. 'She is the most remarkable of girls, an orphan like no other.'

'Quite so,' Thomas agreed readily. 'But Ma'am, it is not Bellinda who interests me at this moment,' he lied. 'Although I shall be taking further interest in her progress in due course. No, it is your husband with whom I would like to discuss a matter of mutual benefit.'

'I am sure that my dear husband would indeed be honoured to talk to one as eminent as yourself.'

Good! His plan was already beginning to work. 'Ma'am, you flatter me too much, I fear. Tell me, is he available at the moment?'

'He is in his study.'

'I shall not be disturbing him, I hope?'

'Indeed not. I can assure you that he has always held you and your family in the highest esteem. Please go to him.'

'Again, Ma'am, I feel flattered,' Thomas said, bowing his head, and he made his way to the study.

191

'Mr Groves-Hawkes,' John Gage greeted enthusiastically. 'How good of you to grace our humble home yet again.'

'Please, I beg you, call me Thomas.'

'Only if you do me the service of calling me John.'

'John, I wish to offer you first refusal on some shares I am about to sell.'

'You do? Well, I *am* honoured, for I know that any equities held by Thomas Groves-Hawkes must be sound ones.'

'Davenports are particularly sound. But the truth is, my dear fellow, I simply have too many of them. I am solvent enough to risk a little speculation. Were you in my position would you not do the same?'

John Gage stroked his muttonchop whiskers and looked pensive.

What was the matter with the man? Thomas fumed secretly. Wasn't he being trusted? 'I can assure you that I have given the matter a great deal of thought,' he told Gage firmly.

'Forgive me, Thomas, I must apologize most profusely. It is simply a habit of mine to consider carefully any proposition. Even one as sound as yours.'

'It is perhaps my motive that concerns you?'

'Unthinkable! One never needs to question the motives of Thomas Groves-Hawkes. If I have given the impression that – '

'Of course not, but I feel compelled to state my reason, for are we all not creatures of purpose and motive?'

John Gage gave him a sly wink. 'Indeed we are. Now tell me how, in return for your generous offer, I can be of service to you?'

'I shall speak plainly. I have everything that a man could desire – ' how he lied, for was not Bellinda all that he now truly desired? 'However, there is one thing – '

'You do not have a title,' John Gage interrupted.

'Precisely.'

Gage gave another sly wink. 'Alas, I fear that my own position, although a most favourable one, will not win me a title. But you, my dear friend . . . Well, I am sure that a word in the right places and – '

'I believe you know Lord Maltravers?'

'Indeed I do, and I could also introduce you to his cousin, Adam Carr. He is a man of limited means who has done well for himself in the City. A fellow worthy of acquaintance if one wishes to speculate, although I will hasten to add that there is no love lost between himself and Maltravers.'

'Capital!' Thomas had no real interest in this Carr fellow, nor Maltravers, but any excuse to keep visiting the house was welcome. 'I should very much like to meet him.'

John Gage beamed approvingly. 'Then may I be so bold as to suggest that you and your good wife do us the honour of dining at our home? I'm sure that the prospect of meeting someone as eminent as yourself will entice Mr Carr to join us. I shall also invite a distant relative of ours staying in London – a brash young American girl, but engaging company, I believe.'

Thomas had no intention of bringing Marguerite to this house, but did not say so. Not when his insane plan was beginning to work. He was succeeding in ingratiating himself with the Gage family, thus providing a plausible excuse to see more of Bellinda. How disciplined and self-controlled he had been in not asking to see her! How innocent his patronage would appear to everyone. How innocent!

Downstairs a dinner party was in progress. Jamie was to be kept amused during the meal

'Who has been invited?' he asked, his eyes shining brightly.

'I have no idea,' Bellinda answered.

'None at all, Bellinda? But you know everything. Everything!'

193

She threw back her head and laughed. 'Oh, what it is to be held in such glorious esteem!'

'But you must have some idea.'

She shook her head. 'If your mama has not told you who is coming then how should I know?'

He crinkled his nose. 'Maybe Uncle Adam will be there. I hope so, I like him. He played with my toy soldiers once, and showed me how they do it in a real battle.'

'There, you see, I don't know everything. What do I know of battles?'

'Then you must speak with Uncle Adam.'

It was hardly the place of a nanny to converse with one of the Gages' guests. Jamie was forgetting that she was only a servant. 'We shall see,' she told him. 'We shall see.'

Jamie then used his toy soldiers to demonstrate the tactics Uncle Adam had shown him. Dutifully, Bellinda did her best to appear interested even though warfare held no appeal. She was relieved when he eventually tired of it and asked her to read to him. However, she had barely finished two pages when Harriet Gage entered the room to take Jamie down to be shown to the guests.

Jamie insisted that Bellinda should accompany him. Mrs Gage protested but her son was insistent. A tantrum threatened and his mother conceded.

When Bellinda saw that amongst the guests were the Groves-Hawkes family she froze. Thomas smiled benignly at her but both Marguerite and Vanity looked at her first with surprise and then with measured contempt. She had hoped never to see those two women again, and they obviously felt the same.

Averting her gaze from them, she took in a deep breath and followed Jamie. Never before had she seen so many finely dressed people gathered in one room, the sound of their chatter booming in her ears.

'Why, he has grown!' enthused a bulbous woman as she knelt down in front of the boy.

'No I haven't,' Jamie disagreed crossly as the woman tried to entwine her thick arms around him.

She laughed haughtily. 'Oh, this child has never craved affection.'

Bellinda knew Jamie to be the most affectionate of children but it was obvious that he had no desire to be crushed by this gargantuan woman. Were she his mother she would have politely led him away, yet as his nanny she could only stay silent.

Fortunately another of the guests came to Jamie's rescue, a spindly grey-haired man who seemed to be held in much higher favour. The Gages were in deep conversation with the Groves-Hawkes and a tall blond-haired man.

'Look, there's Uncle Adam,' Jamie told her, pointing to the blond man beside Vanity. 'He's the one I've been telling you about.'

At that moment Adam Carr glanced over in their direction, and immediately left the group and advanced towards the boy.

Jamie was scooped up and lifted on to a broad shoulder. 'Good to see you, little soldier,' Adam said heartily. 'Good to see you!'

'Can you show me and Bellinda some more tactics?' Jamie asked, his eyes shining.

Adam turned to her. 'Are you Bellinda?' he asked, in a voice that was firm and strong.

'Yes, Sir,' she replied awkwardly. 'I am the new nanny.'

'And the prettiest one in London, I'll wager.'

Bellinda blushed.

He smiled at her and she blushed again.

He looked at Jamie. 'Best I not show your nanny any battle tactics lest her face stay that pretty pink for ever.'

How dare he mock her embarrassment! Undeniably he was attractive – tall and strong, with curly blond hair and piercing blue eyes – yet he was obviously as arrogant and contemptuous of the serving classes as most men of his kind.

195

Harriet Gage had now joined them. She looked at her son still perched upon Adam's shoulder. 'I think Mr Carr wants to talk business with Mr Groves-Hawkes, Jamie.'

How typical, putting business before the children. Was that not why the rich always got richer? Did they not care more about their wealth than anything else?

Carr winked at Jamie before saying predictably, 'True enough, young fellow. A man has to earn his living, you know. Still, some other time, eh?'

'Yes please,' Jamie said as he was lowered to the floor.

'Come now, dear child, a few other people will be wishing to see you before you retire for the night,' Harriet Gage told him before turning to Bellinda. 'You may wait in the hall, I will bring him out to you.'

At this time of the evening the hall was rather dark, lit only by a flickering gaslamp. It was also cold, and Bellinda shivered. Then she heard footsteps descending towards her and smelt pungent cigar smoke. She turned and saw the face of a dark god.

'Well now, who have we here?' His voice was silky smooth.

'I am Bellinda, Sir, Master Jamie's new nanny.'

'But much more than a nanny. At dinner I was told that under your tutelage he has learned a great deal. You are to be congratulated.'

Bellinda opened her mouth but no words came. The half darkness gave this man a tantalizingly sinister appearance. Somehow she could tell that he was a man with strong, powerful desires. The thought uneased her.

'I am flattered, Sir,' she finally managed to say tremulously.

He drew upon his cigar, his dark eyes studying her. 'I meant it as no flattery. No, if I were to flatter you then should I not talk of your innocent beauty, so striking even in this half light?'

Adam Carr had made her blush, surely she was doing the same now. She opened her mouth but could utter no words.

'What a pity that I must go abroad tomorrow. Otherwise we could have become better acquainted.'

Acquainted? Was that what he truly meant? Now she was trembling. 'I must go and find Jamie,' she said hastily.

'Of course,' he agreed smoothly, 'but I'm sure we'll meet again.'

'Yes, Sir,' she managed to say, before hurrying back into the parlour.

'Bellinda, I thought I told you to wait outside?' Harriet Gage asked sharply before smiling down at her son. 'Still, I think that it is perhaps time for you to go to bed, Jamie.'

Ignoring his mother, he looked up at Bellinda. 'Will you read to me before I go to sleep?'

'Of course, I will,' she said, taking his hand and leading him out of the room. The dark stranger was gone. She gave a sigh of relief and followed Jamie as he scampered up the stairs.

Bellinda had read but a few lines before Jamie fell asleep. Then she went to her own bedroom. While she undressed she thought of nothing but the stranger, as she slipped beneath the sheets she thought of nothing but the stranger, and when eventually she did manage to sleep, she dreamed restlessly of the dark and handsome stranger.

'How dare you, Hawkes,' Marguerite raged. 'How dare you!'

'Oh in God's name, dare do what?' Thomas demanded.

'Have you gone mad?' she screamed at him. 'You knew that girl was going to be there. You knew it!'

How Thomas had sweated when he discovered that Marguerite had seen their invitation to the Gages' party before he had the chance to hide it from her. She had seen this as an opportunity for their reconciliation, and what choice did he have but to play along with her? However, he had hoped that Bellinda, a mere nanny,

197

would not have been seen by the dinner guests. Forlorn hope. Now he felt powerless to say anything.

Marguerite's face was crimson with fury. 'Say something, you blaggard. Say something!'

Thomas's mind was in such a turmoil of guilt and anger that he could say nothing coherent.

'You've lost your tongue, have you?' She was now volleying the words at him. 'Well you were not tongue-tied in her company, were you?'

Thomas was confused. He had been careful not to say one single word to Bellinda. Had Marguerite lost her mind? He would deny it. Was it not the truth?

'Your senses have deserted you, woman. I barely looked at her all evening.'

'Liar! You were captivated. Utterly captivated by that – by that – by that American *whore*!'

Utter relief surged through Thomas. His true obsession had not been discovered after all. As if he had been attracted to Amity, a girl who had done nothing but boringly ramble on in her grating American accent about what she had just been reading about London's poor.

'My dear wife, how could you ever believe that I was enamoured with that dreadful girl?' he chuckled. 'Why it was an endurance to sit next to her. An endurance!'

'Endurance! Then why did you not tell her to be quiet?'

'How could one be so impolite? Have you lost all sense of propriety?'

Marguerite seemed less flushed. Was she calming down? 'There is propriety and there is *propriety*, Hawkes.'

'I can assure you once again, my dear, that Amity Smallwood held no appeal for me at all. Had I ever found American women attractive, I would have married one.'

'Oh Hawkes, I really do want to believe you.'

'Then why don't you? It's the truth.'

Marguerite cocked her head to one side and smiled, behaving as if she were a child again. 'Oh Hawkes, I do want to. I really do.'

'Dearest Marguerite, my sole reason for going to the Gages' is for matters of business. John Gage is acquainted with people of great use to me. That Mr Adam Carr – who, by the way, I noticed you ogling – has great and profitable knowledge of the stock market.'

'Why did you not tell me that orphan girl was a servant for the Gages?'

Thomas's heart fluttered as he swallowed hard. 'Oh her, I didn't think that was important,' he said awkwardly.

'Not important, Hawkes? Of course it is important. You behave as if it were some great secret.'

'It is no secret, simply an oversight,' he said tetchily. 'That troublesome girl is no longer in our home. What else matters?'

'Indeed not. How I rue the day that she and that dreadful Sara ever came to Carlyon.'

'I totally agree,' Thomas lied readily.

Marguerite looked at him seductively. 'Hawkes? Shall we go to bed?'

'My dear, it is the afternoon,' Thomas protested limply.

Marguerite toyed with one of her flaxen ringlets. 'And there can be no better time, Hawkes,' she said coaxingly.

Thomas could not be seduced. No woman, not even his own wife, could ever seduce him. He desired only Bellinda. 'I have some urgent business awaiting me in my study,' he said sternly.

'Urgent business. Always there is urgent business!'

'It is business that helps to pay for all your clothes.'

'And it is business that has ruined our relationship. For good!' Marguerite raged before storming out of the drawing room.

Now alone, Thomas reflected upon the rubble of his crumbled marriage. Divorce? No, that would be unthinkable. Mutual separation would be slightly less embarrassing, but even then there would always be an unpleasant stigma. Really, there was no alternative but to endure this cruel charade.

Gloomy thoughts prevailed until he remembered his secret success. Without Marguerite's knowledge he had managed to persuade Harriet Gage of the desirability of allowing Bellinda a whole day off. He had told her that many households were now adopting this generous policy and that should the Gages not comply with the fashion, then they were in danger of losing their most prized servants.

Now every Wednesday his beloved Bellinda would be free to be with him. Together they would stroll through the park or take tea somewhere. He would tell her so much about the myths and customs of other cultures. How quickly his divine beauty would learn and how, perhaps, she would grow to love him for his knowledge and wisdom. Yes, there was a chance that he would have her company for a whole day. He could hardly wait!

A whole day to herself! Bellinda would go to Shoreditch railway station, the church nearby, and even search the streets if necessary, to find her friend Betsy. How it would warm her to see the old woman's face brighten when she received the handsome sum of money that Bellinda intended to press into her wrinkled hand.

On this particular morning she had stayed in bed until eight o'clock. Now she was dressing with an air of eager excitement. Perhaps, with her newfound prosperity, she would be able to take the underground railway or even an omnibus? Yes, this was destined to be a day to remember.

Thomas Groves-Hawkes' coachman had been given two strict instructions. The first was not to gossip to anyone, and the second was to urge the horses forward at a slow trot as soon as he saw Bellinda emerge from the house. This he did with discreet ease.

'Bellinda, will you join me?' Thomas called down to her.

Bellinda felt she had no choice but to concede to his wishes as his coachman clambered down and helped her into the carriage.

'Remember how you once admitted an interest in visiting the zoo? Well, today your wish will be granted, for I intend to take you there.'

'I am most grateful, Sir,' she told him with little conviction.

He turned and looked at her, his eyes questing. 'I am sure that you are grateful, my dear Bellinda, but are you pleased? Are you really pleased?'

'Yes, Sir. What servant girl would not be grateful for the opportunity to go to the zoo?'

Thomas sighed and looked up at the roof of the coach. 'Oh, Bellinda. Bellinda! You are so much more than a mere servant girl. Deep in your heart you know that to be true. Don't you?'

Bellinda did not answer.

'You must regard me as a father figure, a teacher if you like.'

'You have indeed taught me a great deal,' she admitted.

Thomas suddenly clasped her hand in his own. She tried to pull free but it was no use, he held her fast, staring with passion-filled eyes, a desperate unsated passion. 'And I can teach you so much more, my be-, ah, my dearest Bellinda. You are the goddess and I am the oracle from which bounteous knowledge can be drawn.'

Bellinda blushed 'Sir, I am no goddess. Please, I beg you. Do not hold me in such absurd esteem.'

Thomas threw back his head and laughed before letting go of her hand. 'Absurd esteem! Have I not made my point? An orphan with no proper education who can use the English language to such perfection. Are you not unique?'

'I have done my best to improve myself.'

He looked at her again with the eyes of a little boy who longed to be loved. 'And with my guidance you shall go on improving yourself,' he insisted.

'I cannot deny that I do have a voracious appetite for learning.'

'Of course you do, and learn you shall! There can be no impropriety in my teaching you.' He glanced out of the window. 'Ah, our journey is almost over. Now, will you do me the honour of calling me Thomas for the rest of the day?'

'Yes, Thomas, I will,' Bellinda promised awkwardly.

As soon as they entered the zoo she was overwhelmed. Never before had she been to a place like this. People abounded everywhere. Was there any room for the animals?

Their first stop was to see the tigers. What terrifying beasts they were, gargantuan cats prowling their cages and snarling at the onlookers, displaying wicked-looking fangs. Bellinda was grateful for the thick iron bars that separated them from her.

Thomas told her of their Indian origins and how rajahs and other men of importance loved to go on hunting expeditions to seek them out. He also told her it was strongly believed that tigers were often capable of killing everyone in any village they attacked. An exaggeration perhaps, but a vivid illustration of the fear that these awesome creatures generated.

Bellinda listened attentively, the whole experience was fascinating. How massive and utterly peculiar were the elephants with their long dangling snouts, or the mighty hippopotami with their great wide mouths and scaly skins. Then there were the mighty bears with thick woolly coats, standing up on their hind legs to make themselves look even more formidable. The incredible sights of this menagerie would stay in her memory for the rest of her life.

Unfortunately another aspect would also haunt her. Was it right that these animals should be imprisoned? It was the plight of the monkeys that most moved her. She noticed one with sad round eyes, gazing at her longingly. If only she could free the poor little creature. If only she could free them all! However, she did not express this reaction to Thomas Groves-Hawkes, who would not have understood.

Having toured Bellinda round the whole zoo, Thomas now escorted her to a tea room. Limply, Bellinda had tried to decline the offer, but he insisted. It was a grand place with masses of tall luxuriant plants, and every table was draped in fine white linen. Although initially reluctant, Bellinda now found the prospect of taking afternoon tea here exciting. There had been a teashop in High Wycombe that she would have loved to visit had she not been an impoverished orphan.

Not only did Thomas order tea, served in a delicately patterned china teapot, but also a plate of delicious wafer-thin jam sandwiches. There were also hot buttered scones. Bellinda found herself eating heartily as Thomas told her some more interesting facts about the animals in the zoo. However, when they had both finished eating and more tea had been ordered, his mood suddenly changed.

'Bellinda, I must explain my reasons for bringing you here,' he said earnestly.

She looked up from her tea. 'I would be grateful of that, Thomas.'

'Yes, yes, of course you would,' Thomas said, shifting awkwardly in his chair like a chastened boy. 'Well the truth is that I have grown increasingly fond of you.' He paused, summoning the courage to continue. 'Bellinda, you are everything I ever wanted in a daughter.'

Bellinda was stunned. What was possessing him to say such words? She was forced to take a deep breath before speaking. 'Is not Miss Vanity the most perfect of daughters?'

Thomas laughed bitterly. 'Vanity! How well I christened her. No name could have been more suitable for one so vain and self-centred.'

Before she could stop herself, Bellinda smiled.

'There, you agree. Now don't you deny it,' Thomas chortled.

'It is not my place to say, Thomas.'

203

'Of course it isn't. That's why I am saying it for you. Heavens above, the girl becomes more like her mother every day!'

Again, Bellinda smiled.

'Where you are so sweetly innocent, she is already worldly and cunning. Where you are fascinated, as I am, with learning, Vanity finds such matters utterly tiresome.' He paused and looked at her with those sad little-boy eyes. 'Bellinda, only in you have I found a kindred spirit.'

Bellinda stared blankly down at the tea that was being allowed to go cold. 'Thomas,' she began hesitantly, 'young as I am, I have already discovered that there is one law for the rich and one for people like myself. Our positions in life will ensure that we can never become kindred spirits.'

Nervously, Thomas tapped a silver teaspoon against his cup. 'In the past few months I have learned how little a difference in class matters. You, Bellinda, have opened my eyes to so much. So very much!' he said adoringly.

Bellinda was too embarrassed to speak.

Perhaps sensing this embarrassment, Thomas called out to a waitress who rushed over to attend to him. Hastily, he settled the bill before telling Bellinda that he would take her back to the Gages' house.

Thomas spoke little during the return cab journey. He seemed to be brooding over what had been said. Bellinda averted her gaze to the window and watched the bustling world of London speed by.

When they arrived he escorted her to the door and bade her farewell, promising that he would see her again. Slowly, Bellinda mounted the stairs to her room. Her mind was in turmoil. Could there really be any doubt that Thomas Groves-Hawkes was in love with her? She had first dismissed the notion as absurd, but not now. Eventually Marguerite would find out about his obsession, and what would happen to her then?

Chapter 18

'So this is young Master Jamie?'

Jamie stopped his reading of the Bible and, like Bellinda, looked up to see who had entered the nursery. It was the girl with the strange accent who had dined at the house two weeks ago.

'It is, Ma'am,' Bellinda told her.

'And this is the best friend I ever had,' Jamie added, pointing to Bellinda.

The girl smiled warmly at them both. 'Looks like you two have got your own mutual admiration society going on here.' She knelt down in front of the boy. 'Tell me, Jamie, do you know what a mutual admiration society is?'

Jamie frowned as he thought hard. 'Is it? . . . Is it? . . . Is it when a group of people like each other a lot?'

'That's right! My, we are a clever little fellow!'

Bellinda smiled proudly as the girl turned to her.

'I've a feeling you've got a lot to do with Jamie's progress.'

'I have been tutoring him a little, Ma'am.'

'Now don't you be so modest,' she said, wagging a finger at Bellinda. 'You can also forget all this Ma'am nonsense. The name's Amity, Amity Smallwood, and just in case you're wondering why I speak in such a peculiar way, it's because I'm an American.'

'An American!'

'You find that exciting?'

Bellinda turned to Jamie. 'We both find that very exciting indeed.'

'Oh yes, Bellinda,' Jamie agreed. 'Very, very exciting.'

'One day I must tell you all about America,' Amity said to Jamie before turning to Bellinda. 'But first I want to know how you got such a lovely name. Tell me, do lots of English girls get called that?'

'Only if they're orphans. I was born near the sound of ringing bells so they called me Bell, and then Bellinda.'

'Even an orphan can get just a little luck in life – you got yourself a beautiful name.'

'And a good position here at this house,' Bellinda said, putting an arm around Jamie's small shoulders.

Amity gave Bellinda a friendly smile. 'Well, being an American here in England kind of makes me an orphan too.'

'Jamie and I were just about to go to the park, would you like to join us?' Bellinda asked before remembering that it was not customary for nannies to invite their mistress's friends to join them in a walk. However, Bellinda was already beginning to feel relaxed in the company of Amity Smallwood.

'Nothing would please me more,' Amity enthused.

Outside, the unusually clear London air promised of spring. Gone was the biting chill, the gloom of grey clouds. For Bellinda this had been the coldest winter of all. Would the new season bring forth new hope? On this bright day when the sun shone so gloriously, she could not help feeling optimistic, despite the unwelcome attentions of Thomas Groves-Hawkes.

Jamie had now made friends with two other children, and it had become part of his routine to meet them at eleven o'clock every morning, provided that the weather was not too inclement. Bellinda had become acquainted with the nanny of the other children, and on this day Constance kindly offered to keep an eye on Jamie so that Bellinda and Amity could get to know each other a little better.

Amity told Bellinda that she had come to England from Connecticut simply to visit relatives. However, once in London she soon became convinced that her calling was here.

'Tell me, Bellinda, have you ever heard of Henry Mayhew?'

206

'I'm afraid not.'

'Well I was fortunate enough to acquire his book, *London Labour and the London Poor*.'

'That is indeed a subject that needs to be written about,' Bellinda agreed readily. 'I was forced to spend a night on the city streets before finding my present position.'

Amity looked deep into Bellinda's eyes and suddenly there was an unspoken warmth between them, as if they were both standing near a glowing flame, a flame that would burn for ever. 'Bellinda, I want to do something about it. So far I don't know what, but that's why God put me on this Earth, no other reason,' she said passionately.

'Amity, truly there is so much to be done. One law for the rich and one for the poor. How can this ever be right?'

'It can't,' she said gravely. 'Of course, with all my privileges then you'd be justified in thinking of me as nothing but a conscience stricken charlatan.'

'Dear Amity, I have often seen through the pretences of those surrounding me. I can tell that there is nothing but the purest sincerity in your intentions.'

Amity's brown eyes sparkled. 'You believe that? Oh Bellinda, you can't realize how much that pleases me.' She then took Bellinda's hand in her own and squeezed it. 'I need a friend, someone who cares for other things besides their own selfish interests.'

Bellinda could feel the flames of that imaginary fire rising. 'I shall be your friend as long as you want me to be.'

'For ever? Bellinda, I want you to be my friend for ever.'

'Then for ever it shall be, until death us do part.'

'Until death us do part? Yes, a marriage of minds.'

'Amity, tomorrow is my day off. I was wondering . . . '

'If we could spend it together?'

Bellinda smiled. 'Yes, I was wondering exactly that. When I was forced to spend the night in the East End

I met a woman called Betsy, a lovable but wretched soul who was sleeping on the streets. I would so dearly love to see her again.'

'Then see her you shall! I will call for you at eight o'clock tomorrow morning.'

Amity arrived at the house promptly at eight o'clock on the following morning. Fortunately, she had the sense not to mention to Mrs Gage that she was taking Bellinda to the East End.

'Did you sleep well?' Amity asked as soon as they began the hansom cab journey to Shoreditch railway station.

'I didn't,' Bellinda told her. 'I just spent the whole night wondering about Betsy. I do hope she is well.'

Amity took hold of Bellinda's hand and squeezed it. 'You must always hope, dear friend. I too pray she is safe, and I'll do everything in my power to help her.'

'You will?'

'Of course, any friend of yours is a friend of mine too.'

'Oh Amity, I shall be eternally grateful for such kindness.'

'But first we've got to find her, and that may not be easy.'

'You may well be right,' Bellinda agreed reluctantly.

As soon as she alighted from the cab, the horrors of that first night in London returned to Bellinda. She had escaped from that cruel world, leaving poor Betsy behind. Now at last, thanks to Amity, she had a chance to help the sad old tramp to find warmth and solace in her remaining years.

Bellinda was soon able to guide Amity to the graveyard where she and Betsy had spent that bitterly cold winter's night. Betsy had told her that the surrounding area was one of her most common haunts, so it was a good place to begin their search.

They had not walked far when Bellinda recognized the man who, after seeing his friend hanged, had decided to give up his life of crime and become a beggar.

208

With the instincts of someone who had always been wealthy, Amity immediately pressed some money into the man's grimy hand before allowing Bellinda to ask her question.

He looked up at them with sad, bloodshot eyes. 'Betsy's been dead fer over a week now. Couldn't even tell yer where they took 'er.'

Bellinda was incapable of controlling her emotions. Tears flooded down her cheeks. Her body shuddered with sorrow, and she wept upon Amity's shoulder. 'I should have come back for her sooner,' she wailed. 'I should have come back sooner!'

'You mustn't blame yourself. You mustn't!' Amity insisted.

Bellinda was still in a grief-stricken daze as Amity led her back to Shoreditch station and hailed a cab. As soon as they arrived at her hotel, the American girl ordered tea. Only after sipping the hot drink was Bellinda finally able to stop crying.

'One day all this has got to change,' Amity said resolutely. 'We cannot continue to have a world like this. I've already decided to leave this place and find somewhere cheaper. My conscience just won't allow me to stay here in all this luxury.'

'Amity, never before have I ever heard of any rich person making such a gesture.'

'Well you have now,' Amity said before looking at Bellinda with eyes glowing with determination. 'I intend to run a mission. Would you help me, Bellinda?'

'Gladly.'

'All this is destined. You know that, don't you?'

'Yes,' Bellinda answered readily. 'Ever since Sara died I have vowed that I would devote my life to helping others.'

'Who was Sara?' Amity asked, then contritely: 'Forgive me with my foolish American ways. I'm sure you don't want to talk about someone else's death at the moment.'

Bellinda took in a deep breath. 'No, Amity, I think now is the very time to tell you about the wretched life of the girl I always regarded as my baby sister.'

'Are you *sure* you want to, Bellinda?'

'Yes,' Bellinda said emphatically before beginning her story. 'There was once a girl called Sara who I now believe to have come from a good home. Although I will never be able to discover the exact circumstances, it is clear that somehow she became separated from her parents. I believe she fell into the hands of a vile man who – who debased her and then turned her out. Imagine an eleven-year-old child being forced to wander the streets of London, utterly alone, utterly penniless.'

Amity sighed, 'Oh, the poor child.'

'Poor indeed, for in such desperate circumstances my beloved friend was forced into prostitution.'

'A child becoming a prostitute? Bellinda, you have to be mistaken.'

'Mistaken? Then you have not taken a walk in Covent Garden yet. I have seen for myself a girl just like Sara touting for business,' Bellinda said bitterly. 'Apparently there is no shortage of customers.'

'This has to be stopped!'

'How? As far as I know it is not against the law.'

'Oh come now, Bellinda, you're not trying to tell me that it's perfectly legal for men to pleasure themselves upon a child!'

Bellinda shook her head in despair. 'I fear so.'

'Oh dear God, what kind of a world have I been born into?'

'One that then demands the wretched life of someone like Sara,' Bellinda said, grimly. 'Those nights on the streets finally took their toll. She died of the consumption.'

Her story told, Bellinda became silent. Amity said nothing. Neither could do anything but reflect upon Sara's tragic life.

Suddenly, Amity balled a dainty hand into a fist and banged it down hard upon the table. 'One day the law will be changed. For ever!'

'And I shall do everything in my power to help you,' Bellinda vowed.

Amity smiled. 'I knew I could count on you. Tell me, would you really give up your position with Harriet Gage to work with me instead?'

Bellinda returned the smile. 'Amity, have I not already agreed?'

'You have, but are you really sure? I know that you will be taking a risk leaving Harriet and John, they think very highly of you.'

'And I think highly of little Jamie, but I have always had a destiny to fulfil.'

'A destiny the same as mine.'

'Yes, Amity,' Bellinda agreed readily. 'A destiny the same as yours.'

Thomas Groves-Hawkes had been angered to discover that Bellinda preferred to spend her day off with Amity Smallwood instead of himself. Once again he had created a fictitious business trip to London, and all his efforts had been wasted. How dare that American girl steal his divine goddess from him? How dare she!

'Hawkes?'

'Yes, what is it, Marguerite?' he snapped, angered at having his thoughts disturbed.

'I feel strangely tired.'

'How in God's name can you feel tired? My dear, you have only just got up.'

'I know, that's why I'm worried.'

'Worried? Worried about what?' he demanded irritably.

'Worried that I am ill, you insensitive buffoon!'

'My dear, I am not being insensitive, but how can a little tiredness mean that you are ill?'

'How can a little tiredness mean that I am ill?' she mimicked contemptuously. 'Am I really talking to my husband? Am I?'

Thomas slapped his morning paper down on to the table and glared at his wife. 'To count how many times that you have believed yourself to be ill, just because you felt a little tired, would be impossible,' he said sarcastically.

Marguerite, her face crimson with rage, stormed out of the room.

Thomas went to the window. Buckinghamshire was about to bloom again. The trees were beginning to leaf out, verdantly heralding spring. It was a time of rebirth, the winter was done. He vowed to himself that his infatuation for Bellinda would have to end. His marriage was speedily being destroyed.

Within a few days it soon became apparent that Marguerite's tiredness was more than histrionics. Her appetite was suddenly gone and her complexion, usually so fresh and healthy, had rapidly become pale and sallow. She had always had a fear of doctors, and protested when he told her that she was about to receive a visit from one.

'Hawkes, this *petit malaise* will soon pass,' she protested. 'You had no right to call him in. No right at all!'

'My dear, I am sure that there is nothing of real concern. My calling in of Doctor Stokes is a mere precaution,' Thomas lied, for in truth there was every reason for concern, though neither could bring themselves to face it.

Impatiently, his heart pounding, Thomas paced the landing as he waited for Doctor Stokes to emerge. It seemed like an eternity before the bedroom door opened. The grey-bearded doctor had no need to say anything, it was all written on his face.

'Tell me, Mr Groves-Hawkes, has your wife coughed any blood?

Thomas swallowed hard. The question was as inevitable as the answer. He nodded.

'A great deal or very little?'

'Very little so far.'

212

'So far? Then, Sir, you are aware of my fears.'

'Yes,' Thomas said gravely. 'We allowed an orphan girl to stay here during Christmas. Not long after, she died of the con . . . ' He choked, unable to finish the sentence. 'How could Marguerite of all people fall prey?'

'That is difficult to say. Those who are strong in health have less chance of contracting the disease.'

'Until now my wife has always been strong in health,' Thomas said bitterly.

Stokes shook his head. 'Most unfortunate, most unfortunate. Perhaps something was worrying her unduly? Some of my colleagues believe that those who are under great stress can be more vulnerable to illness.'

Under great stress? Of course Marguerite was under great stress. She believed that Thomas no longer loved her, that he had become obsessed with someone else. To his eternal shame she was right.

Solemnly he thanked Stokes for his opinion, knowing full well that there really was no doubt that the woman with whom he had shared most of his adult life was going to die very soon.

'What did he say to you, Hawkes?' Marguerite asked weakly when he returned to the bedroom.

'He said that I must remain constantly by your side, my beloved.'

She smiled, a loving, adoring smile – a smile that reminded him of when they had first met. 'And will you, Hawkes? Will you?'

'Yes,' he vowed softly, as tears began to fall.

'Then I shall get better, I know I will.'

'Without doubt my beloved,' he lied. 'Without doubt.'

'You are making the most foolish of decisions,' Mrs Gage raged. 'I am most inconvenienced by this sudden departure. Most inconvenienced!'

'Ma'am, all I know is that I have a destiny to fulfil, and Amity can help me to reach my goal.'

'And what goal can that be, pray?'

'To stop the poverty and deprivation that is so much part of our capital.'

Mrs Gage sighed before taking a short sniff at her sal volatile. 'Oh child, what foolishness, there can never be an end to poverty. And as for this absurd plan of Amity's, well . . . She has even had the temerity to ask my dear husband for financial assistance.'

'To set up the mission will be very costly, Ma'am, but I can assure you that much good work will be achieved, once it is open.'

'Bellinda, I have no doubt of that, but people will not be willing to part with the large sums of money needed for your cause. We should be poor ourselves were we to donate so generously.'

Bellinda knew that what Amity had asked for was hardly a generous donation. The truth was that people like the Gages were simply unwilling to part with any of their wealth to help the poor. It was tempting to voice her anger. Instead, she asked whether she would be allowed to say her farewells to Jamie.

'Of course you may,' Mrs Gage said. 'Dear Jamie will be heartbroken by your sudden leaving. Utterly heartbroken!'

'I shall miss him a great deal, Ma'am.'

'Then I implore you to stay. I shall increase your wages most substantially.'

'Ma'am, it is not a matter of wages that urges me to leave. I have been most content with my position here.'

'And we have also been content with your services,' Mrs Gage said before adding proudly, 'Jamie has learnt so much from your tuition.'

'And he will continue to learn, Ma'am, provided that he regards any lesson as a game.'

Mrs Gage gave one of her wan smiles. 'I will never forget that. We will be employing a governess with strict instructions to carry on with your good work.'

'I shall always be keeping in touch with him, Ma'am.'

Mrs Gage's smile vanished, her expression suddenly hardening. 'No, I do not think that would be correct.

Even the most highly regarded of servants should remember their place.'

So this really was the last time she would ever see Jamie. How foolish the rich were with their heartless ways.

Jamie was reading *Gulliver's Travels* when she entered his nursery. He looked up from the book and beamed. 'Bellinda, this is a wonderful story.'

'And it is even more wonderful that you are able to read it yourself without having to ask about any of the words.'

He frowned. 'Some of the words are a little hard to understand but I have been able to find out.'

'Splendid!'

'Oh Bellinda, I'm so glad you're pleased. I always want to please you.'

Bellinda took in a deep breath and prepared herself for what had to be said. 'Jamie, you will always please me,' she began hesitantly, 'and you will always be in my thoughts.'

Jamie frowned again. 'Bellinda, you are trying to tell me something, aren't you?' he asked suspiciously.

'Jamie, I must leave this household.'

The child's complexion turned pale. 'You can't. I won't let you go. I won't!'

'Jamie, I must. I have no other choice.'

'You do have a choice. You're my nanny. What am I going to do without you?' Jamie burst into tears.

Bellinda took the child in her arms and held him close to her, patting his head. 'There, there, my little one. Remember all that I have taught you, and in spirit we shall never be parted.'

'Will you come and see me, Bellinda?' he snuffled.

'Jamie, you must be a brave little boy.'

'That means you *won't* be coming!'

'My dear little friend, if it were at all possible then I would,' she said, unable to explain the rigid class structure that denied her future access to him.

He wrapped his arms around her waist. 'I really don't want you to go.'

Bellinda kissed his forehead. 'I know, my little love. I know,' she whispered. 'Perhaps one day we will meet again.'

'Oh Bellinda,' he said, tears streaming, 'I'll never forget you.'

Bellinda kissed him again. 'Jamie, you must never forget all that I have taught you.'

'I won't,' he promised.

Before her own tears began to flow, Bellinda hurriedly made her farewell. She would always fondly remember the little boy who never wanted to grow up.

'Well, this is home,' Amity said as she and Bellinda surveyed the bare, dilapidated walls of the newly acquired mission.

'A lick of paint will make all the difference.'

'You really think so?' Amity seemed unconvinced.

'The Downley orphanage was no worse than this.'

'Then I'm even more glad I wasn't born an orphan. Still, we must never forget how lucky we were to find somewhere in the very heart of Covent Garden.'

'I am still amazed that you were able to raise the money to buy this place.'

'So am I. Had it not been for the generosity of your friend then I would have been forced to back down from the purchase.'

'My friend?'

Amity grinned mischievously. 'Well, I suppose you could call Thomas Groves-Hawkes a friend of yours.'

'You went to see him? Amity, you told me nothing of this!'

'Sorry, I've been so busy while you were finishing out your time at the Gages that I completely forgot.'

'Only an American could forget to tell me something as important as that,' Bellinda quipped.

'How can you say? I'm the only American you've ever met.'

'I'll not comment on that,' Bellinda said with a smile. 'Any more than I'll comment upon how only someone with your persuasive talents could have enticed him into donating.'

'Oh, there was nothing to it, once he knew you were helping me.'

'Why did you tell him that?' Bellinda asked angrily. 'Don't you realize that he will start to pester me again?'

'Calm down, Bellinda, he's not likely to do that while his wife is so ill.'

'Ill?'

'That's right. He told me she'd been bedridden for a whole week.' Amity added grimly, 'He seemed very worried. Very worried indeed.'

Bellinda had no love for Marguerite but she wished no one ill. 'Do you know what the illness is?' she asked.

Amity shook her head. 'I did inquire but he wouldn't say. In truth, I was too obsessed about getting a donation from him to worry as much as I should have done about his wife.'

'We can only pray that Marguerite gets better,' Bellinda said solemnly.

'Yes, we must do that and give our thanks to Thomas's generosity.'

Bellinda nodded in agreement.

Amity clapped her hands together. 'Time to get to work! You'll have to bear with me, a wealthy girl never gets much of a chance to get her hands dirty.'

'When I was a tweeny, Cook was always complaining that I didn't work hard enough. Perhaps you'll be able to teach me a thing or two.'

Previously the house had been a brothel. However, Amity learned that many of the prostitutes preferred to ply for their trade on the street. Little did their neighbours realize that what had once been a house of sin would soon become a mission for all the child prostitutes in the area. After just three days, Number Five Grebe Street was ready to open its creaking door to all the wretched little girls who were forced to wander the streets.

217

Chapter 19

'What is your name, my child?'

The frail little girl remained silent, sad eyes staring up at Bellinda and Amity.

'Oh, please speak to us, little dear,' Amity begged. 'No harm is going to come to you, I promise.'

'E'll 'it me, I know 'e will.'

Bellinda took hold of the girl's hand. 'Who will?'

'The man what looks after me.'

Bellinda knelt and kissed her cheek. 'Knocking someone about is not looking after them.'

Suspiciously, she studied Bellinda. 'You mean if I comes in 'ere then I won't get knocked about?'

Bellinda kissed her on the forehead. 'Of course not.'

'And what is more, no man will ever molest you again,' Amity told her.

'That we can promise you,' Bellinda added.

The child's expression was still suspicious. 'You ain't 'avin me on, are yer?'

Bellinda and Amity shook their heads and smiled down at her.

Suddenly her tiny face was transformed by a gleeful smile. 'Ain't got no second name, but people calls me Polly.'

'I have only ever been known as Bellinda, so you and I have a lot in common.'

'You an orphan too?'

Bellinda nodded before taking the child's hand and leading her inside. After Polly had enjoyed a warm bath and some hot broth, she soon ventured the full story of her tragic life. She neither knew nor seemed to care who her parents were. To Bellinda and Amity's horror, she also told them that her virginity had been lost at the age of five.

218

The wretched child had known no other life but prostitution. Willingly, she promised that while she was under the care of the mission, she would not allow any man to ill treat her. Upon the very first day of opening they had succeeded in giving shelter to one small child. Others would surely follow.

It was not to be. Despite constant approaches to the children soliciting on the streets, they were always unsuccessful. None of the infant prostitutes would come to the mission, even for a short while. Unseen, there seemed to be a threatening influence, an evil pervasion.

Amity and Bellinda had already made contact with the police, who strongly approved of what they were trying to achieve, but could not promise to provide the mission with any protection. However, what help could anyone offer against someone who was always in the background, cunningly undermining their efforts?

Dejectedly, Bellinda and Amity were returning to their mission after yet another unsuccessful day. Neither spoke – there was nothing to say. It all seemed utterly hopeless. Although night had not fallen yet, Covent Garden had darkened beneath a smoke-filled sky. A fog was probably on its way, perhaps then a few of the children might seek shelter from the choking mists. Hope! Bellinda tried to convince herself that one should always hope.

Number Five Grebe Street was just ahead of them, a grim and uncharitable-looking building. If only Amity had the capital to have the whole house painted in smart white, like some of the houses in Mayfair. Bellinda was still thinking about this when Amity screamed, 'What's going on?'

It was only then that Bellinda saw Polly struggling to free herself from the grasp of a strongly built ruffian. Immediately, she joined Amity in rushing to the child's aid.

'Let go of her,' Bellinda demanded as she tried to tug Polly free.

'Stay out o' this,' the unshaven bully growled. 'Otherwise you'll be getting a beatin' too.'

'Let go of her at once!' Amity ordered.

Angrily the ruffian hurled Polly against the wall. 'I'll let go of 'er,' he snarled. 'I'll let go of 'er 'cos she's mine and she knows what's good for 'er.'

'A man like you isn't good for anyone,' Bellinda raged, before the open palm of his hand slapped hard against her face.

Reeling from the stinging pain, she fell back against the house and through blurred vision saw him poised to deliver another blow. It never came. Someone in a tall hat was attacking him, fists flailing. Her assailant groaned as he was punched hard in the stomach. Then another fist was cracking against his jaw.

Although the stinging pain of the slap was still there, Bellinda's vision had returned. She could now see a handsome, well-dressed man standing above the felled ruffian.

'Get out of here,' their rescuer demanded in a cultured voice, and then as the beaten man struggled to his feet, 'You'll talk to no one about this if you know what's good for you.'

The ruffian scurried away, mouthing obscenities, and a leather-gloved hand was then offered to Bellinda. Gladly she took it. His grasp was strong and firm. As she was helped to her feet, their eyes met. His were almost black, a deep ebony that instantly held her spellbound. His skin was richly tanned, a smooth mahogany that had matured without one wrinkle or blemish.

'Did that blaggard hurt you at all?' he asked in a familiar, velvet-smooth voice.

She shook her head. 'I'll survive,' she told the dark stranger. But no, he wasn't a stranger. She had met him once before, in the dark hall on the night of the Gages' dinner party.

His lips curled into a wry smile. 'Then our acqaintance can be renewed.'

'So it seems,' she said breathlessly.

He cast a quick glance at Amity who was now tending to Polly. 'I have already been introduced to your American friend at the Gages' party, but I should introduce myself to you. Hugh Maltravers at your service,' and he bowed before her in a truly dashing manner.

'I am Bellinda,' she told him.

Again his lips curled into a wry smile that could not have been more captivating.

For a moment she remained under his spell before returning her attention to Polly.

'She'll be fine,' Amity assured as she continued to comfort the distraught child.

'Shall we go inside?' Hugh suggested.

'Don't want te go inside with *'im*,' Polly protested.

'Dearest, what is the matter?' Bellinda asked, baffled by the child's reaction.

Hugh knelt down in front of the little girl. 'What is this nonsense, my little friend? You could never have seen me before in your life.'

'Yes, Polly, you must be mistaken,' Amity added.

Polly shook her head and clung to Amity. As soon as they had entered the mission, she rushed upstairs. After tucking the little girl into bed and giving her goodnight kisses, Bellinda and Amity returned downstairs and apologized for Polly's curious behaviour.

'Think nothing of it,' Hugh told them. 'Thank God I was there to save her from worse harm.'

'So far she is the only child who has wanted to stay at our mission,' Bellinda said as she sat beside Amity.

'And how long have you been open?'

'A whole week now,' Amity said dejectedly.

'A week? Is that all?'

'Hugh, that is surely long enough?'

He shook his head and then winked at Bellinda. 'I think our American friend lacks our patient English ways.'

'Perhaps, but I fear I'm like Amity, impatient to begin preventing these outrages.'

221

Hugh stroked his firmly shaped jaw and looked straight at her with his dark eyes. 'How do you intend to prevent child prostitution, Bellinda? Have you not seen how much of it goes on in London?'

'We have indeed,' Amity answered, 'and that is why we shall very soon be leading a campaign to get the law changed.'

He crooked an eyebrow. 'Really?'

'Yes, really, Hugh. And when Amity Smallwood says she's going to change the world, the world gets changed!'

He laughed, displaying a perfect set of ivory teeth. 'Amity, there is nothing that I admire more than a strong-willed girl.'

'In that case you will not mind giving this mission your patronage, Your Lordship,' Amity said forcefully.

'My Lordship! Now there's respect for a man's title,' he chuckled. 'Well, I can assure you that addressing me in that manner will not enhance your chances of gaining my support.' Then he grinned. 'Just plain Hugh will suffice, and naturally I'll help you, in every way I can.'

'You will?'

'Of course, Amity, but for the time being I advise that you forget about trying to have the law altered. More girls will soon be coming to your mission. Just you wait and see.'

'I certainly hope so, but I'm still determined to get the law changed.'

He turned to Bellinda. 'And does that include you too?'

'Most assuredly,' she told him. 'Most assuredly.'

'Another spirited girl, and a very beautiful one at that.'

Bellinda's heart fluttered. Probably, she was blushing. How dare he sit there grinning at her, savouring her embarrassment. How dare he! 'It is the spirited who get things done,' she told him curtly.

His black eyes twinkled. 'I'm sorry if I have offended you by saying that you are beautiful. But really, what

222

else can a man do when confronted by someone like you?'

Bellinda was stunned into silence.

'However, for the moment I think I have outstayed my welcome,' he said, getting to his feet.

'No, Hugh, please do not think that,' Amity insisted.

'It is kind of you to say so, but I really do have urgent business to attend to before the fog descends.' He turned to Bellinda. 'However, you can rest assured that we will soon be meeting again.'

As soon as he had gone, Bellinda turned to Amity. 'You did not tell me that he was a lord.'

Amity shrugged. 'Oh yes, and a lot of women would like to become Lady Maltravers.'

'Does that include yourself?' Bellinda teased.

'That includes just about everyone, but although he will court and flatter a woman, he always seems reluctant to get involved. At least, that is what I have heard.'

'He certainly has a very forthright manner.'

Amity laughed. 'Don't worry about his calling you beautiful. He knows he's a handsome devil and that a lady will forgive any indulgence on his part.'

'Well, I don't think *I* can forgive such blatant behaviour.'

Amity gave a wry smile. 'Come now, Bellinda, he was flirting with both of us – and weren't we enjoying it?'

'We certainly were,' Bellinda agreed with a smile.

'Well, a girl can dream about being married to Hugh Maltravers. But as for me? If he really does patronize this mission then I'll content myself with being grateful for that.'

'And I too,' Bellinda agreed untruthfully.

'Then we are agreed.'

'Amity, we are always agreed,' Bellinda said, and gave her friend a hug.

On the next day a small girl called Mary came to the mission. She told Bellinda and Amity that others would soon be following, and her prediction soon proved true. During the following two weeks, eight other girls came to the mission and eagerly renounced their former way of life. Why this sudden change? There really was no answer. However, it did not matter to them nearly so much as seeing Hugh Maltravers' optimism justified.

The mission now had ten girls in its care, and all within three weeks. Before long they would be too full to take any more. That would be a time to dread, but the ever-determined Amity was convinced that Hugh Maltravers was a prospective benefactor who would be able to finance another mission.

One morning a smartly liveried coachman called to present Bellinda with a large bunch of flowers, together with an invitation to join Lord Hugh Maltravers at his home that evening.

Chapter 20

'Look, if you really feel that way then I won't go.'

'Don't be a hypocrite, of course you must go,' Amity said petulantly. 'Hugh has invited you to supper. What could impress an ex-serving girl more?'

'Oh, so I'm getting above my station in life. Is that it?'

'Of course you are. He sees you as a dalliance, nothing else.'

Anger swelled up in Bellinda. 'You, of course, belong to the right class,' she raged.

'Bellinda, we're not discussing my social position, we are discussing yours. I don't want to see you get hurt, that's all.'

'What we are discussing is your jealousy!'

'Jealousy! How dare you accuse me of that? How dare you!' Amity screamed before storming into the kitchen.

Of course Amity was jealous. What other explanation could there be for such infantile behaviour?

The children were waiting for their meal of potato broth and a trencher of bread each, which should have been ready by now. But it was best to stay out of the kitchen until her friend had calmed down. Friend? For how long would Amity remain a friend?

Bellinda had just finished laying the bowls and spoons on the table when there was a knock at the door. Amity emerged from the kitchen and said coldly, 'You better get yourself dressed for your night out – that will probably be Maltravers' coachman.'

What clothes did Bellinda have but the outfit she had worn when travelling to London? Admittedly it had been well cleaned and her dextrous skills with needle and thread had ensured that no part of it looked either threadbare or holed. It was hardly suitable for dining at the opulent home of a lord. But it would have to suffice, and she would not be ashamed of how she dressed.

She was taken to Belgravia. The house with its white-pillared porch seemed almost palatial. The hallway was even more impressive: a glittering chandelier dangled from a white stucco ceiling and everywhere she looked, tiny gaslamps glowed, creating a glorious illusion of internal daylight. The butler led her up a spiral staircase and into the candlelit dining room.

Lord Maltravers was wearing a well-tailored frock coat in deep burgundy, which emphasized his well-honed physique to perfection. He gave her a welcoming smile. Gladly she returned it, for now that she had arrived, all thoughts of Amity's foolish jealousy were forgotten.

'I must apologize for not inviting you here sooner,' he began. 'Regrettably, I was called away to France on business again.'

'Well, I am most grateful for the invitation, Your Lordship, but why was not Amity invited too?'

'Because it was you I wanted to see, Bellinda.' Then there was a mischievous glint in his dark eyes. 'Does that embarrass you?'

'Just a little.'

'Then I am sorry, but you must not embarrass me by addressing me as Your Lordship. Please call me Hugh, and take a seat here.'

As soon as they were seated at the head of a long, highly polished dining table, the butler and a serving maid entered.

'I hope you enjoy quail?' Hugh asked.

'I have never eaten them. Are they little birds?'

'Yes,' he said, looking at her quizzically. 'Do I suspect a reluctance to eat little birds?'

Embarrassed that she had allowed her true feelings to show, Bellinda lowered her gaze. 'Birds are such adorable little creatures,' she said quietly.

Hugh turned to his butler. 'Tell the kitchen that we shall not be having the quail. The fish course will suffice.'

Wine was then poured by the butler into tall-stemmed glasses. She followed Hugh's example and sipped a little. Although tart in flavour, it had an enticing aroma and lingered on the palate.

'Do you like it?'

'It is delicious.'

'Then let us raise our glasses and drink a toast to the success of the mission.'

Bellinda raised her glass and chinked it against Hugh's. 'I will gladly toast to that.'

'Is it becoming a success?' he asked in a manner that suggested he already knew the answer.

'We have filled the mission. We may have to find another place, if more children come to us.'

'I doubt if there will be many more at the moment.'

Bellinda was about to ask why he should be so sure when the fish course was brought in. Dover sole garnished with a sprig of parsley and boiled potatoes, it looked very enticing. One mouthful confirmed her expectations. It was well up to Mrs Ramsbottom's exemplary standards. There was a pause in their conversation while they enjoyed the meal.

'Once again I recall Harriet Gage telling me that Jamie had actually begun to learn something while you were his nanny.'

'And I recall admitting that I did help a little with his education.'

Again his lips curled into a tantalizing smile. Bellinda was helplessly captivated by Hugh Maltravers, and knew she would remember this evening for the rest of her life.

'That was the modest answer I would have expected from someone as beautiful as you,' he said in his velvet-smooth voice.

He was looking at her intently, his black eyes boring into her. There was a mesmerizing quality about him, perhaps dangerous. She was becoming tangled in his web but, unlike a captive fly, she had no real wish to escape. Already she was a slave to his dark charms.

'I regard modesty as a virtue, for can one ever truly say that one has done enough?' she asked in the hope of diverting the conversation back to its original formality.

'Indeed not, that is why as you leave this house tonight, my butler will be handing you a cheque to the value of one hundred pounds.'

'That is most kind!' she gasped. 'I assure you that the money will be well spent.'

'I shall not consider it well used unless just a little of that money is spent upon yourself. The outfit you are wearing is most becoming but . . . '

'Not worthy of someone dining with yourself? Then I must apologize, but I truly believe there are more important financial priorities than the pursuit of mere fashion.'

Hugh raised his glass and toasted her. 'I am truly humbled, Bellinda. Of course, you are right. If only more women thought like that,' he said with a smile. 'Now, I see that you have finished your sole too, time for the second course. Tell me, does the prospect of an open jelly topped by whipped cream appeal to you?'

Bellinda remembered how appetizing Mrs Ramsbottom's jellies always looked. Tonight she was going to actually eat such a jelly herself. 'It appeals a great deal,' she enthused.

The sweet was created from segments of strawberry and lemon jellies, a base for a mountain of whipped cream. She wondered whether such an indulgence was healthy. No matter, this was a night for indulging.

Once the last heavenly mouthful had been taken, Hugh suggested they retire to the drawing room where a pot of tea awaited them. The walls of his drawing room were adorned with paintings.

'They look very fine. Is this one a Canaletto?' she asked.

He looked impressed by her knowledge. 'It most certainly is, and all part of my inheritance. As you can see, I am a very fortunate man.'

'Most fortunate.'

'Bellinda, I cannot believe that you are envious?'

'Certainly not, except that were I ever to become rich, I would spend it all on helping the poor.'

'Christian charity at its most noble,' he said, passing her a cup of tea.

'I fear not, for in truth I do not accept the Christian concept of God.'

'What blasphemy!'

Bellinda blushed with embarrassment. What had suddenly made her reveal her true feelings about orthodox religion? No wonder she had angered him. 'I am sorry,' she said awkwardly. 'I should not have ventured my opinion in such a forthright manner.'

'You most certainly should have done. When I said "What blasphemy!" I can assure you that I was teasing.'

Bellinda gave a sigh of relief. 'Then I must now apologize for misjudging you, Hugh.'

He gave one of his wry smiles. 'You must, for the religions that fascinate me are far from Christian. Tell me, have you ever heard of the Indian goddess, Kali?'

Bellinda shook her head.

'She adorns herself with a necklace of human skulls. Her followers are known as the Thugs and have strangled literally thousands in the Bombay area.'

Bellinda was interested only in a benign goddess, but did not mention this. Why he should be so interested in the instigator of such terrible cruelty was a puzzle. Hugh Maltravers was a man of dark mystery, an aspect that only served to enhance his allure. There was a frisson of excitement in that room. Deep hidden desires that she had always suppressed were now awakening. Once more his night-black eyes were boring into her.

'I do hope that you will continue with your support for our cause,' she said almost formally, reminding herself of the true reason for visiting him.

'Bellinda, you know I will. But it is not your cause that I wish to speak of.'

Bellinda's breathing had become uneven, her heart-beat was racing. She would have to say something to distract him from continuing on those lines.

'You cannot imagine how I was spellbound by your fresh, virginal innocence when I first saw you.' His voice, his eyes, his very being, exuded a raw passion. 'You have seen and suffered much yet there is a child-like quality about you. I see you as a tiny child in a woman's body.'

Before the teacup could fall from her trembling hands, she placed it on the table. Hugh advanced, and instinctively Bellinda backed away from him. She was not quick enough. His strong hands gripped her by the waist. His mouth fell upon hers. She struggled but he held her fast, his lips driving hard against her own. Her struggling was done. Now willingly, she submitted to the ecstasy of his kiss.

Enraptured, she was transported to a high plateau of powerful delight where her senses soared into a glorious haze and her mind almost ceased to function. She could feel his virile body pressed against her own, and she wanted him. Yes, why should she not give herself to him completely?

'Oh Bellinda,' he whispered when their lips had finally parted, 'stay the night and I shall make you my little queen.'

Despite her surging emotions, Bellinda baulked. Her virginity was all she possessed and she would hold on to it, for it was precious to her. 'Please, Hugh, I am not ready for that.'

'Of course you are, little one. Of course you are.'

'No, please,' she begged, desperately trying to free herself from him. 'Please let me go.'

'If you wish,' he said coldly, pushing her away from him.

Bellinda trembled as Maltravers stood before her, magnificent in his dark anger. She backed away from him, scurried down the stairs, wrenched open the door and bolted into the waiting darkness.

Belgravia was a long way from Covent Garden. It would be wise to hail a hansom cab if one were passing. No, she would not do so. How wrong it would be to indulge herself in such a luxury when every penny was needed for the mission. She soon managed to convince herself that it would be best to walk.

Bellinda hurried through the gaslit streets, not even sure whether she was heading in the right direction, but had not gone far when Maltravers' carriage drew up beside her. 'His Lordship wants me to take you home,' the driver shouted down to her.

'Tell His Lordship that I have no wish to be taken home in his coach.'

'I wish you *would* come, Miss. I could lose me job if I don't do what he tells me.'

Bellinda did not want to do any harm to the coachman. Reluctantly she allowed him to help her in, and very soon arrived at the mission. Thankfully, Amity was asleep when she entered their bedroom.

As soon as she was beneath the sheets, Bellinda's thoughts raced back to the moment when Maltravers kissed her. Part of her wanted him now, right here in her bed. Yet he had behaved in a ruthless and arrogant manner, regarding her, no doubt, as a mere servant girl who would soon give in to his demands – before finding herself pregnant.

What could possibly be attractive about such a self-centred man? Hopefully she would never see him again. Yes, that was what she hoped, but even so, throughout a rage-filled night, her whole being ached to be in the arms of Hugh Maltravers.

Chapter 21

'It was as I feared,' Amity said when Bellinda told her what had happened. 'He just wanted to use you, Bell.'

'I see that now,' she admitted. 'At the time I thought you were jealous of me.'

'And you could not have been more right. Of course I was jealous. What girl wouldn't be?' Amity sighed. 'He is so incredibly handsome.'

Bellinda sighed too. 'Yes, incredibly handsome – but no gentleman.'

Amity chuckled. 'Bell, the more I see of men the more I realize that there are no gentlemen.'

Although no other children came to Number Five Grebe Street, their time was fully occupied with those already there – and in particular, little Florrie, who was dying. They had consulted two doctors about the child's condition and both had shaken their heads in despair. The little prostitute had contracted syphilis from one of her customers. It would only be a matter of time before she died.

Bellinda and Amity wept as Florrie's rapid decline began. However, many of the children seemed curiously unmoved. Their attitude seemed to be: There but for the grace of God go I.

Amity was moved to confess how guilty she felt about having a privileged childhood. Bellinda did her best to comfort her, explaining that guilt was a negative attitude and Amity did seem to find some kind of solace from her words.

When the time came, Florrie would go to a pauper's grave, for there were insufficient funds for a proper funeral. They would dearly have loved to find somewhere better to lay her to rest, but there really was no alternative. That was, until Lord Hugh Maltravers paid the mission an unexpected visit.

'Tell him to go away,' Bellinda said when Amity told her he was standing on the doorstep. 'I have no wish to speak to him.'

'I cannot tell him that. You must do it yourself.'

'I most certainly shall,' Bellinda vowed, her heart pounding.

Hugh Maltravers looked even more stunning than before, immaculate in a smooth grey overcoat with a sleek fur collar. His hat was also of fur, probably beaver. He lifted it with dashing aplomb before bowing his head.

'Bellinda, as always I am your humble servant,' he said in a manner far from humble.

'I have no servants,' she said sharply. 'And were I ever to do so, I would certainly choose one with a little more grace than yourself!'

Maltravers crooked a sleek black eyebrow and smiled. 'At least you are no longer calling me Your Lordship.'

'A proper lord would not have behaved as you did last week.'

'Once more I must accept what you say. Truly I was in the wrong.'

A part of Bellinda wanted to believe in the sincerity of his apology, but could a man as strongly passionate as he ever change? He had a dangerous quality that no amount of charm would ever conceal.

'No apology could suffice for an act as disrespectful as yours,' she told him curtly.

'Oh dear, I fear that now I shall be accused of trying to buy your affections,' he said while delving into his pocket. 'However, before you begin your rebuke I will remind you that I had already pledged this money on the night we met.'

When he produced his cheque for one hundred pounds Bellinda felt she had no choice but to accept it. So much could be done with it, including giving poor Florrie a proper funeral.

233

'I must thank you for your generosity,' she said with measured politeness. 'One of the girls is dying. We will now be able to give her a decent burial.'

'Are you sure that is wise?'

How dare he ask such a question? What arrogance! What business was it of his?

'Of course it is wise,' she retorted.

'Do you really think that this particular girl is the only one who is going to die in your mission? Will you be able to give decent burials and funerals to them all?'

Bellinda remained silent, unable to answer. Florrie would not be the last to die, and Bellinda remembered that at the orphanage, only Sara had avoided a pauper's grave by being buried beneath a tree. Maltravers' cold realism had to be faced. If only he were not right. If only he were not so magnetic, so entrancing.

'Bellinda, how you misjudge me. I may be a man of passion when I fall in love, but I am not heartless.' There was a hint of repentance in his smooth voice. 'I want to do as much as I can to help you.'

'I think I have told you before, one can never do enough,' she said aloofly, desperately trying to hide her vulnerability to his seductions.

His smile was beguiling. 'You have indeed, Bellinda. I believed you then and I believe you now.'

'Your behaviour that night must never be repeated,' Bellinda found herself saying in the manner of an admonishing schoolmistress. Again, she was voicing her true feelings.

There was a melting warmth in his dark eyes. 'I should have taken you to my favourite restaurant instead of inviting you to my home.'

Before she could stop herself, Bellinda nodded eagerly in agreement.

'Ah good! Then you will dine with me again?'

'I did not say that,' Bellinda answered, feeling tricked.

'But surely you will, for is it not wise to maintain a good relationship with a generous sponsor?'

'I refuse to be blackmailed by the promise of more money.'

He gave her a knowing look. 'Not even when it is money for others? Come now, Bellinda. Have I not promised to behave myself?'

'You have, but promises are easily broken.'

'Not so, I really can assure you that any passionate advances will now be made by yourself and not me.'

'What arrogance! I shall certainly not be making any advances.'

His lips curled into a wry smile. 'Good, then I will be able to eat my meal in safety. My coachman will call for you tonight at seven o'clock.'

'I refuse!'

'Seven o'clock,' he directed, unabashed.

Before she could say anything else, he had returned to his coach.

'Bellinda, have you gone truly insane? He will only be making more advances. You *know* he will.'

'I know no such thing,' Bellinda protested. 'He is fully repentant of his behaviour. Fully repentant!'

'Hah!' Amity scoffed. 'Can you really be so gullible?'

'And was I gullible in accepting this?' Bellinda protested before handing her Maltravers' cheque.

Amity's eyes widened before she handed it back.

'You see!' Bellinda said triumphantly.

'I still see a man who intends to take advantage of you.'

'Oh Amity, this jealousy of yours is so ill becoming.'

Amity blanched. 'I think we'd better drop the subject,' she said coldly. 'Perhaps before you meet your beau, you will be kind enough to assist me in the running of this mission.'

'Amity, please,' Bellinda sighed. 'Must we quarrel?'

'Perhaps not, it is your folly, not mine,' said Amity, shaking her head. Although she was delighted by Maltravers' generosity, Amity's coolness lingered.

The rest of the afternoon was spent with the children, keeping them amused and listening to their stories. Much of what they had to tell was too hard to bear. It seemed impossible that grown men would wish to abuse and violate these little girls. What vile beasts they all were. If only there was a way to stop this dreadful trade. Maltravers was a man of influence. Surely he could help them to get the age of consent raised? It was also obvious that some of the girls in their care were less attractive, compared to those who still worked the streets. There was so much to be done.

As promptly as before, Maltravers' coachman arrived and took her to Shepherd Market, a charming and quaint little area that nestled behind Curzon Street in Mayfair. There were several restaurants but she was taken to one that looked more attractive than all the others. It was lit by candles instead of gas, a very romantic setting, and despite herself Bellinda was now relishing the prospect of another evening in the company of Hugh Maltravers.

As soon as their eyes met, she was entranced. No man could ever have been more sensual. How many women had fallen prey to his demands? Could she be the one to tame him? It had become her innermost dream.

'Bellinda, I was dreading that you would refuse to join me.'

'How could I refuse the mission's most generous sponsor?'

'How indeed,' he said wryly. 'Now, what would you like to eat?'

He passed her a beautifully scripted menu. Holding it up to the candlelight she did her best to understand what any of it meant.

'Forgive me, I should have warned you – this restaurant is run by Frenchmen who insist on writing their menus in their own language. Would you trust me to do the ordering?'

'That is about the limit of what I can trust you to do.'

He laughed. 'Oh Bellinda, how I erred that evening. But I know that one day we will be joined for ever and then my passion need never be bridled again.'

Yes, to be at his side for ever. Deep down in her soul she wanted that too. In a blissful marriage their passion would be one, a blazing fire that time would never quench. More than anything she wanted to experience the soaring sensation of his kiss again. 'What would you recommend?' she asked in a less hostile tone than before.

'I recommend that you leave everything to me,' he told her before adding with a grin, 'I promise you that there will be no little birds in my selection.' He summoned the waiter and gave his order in what she assumed to be French.

'I must thank you for the donation,' she said as they waited for the food. 'There is so much needed to improve the mission, or perhaps expand it.'

Momentarily there was a strange expression on Hugh's face, but then he delivered one of his most tantalizing smiles. 'Bellinda, I should have mentioned that I intend to pay *all* your bills.'

'You do?'

'Of course, no one wants you to succeed more than myself.'

'And will you help us in our campaign to get the age of consent raised?'

Maltravers hesitated. 'Yes,' he answered cautiously. 'I will help you in that too.'

Bellinda was thrilled. To have a man of such power and influence as an ally would indeed be a great advantage. Perhaps . . . well perhaps . . . ? Was she not going too far by asking him this? Probably, but the need to get child prostitution banned for ever demanded that she ask. 'Could you not get a bill passed through the House of Lords? Amity believes this could be done.'

'And what, pray, does an American know about the workings of our House of Lords?' he asked scathingly.

'Apparently, she has read a great deal about our political system.'

He gave a mocking laugh. 'So by reading a few books by misinformed do-gooders, Miss Amity Smallwood has become an expert on such matters.'

'Amity should not be underestimated,' Bellinda said in quick defence of her friend. 'If she claims to be knowledgeable about British politics, then I can assure you she is.'

'Once again, I must apologize,' he said wryly. 'What choice do I have, but to help you in that respect as well?'

Bellinda smiled triumphantly. 'None at all.'

Before the matter could be pursued further, Bellinda saw the waiter approaching, gasped, and then looked again.

Being wheeled towards her was a hideous monster. Its shell was an angry red, and dangling over the front of the platter were two vicious claws. Its eyes were like small black buttons and from its tapered head protruded two high antennae.

'What sort of insect is that?' she asked in horror.

Hugh laughed heartily. 'Dear child, this deceased creature is no insect. It is a lobster and comes from the sea.'

Bellinda shook her head in disbelief.

'Here, try some,' he said handing her a plate of rubbery white meat that had just been scooped out of the shell.

Reluctantly she put a piece into her mouth. Undeniably, it was absolutely delicious. She tasted another piece, then another, until all of it was gone.

The chicken cooked in wine was equally exquisite. During this course Hugh spoke of his estate in the country and of how costly it was to run. His smooth voice was as intoxicating as his cologne, and just as on the first night, Bellinda was totally beguiled.

They finished by drinking French coffee. Like everything else that Hugh Maltravers introduced her to, it was excitingly different, having a much stronger aroma than tea and being of a thicker texture.

238

As they drank their coffee, Hugh asked about her past. He seemed very interested in the orphanage and wanted to know the ages of all the girls there. She now felt that beneath the fearsomely handsome facade was a man who cared deeply. That was his secret, a hidden sensitivity that he was all too reluctant to show.

Bellinda did not want the evening to end. It was as if she had suddenly been transported to a Paradise far away from the everyday world. Was that really surprising? Hugh Maltravers was no ordinary man. To her he seemed a proud and magnificent lion, king of all he surveyed.

It was cold outside and when Hugh put an arm around her, Bellinda did not protest. Instantly, the cold was banished. The coachman, his face buried beneath a thick muffler, leapt down and opened the door for them.

In the carriage Hugh wasted no time in putting his strong arm around her shoulders and drawing her towards him. This time she did not protest. More than anything she now wanted to feel his kiss again. As soon as their lips met her heart raced. It was like the drinking of a sacred wine, filling her with an ecstasy that only a goddess could know.

Not until the journey to Covent Garden was over did their passion finally cease. Bellinda could no longer deny to herself that she had fallen helplessly in love.

As soon as Hugh had helped her to alight from the coach, Bellinda saw the body of a child lying on the mission steps. She rushed over. Thankfully, Polly was alive but even in the poor light Bellinda could see the dried blood on her face. She hurried to unlock the door and Hugh carried the unconscious girl inside to a couch.

As far as Bellinda could tell, the wounds were superficial, though her face was lacerated by cuts and deep bruises were forming around her eyes.

Blearily, Polly looked up at them. Her first expression was one of relief, but when she saw Hugh it changed to sheer terror.

239

'The poor child,' he said to Bellinda. 'She must see all men as her enemy. By God, I would like to get my hands on the blaggard who did this!'

Bellinda took the child in her arms before turning to him. 'Now can you not see the urgent need for law reform?'

'I certainly do. And as for this wretched child, she will be given a proper home on my estate as soon as she has recovered.'

Before Bellinda could thank him, Amity burst into the room. 'Dear Heaven, what has happened to her?'

'She has been beaten most severely,' Hugh told her, 'but I think she will recover.'

'Shall I fetch some warm water?'

'Yes, please do,' Bellinda said, still holding the shaking child.

While Amity washed away the blood, Hugh went outside. Thankfully it now seemed certain that no lasting harm had been done but even so, Polly's attacker had been most brutal.

Hugh returned to say that the coach had now been prepared to take the girl back to his home. Upon hearing this, Polly again looked terrified.

'She will be in good hands,' he assured them. 'One of my servant girls can act as her nanny, until I find a proper one for her.'

'Hugh, you're not just doing this to impress Bellinda, are you?' Amity quizzed cynically.

'But of course,' he answered, 'she has opened my eyes to so much. So much!'

Adoringly, Bellinda smiled up at him as Hugh took Polly from her arms. The little girl struggled feebly but he held her firmly while assuring them all that she would be well cared for.

Bellinda accompanied him outside and saw Polly lifted into the coach. Shivering in the cold night air, and while Grebe Street was filled with prostitutes and their prospective customers, Bellinda watched the coach pull away, glad that one child at least was in safe hands.

Before she went to bed, Bellinda tiptoed around the large room that had been converted into a dormitory. All of the children were asleep, contented perhaps that they no longer had to walk the streets and be constantly abused. Yet how many of these, like Florrie, had contracted a terrible disease? Only time would tell. She vowed that one day all this would end. The law would be changed, no matter what the cost!

Chapter 22

'I have come to see Lord Maltravers,' Bellinda announced as soon as the door was opened.

'His Lordship does not see anyone without a proper appointment,' the butler said regally.

'I think he will see me.'

'Not without an appointment.'

Bellinda was losing patience. 'I insist you tell him that Miss Bellinda has come to see him.'

'Miss Bellinda who?'

'Just tell him that I am here.'

'Very well, but I know you'll be told to go away. He never sees any of you girls in the morning.'

Bellinda was forced to wonder what the butler meant by 'you girls' as she waited for him to return.

'His Lordship will see you,' the butler said begrudgingly, and led her up to the drawing room.

Today Hugh was dressed in black, contrasted by a white silk cravat. It was the perfect outfit for someone as swarthily handsome as Hugh Maltravers.

'Bellinda, this is most unexpected,' he said warily.

'Are you not pleased to see me?'

'Of course, but I am still surprised.'

'I do not see why you should be,' she said, still infuriated by his butler's hostile reception. 'Surely it is only natural for me to inquire about the child's welfare?'

'Oh, the battered child. Of course. What a pity you had not come just a little earlier.'

'A little earlier?'

He palmed a hand over his smooth-skinned face. 'I have already had her taken to my estate. Her recovery was remarkable. Absolutely remarkable!'

'It was? Oh praise be!'

'Praise be indeed, but what a shame you could not have seen her. It would have gladdened your heart.'

Bellinda took in a deep breath, steeling herself for what had to be said next. 'Hugh, there is something that I must ask you,' she began, trying her best to control the shakiness in her voice.

His smile was reassuring. 'Please, do not hesitate to ask me anything at all.'

Bellinda hesitated. 'It has been suggested . . . '

'Suggested by Amity no doubt.'

Bellinda ignored his interruption, determined to continue, ' . . . that I am nothing more than a dalliance for you, a mere servant girl who, once she has conceded to your desires, will be promptly discarded.'

There was a flash of dark anger before his expression changed. Now he was smiling. 'Is it just possible that Amity might be a little jealous?'

'Perhaps, but I still want an answer to my question.'

'Of course you do,' he said calmly. 'I suspect Amity also suggested that I would never introduce you to anyone in my own social circle.'

How perceptive this man was. She was too embarrassed to comment.

'Well, I can assure you that she is wrong, for your arrival has saved my coachman the trouble of delivering an invitation to you.'

'An invitation?'

'Yes Bellinda, an invitation. I am holding a dinner party tonight and I want you to be my partner.' He stroked his face again and looked at her pensively. 'However, there is one proviso.'

'What is that?' she asked suspiciously.

'You must allow me to buy you some new clothes.'

Amity had been so wrong. Of course Hugh Maltravers respected her. No, more than that. He had fallen in love with her. What bliss. What utter bliss!

★

Bellinda spent the rest of the day in Hugh's company. They went first to a fashionable dressmaker in Bond Street, where he insisted that she choose three outfits. Her initial reaction was one of guilt – it seemed so wrong to be squandering money on clothes when it could be better spent on the mission. However, if her opinions were to be accepted by society then she would have to dress as they did. And never before had she seen such beautiful dresses! She soon found herself relishing the dilemma of selecting the most suitable.

She chose an evening dress of green taffetta with a fine double stripe woven in black, and a wide piece of lace draped diagonally across the skirt. The bodice had a pleated bertha and puffed sleeves. As Bellinda twirled joyfully in the dress, Hugh voiced his approval, telling her that the green matched the colour of her eyes perfectly.

However, she insisted that her two daytime attires be far less ostentatious. She chose an outfit in pale, stone-grey satin trimmed with black piping, and one of a similar design in a deep forest green. There were also other items to be considered. A spectacular fan created from black goose feathers was accompaniment to the evening dress, and with the day outfits, a matching bonnet for the green, and a black one for the grey. Hugh also insisted that she have two matching parasols as well. Finally, four petticoats were selected, together with three light-boned bodices that could not have been more comfortable to wear.

They ate lunch at a nearby restaurant. Bellinda sampled smoked salmon for the first time, and then a mouthwatering confection of chocolate mousse, a speciality of the house. They lingered a long time over the meal, savouring the growth of their newfound relationship. Bellinda told Hugh more of her determination to crusade against a law that allowed the abuse of children. Hugh then told her of how he came to inherit so much and of how he had never really felt guilty about his unearned wealth until he had met her. Afterwards, he described the many countries he had travelled to.

Nothing could have been more fascinating, for Hugh had journeyed extensively throughout Europe: to Rome, Paris, Berlin. She learned how different each country was from the other, how the Gallic temperament differed totally from the German and Italian.

Eagerly, Bellinda asked about the Coliseum in Rome and the Louvre in Paris. Hugh was only too willing to tell her just what it was like to see those marvels for the very first time. Only Thomas Groves-Hawkes had ever impressed her as being so learned, but then she had not been in love with him. To her, Hugh Maltravers seemed the most informed man in the world.

They returned to his home for afternoon tea, then Bellinda was advised to stay and take a short rest on the chaise longue.

'I should return to the mission,' she protested half-heartedly.

'Bellinda, are you questioning my conduct again?' There was a glint of humour in his dark eyes.

'Of course not, I now trust you to behave with perfect discretion.'

'How disappointing,' he teased. 'However, I really do not see any value in your returning to the mission for a few hours. It is, after all, customary for a lady of position to rest in the afternoons, especially when she will be dining with people as important as your past employers.'

'You mean the Gages?'

'I mean the Gages. Does that worry you?'

'A little, I suppose.'

His smile instantly reassured her. 'You have no right to be worried. As the companion of a titled lord, you are exalted above those two mere commoners.'

'Exalted! Now there's a thing.'

'We will also be joined by my cousin Adam, unfortunately.'

'Unfortunately?'

Another look of dark anger flashed across his face. 'Yes, unfortunately. You might well detect some animosity between us – he is envious of my wealth and title.'

'How foolish. A day amongst the wretched poor would soon cure his envy.'

Hugh smiled approvingly. 'My dear Bellinda, what blessed wisdom comes from your sweet lips.'

'In this instance, I prefer my thoughts to be described as common sense rather than wisdom.'

He laughed. 'Very well, common sense it shall be. Now, I leave you to take your rest, and shall be expecting to hear some more of your common sense tonight.'

Alone, she stretched upon the chaise longue and attempted to take a short nap. It was difficult, for her head was filled with a glorious carousel, spinning with images of the past few hours. At first it seemed impossible that she would ever sleep, but then the wine Hugh had so liberally poured into her glass during the meal began to take effect. Usually, it was sheer tiredness that caused her to drift off, but now it was a warm and glowing sense of contentment.

She was woken by a haggard serving girl who led her to a bedroom where her new evening dress and underwear were laid out. As soon as the girl left she slipped into the petticoats and fastened up the light-boned bodice. Then she stepped into the evening dress before joyfully twirling around the room.

'I can see that I should have made this an occasion for dancing.'

Instantly, Bellinda stopped. Undetected, Hugh had entered the room and was standing before her, stunning in his evening suit.

'Oh yes, how I would love to dance properly,' she said, again twirling around the room. 'One day you must teach me, Hugh.'

'That I shall, but first you must prepare yourself, our guests have already arrived.'

'They're here? But why didn't you wake me sooner?'

'Oh, there was no need for that. Besides, I've a suspicion that you never get enough sleep at the mission.'

'How thoughtful you are,' she said softly.

'Never before have I been attracted to someone of your age.'

'It worries me that I might be too young for you.'

Momentarily, a strange expression flashed across his face, but then he gave a dazzling smile. 'Let me say that my taste in women has taken a turn for the better.' He then retreated towards the half-opened door. 'I must now leave you to put the final touches that will make you even more beautiful than you are now,' he said, presenting her with a silk flower.

During the shopping trip Bellinda had also been treated to some cosmetics. Carefully she applied just a little rouge, enough to bring some colour to her cheeks. Then she brushed and lifted up her hair, fastening it at the back just as the Governess had once taught her to do. The final touch was the silk flower in her hair.

Bellinda looked in the mirror and was pleased with what she saw. In her expensive evening dress and with the extravagantly feathered fan in her hand, she looked every inch a woman of standing. Yes, she would face the Gages on equal terms tonight. Whether they liked it or not!

Confidently Bellinda entered the dining room – and almost dropped her fan. Seated at the table were not only the Gages and the arrogant Adam Carr, but Vanity Groves-Hawkes.

Carr showed the courtesy of standing up and giving a slight bow, but Vanity displayed an expression of sheer contempt before looking away. Hugh then ushered her towards a seat between himself and his cousin. Sitting opposite were the Gages.

While the salmon mousse was being served, John Gage leaned towards her. 'Hugh tells me the mission has become a great success.'

'We are only at the beginning,' she told him. 'It is the intention of Amity and myself to purge the streets of this dreadful trade once and for all.'

'Most commendable, I am sure that everyone in this room will agree with that.'

'Not all of us, I suspect,' Adam Carr said cynically.

'What can you mean by that?' Bellinda asked.

'Without child prostitutes where would our respected men of society go? Eh, Hugh?'

Lord Maltravers made no comment.

'Adam, your cynicism does you no credit,' John Gage said sharply.

'It might not do me credit but the truth is the truth. I neither approve nor do I disapprove of the situation. I simply accept it.'

'If everyone accepted the world as it is, nothing would ever be changed at all,' Bellinda said, doing her best to control her anger.

Adam Carr's blue eyes were full of mockery. 'Such noble zeal, such Christian dedication! I could not be more impressed.' He then turned to John Gage. 'It is just as well that this girl didn't stay for long in your household. She is too good for all of us.'

'I hardly think so, Adam,' Vanity said haughtily.

He ignored the remark and kept his attention focused on Bellinda. 'We are two of a kind, if you did but know it, for I too once fought a losing battle.'

'I shall not lose,' Bellinda said firmly.

He gave her another mocking look before diverting his attention to Hugh. 'I must compliment you upon your choice of companion, Cousin. Not only is she beautiful but spirited as well. But how long can this improvement in taste last, I wonder?'

Hugh glared angrily at his cousin. Bellinda did not understand what Adam meant by 'How long can this improvement last?' but she could almost taste the tension between them. Quickly, she turned to Harriet Gage. 'How is Jamie?'

There was no answer, just a look of disdain. It was now plainly obvious that, like Vanity, Harriet objected to the presence of an orphan and former servant girl at the same dining table as herself. John Gage looked clearly embarrassed by his wife's attitude.

'He is well enough and is now eager to learn more,' he told her.

'What splendid news. I do hope that he continues to improve his mind.'

'Indeed, for we cannot thank you enough for what you did,' John said. 'You must visit him some time.'

'John!' Harriet Gage glared at her husband.

'Well, not at the moment, of course,' he said awkwardly. 'Later perhaps.'

Bellinda was forced to reflect how foolish the Gages were in their behaviour. She would dearly have loved to see Jamie again.

The second course, roast pheasant and a selection of delicious vegetables, was served. Bellinda refused the accompanying claret for she still felt affected by the wine she had drunk during the day.

Resenting the hostility of the other guests, she decided not to speak again unless someone addressed her. It was as if she were a servant once more.

'We do so miss the presence of your father at this table,' Harriet Gage told Vanity in her frail voice.

'He never leaves my mother's side now that she is so ill,' Vanity said without any hint of distress.

'Consumption, I believe?'

'Yes.' Again Vanity sounded quite calm. 'It can only be a matter of time.'

'You poor child,' John Gage soothed. 'It must all be very distressing for you.'

'One does what one can,' Vanity said unconvincingly.

Bellinda would willingly have visited the dying Marguerite and given what comfort she could, had it been permissible. She was musing on the impossibility of this, and the conversation had gone on to other matters, when Adam Carr spoke to her.

'What a quiet companion Hugh has found for himself. I fear that, like me, small talk holds no real appeal.'

'It is not something I am practised in.'

'Nothing to be ashamed of,' he told her. 'I would much rather talk about your work at the mission.'

'But I thought that you didn't approve?'

'I don't, any more than my cousin, but an argument is always more stimulating than light conversation.'

'Hugh happens to be in full support of what Amity and I are attempting,' she said defiantly.

'Ha!'

'What do you mean by that?' Bellinda demanded, angered by his response.

'Adam, I think you should remember that it is me with whom you are dining,' Vanity interrupted sharply.

'How could I ever forget?' he asked sarcastically.

Fortunately, Hugh had now finished his conversation with the Gages and was ready to give Bellinda his full attention. Throughout the rest of the meal they spoke to no one but each other.

However, it was then time for the men to retire to the smoking room to talk business while the ladies took *chocolat chaud* in the drawing room. This was the moment Bellinda had been dreading, for she had no wish to be alone with two women who did not regard her as their equal.

Bellinda was soon to discover that *chocolat chaud* was hot chocolate. The sweet liquid was too hot to drink. Vanity and Harriet chatted as if she weren't there.

'I am so glad that you have befriended Adam Carr,' Harriet said.

'A pleasant enough companion until I find someone of a more worthy status,' Vanity answered coolly.

'Then Adam is not worthy enough?'

'Certainly not,' Vanity said haughtily. 'If it were not for his success in the City he would be a pauper.' She turned to Bellinda. 'No, I am more suited to someone like Hugh Maltravers. It is obvious that as he is in the company of a servant girl, he has yet to choose a proper companion.'

250

Harriet deigned to glance towards Bellinda. 'You could not be more right, my dear,' she said icily.

Enraged, Bellinda clattered her cup on to the table, and told the doe-eyed serving girl to summon the coachman. She stood fuming in the hallway until he arrived.

'Take me home,' she told him. 'I shall not stay in this place a moment longer!'

Throughout the short journey to Covent Garden, Bellinda's anger remained unabated. How dare they treat her so. How dare they!

As usual, Grebe Street was filled with prostitutes plying for trade. One of them spat at her as she alighted from the coach. Another told her in the foulest possible language to go back to wherever she came from and to stop interfering in their way of life. This was by no means the first time that Bellinda had been harassed. She had always shrugged it off, but tonight it was harder to endure than usual. She fumbled for her keys before managing to enter, relieved to shut out their derisive taunts. Quietly, she mounted the stairs. Amity was waiting for her on the landing.

'Where have you been all day?' she whispered angrily.

'With Hugh.'

'Well, while you have been indulging yourself, Florrie has died.'

Reeling from the shock, Bellinda grabbed at the banister.

'It can hardly come as a surprise, Bellinda. You knew she was dying.'

'Yes, but . . . '

'Yes but nothing! You chose to spend the day buying expensive clothes and being entertained. Soon you will become part of the society you have always claimed to loath.'

'That is unfair!' Bellinda protested.

'I think not. Good night, Bellinda!'

Amity turned her back and entered the dormitory. Bellinda went up to their room, removed her taffeta evening dress and hurled it angrily across the room so that it landed in an untidy heap. Weeping, she slipped beneath the rough sheets and vowed that never again would she wear such ostentatious clothes.

In the darkness she waited for Amity to arrive, until it became apparent that she was to spend the night alone. Now even her friend had spurned her.

What had possessed Bellinda to spend the evening with people who despised her? And should she not include Hugh Maltravers? Had he been more considerate she would not have been left in the same room with two women who held her in contempt. And the worst blow had come at the end. She and Amity had known a unique bond of friendship, and Bellinda had carelessly destroyed it. That friendship was gone. It was what she deserved, for to be absent during poor Florrie's final hours was unforgivable. Instead of doing her best to persuade Hugh Maltravers to put a Bill through the House of Lords to raise the age of consent, she had indulged herself in flirting with him. Yes, flirting. How else could it be described?

Despite the storm of sorrow and anger that she knew would keep her awake for most of the night, Bellinda resolved to see Maltravers once more and persuade him to act quickly. She now realized that her conscience would never rest until children like Florrie were saved from a wretched existence, one that could so easily end up in their suffering a slow and degrading death.

'I was not expecting to see you so soon after last night.'

'I am surprised that you expected me to come back at all,' Bellinda said sharply.

Hugh Maltravers crooked a sleek eyebrow, studying her with his penetrating black eyes. 'Then why did you?'

'I have come to urge you to raise a Bill concerning the age of consent.'

'And how will I benefit from such an undertaking?'

Why this sudden change of heart? Yesterday Maltravers had indicated that he would be only too willing to help Amity and herself in their cause. 'It is your Christian duty,' she told him.

His lips curled into a laconic smile. 'My Christian duty? Well, I must not neglect that.'

'Then you will help?'

'Of course, I believe that one of my colleagues is going to raise the matter. You can rest assured that I will be voicing my own opinion.'

'Another lord is involved?'

'Lord Trentham has already campaigned for the age of consent to be raised, but the old fellow has little influence. Nobody ever pays much attention to him.'

'But they will listen to you.'

Again he smiled laconically. 'Oh yes, they will listen to me.'

'Then the day will be won. I know it will.'

'Of course, my blessed innocent, the day will be won.'

'Oh praise be, Hugh. Shall I ever be able to thank you enough?'

'Well, you can start by joining me in a cup of *chocolat chaud*,' he said, adding with a grin, 'I believe you did not finish your cup last night.'

'They behaved abominably towards me,' Bellinda said angrily.

'I have little time for either of those two women, yet what else could I do but to leave you with them? It is customary for the men to retire to the smoking room after a meal.'

'It also seems customary for the rich never to accept anyone for what they are, only for their status.'

'There is at least one exception.'

'Is there?'

'You know there is, Bellinda.'

He was impossible to resist. More than anything else in the world she wanted to become enslaved by that dashing arrogance. One day they would wed and her desire to share his bed would finally be fulfilled.

'Oh I do so want that to be the truth.'

'It is.' His voice held a tantalizing hint of passion that matched her own.

'I cannot wait to try some *chocolat chaud* in the right company.'

He took the silver pot standing on the tray and poured some into his cup. 'I am sure you won't mind drinking from the same cup as myself,' he said, handing it to her.

'I am willing to share many things with you, Hugh'

'That is good to hear,' he said, his dark intense eyes never leaving her.

She sipped at the chocolate – mouthwateringly sweet, a nectar, a love potion, a drink beyond her wildest dreams.

'I can see that you have rapidly developed a taste for the beverage.'

'How could I fail? It is indeed very morish,' she smiled.

'But there is something that tastes even sweeter,' he said, taking the drained cup from her.

'And what can that be?' she asked, knowing the answer.

Bellinda caught her breath as he placed his hands on her shoulders and drew her to his waiting lips. There was a fierce hunger in his kiss, a hunger she felt compelled to sate. Upon a chariot of desire she was transported up into a golden-clouded sky. There she was at one with a mighty god who was holding her tighter and tighter to him, until she could feel the hardness of his manhood.

'Bellinda, you cannot know how I am tortured by you,' he gasped.

She arched her neck for him, revelling in each silken kiss. She too was tortured. How she longed to feel him even closer, to surrender to his fiery wanting.

Again they kissed with a savage passion. How could she resist him? In her mind she had surrendered to him. She was his to do with as he pleased.

'You know why you're here,' he whispered. 'You know!'

Suddenly she came to her senses. 'No, Hugh,' she protested.

'Bellinda, what are you afraid of? I am your eternal slave. Yours until the end of forever.'

Were they not deeply in love? Would that love not be bonded for ever by their lovemaking? Theirs was a desire that would never cease.

No! The Governess had been adamant in her warning. If he really loved her then he would wait until wedlock. A good many of the prostitutes in Covent Garden were single girls who, having found themselves pregnant through love, were now forced to walk the streets. She could so easily suffer the same fate.

'Please, Hugh, no more,' she begged as she tried to free herself from his grasp.

He refused to let her go, tightening his grip. 'You will be mine. You *are* mine!'

'Yes, but not yet,' she protested. 'Not this way.'

His fingers dug deep before he threw her to the floor. 'How dare you refuse me, you little whore!' he raged down at her.

Shocked by this sudden attack, Bellinda struggled to get back on her feet, but before she could do so, Maltravers viciously kicked her. His boot cracked against her shoulder. The pain was incredible. He tried to kick her again but she managed to roll out of the way.

Maltravers threw himself on top of her, frenziedly, wrenching at the front of her dress as she kicked and struggled. He was like a wild animal, forcing her to use all her own animal instincts for survival.

It was no use, she was no match for his angry strength. Having managed to undo the first button, he ripped the others away from their shanks. No longer was he Hugh Maltravers, but a raging madman.

He then hit her hard across the face, before delivering another blow and then another. Momentarily Bellinda passed into an empty, comforting void but then she returned to the horror of reality. No, she must *not* give in, allow him to do as he pleased. Somehow she would have to fight back. Bellinda struggled for control of her senses as the warm darkness beckoned. No, he shall not win. He shall not win!

Bellinda knew that she had only one chance to save herself. There could be no mistakes. She put two fingers together and jabbed. Her aim was perfect. Maltravers howled with pain as the fingers were rammed into his eye. Her parasol had fallen to the floor. If she could reach it . . .

In one desperate movement she grabbed the parasol and brought it down hard against the back of Maltravers' head. He groaned, weakened by the blow. Still on her knees, she hit him once more. This time the sharp handle cracked against his ear. Again he groaned, a hand against his injured eye.

It would not be long before he recovered. Now was her only chance to escape. Still dazed, she struggled to her feet, lurching towards the door and dragging it open. She was now faced with a dizzy descent of the stairs. Holding on to the banister she stumbled down to the hall. The big heavy door was another obstacle to her ebbing strength – and pray God it was unlocked! To her relief, the door swung open easily and Bellinda staggered out into the daylight. She almost collapsed on the porch but managed to regain her balance. Still dazed, she tottered out on to the pavement. A woman with a small child passed by, ignoring her plight. Then she heard the sound of clattering hooves alongside.

'Need any help, Miss?'

Bellinda turned and saw that the voice belonged to the driver of a hansom cab. He leapt down and opened the cab door before helping her inside. After gasping out her address she sank into the padded leather seat. As the cab pitched and rolled its way towards Covent Garden, she was forced to relive the nightmare of what had just happened, over and over again.

'In Heaven's name!'

'Found her wandering the streets like this,' the driver told Amity as he helped Bellinda into the mission. 'Looks like someone's given her a right battering.'

Clutching on to the burly driver, Bellinda watched Amity offer him some money. He shook his head.

'No need for that,' he said. 'Glad to be of 'elp, but best I gets back to me 'orse 'afore he decides to go a'walking off without me.'

After thanking the driver, Amity caught hold of Bellinda and held her close. 'Oh dearest of friends, what has happened to you?'

Bellinda wept with relief, feeling safe at last in the arms of her soulmate. 'It was Maltravers,' she sobbed. 'He tried to rape me.'

'He *what*?'

'He was like a madman. A madman!'

'Then we must go to the police.'

'It's no use, they won't want to charge a lord.'

'But *I* will!' Amity raged.

'I just want to rest, to sleep,' Bellinda said blearily.

'Then sleep you shall. I'll help you upstairs'

As soon as she was helped on to her bed, Bellinda conceded to the dark oblivion that had beckoned during the attack. The fear, the pain, all began to fade. With Amity sitting upon the side of the bed, she felt safe at last.

'Bell, there is someone to see you.'

'Must I speak to anyone at the moment?'

'Not if you don't want to, but he insists that what he has to say is very important.'

'He?'

'Adam Carr.'

'Adam Carr. What can that cynic want? Tell him to go away.'

'Best to see him, Bell. Tell him the truth about his cousin.'

'You mean you haven't?'

Amity shook her head. 'The conversation never got that far – it's you he's come to see.'

The room at the bottom of the house was now un-occupied by children, and the prospect of being alone with a relative of Maltravers made her feel uneasy. She left the door slightly ajar.

Like Maltravers, Adam Carr was undeniably hand-some, dashing in his navy frock coat and slim grey trousers. He looked startled by her appearance. 'What has happened? What bounder has been hitting you?'

Bellinda was impressed by his concern for her, but refused to show it. 'I have been attacked by your cousin,'

'Maltravers did that?' His crystal-blue eyes flashed with anger. 'He'll not get away with it. I'll kill him with my own bare hands, I swear I will!'

Once again, Bellinda was impressed by his attitude. However, it was impossible to forget how cynical he had been about her work during Maltravers' dinner party. 'There has always been a different law for people of your class,' she said contemptuously.

'I doubt if you realize the *full* import of what you have just said. There is much that you should know about my respectable cousin.'

'I now know more than I will ever *want* to about Maltravers.'

'Bellinda, I didn't have to come here, you know.'

'I suppose not,' she conceded reluctantly. 'Please continue.'

'What prompted me to call was something that was said after you left the dinner party,' he began. 'Harriet and Vanity immediately came to the smoking room and joined us. When Maltravers heard what had happened, he guffawed loudly. Yes, all of them were mocking you, Bellinda. My cousin made no secret of the fact that he regarded you as nothing more than a desirable amuse-ment.'

'Amusement? Is that how he defines rape?' Bellinda asked bitterly.

'Rape?'

'He almost succeeded in raping me.'

Anger flashed across Adam's features. 'I'll kill him,' he growled. 'I'll kill him!'

Now Bellinda really was unable to deny how impressed she was by his concern. 'I confess to being flattered by your reaction.'

'Yes, well, in away you should be flattered,' he said grimly, 'there is no more enthusiastic customer of the girls you are trying to save than Hugh Maltravers.' Then he shrugged. 'It's what you'd expect from someone like him, it's never surprised me.'

Bellinda's stomach tightened, for a moment she was rendered speechless. 'You seem unmoved by the plight of the children yet offended by the way he has treated me?' she finally managed to ask.

'Dash it! I know that must sound odd, but I truly admired the way you argued with me.'

'And now you find yourself agreeing with me, I suppose?'

His diamond eyes sparkled. 'Bellinda, I would never agree with everything you said – on principle.'

She was in no mood to be charmed. 'How much more do you know about Maltravers?'

'I know that he frequents this area and when he finds a child who particularly interests him, he takes her back to Belgravia, keeps her there for a few weeks, tires of her, and then throws her out.'

Immediately Bellinda thought of Sara. Had *she* been abused by him? Never did a man deserve to be brought to justice more than Hugh Maltravers! 'I think Amity should be told about this,' she said, and went to fetch her.

'I have just been telling Bellinda about Maltravers,' Adam told Amity.

'That man is going to pay for what he did to Bellinda. I've already been to the police.'

'I didn't know that,' Bellinda said.

'You were asleep.'

'And what did they say?'

'You're right about this country, Bell, there is a different law for the rich,' she said angrily.

'Maltravers can get away with what he likes, I'm afraid,'

Amity turned to Adam Carr. 'Is that what you've been telling Bellinda?'

'I have been telling her a lot more than that.'

Bellinda took Amity's hand in her own and said, 'Maltravers abuses little girls.'

'What?'

'He has been indulging himself for many years, I suspect,' Adam told her.

'Then why was he interested in Bellinda?'

He looked at Bellinda with a beguiling warmth in his eyes. 'Because she is utterly unique. She has a haunting beauty of spirit that is the rarest of rare amongst women.'

Embarrassed by his words, Bellinda averted her gaze. How she detested these attempts to charm her. Could the fool not realize that she now loathed all men? Especially one who was related to Hugh Maltravers.

'Lizzie said something that made me wonder the other day,' Amity said pensively.

'You think she might have been referring to Maltravers?' Bellinda asked.

Amity nodded.

'Then best I leave you two to speak to her.'

'Mr Carr, I cannot thank you enough for telling us this.'

He looked at Bellinda. 'I am sorry if I have distressed you even more than is necessary.'

'It needed to be said, and I am grateful to you, Sir.'

He smiled.

Once again he seemed to be trying to charm her. Once again she felt angered. 'No doubt you will continue to do business with your cousin, despite his ways,' she said coldly.

'Believe me I shall not, even if I starve. Never!'

'Then that is to your credit,' she conceded reluctantly.

He gave another smile. 'I shall treasure the fact that you have given me a little credit, Bellinda.'

As soon as Adam had left them, Bellinda and Amity went upstairs to see Lizzie, a nine-year-old who had always seemed frightened of something, right from the very first day she had walked into the mission.

'The man who came here after Polly had been found beaten, you knew him?' Amity asked her.

Lizzie nodded.

'Then, child, you must tell me what you know.'

She shook her head. 'Can't! Won't!'

Bellinda knelt down and took both of the girl's hands in her own. 'Lizzie, you must tell us.'

'But 'e'll 'it me,' she sobbed. 'Knock me about, like he did last time.'

'Did you go to his house?'

'Yes,' she snuffled. ''E said I was 'is favourite little girl, that 'e was going to look after me.'

'And then what happened?'

Lizzie began to cry profusely, her whole body quivering. Bellinda hugged her until she had calmed down.

''E did things ter me. Tied me up. Knocked me about. Made me do things ter 'im, lots of things.'

'Oh Lizzie, you poor child.'

'Didn't mind at first 'cos he kept feeding me with fancy food and bringing me nice clothes to wear. But then one day he just throws me out.' She blanched, her eyes full of terror. ''E said if I told anyone what he'd bin doing ter me then 'e'd make sure Jack did the business on me.'

'Jack? The business?' Amity asked.

'Don't want a beating from Mad Jack.'

'Yes, but who is he?'

'Jack just does for girls who don't do what they're told.'

Bellinda suddenly recalled the night when Polly had been attacked on the mission doorstep, then saved from further harm by Maltravers. 'Was Polly beaten by Mad Jack that night?'

'Who else?'

'Oh Lizzie, if only you had told us about him,' Amity scolded mildly.

'All of us is too scared ter say anything about Mad Jack or 'Is Lordship.'

Amity turned to Bellinda, her face ashen. 'Come outside,' she said grimly.

'What is it?' Bellinda asked as soon the dormitory door was closed.

'I've just had a terrible thought, Bell. I think Mad Jack was told to stay away from the mission by Lord Maltravers.'

A cold shiver swept through Bellinda's body. 'And now that he has shown himself in his true light, Mad Jack might be told that he can do as he pleases with the mission.'

'Exactly!'

'We must tell the police.'

'Tell the police,' Amity repeated mockingly. 'And what could they do? Put a constable on guard for twenty-four hours a day? No, there can only be one answer. I am going to see him right now.'

'Who?'

'Why Adam Carr, of course.'

'Amity, have you gone insane? I don't trust him.'

'Well I do, I trust him implicitly and I'm going to see him right now. I know where he lives.'

'I don't want a relative of Maltravers staying here, amongst all these children,' Bellinda protested.

'Oh Bell, you cannot judge every man you meet by Maltravers' disgusting standards. We will have to sleep in the dormitory and he can have our room.'

'So now you intend to treat him like a king!'

'Sometimes there is no reasoning with you,' Amity sighed before hurrying down the stairs and out into the street.

Angered, Bellinda now had no choice but to bolt the door and hope that her American friend would be safe. She would count every moment until Amity came back. However, the prospect of her returning with the arrogant Adam Carr filled Bellinda with the strongest misgivings.

Chapter 23

'Oh, Bellinda, isn't it splendid? Adam has agreed to stay here as long as we need him.'

'And where is he going to sleep?' Bellinda demanded, behaving as if he were not present.

'Bell, we've been into all that. Adam can sleep in our room and we'll just have to manage in the dormitory.'

What Amity was suggesting was absurd. There was hardly any room in the dormitory now. How Bellinda resented this man's presence. Adam Carr had no place in a mission for small girls. Despite the circumstances, as far as she was concerned his presence could not be more unwelcome. 'I'll go and move our things before Mr Carr makes himself at home,' she said angrily.

'Why don't I sleep down here on the chaise longue?' Adam suggested.

'Adam, that is impossible. You would be most uncomfortable,' Amity protested.

'I can assure you that I have slept in far worse conditions in the army.'

'You were in the army?'

'I was a captain, during the Crimean War.'

Amity turned to Bellinda. 'Did you hear that, Bell? We have a war hero protecting us.'

Bellinda remained silent.

'What regiment did you serve in, Adam?'

'The Light Brigade.'

'You were one of the gallant six hundred?'

'One of those lucky enough to survive – but please, I have no wish to impose my memories of those terrible times upon you,' he said before turning to Bellinda. 'Don't worry, I will not be staying here one moment longer than is necessary. You have my word.'

263

'I am glad to hear it,' she said coldly. 'Now, I must attend to the children before going to bed myself.'

'I can lend a hand with any chores.'

'You, a man who can do chores?' Amity asked in wonder.

'There was a time in my life when I could not afford any servants. I had to do everything – cooking, cleaning, washing.'

'A captain in the Light Brigade who can do all these other things. Bellinda, just what *have* we found?'

Bellinda was sure he was boasting, or trying to ingratiate himself. Adam Carr was of the privileged classes. Never at all did such people have to soil their hands. Wishing to hear no more, she left the room.

It seemed like an eternity before Amity joined her – with no apology for keeping Bellinda waiting. 'Oh, Adam is indeed a most interesting man,' she sighed. 'That night at the Gages' party I had little chance to speak to him, but now that I have I find him quite acceptable.'

'Really.'

'Yes, Bellinda, really. Why are you so hostile towards him?'

'Because I do not like him. Surely that is a good enough reason?'

'Reason? You have lost all sense of reason as far as I can see.'

What point was there in quarrelling? Angrily, Bellinda blew out the candle at her bedside before turning upon her side, without even saying the customary goodnight. Sheer exhaustion ensured that she soon fell into a deep sleep.

Bellinda awoke to the sound of the landing being scrubbed. Daylight was streaming in through the window as she delicately rubbed the sleep out of her eyes. The hand on their clock showed at eight. As the other hand was missing, she could not tell the exact time, but clearly she had overslept to a shamefully late hour. She dressed hurriedly, while the sound of scrubbing continued.

'Well, at last Her Ladyship has risen,' Adam Carr mocked as he stood upon the landing, dressed in shirt sleeves and trousers. In his hand was a scrubbing brush and beside him a bucket of water.

'Most mornings I am awake before you have even contemplated rising from your bed,' she riposted.

Adam Carr laughed heartily. 'Oh Bellinda, how you misjudge me. Do you really think I could have made any kind of success for myself had I not been up and about, well ahead of my rivals in the City?'

'I neither know nor care,' she retorted. 'It is Amity who is easily impressed by you, not me.'

'I am flattered to hear it, but I didn't come here to impress anyone. I came here to – '

'Bellinda! Adam!'

'What's the matter?' Bellinda asked urgently as Amity hurried up the stairs.

'Have we not forgotten Polly?'

A cold shiver swept through Bellinda. Polly had been taken away by Maltravers. No wonder the poor child had been terrified when he lifted her and carried her to his coach. 'Oh Amity, what have we done? What have we *done*?'

'I don't know, Bell,' Amity said grimly.

'What's the matter?' Adam asked.

'Polly, one of the children, was found severely beaten,' Amity told him. 'Like utter fools, we allowed Maltravers to take her away. He promised to find a place for her on his country estate.'

'Country estate? Maltravers has no country estate.'

Bellinda gasped in horror and Amity clutched at her hand.

'Adam, are you really sure?'

'Yes, Amity, I am quite sure.'

'Then what could have happened to her?' Bellinda asked shakily.

'Now, please, neither of you must rush to any conclusions.'

'It is difficult not to,' Bellinda insisted, her voice quavering.

There was an undeniable warmth in his eyes. 'Needless to say, I will do everything in my power to find her.'

'What do you suggest?'

Adam stroked his chin as he thought hard about the situation. 'We will go to the police,' he finally said.

'I went to them before about Maltravers,' Amity uttered dejectedly. 'They refused to investigate his attempt to rape Bellinda.'

'I am not surprised. Hugh is regarded as too important a dignitary to be accused of such a crime, but if a cousin of his were to go and see them, then . . . ' He stroked his chin again. 'Yes, I think that might be different.'

'Are you going to see the police now?' Amity asked urgently.

'Straight away,' he answered before turning to Bellinda. 'I think it best that you come with me.'

'I would rather stay here and look after the children. Why not take Amity with you?'

He shook his head. 'No, I think you should come to the station. Tell them again about his attempt to rape you. I believe they'll be more likely to listen this time.'

'But then the mission will be unguarded.'

He turned to Amity. 'I have brought my pistol with me. I'll show you how to use it.'

'No need, my papa taught me.'

He grinned. 'Thank God for American ways in times of crisis. I'll hand it over to you before we leave.'

Outside, after listening for Amity to draw the bolts across the door, Adam and Bellinda hastened to Bow Street police station.

'Can I help you, Sir?' a burly sergeant asked as soon as they arrived.

'Yes, I want to see your superior officer,' Adam said with quiet authority.

266

'That'll be Inspector O'Hara. But you'll have to tell me what it's about.'

'I am talking about a possible murder.'

The sergeant raised his bushy eyebrows before leaving the desk and vanishing into the station.

As soon as the word 'murder' had been mentioned, Bellinda's stomach tightened. 'Can you really believe that?' she asked shakily.

'I only said that to gain the sergeant's full attention. There is no need to draw any conclusions at the moment,' he whispered.

Bellinda was far from reassured. There was a very real possibility that Maltravers had actually had Polly killed. It could not be denied. She was now trembling, uncontrollably.

'Bellinda, what is the matter?'

'Nothing, it will pass.'

'Nothing be damned! You must not blame yourself.'

Bellinda could control her tears no longer. 'What else can I do?' she wept. 'What else can I do?'

Suddenly she was in his arms. 'There now,' Adam was saying gently. 'There now.'

'Would there be something the matter with the young lady?'

Through eyes misted by tears Bellinda saw that the lilting Irish voice belonged to a cadaverously featured man with curly grey hair, and yellowing teeth clamped over a smoking pipe.

'I shall soon be in control of my distress,' she told him, fighting to hold back her tears.

'Then best you both be coming into my office and telling me all about it,' he managed to say with his pipe still between his teeth.

There was a cloying fog of tobacco smoke in the Inspector's office and the top of his desk was strewn with papers. 'Look at all this mess,' he said after offering them seats opposite. ''Tis nothing more on God's good earth that I abhor than paperwork.' Then his eyes twinkled. 'But a murder is much more me style. Much more!'

'Especially when a certain Lord Maltravers is involved,' Adam added.

'Lord Maltravers? Murder? What are you saying?'

'I'm saying that you should investigate the disappearance of a child called Polly.'

'From my experience, lords don't go around murdering little girls.'

'Even when you know them to be rapists?'

The Inspector's eyes narrowed. 'Are you referring to the time when an American girl came here with wild claims that Lord Maltravers had tried to molest her friend?'

'I am indeed, and I can assure you that it was no wild claim. This lady was his victim.'

Momentarily, the Inspector stopped smoking his pipe and looked closely at Bellinda's bruised face. 'I'll be honest with you,' he said, 'it doesn't surprise me that he tried to molest you, except that small children are usually more to his taste.'

Bellinda was stunned. 'You know about him yet you do nothing?'

'Yes, Miss. 'Tis to our shame.'

'Because of his friends in high places, I suppose?'

'Yes, Sir. People like him can get away with what they like. It makes me sick.'

Suddenly Adam banged a fist down hard upon the desk, causing O'Hara to jerk back in his chair. The smoking pipe dropped from his mouth and clattered on the floor.

'This time you *are* going to do something about him! Make no mistake about that!' Adam roared.

'And who might you be to start throwing your weight about?' the Inspector demanded.

'Someone who has the connections to make you and your servile colleagues' lives an utter misery, unless you do the job for which you are paid.'

O'Hara glared at Adam after picking up his smouldering pipe from the floor. 'And what do you suggest I do? Go up to his house and question him?'

'It's not a suggestion. It is a demand! I won't rest until the child he has abducted is safely returned to the mission.'

'So now it's abduction, is it? A minute ago you were talking about murder!'

'Look, I shall be dining with the Commissioner next week. It's up to you how I describe your performance over this case.'

'The Commissioner? You're bluffing.'

Adam raised an eyebrow. 'Am I?' he asked coolly.

His face flushed red with anger, O'Hara stood up and kicked his chair aside. 'Come on then,' he growled. 'I just hope you two are right, that's all.'

When they arrived at Belgravia, the butler led them up to Maltravers' study. Before they entered the room, Bellinda shuddered. In the next moment she would be confronted by the man who had tried to rape her.

'Adam, Bellinda, and a police Inspector. Why am I so honoured?' Maltravers asked innocently.

'It's official business I'm afraid, Sir,' O'Hara answered obsequiously.

'Not more burglaries, I hope?'

'No, Sir, it's about – '

'It's about two matters, Cousin. First there is the attempted rape of Bellinda, and then there is the disappearance of a little girl called Polly.'

Maltravers placed both hands upon his hips, threw back his head, and laughed. 'I a rapist? An abductor? Could anything be more absurd?'

'You deny it then, Your Lordship?'

'Yes Inspector, I deny my cousin's preposterous accusation. Utterly! Totally!'

'My God, you're a liar!' Adam stormed. 'Bellinda is still bruised by your vicious attack.'

Maltravers looked straight at Bellinda and smiled. She now saw that smile for what it truly was, as belonging to a man without scruples, utterly wicked. 'Bellinda, my dear, I know that we quarrelled but surely you can't believe that I tried to rape you.'

'Could I be intruding on you to tell me what the quarrel was about, Your Lordship?'

He turned to O'Hara. 'You certainly may, Inspector. Bellinda was offended by my offering to donate five thousand pounds to her cause.'

'Offended? Why should she be offended?'

'These are pure lies!' Bellinda protested.

O'Hara ignored her protests and asked Maltravers the same question.

'Well, I suspect that Bellinda thinks I am trying to take over the running of her mission, but my argument was that none of that mattered, only the welfare of those wretched children.'

'You can't believe any of this, O'Hara!' Adam raged. 'You know the truth about him.'

'Although the Inspector might appreciate the perils of slandering me, dear cousin, it appears that you do not,' Maltravers threatened.

'It's just the truth that I've come to trouble Your Lordship about.'

'And it is the truth that I have given you.'

'Yes, thank you, most grateful, Your Lordship. Most grateful!'

'In God's name!' Adam blazed. 'This man is evil and perverted – and you know it, O'Hara!'

'Bide your tongue, Carr,' Maltravers snarled. 'Bide your tongue!'

'I'll not bide my tongue until you show me where Polly is.'

Maltravers' lips curled into a self-satisfied smile. 'Why, she is here, having just returned from my place in the country.'

'Place in the country? What place in the country?'

'Why, my farm in Kent. If you recall, Cousin, it was you who suggested that I divert some of my capital into such an enterprise.'

'Where is Polly? Where is she?' Bellinda demanded, desperate to see the child.

His expression was smug as he pointed to the door, which was slowly opening. Polly entered. She rushed over and wrapped her tiny arms around Bellinda's waist.

'Oh Bellinda, take me back. Take me back.'

Bellinda clutched the child to her. 'Of course I will, little love.'

'I was going to return her today,' Maltravers said to O'Hara. 'I realized that she would be happiest with Bellinda.'

'I'm sure you were, Your Lordship.'

'In God's name, man! Maltravers had no intention of doing so,' Adam raged at the Inspector. 'You should be asking Polly whether she's been ill treated.'

O'Hara jabbed a finger at Adam. 'I'll do no such thing. Not only have you accused His Lordship of murder but of molesting the young lady too. I ought to be arresting you both for wasting the police's valuable time!'

'It is all right, Inspector, I will make no complaints against my hot-tempered cousin. Nor Bellinda, whose fertile imagination seems to have run riot,' Maltravers said arrogantly.

Bellinda saw Adam's face turn crimson, a hand already bunched into a fist. 'Please, take us home,' she begged, hoping to divert his attention before anger got the better of him and he lashed out at either Maltravers or the Inspector.

'Yes, of course,' he told her before turning to his cousin. 'This will not be the end of the matter, Maltravers.'

'I think it had better be, for your sake,' O'Hara warned. 'There's no need for you to go telling your friend the Commissioner. I shall be doing that myself.'

Once again Maltravers threw back his head and gave a scornful laugh. 'Carr told you he knew the Commissioner? At last we really have heard a proper lie. He is no more acquainted with that gentleman than I am.'

271

Once again Adam's hand was bunched into a fist. 'I'll not rest until you're in Newgate,' he growled before Bellinda took hold of his other hand.

'Please, we must take Polly away from here,' she begged.

Adam nodded, glared at his cousin and escorted Bellinda and Polly out into the street. As they stood on the pavement, hoping to catch the attention of a passing hansom cab driver, Bellinda was still holding Adam's hand.

Thankfully, a driver soon stopped for them. Throughout the journey back to Grebe Street, Polly did not stop crying upon Bellinda's shoulder.

At the mission, Amity took hold of the child and hugged her. 'Oh Polly, you're safe. You're safe!'

Adam turned to Bellinda. 'You must be feeling very relieved.'

'I was convinced that she had been murdered.'

He smiled. His anger was gone, replaced by an aura of strong and reassuring tenderness. 'I have to admit, I too feared that.'

'Yet, we do not know what Maltravers has been doing to her.'

'No, but I can imagine.'

Bellinda turned and looked down at Polly who was now clinging to Amity's waist. 'Such vile acts are unthinkable.'

'They are,' Adam agreed as Beattie, a freckle-faced child who always reminded Bellinda of Sara, took hold of Adam's hand.

'You seem to have a way with the children.'

He laughed, his blue eyes sparkling. 'Can't think why, I've never had any of my own.'

'Then this will serve as practice for you,' she said, now without any hint of animosity in her voice.

'Bellinda, I can assure you that I am very different from my cousin.'

'I'm beginning to realize that,' she said softly, 'but first I must help Amity to assure Polly that her nightmare is finally over.'

His smile made her feel warm inside. Yes, he was indeed very different from his cousin. 'No matter how you regard me, I shall never be able to compete with your good causes,' he said affectionately.

'Polly must come first,' she said, returning his smile before hurrying over to the frightened child.

'Oh Bellinda, he won't ever come 'ere again will 'e?'

She kissed the child's forehead. 'No, my little love, I promise you Maltravers will never darken this door again.'

'Men was always doing things te me,' Polly said, tears still streaming down her cheeks. 'But 'e was the worst. 'E was cruel.'

Bellinda turned to Amity. 'Why is this world so abominable?' she raged.

Amity took hold of Bellinda's hand. 'If it were not so, Bell, then there would be no need for either of us.'

Bellinda returned her attention to Polly. 'Maltravers told me that you were going to be looked after at his country estate.'

Polly shook her head. ''E was lying. 'E had me locked away in 'is attic. I even 'eard your voice once. I wanted to cry out but I knew if I did, then 'e'd beat me 'ard.'

'Had he been beating you when we found you at the mission door that night?'

She shook her head. 'That was Mad Jack.'

'And why did he beat you?' Amity asked.

''E said it was a warning, so that I'd keep me mouth shut.'

'Keep shut about what?'

She looked up at Amity. 'All us girls 'ere 'as been told ter come ter the mission.'

'I don't understand,' Bellinda said.

'Mad Jack just came up ter some of us. Said we better go ter the mission or it would be the worse fer us.'

'Why?'

Jenny shook her head. 'Dunno.'

'I think I do.'

Bellinda turned round to discover Adam standing behind her. 'What can be the reason?' she asked.

'Right from the start, my devious cousin encouraged the running of this mission. Am I correct?'

'I remember Maltravers predicting that within a few days after his visit, our mission would be full,' Amity said thoughtfully.

'And was it?' he asked knowingly.

'At the time it seemed like a miracle,' Bellinda told him.

'It was no miracle,' Adam said grimly. 'With the help of this Jack fellow, he made sure that your mission succeeded.'

'Don't make no sense ter me, Mister,' Polly said.

Adam knelt down and tousled her hair. 'Probably doesn't, little one, but I want you to tell me where Mad Jack lives.'

'Down other end of Grebe Street,' she told him readily. 'Got a room at forty-one.'

'Adam, you're not thinking of going down there. He's a very dangerous man!' Bellinda gasped.

'So am I,' he told her. 'So am I!'

Chapter 24

It had been one of those nights. Jack had only intended to down a couple of ales before going about his proper business. Unfortunately a pair of tarts, who should have been out on the streets touting for business, had persuaded him to make a night of it. One drink led to another, and then another.

What a skinful! Now his head throbbed, his mouth was dry, and worst of all, he kept wanting to vomit but couldn't. All Mad Jack wanted was to go back to bed and sleep it off. Would have done so, had not His Lordship been wanting to see one of Jack's latest offerings. Just eight years old she was, and a real virgin. Not many of those about these days. There'd be a pretty price to pay for the chance to violate her. All that terror and confusion and pain. How Lord Maltravers would enjoy himself. Of course the man was touched in the head, but that was no concern of Jack's. The rich could do as they pleased, so long as they kept lining his pockets.

Maybe a wash would liven him up? Usually, Jack had no time for water. Sometimes people would complain about how he smelt so bad, but it never worried him. Ever since he'd nearly drowned in the Thames, he'd got to hating the stuff more and more. Today was different. A couple of splashes in the face might just liven him up.

In his room was a washbasin, covered in grime and with a crack that oozed water when the basin was filled. As soon as he lowered his head, it began to throb even more. Just how many ales had he got through last night?

He turned on the tap and some brown water dribbled out. If he waited it might clear. Anyway, what was he doing in this hovel, a man of his position? These days people respected him, a man with some money in his pocket. It was about time he got himself a proper room and a regular woman, instead of using whores all the time.

The door crashed open. He turned around, but too late. A fist hammered into his face. He reeled against the basin, and a fist jabbed hard into his stomach. As Jack doubled up with pain, he was hit hard on the jaw. Now, the agony was unbearable. The whole of his face burned and his stomach was aching sharply.

He managed to parry away the next blow. Now it was his turn to do the hitting. Angrily he lashed out at his attacker. The man staggered from his punch. Jack would press home his advantage. Very soon this bastard would be begging for mercy. Too late. His assailant recovered quickly, catching Jack off guard. A fist smacked into his face. Again he lashed out but this time all he hit was air. He'd left himself wide open. The next punch was the worst so far, almost knocking him unconscious.

Thrown against the wall, Jack cowered, waiting for a rain of blows to add to his torture. They never came. Through blurred vision he looked up. Even in this state he could tell that this bloke was a gent. But who?

'Listen to me.' The voice was menacing. 'This little beating is just a taster. Understand?'

Jack nodded, blood gushing from his nose.

'I never want to see your face in London again.'

London was Jack's home, his life. Where else could he go? Limply he shook his head in protest. He should not have done that. The beating started again. Blows rained down upon him – to his face, his body and, finally, one that cracked against his already broken nose. Jack was now terrified for his life. He was dying. In a way that was what he wanted. The agony was unbearable.

'Get out of London, or you'll be dead. Understand?'

This was no threat. This was a promise, Jack realized now. He nodded again, this time with more urgency.

276

He would even have said something had not his mouth been too painful to open.

'Good, now we're getting somewhere. Before this day is out I want you gone from here.'

Again, Jack nodded. There was definitely a merciless quality about that voice. The gent was no stranger to killing, he could tell.

Mad Jack had hoped that the beating was over. It was not to be. Another cruel blow was delivered straight to his eye, momentarily blinding him. He collapsed, groaning.

Although he then heard the man leave, Jack now had every intention of doing what had been commanded. He would get out of Grebe Street, even London. Probably end up starving to death, but what else could he do? He was now too scared to stay. That was for sure.

'Adam, are you all right? What's happened to your hands and face?' Bellinda asked anxiously.

'Just a little bruised,' he answered casually.

'You found Mad Jack then?'

'We had a little talk,' Adam said wryly. 'He has decided to leave London.'

'Did you hear that, children?' Amity said loudly. 'Mad Jack will soon be gone!'

Betty, who had always prided herself upon being the noisiest child in the mission, gave a loud cheer. The others joined in, screeching joyfully as they flocked around Adam.

Bellinda noticed that his first reaction was embarrassment, but then his expression changed to sheer delight.

'Muffins for all!' he announced. 'We shall be having hot muffins for supper.'

Then, as if he were the Pied Piper, he led them all out into Grebe Street. Bellinda turned to Amity and they both laughed before joining in the procession to the muffin man.

Fortunately, the bemused muffin seller was able to provide each child with a muffin. Paternally, Adam watched them enjoy the treat, then he led them to the chestnut seller and, after they had feasted upon chestnuts, to a pie shop. Afterwards he turned to Bellinda and Amity. 'My money is spent,' he declared laughingly. 'Now a pauper, I must seek refuge in your mission.'

Bellinda grabbed one arm, Amity the other, and together they threaded their way through Covent Garden, the children following. Back at the mission, the kettle was boiled and piping hot tea was made. Many of the children then pestered Adam to hear every violent detail of how he had persuaded Mad Jack to leave London. Adam declined, constantly. The girls were becoming a nuisance. Amity and Bellinda jointly decided to send them to bed for an early night.

'Peace at last,' Adam said as he slumped into the chaise longue, stretching out his legs.

'You, the centre of so much attention, now crave for peace?' Bellinda teased.

'I do! I do!' he chuckled.

'Well you're not going to get it,' Amity told him. 'It might not have been suitable for the children's ears but *I* want to hear how you dealt with that villain, blow by blow.'

Adam shook his head. 'I am afraid not, I get no pleasure from such a task. Violence is sometimes necessary, but always terrible. I learned that in the Crimea.'

'I suppose you don't want to talk about that either?'

'No, Amity, I'm sorry to disappoint you. Believe me when I tell you that there is nothing glorious about war. Nothing at all.'

'Of course war is glorious. Valiant are the brave! My brother Tom fought for the Union army and lost his life,' she said angrily. 'How dare you cast a shadow upon his hallowed name!'

'I meant no offence.'

'That may be, but offence has been taken.' Amity's face was now flushed by anger.

'Then I apologize.'

278

Amity suddenly burst into tears. Bellinda rushed over to put an arm around her shoulder. The offer was shrugged away. 'I just want to be alone,' Amity wailed, and left the room.

Bellinda was tempted to follow her friend up the stairs, but resisted. The death of Tom Smallwood had made a deep emotional scar, and it was best to leave Amity to grieve by herself.

Adam stood up from the chaise longue. 'I think I should be leaving.'

'Adam, you are not responsible for what has just happened. Please believe that.'

His crystal-blue eyes were glowing with a deep affection. 'Oddly enough I believe most things you tell me, Bellinda.'

'And I believe you when you say that war is not the glorious affair that books and newspapers would have us believe.'

'Never have truer words been spoken,' he agreed solemnly before sitting down again. 'However, I can understand how Amity feels. The American Civil War must have been the very worst kind of war of all. Americans killing Americans.' He shook his head. 'That just does not bear thinking about.'

'I am sure Amity will have forgiven you by tomorrow.'

'I hope so, it was tactless of me to say that about warfare.'

'You were not to know.'

'No, I suppose I was not. However, I knew what I was saying when we met at that dinner party.'

'Yes, your cynical attitude towards our mission was far from impressive.'

He raised a blond eyebrow and grinned. 'I feel suitably chastened. But please let me explain my attitude at the time.'

'By all means.'

'I learned to accept so much horror,' he began, already showing the expression of a man haunted by the past. 'I have seen the faces of men being blown away by gunfire. Others I watched screaming in terror as arms and legs were sawn off by surgeons. Of course it was not only humans who suffered, but horses too.' He looked at Bellinda with pain-filled eyes. 'Those poor dumb beasts were terrified.'

'Oh Adam, it must have been a dreadful nightmare.'

'A nightmare that will never leave me.'

'I see now how such an experience hardens a man.'

He nodded. 'You develop a talent for turning your gaze away from it all – the disgusting and painful things, the wrongs.'

'No longer, I suspect.'

'It is you who have taught me to care again.' His blue eyes twinkled. 'I am almost as fond of these children as you are.'

She laughed. 'Oh Adam, how I misjudged you.'

'No, I misjudged myself. All of a sudden I seem to have become human again.'

'Now there's a thing.'

'Yes, there indeed is a thing,' he agreed warmly.

For one moment they were silent, pondering. Bellinda found herself savouring the bonding of their relationship.

'What made you join the army?'

He shrugged. 'Why does any red-blooded young buck want to go to war? It was all I ever wanted to do.'

'I suppose so, but then when it was over you made your fortune in the City.'

He laughed. 'No, Bellinda. Not I, most of my so-called fortune has gone into keeping my eccentric parents in the way they have become accustomed to.'

'How wonderful to have eccentric parents,' Bellinda said wistfully. 'How wonderful to have parents at all!'

His expression seemed full of understanding. 'Don't ask me how, but I always knew you were an orphan. I must introduce you to my own parents, I am sure that you and they would get on famously.'

'Is that why you were determined to prosper in the City, for their sakes?'

280

'Nothing like desperation to bring forth undiscovered talents. Father had lost everything through poor speculation.' He shook his head. 'It was madness, some of the schemes that he got himself involved in. Utter madness!'

'And so you gambled all that you owned upon saving your parents from ruin.'

'No, my dear Bellinda. Not gambled, calculated. I studied and studied the market before parting with a single penny. My father was getting impatient, the bailiffs would soon be on their way, but no matter. As far as I was concerned I could not afford to lose, and lose I didn't.'

'And then you became so skilled that even your hated cousin used your services.'

'Yes, even he had to admit that my brokerage was the best in London. It was the first and only time he and I have ever shared anything in common.'

'I'm very pleased to hear it.'

His blue eyes searched hers. There was a sudden, beautiful stillness in the room. The moment lingered.

'I shall cherish the recollection that at least once I managed to please you,' he said mischievously.

She smiled and gazed into his eyes again before saying reluctantly, 'I'd best go to bed.'

'Sleep well,' he said gently. 'Sleep well.'

'I made such a fool of myself down there,' Amity said when Bellinda entered their bedroom.

'Amity, he understands. To lose your brother must have been so heartbreaking.'

'It was, but I should never allow my heart to rule my head. It always causes trouble.'

'I know exactly what you mean,' Bellinda said before tucking in Amity's blanket and kissing her friend upon the head, as if she were putting one of the children to bed.

As she slipped into her own bed, Bellinda recalled how quickly she had fallen in love with Maltravers and had just as quickly paid a heavy price. Never again would she allow herself to be ruled by her emotions. No matter what Adam Carr's attitude towards her was, she could never fall in love with him. All the love she possessed belonged to the children, no one else.

'I am afraid I have some bad news,' Adam announced.
'What is it?' Bellinda asked anxiously.
'Here, you'd better read this,'
He handed an opened copy of *The Times* to her and pointed to a headline.

THE HOUSE OF LORDS REJECTS A BILL TO RAISE THE AGE OF CONSENT

Lord Trentham unsuccessfully attempted to have the age of consent raised to sixteen in the House of Lords yesterday. Several lords were in agreement but the Bill was finally rejected due to a forceful speech by Lord Maltravers. His Lordship began by informing his fellow Peers that he was a benefactor of the Smallwood Mission for Abused Children and fully supported their work in providing a home of Christian comfort to children who had so unwisely turned to prostitution. He was sure that with his continued support, many more such places would soon be opening. He explained that this was the proper way to overcome the problem, not through legislation. It was a most convincing speech and soon won the general support of the House.

Bellinda hurled the newspaper across the room. 'What fools those people are,' she raged. 'What utter fools!'
Amity came in, picked up the discarded paper and read the article. 'In God's name, why are these men so easily duped?'
'Because, I dare say, several of Maltravers' fellow Peers abuse these children themselves,' Adam answered.
'Then what can we do?' Bellinda asked desperately.
'Yes, we must do something,' Amity added.

282

'Ladies, all is not lost. The campaign has barely begun. Did you really expect victory so early on?'

'I cannot believe that he wants more missions to flourish.'

'No, Bellinda, he does not, but with men like Mad Jack out of the way, hopefully more children will be less afraid to come here.'

'But you cannot stay here to protect us for ever,' Amity said. 'What then?'

He looked at Bellinda. 'Should you permit me, then I would like to remain here a little longer.'

'What about your business interests?'

'I have sufficient capital to see me through for a couple of years at least.' He then stroked his chin thoughtfully. 'I have every confidence that I could persuade Twiffers to come here during any absence.'

'Twiffers?'

'Captain Percival Twyford. An old army chum of mine.'

'Well . . . '

'That would bother you, Bellinda?'

'I am sorry. I suppose after my experience with Maltravers and knowing how vile so many men can be, I am cautious.'

'I think you mean overcautious,' Amity said.

'Perhaps.'

'I dare say Twiffers has been to a few brothels in his time but a more decent and loyal fellow would be hard to find,' Adam said proudly.

'Do you really think that he would help?' Amity asked eagerly.

Adam grinned. 'Twiffers is one of the idle rich. It's about time he did something useful for a change. Look, I'll go and fetch him and then you can judge for yourselves.'

'That sounds a splendid idea,' Amity told him.

Adam was gone for only an hour before returning with Captain Percival Twyford. He was extremely tall, red haired, and sported a bushy moustache joined by two equally bushy sideburns. Upon entering he bowed gracefully.

'Glad to meet you, ladies,' he said jovially.

'And I am glad to meet you, Captain,' Amity said enthusiastically.

'Well now, that would not be an American accent I hear, would it?'

'Sir, you know very well it is for I am sure Adam has already told you about my origins.'

Once again Captain Twyford bowed his tall frame. 'Touché, Ma'am. Touché!'

'Adam tells me you were in the army together,' Bellinda said.

'Correct, deuced fine comrade he was too. Risked his own life to save mine.'

'Well, now you can return the favour, Twiffers,' Adam told him. 'It's about time you did something besides betting on nags that never win.'

'Unfair that, one of mine did come home first the other day,' Captain Twyford said before laughing heartily. 'Dash it! I then put all the winnings on a horse that came home last.'

'What pleasure can there possibly be in such an aimless pursuit?' Bellinda asked critically.

Twyford looked at her quizzically before shrugging. 'Hanged if I know. Something to do, I suppose.'

'Would you like to sit down, Captain?' Amity asked.

'Wouldn't say no,' he said eagerly.

Slowly and awkwardly, Captain Twyford lowered himself down to the chaise longue. Throughout the whole movement his left leg had remained straight. He looked up at the two women, obviously sensing their embarrassment.

'Adam should have warned you. He has got a cripple to guard you,' the Captain said glumly.

'Please do not call yourself that,' Bellinda insisted.

'Kind of you to say so, but truth is I am not much use in a brawl.'

284

'Nonsense, Twiffers, your other leg's now better than ever. Anyway, who's going to be foolish enough to challenge a six-foot army captain?'

'Exactly,' Amity agreed with Adam. 'I'm quite sure that we will all be safe in your capable hands, Captain.'

'Good of you to say so, Ma'am. But please, the name is Percy.'

'And I am Amity Smallwood.'

He smiled up at her. 'Very glad to make your acquaintance, Amity.'

'And I yours,' she said coquettishly.

'Shall I make tea for us all?' Bellinda suggested.

'That would be a splendid idea,' Amity said without averting her gaze from Percy.

Adam soon joined Bellinda in the kitchen. 'I know what you're thinking,' he told her.

'You do?'

He smiled knowingly. 'You may well be a little wary of Percy.'

Momentarily, it was impossible for her to answer as water from the tap thundered into the kettle. She thought hard of what answer she should give. Was not honesty the best way of replying?

'Yes,' she confessed. 'But I am sure I am being foolish.'

'No, Bellinda,' he said as he helped her to place the heavy kettle on the hob. 'After what you have been through, it must be more than tempting to judge all men as if they were Maltravers.'

'I do not compare you to him.'

'Bellinda, you cannot realize what music that is to my ears.'

She looked straight at him. With his hair bathed in the sunlight streaming through the window, he seemed like a sun god. Had they known each other in past lives? His eyes were the colour of a timeless blue sea with an eternal tide that ebbed and flowed through the centuries. She was entranced until three of the children burst into the kitchen, noisily demanding to know who the stranger was.

285

'Do you like Captain Twyford?' Adam asked.

'Yes,' they all cried. 'Yes!'

He turned to Bellinda. 'Percy has always had a way with children. Always.'

'You are not so bad with them yourself.'

'I do not seem to be,' he chuckled as some of the children flocked around him. 'Must admit, though, I never saw myself as a missionary.'

Bellinda was about to comment upon how well he had settled into the role when Amity came into the kitchen.

'Bellinda, you have a caller,' she announced. 'Thomas Groves-Hawkes.'

Chapter 25

Thomas Groves-Hawkes seemed to have aged rapidly. His face had become drawn and thin, his grey eyes were haunted by deep anguish. He stood before her, awkward and ill at ease.

'Bellinda, I am so glad that you did not turn me away.' His voice sounded weaker than she remembered.

'Why should I do that, Thomas?'

'Marguerite has died,' he said before his whole body began to convulse.

'Please, Thomas, I beg you. Take a seat.'

He slumped to the chaise longue, staring down at the floor with tear-glistened eyes. 'She was so afraid of dying,' he wept. 'So utterly afraid.'

Bellinda knelt down and took his trembling hand. 'Oh Thomas, how you must be suffering.'

'I would suffer less if you were to tell me that you have forgiven me for my foolish behaviour towards you.'

'There is nothing to forgive,' Bellinda said gently. 'I have learned so much from you.'

'If only Marguerite had shown some interest in my collections,' he moaned.

'The deeper aspects of life are not for everyone,' she comforted softly. 'Yet Marguerite loved you greatly.'

'And I on my part failed to return that love.'

Bellinda felt powerless to say any other words of comfort. 'How are the children managing to cope?'

'Robert is most distraught but Vanity seems to be totally unaffected by it all. She is more concerned with the courtship of Lord Maltravers,' he said with bitter resignation.

'Thomas, you must stop her!' Bellinda gasped.

'Why?'

'He is not what he seems.'

'Not what he seems? But he is a man of extremely high standing.'

'Oh yes, none could question his position and wealth,' she said ironically. 'Those who do not know his dark secrets can be so easily duped.'

'What dark secrets?'

'There is no greater abuser of young children than Maltravers.'

Thomas's tear-filled eyes widened. 'This cannot be so. It cannot!'

Bellinda nodded.

'But how do you know? Are you sure?'

'I could not be more sure. The children here have told us all about him. And he revealed his true nature when he attempted to rape me.'

'He *what?* I shall see that he is ruined for such an outrage!' Thomas's face was now flushed by rage, his knuckles whitening as he clenched his fists. 'And now that man is courting my daughter?' he growled.

'You must warn her.'

Suddenly he laughed, but it was not a joyous sound. 'Do you know? I truly doubt that this fact will actually concern her.'

'Thomas, it is bound to.'

He shook his head. 'Wealth and position are all that matter to Vanity. And as for my giving her permission? Why, that would not concern her either. She has no respect for her father. None at all.'

Poor Thomas. Bellinda suspected that for much of his life he had been shielded from grief and misery. Not now. This was a time of atonement for him, even re-tribution. She sat down beside him and took his hand. 'Then Vanity is a fool,' she told him. 'You are a man most worthy of respect.'

He turned to her and smiled weakly. 'In spiritual terms I have achieved so little. Yet . . . ' again he smiled ' . . . I think you will approve of what I have done at the Downley Home.'

'And what is that?' she asked eagerly.

He stood up. 'I wanted to see you alone first but I have brought you another visitor. The Governess is waiting in my carriage. I will go and fetch her.'

Joy surged through Bellinda. 'The Governess is here! Miss Waring is here?'

'Yes.'

Bellinda did not wait for Thomas to fetch her. She rushed outside and there, peering from the window of his carriage, was the crumpled face of the Governess.

'Bellinda! Is it you? Is it really you? Miss Waring almost fell on top of Bellinda as she tumbled out of the coach. 'Oh, it is so good to see you, child. Oh, it is so good!'

'You must tell me everything about the orphanage. Everything! Do you hear?'

'It is not the place you remember. Not at all,' the Governess said. Once inside the mission, she turned to Thomas. 'Sir, have you not told Bellinda of your generosity?'

'I have merely done my Christian duty, nothing more.'

'Well if I may be permitted to say, Sir, you have gone well beyond the bounds of Christian charity in your generosity. Well beyond the bounds!'

'In what way?' Bellinda asked.

'Why, you would not recognize the place. Mr Groves-Hawkes has called in the builders and made it seem like somewhere new.' Her face was shining with pride. 'Not only that, he has ensured that all the children are properly clothed, with extra garments for the winter. They now have two full meals a day, no less. Two full meals!'

Bellinda looked at Thomas. 'Can there ever be any joy in wealth unless one gives generously?'

'I confess not. It was you who touched my heart.'

'Bellinda touches all our hearts,' the Governess said before gazing around the room. 'Looks like you could do with a lick of paint for *this* place.'

289

'In due course,' Thomas told her. 'Bellinda and Amity will soon be receiving my full support.'

'Then Amity must be informed,' Bellinda said, thrilled by what she had just learned. 'I shall go and fetch her and Adam Carr.'

'Adam Carr? It was he who escorted Vanity to the Gages'. I was most impressed by his manner, but of course he was not wealthy enough to impress my daughter.'

'Well he has certainly impressed us, for he and his friend Captain Twyford are providing us with protection at the moment.'

'Then Adam Carr has risen even higher in my esteem. A bachelor, worthy of taking your hand in marriage.'

Bellinda blushed. 'I have no wish to marry anyone,' she said before leaving the room and fetching Amity, Adam and Percy from the kitchen.

'Bellinda has been telling me about Maltravers,' Thomas began when they were all assembled.

'Few men deserve more contempt than my cousin,' Adam said coldly. 'No longer shall I turn a blind eye to his perversions.'

'He must be revealed at all costs.'

'Not an easy task, as Bellinda and myself have recently discovered. A man of such influence can do exactly as he pleases.'

Thomas stroked his chin thoughtfully. 'I now recall reading about his persuading the House of Lords to reject a Bill raising the age of consent.'

'He did indeed,' Amity responded. 'It was in his own corrupt interests to do so.'

'And is he a benefactor of this mission?'

'We now know that most of the girls here were bullied into coming by his henchman, Mad Jack.'

'Then this Jack must be dealt with.'

'That has been done,' Adam said casually. 'I gave the fellow a good hiding before telling him to get out of London.'

'Will he go?'

'I am convinced he has already gone.'

'Then I must congratulate you, Adam.'

'Rest assured, if that scoundrel has had a beating from an officer of the Light Brigade then he'll not be back in a hurry,' Percy Twyford boasted, tweaking his moustache.

'Unfortunately, Maltravers is still free to do as he pleases,' Amity said. 'Even the police are afraid to act.'

'Then it is a matter for the Queen,' Thomas said gravely.

'The Queen?'

'Yes, Bellinda. Find favour with her and your campaign to end this abominable trade will be greatly enhanced.'

'You really think that she will give it her attention?'

'Should you and Amity approve, then I will write to her myself.'

'We would be most grateful,' Amity said.

'I did work with the late Prince upon several of his projects, including the Crystal Palace. Were he still alive then I too might have become a lord, a knight even.' Thomas shrugged. 'No matter, what does matter is that the Queen still remembers me. Besides, she has a right to be told about a man who has the ambition, the political influence and the wealth to become Prime Minister.'

'That cannot be?' Amity gasped.

'I am afraid Thomas is right,' Adam said grimly. 'Hugh once boasted to me of his intention of becoming Prime Minister.'

'That is unthinkable!' cried Bellinda.

'But nevertheless a terrible possibility.'

Adam was interrupted by two of the children, Elsie and Beattie, bursting into the room.

'Why, what adorable little mites!' The Governess's face crumpled into a smile before she swept Beattie up into the air.

Bellinda watched Beattie respond by flinging her arms around the old woman's neck – reflecting that this very child had been abused by the vile Maltravers.

291

In the next moment, all the children were swarming into the room. Although the Governess seemed to be relishing the experience, Bellinda could tell that the grieving Thomas was overwhelmed. Quickly, she led him into the kitchen and closed the door behind them.

'Bellinda, now that we are alone I have a suggestion to make,' he said cautiously.

'Please, Thomas, go ahead.'

'I propose that Miss Waring stay here for a while – Mary Alewin can continue to look after her charges – and you, my dear Bellinda, should visit the orphanage.'

'I would dearly love to see the children again.'

He smiled paternally. 'I am sure you would, just as they would love to see you.'

'Perhaps I shall get the chance to sleep in my old bed again,' she quipped.

'If you wish, but the whole of Carlyon House will be at your disposal, for I will not be there.'

'You will not?'

He shook his head. 'I think it best that I stay in London for a while. I have taken rooms at the Savoy.'

'What about Vanity and Robert?'

'They are staying with their aunt in Sussex. Carlyon will be empty, except for the servants.'

Bellinda kissed him on the cheek. 'Thomas, how can I thank you?'

'Simply by being happy, my dear. There has been so much pain and sorrow in your life. You above all deserve just a little happiness.'

'To see your own torment come to an end would bring me great happiness.'

'I fear that for the rest of my life God will be demanding my repentance for the selfish and indulgent way that I have conducted my affairs,' he said ruefully.

'Thomas, it is not a matter of repentance but of realization. Was it not you who taught me about reincarnation, that those of the East believe each life is a lesson of our choosing?'

'Oh Bellinda, how well I taught you.'

292

'I know that it is most unchristian,' she began awkwardly, 'but in times of strife it is Kuan Yin that I turn to, not God.'

'Then when you grace my house with your presence, you must take down that most blessed of idols from its place on the shelf and keep it for ever.'

'Oh Thomas, how can I ever thank you enough?'

'There is no need,' he said with a smile. 'And what is more, my coach and coachman will also be at your disposal.'

'That would make me feel ill at ease.'

'Why?'

'I, an orphan, must now say the words, "Drive on, coachman"?'

He laughed, colour momentarily returning to his ashen face. 'There will be no need to say that. Parsons is perfectly adept at going places without any command at all.'

'Then I shall gladly accept your kind offer.'

Thomas smiled approvingly. 'That pleases me a great deal. However, after hearing about Maltravers and Mad Jack I am concerned that you will be unprotected.' He paused. 'Might I suggest that Adam Carr escorts you?'

'Well . . . '

'I am sure that he would behave with the utmost propriety.'

'After my experience with Maltravers it is difficult for me to accept that any man can act with propriety.'

'I know that we have both misjudged Maltravers but I could tell, simply by a glance, that Adam holds you in the highest esteem.'

'I am beginning to hold Adam in a certain amount of esteem myself,' she confessed with a willingness that surprised her.

'Then that is settled, you and Adam can leave as soon as it is convenient.'

'To see the children of the orphanage again,' Bellinda sighed. 'Oh Thomas, what in the world could be more pleasing.'

Chapter 26

Little was said on the journey, for Bellinda soon drifted off to sleep. The past few days had taken their toll upon her. Now she could relax, for here in this coach there were no responsibilities, no worries.

She was awakened by a gentle tap on her knee. Blearily, she opened her eyes and saw Adam, his corn-gold hair tinted by a beam of evening sunlight.

'We have arrived at Carlyon,' he announced.

Still sleepy-eyed, Bellinda looked out. They were approaching the opulent home of the Groves-Hawkes family. With its white walls glowing in the dusk, it looked as imposing as ever.

The past returned. Adam was gone. Instead, a trembling Sara was clutching to her. How awesome Carlyon had seemed then. A black tide of sorrow surged through her as, vividly, Bellinda recalled the bitter time when Sara became ill with the consumption.

'I cannot go back,' she wept. 'I cannot go back.'

In the next moment she was crying upon Adam's shoulder. Tears flooded from her as the wretchedness of those times returned with vivid cruelty. He cradled her in his strong arms as she continued to sob.

'There, there, sweet Bellinda,' Adam whispered. 'There, there.'

He rocked her gently in his arms as the coach drew to a halt.

She heard the coachman climb down, ready to escort them to the house. His was the role of a hangman and she the condemned. As the door opened she held on to Adam tightly.

'Tell me, Parsons, is there a good place to stay near hear?' she heard Adam ask.

'But I thought–?'

'No, not tonight.'

'I see, Sir. Well they say the George and Dragon in West Wycombe is a good coaching inn. They'll probably have rooms.'

'Then take us there.'

'Well, if that's what you want, Sir.'

'It is.'

Bellinda felt relieved as soon as the coach was on the move again. She looked up at Adam with tear-misted eyes. Once more he was the sun god she had first seen in the mission kitchen. It was his gentle strength that had caught her attention then, that was captivating her now.

'Have I made the right decision?' he asked

'Yes,' she answered, still nestling into his arms, 'you have made the right decision.'

'Then all is well,' he said softly before kissing her on the forehead. 'All is well.'

Although the village of West Wycombe was little more than a mile from Downley, Bellinda had rarely visited it. During what little opportunity she had ever had to leave the orphanage, she had gone to High Wycombe. She had always regretted this, for West Wycombe was the quaintest of places with its low-roofed cottages standing below a mighty hill, crested by the mausoleum of the Dashwood family and an imposing church with a large golden ball upon its tower.

As the coach bucked and lurched its way towards West Wycombe, Bellinda was still haunted by images of the past. When Thomas had suggested that she return to Wycombe she had been thrilled. No longer. Returning had brought back all the sorrow and anguish of those times. Part of her wanted to return to London, yet part of her, despite everything, was still eager to revisit the Home.

They waited in the coach while Parsons went inside to inquire about rooms. 'They've got two available, sir,' he soon told Adam.

'Then it is here that we shall stay. I'll help you with the luggage.'

'Very kind of you, Sir.'

Nervously, Bellinda waited until Adam was ready to escort her inside. Upon his return he held out a hand and helped her down to the ground. As he did so, he showed her a gentle, reassuring smile.

The inside of the George and Dragon was as she had imagined it to be, a coaching inn in the Georgian tradition with a high-beamed room where men sat nursing jugs of ale and puffing upon clay pipes.

'Will 'e be staying long?' the plump proprietor asked hoarsely.

'Depends,' Adam answered before turning to Bellinda. 'We can stay here until you are ready to face everything.'

'Course 'e can, Miss, I'll show 'e to your room.'

'Shall we go for a walk first?' Adam asked.

It was as if he had read her thoughts. She nodded.

'Well, your rooms'll be ready when 'e are,' the innkeeper told them.

Once outside, Adam took hold of her hand as they began to walk beside the road that ran through the tiny village. She felt calmer. The past was still haunting her, but what mattered most now was that Adam was here, by her side.

A lowering sun was still glowing over the rooftops, birds were trilling their eventide songs from the trees and in the fields sheep were bleating contentedly. Was she contented? She doubted if she could ever be that, for was not contentment reserved for those who did not truly care about the world and its multitude of problems?

'How far to the church?' Adam asked.

'If I recall there is an entrance beside the village hall, then you go straight up a lane that leads you all the way there.'

'Shall we walk a little of the way?

'It will do us good, it was a long time to spend sitting in that coach.'

'I never noticed,' he said tenderly.

She looked up at him. His eyes were full of adoration. Yes, there was passion there, but not the unsated hunger that had overwhelmed her when she had gazed into the eyes of Maltravers. Adam's look was reassuring. No, it was more than that, much more.

The way up to the church and mausoleum soon steepened. Adam's stride did not falter until he realized that Bellinda was struggling to keep up with him. Instantly, he offered her a hand. Gladly she took it.

When they reached the top, Bellinda told Adam that the mausoleum was the burial place of the Dashwoods who in the last century had formed the infamous Hell-fire Club, an organization which was suspected of devil worship. Although he showed interest Adam seemed keen to carry on up to the church.

'Do you think they will be holding a service tonight?' he asked.

'I doubt it.'

'I doubt it too,' he said enigmatically.

Bellinda was at a loss to understand why he should be so interested. Why was it so important to him that he should see the inside of St Lawrence? They were now upon the summit. To their right lay a greensward, to their left the parish church of West Wycombe. They went into a clustered graveyard sheltered by trees sighing quietly in an evening wind, then into the church itself.

A kindly clergyman with white wispy hair was standing in the aisle. It was almost as if he were expecting them.

'Can I be of assistance?' he asked.

'We have come to admire your church,' Adam told him.

'There is much to admire, for although it is plain it does have a charm of its own. Do you not think so?'

Adam looked around before returning his gaze to the Vicar. 'Yes,' he agreed. 'A place fit enough for a fellow to be married in.'

'Are you anticipating such a joyous occasion?'

He grinned. 'One cannot stay a bachelor for ever.'

The Vicar turned his attention to Bellinda. 'And are you to be the bride, my dear?'

She shook her head. 'I think that my companion was speaking hypothetically.'

The Vicar gave a knowing smile. 'Quite so. Quite so,' he said before pointing up at the roof. 'Did you know that the golden ball is hollow, that one can actually stand inside and view the surrounding countryside?'

'I was told that once,' Bellinda said. 'I found it hard to believe.'

'Then I must prove it to you,' he said, indicating a staircase that would take them right to the top. 'Up you go.'

They climbed until suddenly, as the Vicar had predicted, they were inside a huge metal ball. Although claustrophobic it was nevertheless an exciting experience for Bellinda. Holding each others' hand they peered out of a tiny porthole.

Directly opposite was the side of the hill upon which Downley stood. From high up in the globe it seemed so far away. To the left were the rolling hills and lush woodlands that stretched all the way to Princes Risborough. Fascinated, she scanned the countryside before returning her gaze to Adam.

Once again his gold hair was tinted by the evening light and once again, his diamond-blue eyes were filled with adoration. Her heart began to beat faster as his lips lowered towards her own. His was the kiss that deep in her soul she had always longed for. In that strong, powerful embrace was the love of a father and mother which she had always been denied; the rock that had never been there for her to cling to, no matter how terrible the storm.

When their lips parted he continued to hold her close to him. 'Bellinda, if only you would open your heart to me. I know that God intended us to be together. I know it!'

'Adam, I am afraid to, so afraid.'

298

'Are you to go through life judging all men as if they were Maltravers?' he asked gently.

'I know you to be a far better man than Maltravers. But . . .'

' . . . you find me too worldly?'

She shook her head. 'No, Adam, if you are too worldly then I am not worldly enough.'

'You could never be worldly,' he said adoringly.

'Sometimes I feel that I hardly belong to this world at all, that I should have been born somewhere else.'

Adam kissed her again, a long loving kiss. She felt at one with him – as if she were in Paradise, a Paradise that belonged only to themselves.

Outside, the sun was sinking below the Buckinghamshire hills as in a mutual, loving silence they stood in the darkening globe, listening to the sound of their own excited hearts. Then they descended the staircase, smiling at the Vicar who was waiting for them at the bottom.

'I hope that you were able to see something before darkness fell,' he asked hopefully.

'Yes,' Bellinda told him before looking up adoringly at Adam. 'Up there I saw so much. So much!'

He nodded. 'I am very glad.'

'We shall meet again, Sir,' Adam said.

Again, the Vicar smiled knowingly. 'Yes, I do not doubt it.' They said goodbye to the kindly old man and returned to the graveyard and the sighing trees. There was a chill now and Bellinda found herself shivering in the night air, before Adam wrapped a strong and protective arm around her shoulders. Instantly the chill was banished, her shivering stopped. It was true what they said about the warmth of love.

They lingered over the descent to the village, in no hurry for the evening to end. When they reached the bottom, Adam suggested that they eat. Bellinda agreed readily, knowing that it might well prove to be the most memorable meal of her life.

'Only got some cold meat left,' the proprietor of the George and Dragon said unapologetically. 'You're welcome to some of that, washed down with a jug of ale perhaps?'

Adam turned to Bellinda. 'What do you think?'

'Not far from here I was once grateful for any meal.'

'Of course, then we shall enjoy a cold supper – but not with mugs of ale.' He turned to the proprietor. 'Is there no wine in the house?'

The innkeeper peered at them from under sagging and wrinkled eyelids. 'Suppose wine would be more romantic. I'll see what I can do.'

As soon as he had vanished into the kitchen, Bellinda turned to Adam. 'Is our romance so obvious?'

'Yes,' Adam said lovingly. 'I am afraid it is.'

They took seats at a table by a tall window looking out on to a West Wycombe now cloaked in dusk. Neither spoke, preferring to savour the moment. The proprietor soon emerged from behind the bar and placed a bottle of claret and two glasses on the table. As soon as the glasses were filled they raised them, gazed intently into one another's eyes, and sipped. Bellinda saw it as a Holy Communion. Instead of drinking the blood of Christ she was imbibing the sacred, ancient water of love. No longer was she resisting the inevitable. Their destinies were entwined and she was glad, so very glad.

The meal provided was simple – cold mutton, trenchers of bread, and apples from the inn's own trees – and they ate heartily.

'That was the finest meal I have ever eaten,' Adam declared after dabbing his mouth with his napkin.

'I am sure you have enjoyed far more lavish fare than this.'

'True enough, my love, but the company has never been surpassed, and it is that which makes it a meal fit for the Gods.'

Bellinda laughed joyously. 'Oh Adam! You and I, we are so alike.'

'I have known it all along. It just took you a little longer, that is all.'

300

'Well, I got there in the end.'

'Yes,' he agreed lovingly. 'You got there in the end.'

The whole room appeared to be bathed in golden sunlight when Bellinda awoke. Her usual habit was to rise up from her bed straight away. Not this time. The pleasure of the evening spent with Adam lingered, and she would lie here for a while to savour every joyous moment. After their meal they had talked and talked. Never before had she felt so at ease with anyone, not even Amity.

Adam had insisted that she tell him everything about her past. At first she was reluctant but then after another glass of wine, the sadness and heartaches of her life began to unfold. Never before had she confessed so freely all her anxieties and self-doubts. Adam listened attentively, lovingly, and then delivered words of reassurance and comfort.

She had not wanted the evening to end – and, she suspected, neither had he.

She had finally gone to sleep at one o'clock, blissfully tired. There was no clock in her room, but she was sure she had slept well past her usual time.

Her thoughts were disturbed by a knock on the door. 'Bellinda, are you awake?' she heard Adam ask.

'Give me a few minutes and I will join you downstairs,' she said dreamily.

Hurriedly, Bellinda washed and dressed, eager to be in Adam's company once again. As she entered the bar she saw that he was sitting at exactly the same table as before. He smiled appreciatively as she approached.

'Did you sleep well?' he asked.

'Yes, I did. No doubt my dreams were sweet after such a heavenly evening, but to my shame I cannot remember them.'

'Was it not all a beautiful dream, Bellinda?'

'Yes,' she said gazing into his eyes. 'It was the most beautiful of waking dreams.'

'The proprietor is boiling some freshly laid eggs for breakfast.'

'Delicious!'

'Parsons has also arrived. The coach is outside, ready to take you wherever you want to go.'

Carlyon House, the orphanage. Bellinda had suddenly been reminded of the true purpose of her visit. The dream was gone. She was only here at the George and Dragon because she had been unable to face the bitterness of her past. However although she still had no wish to return to Carlyon, she now relished the prospect of seeing Downley again.

'Can you afford a few more nights here?'

'Bellinda, if you so desire then we shall stay here until my last penny has been spent.'

She laughed heartily before the innkeeper proudly placed a tray laden with boiled eggs and more trenchers of his coarse-grained bread upon their table, together with a large china pot of tea and cups displaying the Dashwood crest.

'Present from His Lordship, they was,' he said proudly before pouring them each a cup.

Bellinda ate three eggs and two of the thick slices with hungry relish.

'Bellinda, I have a strong suspicion that there are times when you do not eat properly.'

'There are times,' she confessed. 'Often when we have fed the children there is very little left for Amity or myself.'

He shook his head. 'Oh, Bellinda, that *is* foolish. What use to the children will you be if you do not eat properly?'

'Are you lecturing me?' she retorted.

'Yes!'

'Someone who cares for my welfare as much as I care for theirs. What luxury. What utter luxury!'

'Can you wonder why I have fallen head over heels in love with you?'

'You talk as if I am perfect.'

'You are.'

'Nonsense, no one has ever been that.'

He stretched an arm across the table and took her hand. 'No, but please believe me when I say that you come the closest of all.'

'Will you still be thinking that in twenty years' time?'

'Always, my love. Always!'

Once more they gazed into each other's eyes. How exquisite Adam's eyes were, sometimes as sharp and clear as diamonds, and at others as deep as the blue ocean. What lay in those depths she longed to explore?

Shortly, she set off for the Downley Home for Distressed Minors. As the coach reached the bottom of Plomer Hill, Bellinda remembered the day when she had descended it to begin her journey to London. So much had happened since then. Would she now be a stranger to them all?

From the outside, the orphanage was almost unrecognizable. Its flint masonry had been cleaned, giving it the look of a rich family mansion. What changes had been made inside? Bellinda was now eager to find out.

'Bewinda! It's Bewinda!'

Although little Nancy's pronunciation had not improved, she was now ruddy cheeked, her button eyes glowing with health. Bellinda hugged the tiny orphan before others swarmed around her.

'My, my, little loves. How well dressed you all are. How well scrubbed!'

'We get two full meals a day now,' a newly plump Lily told her.

'I know, the Governess told me,' she said before adding laughingly, 'I should never have left.'

'Why not? Looks like you've done yourself proud.'

The question had been asked by Mary Alewin, the washerwoman from Carlyon House.

'Mary, it is so good to see you.'

'Master says that looking after this lot will give me good practice for when I have one of me own.'

'You are married?

'Me and Jake is as happy as lambs in springtime,' she said coyly. 'But that don't answer me question.'

'I am helping to run a mission for abused children,' Bellinda answered.

'I might have known. God always intended you to help others.'

Bellinda laughed in agreement before asking each of the children how they were.

She spent the whole day there. It was as if she were helping the Governess to run the orphanage again, except that now everything was clean and fires burned heartily, banishing the cold and dampness that had always lingered, even in summer.

However, there was a moment when this joyous day was tinged with sadness. The beech tree was in leaf again, a verdant, beautiful canopy beneath which Sara now rested at peace, free from the world that had treated her so cruelly. Bellinda knelt there in silence, remembering the girl with the multitude of freckles who more than anyone else had helped her to endure the pain and deprivation of her time at the orphanage.

As promised, Adam arrived at five o'clock. He had walked from West Wycombe and intended to walk back, this time with Bellinda.

They descended the hill hand in hand as she told him about her day, and of how she had so enjoyed seeing all of the orphans again. They then spent another blissful evening in West Wycombe.

Every moment was a shared one, a joyous celebration of their love. Bellinda visited the orphanage on the next day, this time accompanied by Adam. Like the children of the mission, the girls warmed to him instantly. Then in the evening they returned to West Wycombe, there to wander, holding each other's hand and talking in the secret, reverent tones of lovers. They were one soul now. At last Bellinda had found the rock that in her heart she had always been seeking.

Chapter 27

'Oh, Bell, I am just too frightened to enter.'

'Amity, you must take a grip of yourself,' Bellinda whispered to her friend.

'It's all right for you, you're not an American,' Amity said shakily. 'We don't have this kind of thing!'

Despite her own fluttering heart, Bellinda managed to show her friend a reassuring smile. 'How often do you think *I've* been here?'

Amity giggled nervously. 'Why, every day, Bell. Every day!'

Before anything else could be said, the gold handles of the highly burnished double doors slowly began to open. Bellinda took in a deep breath and thought of Kuan Yin to calm her mounting nervousness.

As the doors swung wide they were confronted by a tall man with a bushy beard and wearing a kilt.

'Ye can come in now,' he told them, his eyes twinkling.

There was a fatherly quality about him that immediately helped to put Bellinda at her ease; she hoped he was having the same effect upon Amity.

As soon as they entered, the Scotsman stood aside. There before them, not sitting upon a high grand throne in ermine regalia, but upon a low-backed chair, was a small middle-aged woman in disappointingly plain and matronly clothes. Could this puff-cheeked lady really be Queen Victoria?

'That will be all, John,' the Queen commanded in a high-pitched voice.

'Aye, but I shall be close at hand if ye need me,' he said to her with a surprising lack of reverence.

As soon as John had departed, the two girls curtseyed before the sovereign.

The Queen nodded approvingly. For a whole week they had been practising their curtseys. Bellinda felt relieved – seemingly they had performed the movement correctly.

'You may sit,' Victoria said regally.

'Thank you, Your Highness,' Bellinda said, Amity adding her own thanks in a nervous voice. They then sat carefully upon the chaise longue opposite.

Large round eyes examined them with an almost maternal gaze.

'Tell me, how old are you two young ladies?'

'I am eighteen years old, Your Majesty,' Bellinda answered.

'And I am twenty,' Amity told her.

The Queen sighed. 'So young! So very young to be involved in such disturbing charity work.'

'Work that we believe to be very important, Your Majesty,' Bellinda said.

'Oh indeed, child. Indeed!'

'Yet there is no law in this land that prevents this vile trade,' Amity added forcefully, her nervousness seemingly gone now.

'Is that the accent of an American?'

'Yes, Your Majesty, but I live here now.'

'And devote your time and energies to trying to save these wretched children from ruining themselves.'

'As best I can, but most of these poor little girls do not take to prostitution by choice.'

Prostitution! Was that a proper word to use to a queen? Bellinda could only hope that Her Majesty would make allowances for Amity's bold American ways.

'Are you saying that men are enslaving these poor children?'

'In some cases, Your Majesty, but the real truth is that the poverty in this land is so great that many children are ready to do anything to survive.'

The Queen shook her head vigorously. 'Oh, what shame upon our Christian souls do the poor of this

306

land bring,' she said angrily. 'I who must spend the rest of my life grieving over the departure of my beloved Bertie, must also grieve for the destitution of so many of my people.'

'I am sure that you are not to blame, Your Majesty,' Bellinda said.

The Queen shifted uneasily in her seat. 'As sovereign of this land I am forced to share the burden of my country's ills. In truth I have been too preoccupied with my own widowhood to exercise proper concern.'

'Then you will help us in our cause?' Amity asked eagerly.

'Indeed, for the law must be changed.'

'You will change it, Your Majesty?' Bellinda gasped.

'Dear girl, I have not the power to change the law overnight. The age of consent can only be raised by the success of a Bill through Parliament.'

'Lord Maltravers convinced the House of Lords that it was unnecessary to increase the age of consent. He also has ambitions to become Prime Minister,' Amity said grimly.

'So Mr Groves-Hawkes informed me,' Queen Victoria said with equal grimness. 'Be assured that I shall do all that is in my power to prevent this abominable man from achieving his ambitions.'

'We should be most grateful for that, Your Majesty,' Bellinda said.

'I think that the whole nation would owe me their gratitude. I know that if dear Bertie were still alive he would have taken the same view,' she said before adding wistfully, 'He was so very fond of children. So very fond.'

Bellinda suddenly saw Queen Victoria in an entirely different light. Like herself, the Queen had suffered the loss of someone close. Despite her regal manner, she was a sad and lonely figure. 'I hope that I am not being impertinent, Your Majesty,' Bellinda began cautiously, 'but may we offer our condolences over your bereavement?'

The Queen lowered the fan she had been holding against her chest and studied Bellinda with warm and affectionate eyes. 'Have you also lost a dear one recently?'

'Yes, Your Majesty,' Bellinda answered quietly. 'Sara was an orphan who had been abused by men like Maltravers, and died of the consumption.'

'May God grant you solace during these tragic times. Perhaps a husband will help to heal the wounds?' Again her expression became wistful. 'There is no greater joy than a love that is shared between husband and wife. Dear Bertie and myself were so very happy together.'

'I shall always treasure your advice, Your Majesty,' Bellinda said reverently.

The Queen gave her a gentle, motherly look. For one moment Bellinda almost felt that she were one of Her Majesty's own daughters. 'Do more than that,' she was told. 'Act upon it, and when you have found your true love, savour each day as if it were your last together – for as I know to my own bitter cost, it might well be so.'

A solitary tear suddenly rolled down the Queen's cheek. It was obvious that even after such a long period, the poor woman was still deeply affected by Prince Albert's premature death.

'Shall we take our leave, Your Majesty?' Bellinda asked quietly.

Queen Victoria nodded while dabbing her eyes with a handkerchief. 'Forgive me, but sometimes my sorrow overwhelms me,' she said, her voice trembling with emotion.

Bellinda and Amity stood and curtseyed in unison before leaving the opulent room. Outside, the Scotsman called John was waiting for them. Again they were to experience a walk through the vast and imposing corridors of Windsor Castle, until reaching the hired coach that would take them home.

As they were sped back to the mission, Bellinda and Amity were overcome by a feeling of sheer exhilaration.

308

They had actually met the Queen. Even more important, she had given her blessing and support to their
cause. The time might still be far away, but the day
would surely come when the vile trade of child prostitution would finally end.

'Marry you?' Vanity Groves-Hawkes scorned.
'But I thought that all you ever wanted in life was
wealth and position?' Maltravers insisted.
Vanity threw back her head and laughed contemptuously. 'Wealth and position, is that what you have?'
Dark anger swelled inside him. 'How dare you mock
me,' he growled. 'I am still Lord Maltravers, one of the
richest men in the land.'
'And also a child molester.'
'Oh come now, Vanity, do my little pleasures really
disgust you? I doubt it.'
'Of course they disgust me. And you are asking me
to share the same bed with a man who . . . who . . . '
'And am I the only man ever to have enjoyed a
nymph? Who knows? Perhaps your own dear father has
been a customer at some time.'
Vanity's face was now flushed by rage. 'How dare you
say that!' she screamed at him. 'How dare you!'
To make such an accusation had been foolish. The
little bitch might still have had some mild affection for
her father. He had never found her attractive at all, but
it was time he got a wife, now more than ever.
'Listen,' he said calmly, 'I am not going to be
shunned by society for ever. And with you by my side
people will soon begin to accept me again.'
'Maltravers, it is not just people who have shunned
you but the Queen of England. You are persona non
grata. You are finished. Do you hear? Finished!'
Now that murderous anger could hardly be contained.
'Get out of my house before I kill you,' he snarled.
'I shall not give you that pleasure,' she said haughtily.
'Besides, should you not be thinking about killing yourself?'

With that she turned her back on him and left the room. The anger remained. In his rage Maltravers kicked over an Adam chair, hurled a cut-glass decanter against the wall, showering himself in broken glass, and then hammered his fist down upon a table until its glossy surface became smeared with blood.

At last the burning rage ebbed. Now only a dark emptiness remained. He was utterly alone, shunned by the whole of society. Queen Victoria had made public her disgust over child prostitution and in private had hinted to perhaps no more than one confidante that she regarded Maltravers as an undesirable member of society. That one aside had been enough. Suddenly he found himself being ignored at his club, not invited to any functions, and referred to in newspapers as the man who did not want the law changed so that he could continue with his depraved ways. He had threatened one journal with a libel action, but had soon been advised that it would be a case he was bound to lose.

The pain from his damaged hand throbbed, and his face was stinging from the cuts made by the decanter shards. Vanity had suggested that he kill himself. If only he had the courage to pull the trigger he would, for what was there to live for now? He was ruined. Utterly ruined!

William and Josephine Carr were indeed as eccentric as Adam had promised. Their home must once have been grand but was no longer imposing. Almost totally buried beneath a forest of ivy, it was now a place of rambling charm.

Bellinda met Adam's father as they arrived. He was a rotund man with a jolly countenance and wore a waistcoat of lurid yellow. She took an instant liking to him.

'Adam, dear boy, how good it is to see you.'

'Likewise, Father. May I introduce Bellinda?'

His eyes sparkled. 'Ah yes, I have been told all about you.'

She glanced at Adam before answering, 'All good, I hope.'

'The very essence of approbation, my dear. The very essence of approbation! Now, come inside, Bellinda. Pray do join us.'

Josephine Carr was as thin as William was round. 'Oh my girl,' she said in a quavering voice, 'you are so very pretty,' and then turning to her husband, 'Isn't she, Mr Carr?'

'Certainly is, Mrs Carr, certainly is.'

'So clever to be running a dress shop at her age.'

Adam laughed. 'No, dearest Mother, Bellinda does not run a dress shop, she runs a mission for foundling children.'

Josephine turned to her husband. 'Oh dear, Mr Carr, have I got something wrong?'

''Fraid so Mrs Carr. 'Fraid so.'

She turned to Bellinda. 'I never listen properly,' she confessed before coming closer to whisper in her ear, 'Mr Carr does, but then he always gets things wrong. It was he who told me you owned a dress shop.'

'Who knows? Perhaps one day I shall.'

The old lady's face crinkled into a smile. 'Yes, you should. Women will always want dresses. Always!'

'Quite so, Mrs Carr,' her husband agreed readily. 'Quite so!'

Josephine then clasped her son's hand. 'Does the prospect of one of Mr Carr's famous meat and potato pies meet with your approval?'

Adam turned to Bellinda and smiled. 'Well, do we approve?'

'It sounds delicious.'

Again Josephine Carr whispered in Bellinda's ear. 'Mr Carr loves cooking, my dear. We need never employ anyone in the kitchen. He does it all with such great aplomb. Oh such great aplomb!'

Those words were soon to be proved true. Brought from the kitchen was not a mere pie but a gargantuan pastry edifice. Never in her life had she seen a pie so huge. The helping filled the whole of her plate and seemed impossible to finish. However, it was undeniably delicious and Bellinda did manage to eat half of it before learning that the second course was to be another pie crammed with blackberries and apple. Gamely, she managed to tackle some of this pie while continuing to participate in and occasionally just listen to the family conversation.

However, now more than ever Bellinda realized just how much she had missed by being an orphan. What joy there was to be found in the natural rapport of mother, father and son. They were one body, relishing that unspoken web that knitted around them. Could she ever hope for that web to enfold herself? She was an outcast, born to tread her path alone. These people were genuinely kind and there could be no denying that Adam loved her deeply, but something was amiss. Something would always be amiss.

'Why not take Bellinda for a walk in the woods, Adam?' Josephine suggested when the meal was finished.

William Carr winked at Bellinda. 'Good idea. Mrs Carr and myself did some courting there.'

'Mr Carr, behave yourself! Giving away all our secrets like that.'

'What's the point of having secrets if nobody knows about them?' he chuckled.

Adam laughed heartily. 'As always your logic is astounding, dear Father.'

Again William Carr turned to Bellinda. 'Never did have much sense, this lad of mine. Nearly lost all his money once. It was only thanks to me that he got it back again.'

Bellinda knew that the situation was quite the reverse, that it was Adam who had saved William Carr from ruin, but were not some illusions to be treasured? She smiled knowingly at Adam's father as if she knew that he were right.

Outside the air was fresh and clean. There was a scent of honeysuckle as they walked through the gar-

312

den, a lavish riot not only of honeysuckle but of roses, towering hollyhocks, and laden apple trees. It was like a walk through Paradise.

'It would have been so heartbreaking to lose all of this,' she said to Adam while relishing the exercise as an antidote to the bloating effect of William Carr's gargantuan pies.

'The loss would have killed them, I know it would have done,' Adam told her before lifting the latch of the back gate.

In blissful silence Adam and Bellinda walked across the field to the woods. A magnificent magpie swooped amongst the high branches as they entered the place that reminded her so much of Tinkers Wood in Downley.

At their feet was a carpet of bluebells, almost glowing in the filtered sunlight. Adam took her hand, and never before had his felt so warm, so reassuring.

'You felt a little awkward during the meal, I could tell,' he said as they trod a path that led between silent but all-seeing trees.

'Your father's pies are indeed very filling.'

Adam stopped, took hold of her shoulders and looked straight at her. 'Bellinda, don't hedge. You know what I was really saying.'

She nodded. 'I am an orphan, an outcast. It is so difficult to belong. Oh, Adam, I have never belonged anywhere but the orphanage. Not at Carlyon, not at the Gages'. Even now I simply belong to the mission because that is my calling.'

Suddenly she burst into tears. Since Maltravers that cruel isolation had tightened its grip. How could she explain that to Adam? How could she ever make him understand?

As her tears began to fall, Adam kissed her and then kissed her again. She responded, wanting him, needing him. 'Oh my darling,' he whispered. 'Oh my blessed darling. Cannot you of all people believe in the power of love?'

'I love you, but – '

'But nothing! Have I not just shown you two people in love? Have you not seen the joy of contentment for yourself?'

'Oh Adam, there is more to life than contentment,' she argued 'There is starvation, poverty and wicked depravity!'

'And I who have been through one of the bloodiest wars in history have not seen any of this, I suppose?'

Bellinda could not answer.

'Look, I care as much for your work as you do. I want for nothing but your happiness. I am wise enough to know you could never be happy if I were to take you away from what is most important to you.'

'Adam, you really mean that?'

'As these trees are my witness, with all my heart. Yes, with all my heart, for you above all others deserve to be rich in Paradise.'

'Rich in Paradise? How eloquent you can be.'

He smiled. 'I have my mother to thank for that. On cold winter nights the family would gather round the fire while she read her poems to us.'

'Already I am deeply fond of your mother.'

'And I can tell that she is deeply fond of you. In time my parents' love for you will only ever be surpassed by my own. I promise.'

Now her tears were gone, there was a sudden joy in her heart. This wood, where William Carr had courted Josephine, seemed filled with an ambience of love and beauty. Now she was trembling, nervous and fearful of what was soon to be said.

'Bellinda, are we going to allow Amity and Percy to pip us at the post? Already they're talking of marriage.'

His hair was golden in the sunlight and his eyes were a crystal blue. Her adoration for him was unbridled now, but then his expression changed and he looked like a man about to receive a death sentence. 'It need not be in a conventional church,' he said awkwardly. 'If there is a temple of Kuan Yin then . . .'